*For Barry, my guiding star*

And we are put on earth a little space,
That we may learn to bear the beams of love

*William Blake*

# ONE

# *Particles*

The postcard arrived on the same day as their twenty-first wedding anniversary. It slipped into the green mailbox, landing inside its morning-cool interior without ceremony. A silent intruder.

Twenty minutes later Lewis Bell emerged from his house. He walked across his dusty front lawn in an old Hawaiian shirt, jeans and flip-flops.

Lewis opened up the mailbox and reached inside. At first, he thought it was empty, but then his hand touched the glossy side of the postcard. He pulled it out and looked at the image on the front. He wondered if he was imagining what he saw.

A neighbour started up his growling old pickup and pulled out across the road from him, but Lewis didn't look up. Nor did he hear the yelps of the children playing in the front yard of the house two down from him. On Lewis's Cactus Road all sound had been pulled into a vacuum; all motion had been stilled. His universe had narrowed to what he was looking at.

1

It was a sea view. In the foreground of the image there was a cliff edge covered in verdant grass, which fell away to reveal seaweed-strewn rocks and a family of bathers. The aquamarine sea was capped by gentle waves, and behind it the curve of a sandy beach rose to another mossy cliff with a small white cottage atop it. In the far distance a flat-topped mountain made an indigo silhouette against a blameless blue sky. It was a view he had never forgotten, even now when his life showed no trace of who he used to be. A place lodged in a mist of nostalgia in his memory. If he was in any doubt, all he had to do was read the text beneath the photograph: 'The Beach, Rosses Point and Ben Bulben, Co. Sligo.'

Who had sent him a postcard from Ireland?

He knew the answer of course, yet he could not quite believe it.

He turned the postcard over. His heart constricted as he read it, and the world around him shrank to the six words swimming in front of his eyes. In the distance, he could hear his wife calling to him, but he was unable to move.

Something was shifting. As if the lawn were sliding away beneath his feet; as if the world were on a tilt. His breath caught in his throat.

'Lewis!'

Samantha's voice eventually roused him – pulled him back with a gasp as if an icy palm had slapped his back.

He moved forward, walking back towards the house, the postcard gripped in his hand. He paused on the threshold to take one last look at the card, convince himself that it really did exist, before slipping it into his jeans pocket and stepping inside.

Joy Sheldon sat in her kitchen, mug of coffee steaming in front of her, the paper opened upon the table. It was her morning ritual. Ever since the kids had started school, even now they had grown up and left home, she read *The Arizona Republic* every day before she started the cleaning and laundry. She knew everything going on in Arizona. Who had died, what new political wrangle was going on in the state and what new housing developments had been built. She even read the adverts, fantasising about being able to apply for one of the jobs.

After she'd read the newspaper she sat at her kitchen table, watching the world spinning by outside her window, then gathered herself up. She had done this every weekday, year in year out.

Yet, since her father's passing, her ritual was not enough to get her through the day. These past few months, she'd felt more and more restless.

In a few weeks, he would be dead one year, and still she could not quite believe she would never see him again. Her daddy alone had understood her love for nature because he had shared it, nurtured it in her. Who said that the desert was barren? Not Joy's Arizona where, each spring, banks of golden poppies, purple chollas, desert chicory and Indian paintbrush would erupt from the gritty earth. Each time it felt unexpected and spectacular. It was an experience she had always shared with her father, the two of them setting off for hiking trips before the summer came and it got too hot to move that far south.

Joy and her daddy had shared this annual event each

year of her childhood. Her mom had pretended to be happy about it, but Joy knew she'd felt left out. Yet when her dad suggested she come along too, her mom would shake her head.

'Oh, no, Jack, you know I don't like nature.'

Joy always found this the strangest of statements. Her mom, perfectly at ease riding a horse down the main street of Scottsdale, would never consider hiking in the Tonto National Forest with her family.

'I'm a city girl at heart,' she'd say, tucking Joy's shirt into her jeans and placing a wide-brimmed hat on her head. 'Now you stay covered up. I don't want you getting burned. It's bad enough that you're covered in freckles.'

Joy's father had died at exactly the time of year when they would have gone on their annual hike. Yet it was not just his death that bothered Joy. It was what he'd said to her the day he died. How, reeling from the shock of his words, she had suddenly understood why her mom had never really been happy with her.

Joy had no brothers or sisters. If her mom had been distracted by siblings, maybe she wouldn't have had so many expectations for her only daughter.

'There are plenty of opportunities for girls now,' she used to tell Joy when she was still in school. 'You can do whatever you want. Go to college. Have a career.'

Joy had heard that thwarted ambition in her mom's voice. She'd been told that when her parents met her mother had been studying law in New York. She'd given it all up to be a wife and mother. Joy owed her mom a career. Yet she had struggled with books and learning.

She had no inclination for the intricacies of law. She much preferred the sensory world of plants.

Her parents had saved up for her college fund since the day they'd moved to Scottsdale. Joy guessed the money was still sitting in the savings account. She had never gone to college. She had failed them. In fact, she hadn't even finished high school, and her mother had never forgiven her. Even now, over twenty years later, she would harp on about it.

'You could have done so much with your life,' her mom often berated her. 'But you had to go and fall in with that Eddie Sheldon.'

She still said her son-in-law's name as if it left a sour taste in her mouth.

'I didn't fall in with him. I fell in love with him,' Joy would reply, and her mom would look at her with disdain.

'Oh please. You were seventeen. You didn't know what love was. You were behaving badly. God only knows why because I never brought you up that way. You got caught out.'

'Please, Mom, that was so long ago, can we not talk about it?'

It made Joy miserable to hear her mother go on like that. To be reminded how she'd never had any faith in her and Eddie. She'd never understood the bond that tied them together. It was stronger than love. Love was such a delicate thing, so easily crushed. She and Eddie were joined by something more robust. Joy thought of it as a sort of primal connection. That's why she'd got pregnant the very first time they had sex. How incredible was that? And as Catholics what else were they supposed to do? They were meant to be married. Of course, they'd had their ups and their downs like any couple, but Joy couldn't imagine her life without him.

She took a sip of her coffee, glanced back down at the paper and for once a headline leaped out at her.

'Northern Lights Give Arizona a Rare Show'

Her father had often talked about seeing the Aurora Borealis when he was a young soldier stationed up in Alaska. He'd told her it was something she should make sure she saw one day.

> 'Thanks to an unusually violent storm on the sun's surface, people throughout Arizona are getting a rare view of the Northern Lights, colourful displays created when tiny particles from the sun strike the Earth's upper atmosphere.'

Joy read on, her disbelief turning to excitement. How could it be possible to see the Northern Lights all this way south?

> 'Astronomers say to look for a bright glow shortly after 4 a.m. in the northern sky just below the Big Dipper.'

The article went on to state that city lights would intrude on the view and recommended driving out into the desert.

Her first instinct was to pick up the phone and call Eddie.

'I just saw in the paper that you can see the Northern Lights from Arizona!' she told him.

'The what?' he asked, sounding irritated.

'You know, the Northern Lights! You usually only see them up in the Arctic or Alaska, but for once they're this far south. If we drive out into the desert at four in the morning, we'll be bound to see them.'

'Joy, I'm in the middle of something here, can we talk about it later?'

'But can we go? It will be so special.'

'I'm not sure, Joy. You're talking about four in the morning. I've got work.'

'But it's a once-in-a-lifetime opportunity ...'

'Okay, we'll see,' he said, not sounding the least bit excited. 'I've got to go, honey.'

He hung up on her and she felt like she'd been slapped in the face, despite knowing he hadn't meant to be rude. He was just busy.

He was always working. Making money, he said, for her, for their daughter's wedding in April, for the future. But what about now? Why did her husband never have any time for her any more?

★

All day long Lewis saw that postcard in his head. He tried to focus on the job in hand. He was typesetting a leaflet for Scottsdale library but as he laid each letter out he saw the image on the postcard. He could hear the Atlantic Ocean crashing against the western coastline, smell the salty air, almost taste it on his lips, and beneath the sound of the waves he imagined he could hear laughter bubbling with suggestion. These images and sounds were haunting him to such an extent he nearly forgot to call into The Pink Pony to book their table. Every year they went to the same restaurant on their wedding anniversary. He asked himself why he couldn't think of taking Samantha somewhere new. He wasn't sure whether she would be pleased or not at the change. After all this time, he still couldn't be sure what his wife wanted.

Tonight Samantha was in a coral top that flattered her fair hair and sun-kissed skin. He could see a shade of the pretty girl he'd met all those years ago. What had happened between them had been so sudden, so fast, and yet they had stuck together all these years. They should have been proud of the achievement of their marriage, yet this anniversary meal didn't feel like a celebration.

'You look lovely tonight,' Lewis said, taken by a spontaneous urge to see Samantha smile.

His wife looked up in surprise. Her expression was stern.

'It's a long time since you paid me a compliment, Lewis.'

Why did she always do that? Twist something that was positive into a negative? Take the joy out of a simple compliment?

He shrugged, deflated. 'I'm just saying you look good.'

'Well thanks,' she said, picking at her steak.

Lewis could sense her unhappiness, but he was reluctant to ask what was wrong.

'I'm going to Santa Fe with Jennifer at Easter, is that okay?' Samantha asked him, pushing the rest of her food to the side of her plate and laying down her knife and fork.

'Aren't we spending it with your parents?'

'You can go if you want,' Samantha said. 'They seem to like you more than me anyway.'

'Come on, Sam.' He reached out for her hand, but she pulled it away, picking up her glass of wine. She sipped it as she held his gaze. For a moment he thought she might cry, but then her expression shifted.

'I need a break,' she said, not a trace of emotion in her face.

Of all nights, this should be one when he made love to his wife, yet when Samantha said she was tired and off to bed Lewis didn't stir from the couch. Instead, once she was gone, he went in search of the postcard, retrieving it from the jeans he'd discarded on the bathroom floor before they went out. He carried it back downstairs and into the kitchen. He wasn't quite sure what to do with it. If he loved his wife, shouldn't he throw it away? And yet he couldn't.

The words on the back of the postcard were written in block letters, a neat black print.

**EVENTUALLY THE TRUTH WILL COME OUT**

Lewis read the words again, and again, until they brought him back to the morning upon which they had been said. He could almost hear her voice. He imagined her soft Irish lilt, and it took him back in time, transported him to another world altogether, when he was a different man.

He placed the card gently on the counter in front of him then looked out of the window at the star-strewn night hanging above the dark silhouette of the McDowell

Mountains. He was right on the edge of the desert and its vast sky, like those words, gave him hope.

He leaned on the sink, gazing out into the Wild West. He still felt a sense of awe at being an Englishman, an outsider, in cowboy country.

He was about to pull the blinds down when he saw a shimmering red light in the desert sky. It intrigued him for the sun had long set. The red light turned into swathes of fuchsia, and bright green, moving in waves above the mountains. He'd never seen anything like it.

★

It was the darkest hour before dawn. Joy was sitting on her old Navajo blanket spread upon a rocky mound on the Papago Butte. Eddie had refused to drive out to the desert. He'd told her he was too tired and warned her not to go on her own.

'Anyone could be lurking out there,' he'd said.

She hadn't told him that she went out to the desert on her own all the time, although maybe not at night.

When they'd gone to bed, she'd tried to give up on the idea. But she'd been unable to sleep. Her daddy had told her about the wonder of the Northern Lights – that she must see them. And here they were on her doorstep. She never went anywhere. It was now or never.

She'd waited until Eddie's breathing shifted to a deep sleep and slipped out of bed. Made herself a thermos of hot coffee and crept out the house before she had a chance to change her mind.

Now, in the desert, she was not alone. There were

several couples nearby, arms around each other, as they waited. A few whispers, but nothing more. There was a hush of anticipation as she looked up at the sky again. Was she imagining it, or was the dome of the night sky crackling with a kind of electricity? Shivering, she pulled the blanket tight around her shoulders and cradled her hands around her cup of coffee. She was going to sit here all night if she had to, for Joy had faith in her daddy's words.

★

It was only when Lewis had pulled in at the side of the road and begun to climb up Papago Butte that he realised he should have woken Samantha and brought her with him. He had taken off on the spur of the moment, but surely this vision was something he should share with his wife. Would it not have been the perfect symbol for their twenty-first wedding anniversary?

But the truth was he was glad to be on his own. Samantha would know exactly what was causing this light display in the desert sky. She would take all the magic out of it with her scientific explanations, and for the moment he didn't want to know.

He drank in all the colours in the sky. Deep shudders of purple, ecstatic pink and luminous green shot through him. It felt like a message. Things could change. The unexpected could happen. The postcard could be just the beginning.

If only he was brave enough.

Lewis kept climbing up Papago Butte, his way

illuminated by the fantastical lights, his heart pounding. He felt exposed, thrilled to be doing something out of the ordinary.

★

Joy looked up and what she saw took her breath away. It was beyond anything she could have imagined. Clouds of vivid reds and purples, shot through with a mystic green, shifting high in the sky, shimmering over the distant desert.

She was aware of those around her standing up. The clicking of cameras as they tried to capture this rare Arizona moment.

Joy took a step away from the flash of cameras, bumping into someone as she did so.

'Excuse me,' she said, losing her balance slightly as she stumbled.

A hand reached out, caught her by the elbow and steadied her. 'Careful – you don't want to fall.'

It was a man's voice. An English accent.

Something about it reassured her. He was tall, but she couldn't make out his face in the dark.

'This is amazing,' he said.

'I know,' she whispered.

They watched in silence. She realised they were the only two not taking photographs. She wanted to tell the other people to put their cameras down. By creating that barrier between themselves and the experience of the lights, she felt they were missing it.

She glanced at the man standing beside her. He was still, as if held in a spell.

She could see his eyes now. They were filled with reflections of the Aurora. She felt a longing for her husband. If only she could share this special moment with Eddie and see stars in his eyes.

She thought of that first time Eddie had noticed her. He had been in the year above her in high school, and all the girls had a crush on him. The young Eddie had embodied everything intoxicating about the Arizona cowboy spirit: strong, lean, lithe. He was as natural on his horse as if he were born welded to it.

Eddie had never said too much, unlike the other boys who goofed around all the time. He would just watch. Lean back against the fence by the schoolyard, arms crossed, eyes blue slits and take in the rest of them. Now and again, Joy would see a girl with him, in the movie theatre or walking down Main Street, or coming out of the Sugar Bowl after sharing an ice cream. Usually it would be one of the 'Howdy Dudette' girls, the prettiest, most popular girls at school, and he would have his arm around her waist. He had been so sure of himself and his power over the girl. It had fascinated Joy. The way he walked, so at ease in his skin and his physicality.

And then one day, something quite remarkable had happened. She had been in the Sugar Bowl with Mary Lynn Baxter, sharing the 'Sugar Bowl Treat Banana Split', when Eddie had come in. He'd turned towards her – and actually looked at her.

'Can I join you ladies?' he'd asked.

In that instant she had been hooked. Mary Lynn had seemed to be similarly dumbstruck because neither of them had replied, both turning a deep shade of pink as

13

they'd stared down at their half-eaten dish of ice cream.

That hour had changed Joy's life. In the years that followed she would often ask Eddie why it was that he'd sat down with her and Mary Lynn. He would tease her that he had been after her friend and she had been his second choice, but in more serious moments Eddie had said it was because of her eyes. When he'd walked into the Sugar Bowl that day and caught her looking at him, she'd stopped him in his tracks.

'You looked so different from the other girls. You were like Elizabeth Taylor with your black hair and pale skin. I wanted that difference.'

They had dated, and the whole of Scottsdale High had been in uproar at the news. Why was Eddie Sheldon dating little Joy Porter? She wasn't a 'Howdy Dudette' gal. She couldn't even ride a horse.

Joy had always been intimidated by the pretty girls of Scottsdale High, most of whom had their own horses. She had preferred to hang back with the less popular crowd. Mousy Mary Lynn Baxter with her thick spectacles; Rosa Fowler, the only mixed-race kid whose white father had somehow managed to get her into the high school, and Brian Delaware – not a weedy boy but an outcast because he seemed to fear horses just as much as she did.

Her parents had found it hard to understand her terror of horses. Yet right from the first day that they'd tried to put her on her mother's mare at the age of four Joy had screamed her head off. Her mom put it down to wilfulness, but her father had tried his best to understand her terror. He would coax her gently, getting her to help him groom his own horse, and trying to help her connect with the animal, but all Joy saw when she looked into a horse's eyes was madness – something not to be trusted.

She had wanted so much to please her parents, but no matter how hard she'd tried, she couldn't get over her fear. In Scottsdale not to have a horse, not even to ride, was a major social disability. All those boys had cowboy souls, and they wanted western girls just like them.

Yet Eddie had wanted her, and because of that she'd even got on a horse for him. She'd been that crazy about him. He'd told her he would be right there, holding the reins and leading her, so she'd let him give her a leg-up, and she'd clambered on to Amber, a huge Arabian mare.

She hadn't liked it. Had felt the beast shifting beneath her weight, as if it could sense her fear.

'Can I get down now?' she'd asked Eddie.

'Not yet, Joy. Trust me.'

They had been up at Gainey Ranch where his dad worked. But that day there was no one else around.

'This here is where we take those Arabian beauties through the motions,' he'd told her as he led her round the arena.

'Do you help your dad?' Joy had asked him.

'Sure do.'

She had gripped the horn of the saddle, felt the horse shifting from side to side, but it was okay. She could do it.

'Do you want to work here when you leave school?'

'No way. I don't think this place can run as a ranch much longer. I'd say it'll be turned into a development soon. I'm going to get in where the money is.'

He had looked up at her then, and she'd noticed how different he appeared from his usual cool self. He had let his guard down. His cheeks were flushed, his fair hair damp on his forehead, one big blonde curl stuck right in the middle. She had wanted to slide off the horse and kiss that curl.

'Property. That's what I'm going to get into,' he had said. 'You just watch me, baby. I am going to make it big.'

She had loved his ambition. It had thrilled her. What would life be like with a guy like this? she had wondered. They would go places together, have adventures, live the big dream. He would take her all the way to Mexico to swim in the Sea of Cortez.

'Okay,' he had said, stopping for a moment and handing her the reins. 'Now you take those in your hands like so. You're gonna try to ride Amber on your own now.'

'Now? I can't, Eddie.'

'Course you can. You're a Scottsdale girl, aren't you?'

She had gripped the reins in shaking hands. Felt a swell of nausea inside her belly, a dizziness buzzing around her head like a swarm of flies. She had wanted to get down. But she had wanted Eddie more, and if she got off his horse he would never want to see her again. He would think she was pathetic.

'Go on now,' he'd said, giving the horse a slap on the rump.

Amber had started trotting, Joy bumping around on her back like a sack of potatoes, but the horse had sensed her lack of control and speeded up, and before Joy knew it she'd been cantering. Fear had soared through her. She had wanted to stop but didn't know how. She had tried to pull on the reins but Amber had ignored her.

'Just go with it, Joy,' Eddie had called.

There had been a moment when Joy had felt it, that free

spirit that all riders must feel at one with their horse, but it had been fleeting. Then terror had taken over as Amber moved faster and faster.

'Pull on the reins, Joy – stop her!' Eddie had shouted.

But Amber had known she was in charge. The horse had surged towards the edge of the arena, and too late Joy had realised that she was jumping the fence. She had screamed as she let go of the reins and fell off the horse onto the hard sand.

Eddie had scooped her up into his arms, and she had buried her face and her humiliation in his chest as he stroked her hair.

'I'm sorry, baby, I'm sorry.'

Eddie Sheldon had apologised to her, but she had been unable to stop the tears as they leaked from her eyes.

'I'm so stupid,' she'd said.

'I shouldn't have made you do it.' He'd stroked wisps of hair off her forehead. 'I promise I'll never make you ride again.'

'Where's Amber? Has she run off?'

'Nope.' Eddie had given her one of his dazzling smiles. 'She's right there, the minx. She was just having some fun with you.'

That night they had made love for the first time in the back of Eddie's Plymouth. She could still remember the trembling thrill in her breast at the sensation of his fingers pushing under the waistband of her jeans, unbuttoning them. She should have stopped him. She had been raised a Catholic – they both had – and they knew they were sinning. But her vulnerability and his strength had been irresistible, and they had been unable to deny each other.

17

She had wanted him. She had encouraged him. They'd peeled off their clothes and climbed into the back of the Plymouth, and for a while they'd just explored each other's nakedness. She had never seen a man up close before. She'd thought she would be afraid, but instead she'd thought he was beautiful and she'd wanted to know how it would feel to have him inside her. How were they to know that one moment would change both their lives forever?

Nine months later they would be married, moving into their own little house in Scottsdale, and they would have a baby boy – Ray. Two years later their little girl Heather would arrive. She and Eddie had made a family so quickly.

'In the blink of an eye,' her father had said, none too happy.

Thinking of her father again reminded Joy of those last words he had said to her before he died. They felt like old stab wounds, throbbing beneath her skin. She had given her mom a whole year to talk about it, but she'd never said a word. Not in all the times they had spent together since.

Joy wasn't going to wait any longer. Her father had only told her a little part of the truth. She needed to hear the whole story.

★

It had been one of those rare moments of familiarity with a stranger. It had happened to Lewis before on trains, or planes … sometimes in a bar. The sharing of an experience – an understanding that you and your unknown companion were both in your private worlds and thoughts. The woman had split her Thermos of coffee with him. It had seemed perfectly natural, as if they were old friends. But after the lights had faded away, he had said goodbye and climbed back down Papago Butte without even exchanging names.

He was home again now. He doubted Samantha had even noticed that he'd gone out in the middle of the night. He picked up the postcard from where he had left it in the kitchen and brought it out to the garage, storing it underneath the top tray of his toolbox. He was hiding it from Samantha as if it was his own secret treasure.

That very night he dreamed about Marnie. She was in her signature green coat, dark hair glossy as horse chestnuts, umbrella in hand. She was expecting rain. Yet she was walking barefoot under the midday glare through the Sonoran desert, surveying his landscape. Colour and form shifted at her command. The cacti sprouted desert blooms; the arid plains filled with banks of golden poppies. She was conducting an orchestra of vision. She was designing another new land just for them.

## London, 13 April 1967, 7.15 a.m.

Lewis stood outside Marnie's flat, ringing the bell. A few minutes later, she opened the door to him, her eyes still sleepy. She was wearing a black chiffon nightdress, and her dark brown hair was loose, tumbling around her dreamy face. But it was her plush lips that drew him across the threshold. He leaned forward, kissing them without a word and she kissed back. He put his arms around her and buried his face in her chest. She smelled of her favourite perfume, Ma Griffe.

19

'What are you doing here at this hour?'

'Don't talk…' He put his finger to her lips and continued to kiss her, pulling the straps of her nightdress down so it slid off her to the floor. He threw off his coat and walked her backward into her bedroom and onto the lopsided bed.

She was as bold as he, pulling off his clothes until they were both naked. They rolled on the bed, caressing each other until he entered her. He looked down at her. Her eyes were closed, her mouth a little open, her pink tongue pushed against her teeth. The window was unlatched, and the curtains fluttered against the bed. He could smell cherry blossom on the trees outside, and hear the patter of rain as it fell on the leaves. All of this was part of making love to Marnie. The glory of London on a spring morning, the scent of wet cherry blossom, the rainbow-filled puddles and the promise that came with a new day.

Afterwards they lay on their backs, sharing a cigarette. He watched the smoke coil above him, like steam rising from their bodies.

'We had better get up and go to work,' Marnie said at last, sitting up and pulling her hair into a knot on the top of her head.

Now all of sudden she was bashful as she slid off the bed, clasping her black nightie to herself, not quite hiding her nakedness completely. She tried to suppress this wildness within her, but it was her free spirit that had drawn him to her.

Lewis remembered the first day he had met Marnie. Six months ago George Miller had brought her into the design studio, introducing her as their new girl Friday.

'What do you think, lads? Very pleasing on the eye,' George had said as soon as Marnie had gone into the kitchen to make tea for them all. 'Do you think she's a modern girl, eh, Pete?'

Lewis's colleague Pete Piper had looked embarrassed and mumbled something indistinguishable. Frankie, the Italian designer at the studio, had slapped Pete on the back. 'Is she too much woman for you, Pete?'

But George had been wrong. Marnie had not been easily seduced, and she had been faultless at her job. The agency had never run so smoothly. Lewis had found Marnie's cool indifference attractive. He liked a challenge. In his experience, no matter how aloof a girl might seem, there was always a chink in her armour.

Marnie's chink had surprised Lewis. It hadn't been flattery or gifts, like the bunches of flowers George had bought her or the chocolates Frankie had left on her desk. They were both married men, and she had no intention of responding to their constant requests for a quick drink after work.

What had turned Marnie on was, in fact, her love for art and design. Lewis had discovered all this at the Christmas party, plying her with so many gin and tonics that her ice-queen veneer had finally slipped. He had been bewitched by her as she'd talked about her dreams of being a designer herself. Had Lewis seen something in Marnie that he'd identified with? Only a few years ago it had been hard to distinguish between a commercial artist and a graphic designer, but he had sought out the new leaders in the design field. That's why he'd pursued George Miller and persuaded him to give him a job fresh out of art school. Marnie had reminded him of his passion and drive. If she had been a man he would have felt threatened by her, but he knew her gender was against her. She had become a collaborator rather than a competitor.

After the party Marnie had let him accompany her home on the Underground. They had kissed on her doorstep, and after a moment's hesitation Marnie had invited him in for a cup of tea. To his surprise, Marnie had showed him a series of designs she had made for the Macht shaver advertisement he had been working on. Using photomontage she had created a sleek design, alluding to the current fascination with all things space-age. He had told her how good he thought her designs were, though at the same time he had felt a little piqued. Why had this girl been gifted with such a talent?

'Do you think I should show them to George?' she'd asked him.

Lewis had wanted to help Marnie, but George was such a chauvinist. His boss would not have taken her work seriously no matter how good it was.

'I think it might be better if I presented them to him for you,' Lewis had suggested.

'Do you mean pretend you did them?'

'No, but maybe say that we worked on them together as a team.'

'But we didn't.' And she had given him a wary look.

'George is very old-fashioned. We'd have to build him up to the idea of having a woman designer at Studio M.'

'Do you think they're that good?'

'Yes, Marnie, I do.'

He had got up onto his knees and crawled over to her, through the pictures.

'Mind them! Careful where you're going,' she had said, giggling.

'I have an idea.' He had snaked towards her.

'And what is that?' Marnie had asked, letting him undo her blouse, button by button.

'Let's set up our own design agency.'

'Oh yes!' She had sat up abruptly. 'Do you mean it?'

It had been the alcohol talking, but it had seemed like such a good idea at the time.

'With your talent and my sales banter, we would be unstoppable.'

'When can we do it?' she had asked, pulling her shirt off, her breasts spilling out of her bra.

Their desire for each other had never seemed to wane. When would it end? It worried Lewis. He felt he should be playing the field, but he couldn't help wanting only Marnie all the time.

During the first few weeks they had been together Marnie had often asked him when they were going to set up their design practice. He had tried to explain that his drunken state had made him a little premature in his enthusiasm.

'Not yet,' Lewis would tell her. 'I need to get more clients. You need more design experience.'

After she had assisted him on three more campaigns, she'd begun to ask him why he couldn't tell George about her. Could her boss really be that against female designers? Now and again they had dealt with other women in the business.

What was it that was stopping Lewis from telling his boss that she should be promoted?

Was he jealous of her talent? No, of course not. He was proud of her. So what was it?

It was to do with George Miller, he realised in the end. His whole life Lewis had trained himself to avoid conflict, and he knew broaching the subject with George would be difficult. Would the great man think less of him and his capabilities as a designer? Would Marnie rise without him – and once she was successful not want him any more?

Marnie emerged from the bathroom. Her hair was piled on top of her head, two long russet curls spiralling either side; her lips thick with gloss. She had on a sapphire shift dress, which matched her blue eyes and went beautifully with the shimmering viridian eyeshadow she was wearing. Everything about her was glowing and iridescent, as if she were a girl from the stars. Tomorrow's Girl. She smoothed her dress down with her silver-tipped fingers. It rippled over the contours of her body like a waterfall. He grabbed her by the waist.

'I want you,' he said.

'We don't have time,' she protested.

'Come on, baby. We can be quick.'

He was pushing it. They were short of time as it was, but he wanted Marnie right then more than anything in the world.

Marnie twirled her silver bracelets. They looked like miniature planets orbiting each other.

'If you give me a lift to work we might have time.'

'You know I can't. We agreed that we can't arrive together.'

She took her green coat off the hook on the back of the door.

'Well, then I had better be going. It can take over half an

hour to get from South Ken to Russell Square, especially when it's raining.'

He tugged at the sleeve of her coat.

'Now don't make me feel bad, will you?'

It had been Marnie who had first wanted to keep their affair a secret. She hadn't wanted George thinking Lewis was giving her design work because they were sleeping together. She had wanted to be recognised for her own talent.

'I could drop you at Green Park?' he suggested.

'And if you tell George about me today, we can drive the whole way in together tomorrow.'

There was a cheeky glint in her eye.

He watched her as she covered her lips with another smear of pale gloss.

'Okay, darling.' He kissed her again, tasting the synthetic lipstick, and still desiring her. 'God, you're gorgeous.'

She smiled at him, but there was that look in her eyes. She was stepping back from him – he could feel it.

'I'm just a girl,' she told him. 'Like any other.'

'You will never be just any girl, Marnie. You are my shining star.'

'Oh what a charmer you are, Lewis Bell.' She gave his face a gentle slap. 'You don't know how lucky you are. Just to be a man. It's so much easier for you.'

She linked her arm in his as they went down the stairs.

Out on the street, she opened up her umbrella and they huddled beneath it. He put his arm around her, squeezed her to his side. They walked in unison, around the puddles. They could be invincible. Not a couple, yet more together than most marriages ever were.

'Lewis, you *will* tell George about my design work today, won't you?'

'Of course I will.'

He meant every word.

'You promise?'

Why couldn't she trust him?

'I have to be tactful. You know how old-fashioned George is ...'

'Sexist, you mean,' she said, sounding glum.

She said nothing more for the whole ten-minute drive to Green Park. As she got out he leaned across, touched her arm.

'Marnie?'

'Yes.' She turned to him.

'I love you.' He pulled her down and kissed her on the lips, but she was cold beneath his touch.

'Trust me.'

'Eventually the truth will come out, Lewis.'

She smiled yet it didn't reach her eyes. He waited for her to tell him she loved him too, but instead she got out of the car, giving him a weak wave before stepping away.

He watched her walk across Piccadilly and down the steps into the Underground station, men turning to look at her as she went. There was no doubt about it, she was a stunning vision, her waist tiny, cinched in and belted in her green mackintosh, her russet hair like a crown upon her head. She was a jewel – something quite extraordinary in the dull London rain.

# TWO

## *Magnetic Field*

It was exactly two years ago that Joy and her father, Jack, had taken the Apache Trail. It had been the last time they'd gone on a wildflower hike together. It was during that trip that her father had told her he had cancer. She remembered the exact moment. They had been standing on the desert slopes beneath the Superstition Mountains, among the Mexican gold poppies and wild hyacinth. She had felt an overwhelming sense of dread. The dark mountains had gathered above her, reaching out with their long shadows into her soul.

'What kind of cancer, Daddy?' she had asked him.

'Lung – but, honey, I'm going to get chemo. Everything is going to be okay.'

'Of course, Daddy.' She had clutched his hand and pushed her palm against his hard, worn skin. 'You're a fighter. You can beat it.'

She had tried her best to stay upbeat for her father, but their trip had been marred. The drive along the Apache

Trail had lost its magic. They hadn't done it since she'd been a little girl, and they had been planning this time together for the whole of the previous year. As she had crawled up the steep and precipitous Fish Creek Canyon she'd had the urge to let go of the wheel, let the car just slide back down and off the edge into oblivion. How could she live without the rock of her father keeping her upright?

'He is not going to die,' she had told herself. But in her gut she had felt something different. She had watched her father as they'd explored the fields of wildflowers. He with his little notebook and pencil, scribbling down drawings and notes, and she with her camera, attempting to take a few decent shots. Already Jack Porter had seemed less substantial. How had she not noticed that he'd lost so much weight recently? His skin wasn't the right colour, and his rich brown eyes were cloudy.

Then there had been the day he'd disappeared. They had been wandering along one of the many paths the Salados had created, gazing at impenetrable canyons, exploring all the hidden caves. One minute her father had been right behind her and the next he was gone. She had retraced her footsteps along the path, calling out his name, but all she had heard was its echo. She had gone back to where they had been and still he was nowhere to be seen, so she'd returned again to where they'd started along the path and suddenly there he was.

'Where'd you go, Daddy?' she had asked him.

'Nowhere. I've been right in front of you. What's up?'

She had bitten her lip, shaken her head. She hadn't wanted to frighten him. He had slipped away just for an instant. He had come back that day, but she had known he would go eventually.

That last day they had reached the Tonto National Monument and looked down upon the sapphire waters of Roosevelt Lake. The centuries-old saguaros reached up to the skies, their fat prickly fingers pointing to heaven.

She remembered her father had coughed as if to clear his throat. He had wanted to tell her something, but she had not wanted to hear it. She had thought it was more about the cancer and she had not been able to talk about it again. She had wanted to push the reality away from her. Joy reflected that it had most likely been the moment he had wanted to tell her the truth about herself. She was sure of it.

Her father had started to speak. 'Joy, I need to tell you something…'

But she had pretended not to hear him. She had got back into the car and turned the engine on.

'Come on, Daddy, we have to get home.'

She had driven fast, and in silence. An impenetrable quiet that neither she nor her father had been able to breach until they reached Scottsdale, and could leave those unsaid moments far behind.

'Are you okay, honey?' her mom asked her.

Joy was shivering, but not because she was cold. Never before had she had to stand up to her mother. They were sitting at the kitchen table. Her mom was still in her dressing gown. Joy had driven straight over to her house as soon as the sun had risen on Papago Butte. She hadn't wanted to go home first because she knew Eddie would have changed her mind.

29

'Mom, I need to talk to you about something.'

Her mom looked at her warily. 'Well, it better be important since you dragged me out of bed so early in the morning.'

'Mom, I haven't brought this up before because I didn't want to upset you. I know this past year's been hard, but I have to ask you about something Daddy said to me the day he died –'

'No!' Her mother's voice was suddenly sharp.

It was clear all of a sudden. Her mother knew she knew. How could she pretend nothing had ever been said? How could she never have mentioned it for a whole year?

★

When Lewis woke he felt different, as if he was still half submerged within his dream. He slipped out of bed, glancing at the alarm clock. It was 6 a.m. Samantha was turned away from him, a motionless shape under the covers.

He went downstairs into the garage, its heavy door banging against the wall behind him. He pulled out his toolbox, fumbling with the lock, and lifted the top tray off, showering screws and nails around him, his heart thundering. He saw it immediately, lying innocently on top of his hammer. He was not going crazy. This message from the past really did exist.

He picked it up, stared at the family-bathing scene on the beach in Ireland and flipped it over again to read the message. He tried to convince himself that he was only being sentimental for a time in his life that he had long since lost. This postcard represented an impossible dream. And yet here it was in his hands: a real possibility.

## EVENTUALLY THE TRUTH WILL COME OUT

That was the only writing on the card. No name or return address. Just those words – and his own address on the back to leave him in no doubt that this lone sentence was for him. He tried to remember Marnie's handwriting but found it impossible.

He looked at the stamp. It had Eire written on it. He knew that was the Irish for Ireland. It had to be Marnie because it was from her homeland with her words.

What truth was Marnie referring to? he wondered. The truth of their love for each other? Or the truth of his betrayal? In all these years he had never heard from her so why now?

★

By the time her daddy had got around to telling her, he had been able to say so little, but Joy remembered how he had gazed at her. She had felt his regret as he squeezed her hand tightly in his.

'Joy, I have to tell you something…'

'Don't talk, Daddy – just rest.'

He had struggled in the bed as if he wanted to raise himself.

'I've time for resting soon enough,' he had croaked, trying to give her a smile. 'There's something I need to tell you, and I won't be at peace until I have.'

31

'Daddy, please don't worry – it doesn't matter.' She had tried to placate him, get him to lie down again. But Jack Porter had been determined. He had lifted himself a few inches on his elbows and fixed her with a frantic stare.

'Promise me that you'll forgive me, darling.'

She had felt a thick smoke of fear seeping through her. What was he talking about? What could he have done?

'Daddy, I love you. You could do nothing that would change that.'

'Darling girl,' he had whispered, closing his eyes for a moment as he dropped back onto the bed. 'Your mother will be mad at me for telling you, but I just have to ...'

'It's okay, Daddy, you don't have to tell me anything –'

But her father had interrupted her with a rare spurt of energy. His voice had been suddenly crystal clear.

'Joy, you're adopted.'

She had nearly dropped his hand, almost fallen off the chair. It had been the last thing she'd expected her father to say.

'No, Daddy, that can't be true ...'

But her father had talked over her. He'd told her that he and her mother had discovered that they couldn't have children about five years after they had got married. He'd told her how hard it had been on her mother; how badly she'd wanted a baby. A cousin in New York knew of a young girl in Ireland who had wanted to give up her baby for adoption. It seemed meant to be. When they had brought baby Joy back to America they had decided to start fresh somewhere no one knew them or that their daughter was adopted. That's why they had moved to Scottsdale – why they had never returned to New York.

Joy had felt dizzy, her head spinning in her father's airless bedroom.

'I'm so sorry we never told you before,' her father had whispered. Already he had looked different to her. 'Your mother thought it best.'

'But, Daddy.' She had felt tears filling her eyes. Why did he have to tell her this now? Break her heart apart at the very time she was about to lose him.

'Do you mean that you aren't my real father? And Mom isn't my real mother?'

'Oh of course we are, darling. I loved you from the moment I saw you. You have always been my daughter.'

She had felt him muster all his strength – squeeze her hand.

'As soon as I saw you I knew you were my girl,' he'd whispered. 'You just reached out for me, darling, and I took you up and in my arms. We chose each other.'

Joy hadn't wanted to push him for more details. He had been so weak and frail, and this revelation, as mind-blowing as it was, had been nothing compared to the fact that her father was dying. She hadn't asked him why he had to tell her this now. She hadn't asked him about her birth mother.

Joy had shoved the fact of her adoption to the back of her mind. She had even managed not to say anything to her grieving mother. Not one word in the past year. But the truth was tearing her apart.

Her adoption explained so many things. The fact she didn't look like either of her parents. Or how she sometimes felt like an outsider in her own life; how she hankered for something she could never find in Arizona.

Those dreams filled with the scent and sight of places she had never been. The land she was from and knew nothing about.

At first she had tried to talk to Eddie about it. He had been as shocked as her.

'Well, how do you like that?' he'd said, scratching the back of his head and looking at her as if with new eyes. 'You're not a true American after all. You're an Irish girl.'

'I want to find out more. I want to know where I'm from.'

'It's not worth it, Joy,' Eddie had advised her. 'Your parents are the people who raise you. Just give it up. You'll only get hurt, baby.'

The problem was Joy couldn't give it up. She had to know who she was.

*

Lewis put the postcard back into the tool tray. He was being an idiot to even think about Marnie. He and Samantha had been married for so long. That had to be worth more than a fantasy from his past.

He made amends by putting together a fruit platter for Samantha's breakfast: pineapple, strawberries and slices of orange, arranging it all on one of her colourful Mexican dishes. He brought it up to her in bed with a cup of coffee.

'Oh ... thanks, Lewis.' Samantha sat up, looking surprised by his sudden attention.

'It's what you like, right?' he said, placing the tray on her lap.

'You haven't brought me breakfast in bed for years.'

'I know; I'm sorry.' He leaned forward and pushed a

loose tendril of her hair behind her ear. 'And I'm sorry about last night.'

'What do you mean?' She looked at him warily.

'I should have made it more special.'

'It was fine, really, Lewis.' She popped a strawberry in her mouth.

'Let's go on a vacation,' he said, seized by the moment. 'We could take off for Easter. What about Hawaii?'

'I can't, I'm going to Santa Fe, remember?'

'But wouldn't you rather go away with me?'

'It's not that,' she said, not meeting his eye. 'I've promised Jennifer...'

'Right.' He didn't understand it. What was he doing wrong?

'I'm sorry, Lewis.'

He tried to hide his disappointment, walked over to the wardrobe and pulled out a clean shirt.

'Well, why don't we go away this summer?'

'Okay.' She didn't sound enthusiastic.

'It always gets so hot here – it would be good to go somewhere cooler.'

He watched her in the mirror. She picked up a piece of pineapple, bit into it.

'Let's go back to London,' he said.

Her eyes widened in shock.

'Are you crazy?'

He walked over to the bed. 'It's been so many years, Samantha. I want to visit my home.'

'But why? The London we knew is long gone, Lewis.'

She stroked his arm, and when he looked into her eyes he could see her fear.

'I can't go back,' she said, shaking her head. 'You know I can't.'

He saw tears springing. He wasn't sure if they were real or not, but it moved him to kiss her – and for once she was kissing him back. She pulled him down to her and the fruit platter slid off the bed, spilling its contents onto the floor.

Lewis made love to his wife for the first time in months, and yet even in the heart of their passion, neither of them were able to look into each other's eyes. It was a release, yes, but it also felt like an apology.

★

'Daddy told me I was adopted,' Joy ploughed on despite her mother's protests.

'I don't know why he had to do that, Joy.'

'So it's true?'

'Yes,' her mom said, sounding agitated. 'It's true.'

'Why did you never tell me?'

'Because we didn't want to hurt you ... and we thought, what was the point?' Her mom looked right at her. 'What use is it to know that you're adopted?'

'Because it's who I am, Mom.'

'Who you are is Joy Porter, our daughter, a child of Scottsdale, Arizona. That's who you are.' Her mother sounded defiant. Joy tried another tack.

'Please, Mom, I love you, and I loved Daddy.' She grasped her mother's cold hands. 'I know I couldn't have had better parents but Daddy said my birth mother was Irish. I just want to know who she was and her story...'

'Oh, Joy, *why* do you want to know? Why on earth

would you want to find out the details of a woman who rejected her baby? What kind of woman is that?' She looked at her daughter with pleading eyes. 'Can you tell me? What woman willingly gives up her child?'

'But maybe there's more to the story –'

'Surely you of all people should understand? What did you do when you got pregnant at seventeen? You didn't give your baby up for adoption, did you? You married Eddie.'

'But that's only because he asked me –'

'Darling, I know who you are.' Her mom's face softened. 'Nothing in the world would have made you give up Ray. Yet *she* gave *you* up.'

Joy couldn't deny it – her mom was right. And yet she felt strangely protective of her unknown Irish mother.

'Your Daddy loved you so much, Joy.' Her mom's voice was loaded with emotion.

'I know, Momma.'

'I miss him. Sometimes so much I find it hard to breathe.'

'You'll get through, Mom.'

'I don't know, darling; I just don't know if I can. He was everything to me.'

Tears were running down her mother's face, and Joy felt terrible. What was she doing? Hounding her poor mom for details about a woman who clearly never cared about her.

'I'm sorry,' she said, hugging her mother hard and praying she would learn to appreciate all that she had rather than hankering for the unknown.

★

Samantha had already left for work. Lewis looked in the wardrobe mirror. What would Marnie think if she saw him now? He had filled out since he was twenty-five, his face was marked with lines and his skin was darker after all his years in Arizona. His hair was streaked with grey. He had aged, no doubt. Yet he felt just the same inside. Once he peeled back the layers of all those years, he was still that young man living the dream in London.

Not only had he tried to delete his past, but nothing in his present life expressed who he was. He had slept in this bedroom for fifteen years yet nothing in it represented him in any way. It was all Samantha.

His wife loved bright colours. Three of the walls were painted peacock blue and the fourth – behind the bed – was a vibrant orange. He couldn't believe he had let her decorate their bedroom like this but he supposed he had been trying to keep her happy.

'You're such a visual snob, Lewis,' she'd complained. 'I want to make our place free-spirited!'

Combined with the vivid hues of the walls were rainbow shades woven into the rugs, a rustic Mexican dressing table and matching wardrobe. Samantha was obsessed with multicoloured Mexican beadwork, and the bedroom was filled with her hoard: little bead dolls of men and women, bead bulls, bead fish and two skulls painted vibrantly: one beaded, one plaster. She had put one skull on the table right next to their bed. Lewis hated it. But worst of all was her statue of Our Lady of Guadalupe on the dressing table. She thought it quaint, but that's because she hadn't been raised Catholic. Lewis detested looking at that statue and wondered what would Marnie have made of it.

On a spontaneous, rebellious urge he picked it up off the dressing table and dropped it in the basket bin. This was one thing he was going to insist on when Samantha got home. No more religious stuff.

His wife was also passionate about the Mexican artist Frida Kahlo. Much as Lewis appreciated Kahlo's artistic vision from a historical point of view, he found it difficult to look at the print of the painting 'The Henry Ford Hospital', depicting the artist writhing on a bed following a miscarriage, red tubes emanating from her bloody body and connecting her to surrealist objects, one of which was a red foetus. What exactly had Samantha been trying to say when she put that picture above their fireplace?

In all their years of marriage they had never discussed children. Samantha just never got pregnant. He had thought that she didn't want children, but maybe his wife had hidden a private sorrow from him all these years.

It was too late now. He was forty-seven and Samantha was forty-five. He had convinced himself it was a good thing they hadn't had any children. He had no idea how to be a good father.

★

After Joy had tucked her mom up in bed again, as if she were the child, and closed her curtains against the brightening day, she drove home to make Eddie his breakfast.

She could hear her husband singing one of his cheesy cowboy songs in the shower as soon as she walked in. It made her smile – it reminded her of when he used to play the guitar the times they'd gone camping, when the kids were small.

She hurried into the kitchen, took out the pan and put it on the stove, then pulled a tray of eggs out the fridge.

'So did you see them?' Eddie asked her as he walked into the kitchen. 'I saw your note.'

Her husband looked sharp in his suit, his blonde hair slicked back and his face clean-shaven.

'It was spectacular,' she told him. 'I wish you could have been there.'

'You know I'm not really into stars and that kind of stuff, Joy.'

She wanted Eddie to come over and kiss her, but he had already sat down at the table and opened the newspaper, waiting patiently for his eggs. She turned the heat down under the pan and walked over to stand behind him then bent down and kissed his cheek. He looked up at her, surprised.

'What was that for?' he asked.

'Because I love you,' she said.

'Well, that's nice,' he replied, looking back down at the paper. 'So are you gonna make me an omelette? I have to get going.'

'Sure,' she said tightly, returning to the stove and turning the heat back up. She had been about to suggest they took a tumble on the bed but now her courage had deserted her. It had already been a few weeks since they had last made love. It wasn't like him. She and Eddie had never stopped wanting each other.

'Is everything all right, Eddie?'

He looked up. 'Sure – of course. I'm just super busy,

baby. Trying to make all this money for Heather's wedding.'

His eyes were dancing, unable to rest on hers.

'Don't forget to order the invites today,' he reminded her, folding up the newspaper and putting it down on the table as she placed his omelette in front of him.

'Honey, do you think Heather's doing the right thing?'

'Course I do. Darrell's a good kid,' Eddie said, picking up the salt and ruining her omelette with it.

'But they're so young.'

'We were younger.' Eddie looked up, those dancing eyes still refusing to meet hers.

'Yeah but that was different.'

'Well, yes, at least Heather isn't knocked up.'

She winced. It pained her to imagine that Eddie had only married her because she had been pregnant. In her heart she knew it wasn't true. Eddie had been wild, edgy and irresistible to her when she had been seventeen, and she knew she'd had a similar effect on him, yet she saw none of that chemistry between her daughter and her fiancé. There were no sparks flying. It was as if Heather and Darrell were playing at being in love, all 'darlings' and pecks on the cheek.

'I mean, we were crazy about each other.'

Those weeks before Joy had discovered she was pregnant had been so exciting. Eddie would roll up at her house in his fast car and take her off under the disapproving gaze of her parents. They would ride right into the desert where no one was witness to their passion apart from a jackrabbit or a pack rat. She squeezed her thighs at the memory of all that sex. They hadn't been able to get enough of each other.

41

'Other things are more important, Joy,' Eddie said, cutting up his omelette. 'Darrell's a good guy. He's already asked me to find them a house in Scottsdale. Told me it's the best place to raise a family. He'll be a good provider.'

Joy was shocked by her husband's words. How could anything be more important than being in love?

'A few weeks ago I overheard Heather and Carla talking about the wedding and it sounded like Heather might have some doubts –'

'Carla's jealous of Heather. She's stirring her up, that's all. She's just like her mom was, jealous of you and me.'

Joy looked at her husband in surprise.

'Rosa's never been interested in you, Eddie. She's my friend.'

'If you say so, darling,' he replied, polishing off the last piece of omelette. 'I don't have time to chat about this any more.' He got up from the table and dusted down his lap. 'Don't be filling Heather's head with nonsense. I've paid so much up front we can't cancel the wedding now.'

He patted her on the head as he went towards the door. She knew it was meant to be affectionate, but it just felt patronising.

Their conversation hadn't stopped her from worrying. Ever since she had overheard Heather and Carla arguing out on the porch, she'd had a growing feeling that her daughter was about to make the biggest mistake of her life. She remembered Carla's last words: 'This is your life, Heather – think about what you really want. You know you don't love him!'

Joy hadn't seen her daughter's best friend since.

Darrell wasn't a bad kid. Like Heather he was Scottsdale

born and bred, studying to be an accountant with plans to set up a business in Phoenix. He had never expressed any desire to travel outside of the state, let alone leave America.

Was this her daughter's future, to be stuck in Arizona just like she was? Her light to be hidden away, the star that could never be allowed to shine?

★

The last thing Lewis expected to find was a second postcard lying in his mailbox. He stood paralysed on the front lawn, his chest constricting. What if Samantha had checked the mailbox before she'd left for work? How could he have explained that what was happening was so unexpected? She wouldn't have believed him, of that he was sure.

Again all that was written on the back was one line. This time a question:

### AM I YOUR SHINING STAR?

There was no name, no return address. The postmark was Ireland again.

The picture on the front of the postcard was of a lighthouse. The image was made up of tones of blue: the sea was calm, night navy, and the coastline zigzagged through it, layers of wet, jagged indigo rocks. In the background was the lighthouse. A beacon of blue and white stripes, surrounded by white cottages, and topped by its light shining out into the night. It was right on the edge, tipping the navy clouds, with the glimmering light of the dying day seeping through.

Lewis flipped the card over and read it again. The words reminded him of *The Great Gatsby,* one of the few novels he had read and liked. Gatsby had been transfixed by the green light at the end of Daisy's pier.

Were the image and the words upon this postcard Marnie's beacon? Was she waiting for him to see the light? He had once called her his shining star, and he had meant it, not just because of the talent that brimmed out of her, but also because she had been a bright light in his life. She had made him want to be better than he was, and when he'd been with her he had managed to forget his sorry childhood – the demands made by his mother and sister.

At the end of the day he hadn't chosen her light, had he? He remembered how that last day had unfolded between them. Its passionate beginning, and his plan to tell his boss George about her. His intention had been to end the day on bended knee, asking her to marry him. How could it be that everything had happened so differently? During the hours of just one long day he had let everything fall apart.

## LONDON, 13 APRIL 1967, 8.43 A.M.

Lewis manoeuvred his racing-green roadster into a tight spot. Steam was rising from the wet pavement as he walked briskly across Russell Square. The air was glossy with morning light, as if it had only rained for the purpose of brightening up London, reminding him that he lived in the best city in the world.

Three girls in miniskirts walked in front of him. The two on the outside were wearing black, the one in the middle white. They all had the same haircut: a short geometric bob. He imagined their shared flat, the mixture of all their scents with pairs of black and white stockings hanging off radiators, empty wine bottles with candles in them littering the tiled floor and a folded-back paperback of *Lady Chatterley's Lover* on the side of the bathtub. A saggy sofa covered in a stack of bright cushions, crumpled from the night before, and the imprint of red-lipsticked lips on a tissue, discarded on the floor like a lost kiss. Lewis loved the new modern girl. These three looked like op art as they bounced up and down in front of him. It made him think how effective that style might be for the poster he was designing for Dalliance Shoes.

These girls were forthright, just like his sister Lizzie; just like Marnie. He took a cigarette out and lit it up. He wasn't going to think about his feelings for Marnie now. He was going to focus on work.

Lewis didn't know any other advertising company in London that was as up to the minute as Studio M. It was a bold new world, full of colour. It was time to live in the now and not worry about tomorrow.

But he did want to think about tomorrow. He wanted to be remembered for groundbreaking designs, like his boss. He couldn't help this constant need for George's approval, and he knew it was why he had avoided the subject of Marnie with him for so long.

He took a last drag of his cigarette, glancing back down to the end of the street, hoping to see Marnie marching towards him in her emerald-green coat, but she was nowhere. A double-decker bus swept past, leaving a swirl of exhaust behind it as he hurried inside Studio M.

Despite its impression of modernity, Studio M was run very much like the painting studios of the seventeenth century – George Miller was the master, and Lewis, Pete and Frankie were his underlings.

Every designer or commercial artist Lewis knew coveted a job at Studio M, yet he had managed to pull it off not so much on the basis of his portfolio but with his charm. From the moment he and George had met they had got on. Yet during his first two years of working at Studio M he could tell that George had been a little disappointed in him. If Marnie hadn't come along Lewis wondered if he would still have a job. Thanks to her, Lewis now suspected that George was grooming him for partnership one day.

'Boys, I'm not getting any younger you know!' he'd say every now and again over tea and jam tarts during their afternoon break. He would follow this up with, 'I need someone young to keep the flag flying at Studio M,' and Lewis, Pete and Frankie would all eye each other over their mugs.

Although he was talented and industrious, Lewis could tell that Pete irritated George slightly. He was too meek. Yet Lewis liked Pete. He was hard-working, with no airs and graces. He was also honest. Lewis was more wary of Frankie, their Italian designer.

Both Pete and Frankie were already at work when Lewis walked in. The blinds were still down and the room was full of cigarette smoke.

'Christ, it's suffocating in here.' Lewis pulled up the blinds then opened the window. 'Come on, men; let's get some light and fresh air in.'

'What fresh air?' Frankie complained, putting out his cigarette and sweeping his arm dramatically. 'It's a load of car fumes outside.'

'Where's Marnie? I'm dying for a cuppa.' Pete leaned back in his chair, hands behind his head as he surveyed his handiwork.

As if on cue, the door opened and in walked Marnie.

'Good morning, Miss Regan,' Lewis said, helping her off with her coat.

'Good morning, Mr Bell.'

This pretence turned him on no end. Marnie busied herself at her desk, whipping the cover off her typewriter, putting a new ribbon in and sharpening her pencils. He couldn't take his eyes off her. Did the others sense what lurked beneath their professional veneer?

'Tea for all?' Marnie asked once her desk was all set up for the day.

'I thought you'd never ask.' Pete smiled at her in appreciation.

'Coffee, *mia amora*.' Frankie blew her a kiss from across the room.

She shook her head at him, but she was smiling too. Lewis felt a twinge of jealousy.

'Yes.' He pulled at her arm. 'Tea for me too.'

Pete looked at him in surprise. 'Hey, stop manhandling the girl Friday, mate.'

Marnie shook him off and went into the little kitchen to the side of the office, and Lewis heard her bustling around with the stove and kettle.

Then Marnie popped her head round the door. 'Is Mr Miller in?'

'No, not yet,' Pete told her.

Marnie caught Lewis's eye. As if he could forget his promise to her. He looked down at his drawing board, picking up a pencil and pressing its lead tip against a blank piece of paper until it snapped.

How would George react when he knew the full extent to which he and Marnie had teamed up? He had lied. There was no getting around the fact. It was all getting too complicated. Marnie wanted them to set up together as designers. It was a big risk. What if George offered him a partnership? Once he had that in the bag he could look after Marnie and make her part of the team. Why couldn't she just wait?

Lewis sat down. His eyes fell on a framed photograph on his desk. It was of himself and his sister Lizzie, taken just last year at her first art exhibition. She had said that since there were no surviving pictures of them as children she'd wanted to have some happy memories to collect.

She looked radiant, her hair swept up off her face, red curls tumbling out of a loose bun. She was wearing a scarlet maxi dress and she wasn't as thin as she was now. She was smiling, for real, and so was he. He had been so proud of his sister that night. Her show had practically sold out. At last she was getting the adulation she deserved. And yet her night had ended in drunken tears. The one person she had really wanted to come and see her pictures never showed up. Their mother. It frustrated Lewis that Lizzie still cared. He had long since stopped giving a toss what his mother thought of him.

# THREE

# *Connection*

As Lewis drove past Langely Art Gallery, he could see Doug inside wearing his signature black Stetson. Samantha hated her father dressing up like a cowboy, especially since he was Boston born and bred, but Lewis had always found Doug Langely's love of cowboy culture endearing. And the old man had picked the right town to live in.

Every day Lewis drove past the large cowboy signboard on the corner of Scottsdale Road and Main Street proclaiming Scottsdale as 'The West's Most Western Town'. Around the time his in-laws Doug and Dora had moved to Scottsdale in the early seventies, a replica 1880s Old West town was built at the south-east corner of Scottsdale and Pinnacle Peak Roads. Millions came from around the world to 'play cowboy' for the day.

When he and Samantha had first arrived in Scottsdale, Doug used to drag him along to see staged gunfights on Main Street, or ride a hay wagon into the desert for a cookout under the stars. He'd never had the heart to tell Doug that, much as he admired his father-in-law's passion, he couldn't identify with cowboy culture himself. In fact Lewis found it a little distasteful the way the Native Americans had been passed over. There were the cursory souvenirs in the shops, and bits and bobs of native artefacts they would sometimes come across, but the truth was it was rare to see one of the Native Americans from the Salt River Pima Maricopa Community in town.

He had heard Scottsdale described as the town millionaires built, and there was no denying that it attracted the rich and famous. With his background in art and design, Lewis should have thrived here. That was what Samantha had expected of him, but instead of setting up on his own he had taken a job in his father-in-law's art gallery, assisting him with typesetting jobs and print work when it came along.

Where had his old world gone? How had he ended up in this urban desert doing such a menial job? He was supposed to have become someone.

He had to stop thinking about the past and move on. This business with the postcards was just making him feel bad. He had to keep reminding himself that there was nothing to go back to. His life in London had been wiped out. It wasn't the same any more. He was married to Samantha. She was the woman he was meant to be with, not Marnie. Her family had taken him in when he had been so completely alone in the world, and he was genuinely fond of his in-laws. They were good people, and they had taught him a lot too. Doug in particular. Time and again, Lewis found himself staying late to help

Doug with flyers for all the local fundraising events he took on. He could relax with Doug in a way he had never been able to with his old boss George. His father-in-law made him feel that he was appreciated, no matter what he did.

'Morning, Lewis!' Doug gave him a cheery wave as he walked into the gallery space. 'There's fresh coffee in the pot.'

Lewis grabbed a cup before sinking into his chair in the back room, which despite Doug's best efforts was still rather dingy and dark, but at least it was cool. These spring days were pleasant, but once they hit the summer months he found the intense heat almost unbearable.

All year round in Arizona the air was so dry. Sometimes he felt like he was literally pruning, his skin itching, his lips parched and his hair so flat and static. He missed the rain. He wished for showers of sleet and wet, blustery days.

It rained a lot in Ireland. Just the idea of standing on a beach in the west of Ireland and feeling the spray from the waves, letting the rain just soak right down into his very bones, was the most blissful fantasy. In Arizona day after day all he might see were clear blue skies. He found himself chasing elusive clouds, praying for them to spill open.

He picked up his cup of coffee, took a sip. Thinking of Ireland brought him back to those postcards yet again. What did Marnie want from him?

★

Joy's parents were both from New York City, a place so exotic that her heart would race with the idea of living there. She had always felt out of place in Scottsdale. Yet her parents had avoided talking about their family in New York – not once did they visit during her childhood.

'Here in Arizona your dreams can come true,' her mother would sometimes tell her.

'Did yours, Mom?'

'Oh yes,' she'd say, flashing Joy a rare and genuine smile. 'I have you.'

They'd had a big house near the centre of Scottsdale that her parents had had built out of adobe blocks when they'd moved to the town in 1953. Her father would entertain her with stories of all the pioneer characters he knew in the early days when the town was small and everyone mixed, whether they were old timers, friends within the Mexican immigrant families or old Chief Joseph from the Salt River Pima Maricopa Community. Things had changed so much since those days. The town of Scottsdale had grown up into a city, and then just kept on growing. It was pushing into the desert and that had worried her father.

'We've got to protect the nature out there,' he'd told her. 'We'll never get it back if we let it go now.'

Joy had recently joined a group of Scottsdale residents who were trying to get the McDowell Mountain desert turned into a preserved area. She was also working as a volunteer at the Desert Botanical Garden. If she had left Scottsdale to live in New York she wouldn't have these things in her life. Moreover she could not deny the seduction of an Arizonan spring – the heady fragrance of all the blossoms as she walked down the street this very morning. She surveyed all the flowers opening their petals, a cacophony of colour and scent in this desert oasis, reminding her of the miracle of those iridescent Northern Lights. She felt like there was a shift in the air. Something was about to happen.

★

There was a stack of work waiting on Lewis's desk. He leafed through the jobs lined up for the day, but rather than feeling safe in his little back room and engrossed in the meditative task of aligning letters, he felt restless.

'Hey, Lewis.' Doug was standing in the doorway. 'I have to go out. Can you look after the gallery for a couple of hours until I get back?'

'Sure,' he replied. 'I fancy standing out front for a bit anyway.'

He followed Doug out onto the gallery floor. The main space of Langely Art Gallery was filled with a variety of paintings, sculptures and crafts, which to Lewis's eyes seemed to have no set style. Even after all these years he couldn't work out what Doug's taste was. Some of the work Lewis found unappealing: the overly naturalist oil paintings of children and little dogs, and the watercolours of the Arabian horses that always proved a bestseller during the annual Arabian Horse Festival. Yet he never criticised. Who was he to put down someone who was brave enough to put their work out there?

Sometimes, though, art came in that Lewis really did admire. At the moment they had a small exhibit of bird paintings by the artist Charley Harper. He loved the

53

graphic quality of Charley's work, and the humour he infused into his pictures. It reminded Lewis of his own design days – how this artist was aiming to communicate as much with the viewer as to express himself.

'So are you and Sammy coming over for Easter this year?' Doug asked, hovering around the exit.

'No.' Lewis shook his head, avoiding his father-in-law's penetrating gaze as he reshuffled their flyers by the cash register. 'Samantha's going to Santa Fe.'

'Are you not going with her?' Doug asked.

'She's going with Jennifer. Staying with Jen's sister. Not my scene.'

'Well, you're welcome to come on over. Dora and I would love to have you.'

'Thanks, Doug, but I'm going away too.'

'Really? Where?'

'Ireland,' Lewis heard himself say.

'Ireland! That's a hell of a way to go for your Easter vacation. Why do you want to go there?'

'I've friends there,' he lied. 'I haven't seen them in years.'

'You never mentioned anything about Ireland before,' Doug said, his expression curious.

'Actually my mother was Irish.' Lewis considered telling Doug more. In all these years he had never told him the whole story about his childhood. But somehow he couldn't bring himself to do it. He didn't want Doug to feel sorry for him.

Once Lewis was on his own, he poured himself another cup of coffee. Already the heat was blazing on the street outside, and he watched Scottsdale folk walking up and down, some holding up umbrellas to keep off the sun. *This is my home*, he reminded himself. But he knew he was just fooling himself. Were any of these people fugitives as well?

He watched a voluptuous dark-haired woman in a flowery red top, denim shorts and a pair of splendid blue cowboy boots as she walked down the street. Unlike everyone else she seemed to be taking her time. He saw her pause by one of the old olive trees, its base surrounded by bright pink flowers. She was looking at something. He strained to see what it was. She stepped back to reveal a hummingbird feeding at the flowers. He had never seen anyone so close to one of them before, and for some reason he was quite excited to watch. The hummer was fluttering right in front of her, unperturbed by her presence. Then it was by her arm, and he could see the woman was staying very still, holding her breath and watching the bird as it hovered beside her.

It landed on her sleeve. He looked at the woman's face, and he could see that she was transfixed, just like him.

Then, suddenly, the hummer darted away, its movements more bee-like than bird. The woman slowly turned away from the flowers and continued on her way. He watched her as she got closer. There was something familiar about her. In fact he wondered if he might have met her before, maybe through Samantha.

To his surprise the woman stopped right outside the gallery. She took a piece of paper out of her bag, read it, looked at the door and then pushed it open.

★

Joy started when she opened the door to see a man standing right in front of her, holding a cup of coffee in his hand. Moreover he was staring at her. She could feel an unwelcome blush creeping up her chest and neck, towards her cheeks.

'That was amazing,' he said to her.

'Excuse me?' she said, confused.

'I saw you with the hummingbird.'

'Oh, well, if you stand very still they will come up close. It was probably attracted to me because I'm wearing a red shirt.'

The man was still looking at her. She was embarrassed by his scrutiny. She opened her bag and rummaged around inside it.

'I have something that needs to be printed up,' she mumbled.

He seemed to stir himself and put down his cup of coffee.

'Of course, and what would that be?'

His voice – she had heard it before. She looked up with a start.

'Oh, it's you,' she said.

No man had looked at her like this in years. She should be getting annoyed. Yet for some reason she liked it.

'I'm sorry,' he asked her, 'but do we know each other?'

'Last night. On Papago Butte – the Northern Lights. You were there.'

The hummingbird woman was looking at him with interest. Her blush had subsided and she was now pale again. He wondered how she kept her skin so unmarked by the sun, living in Arizona. It looked like cream to him.

A complexion more common in England than America.

'So that's what they were,' he said. 'I thought you could only see them in the Arctic.'

'Usually. It was a very rare event to see them so far south.'

'I'll say.'

She smiled at him. It opened her eyes up. He noticed how blue they were. He pulled his gaze away and gently tapped the piece of paper in her right hand.

'So how can I help you?'

'Oh, yes,' she said as if woken from a reverie. 'I've come to order some wedding invitations.'

'Congratulations,' he said, experiencing an unexpected surge of disappointment. 'Let's see what you want.'

'Oh no,' she said, colouring up again. 'It's not *my* wedding. It's my daughter Heather's wedding.'

He couldn't help smiling at her. 'Well, you just don't look old enough to have a daughter who's getting married.' He beamed.

She gave him a shy smile back. 'That's real nice of you to say that but actually I have a son who is older than Heather. Ray is twenty-one.'

Lewis would not have put this woman past thirty yet she had to be almost forty. Nearly the same age as him.

'Well,' he said, 'you must have been a teen bride yourself.'

'I was,' she said, her smile fading.

His eyes brushed over her left hand and he saw her wedding band, solid and bright in its statement of possession. She was not divorced, yet there was a sense of a woman who wasn't used to being complimented. And more than that, a sadness tinged her shyness.

'It's a pleasure to meet you,' he said, holding out his hand. 'Lewis Bell.'

She seemed startled by his formality. 'Joy Sheldon.' She shook his hand in return.

He suddenly felt embarrassed. What exactly was he doing? Was he flirting with a married woman?

'Okay, so let's take a look at this invite,' he said, trying to regain some kind of professionalism. 'When's the wedding?'

'April twenty-ninth at the Princess Resort.'

He gave a whistle. 'Fancy wedding?'

'Yes, her daddy wants her to have the best. I think she's too young though,' she said in a hushed voice.

'I see, but there's no persuading her?'

'You got it. I guess I was the same. Thought Eddie was the love of my life.' She blushed again. 'Course he still is.'

She went over all of her daughter's requirements for the invite. He noted that it was Eddie and Joy Sheldon who were inviting the guests to the marriage of their daughter Heather to Darrell Winters. There were two golden hearts to be printed at the top of the invite and they had chosen a romantic Gothic font.

When Joy left thirty minutes later, her presence lingered in the gallery, as if the scent of all those spring blossoms around the olive tree had found their way inside.

★

The incident in the gallery had unsettled her. Joy couldn't forget the way that Englishman had looked at her when she'd first walked in. It was with such admiration, as if she was a beautiful thing, just like the pictures on the walls or the flowers outside. She couldn't remember the last time Eddie had looked at her like that.

She chastised herself as she walked back down the street to her car. She was lucky. Eddie might not display that raw desire of their early days any more, but that was only natural. They shared a bed, and they still made love. Most of the other women Joy knew were either divorced or trapped in loveless marriages where their husbands no longer desired them, and they slept in separate bedrooms. Men had become their enemy.

Darrell's mother Erin was one of those women. Recently divorced, she was constantly putting down her ex-husband, even in front of her son. Joy found it uncomfortable. Whenever they had Erin over for dinner it seemed as if she was scrutinising her and Eddie, looking for cracks. She could also be quite rude to Eddie sometimes, although for some reason her husband never complained.

'Don't you mind Erin talking over you?' she had asked Eddie after the last time Erin had come over for dinner.

'Does she?'

His answer had surprised her. One of Eddie's criticisms of Joy was that she talked too much when they had company.

'Have you not noticed?' Joy pushed her husband. 'She's always talking over you and running men down...'

'Well, you can hardly blame her. Her husband ran off with a younger woman. Of course she's sore.'

'But do you like her, Eddie?'

'Of course I do. She's going to be family soon. And she's giving Heather a job.'

Joy stopped walking all of a sudden. She was standing outside a new art gallery that had just opened up. She stared in at a display of Navajo basketry, but she wasn't really looking at it. Her brain was ticking over. What day was it? She opened her bag and hunted around for her diary. Her stomach sank when she read her entry for today. She had been invited over to Erin's house to meet some of her girlfriends tonight and there was no getting out of it.

'The girls want to welcome you into our gang,' Erin had said on the phone.

Joy couldn't think of anything worse than an evening with Erin and her friends.

She had already tried suggesting she cancel, but Eddie had insisted that she should go. It had surprised her, because he usually never liked her to go out without him, but he said it was important for her to get on with Darrell's mother. The wedding was just six weeks away, and after the honeymoon, Heather was going to be working at Erin's beauty salon. It was important that Joy bond with Erin for her daughter's sake.

Erin Winters might have been a divorced woman, but she was certainly no victim. From her settlement she had not only kept hold of a big house in one of the new housing developments in Gainey Ranch, but she also had enough money to set up a beauty salon at the exclusive Hyatt Resort. Despite being older than Joy, Erin had flawless skin and not an inch of fat anywhere on her body, apart from her ample breasts. Her hair was long and golden, always glossy and expertly styled, and she wore just enough make-up to enhance her features: perfectly arched eyebrows, long dark lashes, pale pink lips. Joy couldn't think how Mr Winters had managed to find a better version of Erin, but according to his ex-wife, the 'bitch' as she called her was the same age as her son, Darrell (who was twenty-three), and stunning to boot.

'An underwear model,' Erin had told her. 'Talk about my husband being a cliché. There'll be war if that bitch comes to our kids' wedding!'

Being around Erin always made Joy feel frumpy. Joy had good days and bad days, but any day she saw Erin was always one of the worst. She would have a pimple on her nose, or her hair would have tangled itself into knots, or she'd be unable to squeeze into her best jeans.

Nothing she possessed was smart enough, or classic enough. Erin always looked immaculate in her high heels and skirt suits, and tonight Joy couldn't wear jeans, her fail-safe staple, because all the other women would be dressed up in silky wrap dresses like cast members of *Dynasty*. In the end she put on the dress her father had liked the best: a simple, short-sleeved jersey dress with a pattern of red roses on it. She tried to arrange her hair, piling it on top of her head, but gave up and let it fall loose. She did attempt some make-up though, painting her lips the same shade as her dress.

It turned out that Erin was an excellent cook too. She had invited Joy into her closest enclave. Her best friends, Alison, Tammy and Dana, were joining them for the evening and she fed them a full three-course dinner.

At first things were fine. In fact Joy was almost relaxing. The women asked Erin about her beauty salon and if there were any new treatments to make their skin stay wrinkle free. Joy tried to take note of all of this for Heather's sake, but as soon as the other women hit their third bottle of Chardonnay the tone of the conversation changed.

They were sitting out on Erin's patio by the pool, surrounded by a hotchpotch of cacti and half-dead plants. It surprised Joy that a woman who put so much care into her own appearance could be so blind to the sorry state of her garden. Joy was itching to get up and tend to Erin's abandoned flora yet she was forced to stay put and listen to stories of Erin's friends and their husbands' infidelities. It seemed that not one of them was in a normal committed relationship.

The intimate nature of the conversation was embarrassing her. She tried to shrink into her chair, sipping on her wine spritzer, and merge into her leafy surrounds, but it was no good. Eventually all their attention turned to her.

'So what about you?' Erin asked, hooking her with her beacon stare.

Despite her great body and outward beauty, Joy found Erin's eyes chilling. They were pale blue and watery, big and round, devoid of any kind of emotion no matter what was coming out of her mouth. Darrell had the same feature. Joy often wondered what her daughter found attractive about him. Something about his eyes made her spine crawl.

'Have you ever, you know, slipped up?' Erin pushed, her eyes still expressionless.

All four women stared at her, as if waiting with the bated breath of one.

'Oh no – no,' she said, blushing.

'Surely you have?' Erin continued. 'I mean, you've been married to Eddie for years – since you were kids –'

'How old were you when you got married?' Dana, a plump blonde woman interrupted Erin.

'Seventeen.' Joy's voice dropped to an embarrassed whisper.

'Gee! That must have been a shotgun wedding,' Tammy commented.

'Well, yes, I was pregnant with Ray at the time, but we were in love, you know. We still are.'

Erin raised her eyebrows, although those big fish eyes remained blank.

'Oh please!' Tammy groaned, grabbing the wine bottle and refilling her glass.

Joy felt her blush deepening.

'I think you're lying,' declared the brunette, Alison, the only other divorcee there besides Erin. 'I mean, you've gone as red as one of them Barrel Cactus red blooms. Come on, Joy – spill the beans. Surely you've slipped up once?'

'No, I haven't … I believe in my wedding vows,' she said defiantly.

'Christ how boring,' Tammy said, knocking back her wine. Joy tried not to be offended – the woman was obviously drunk.

'We don't believe you,' Alison said, grinning at her. 'No one is perfect. I mean, how long have you guys been married?'

'Twenty-one years,' she said stiffly. She felt like she was under interrogation. She wished she had the courage to get up and walk out, but she needed to get on with Erin. Her daughter would kill her if she fell out with her new mother-in-law, and employer.

'My, you deserve a medal,' Erin said, but her voice was laced with cynicism.

'And are you really telling us that you haven't cheated in all these years?' Alison asked again, disbelief plastered on her face.

'That's right,' Joy said tightly. 'I've never wanted any other man.'

'Oh that is so, so sweet, isn't it, girls?' Tammy declared, but Joy had the feeling she was being as sarcastic as the others.

'You're so lucky. Does your husband still have sex with you?' Dana asked. The impertinence of her question was softened by the genuine curiosity on her face.

'Are you and Eddie still getting it on, Joy?' Tammy drawled, giggling.

Joy took a slug of her spritzer, trying to quell her anger at this stupid woman. She hated this kind of chat, but she knew if she refused to answer they would all think the worst, and then she would become part of their gossip. She wanted to show them that she wasn't some sad little housewife. Her husband still wanted her.

'Of course,' she said boldly. 'We've always had a good sex life. We just met each other young, that's all. We're meant to be together.'

'You really believe that?' Dana asked her. 'When I was a kid I thought it was true, you know, that there's a "one" – your very own Prince Charming – but now I think that's just some stupid fairy tale they tell girls.'

'Yes, I do think it's true,' Joy declared. 'For everyone there is someone, and some of us just find that special person early on in life. It's not something you can be logical about...'

'Oh please!' Tammy hooted. 'That's just crap. You might not have cheated but believe me I bet your husband has. Men like variety.'

'Shut up, Tammy,' Erin said. 'I think it sounds very romantic. You're a lucky girl, Joy.'

Again Joy had the feeling Erin was making fun of her.

'You sure are. For most the passion wears off after a few years,' Dana said glumly. 'And then they start cheating.' She sighed, gazing into her glass of wine. 'And I guess once your husband starts playing around, why the hell can't you do the same back?'

'But wouldn't it be easier just to break up?' Joy suggested. 'Wouldn't that be more honest?'

'Oh listen to her! Yeah honesty is all great and good, but you got to think of the kids, and then money... Most wives would be up shit creek if their husbands dumped them,' Tammy said hotly.

'No more afternoons at your salon,' Dana said, patting Erin on the knee.

'I think Joy is right,' Erin said, looking at her again with those dead eyes. 'I feel so much stronger since I broke up with Clive. It's hard, of course, but now I've my own house, my own business and...' She paused, smiling slyly. 'My own lover.'

'Go, girl!' Tammy raised her glass.

'I'm with Erin,' Alison said, her voice cracking. 'I might not have met anyone else yet, but I don't care if I'm on my own forever. I'm never going to let another man have control over my life.'

'Alison's husband was emotionally abusive,' Dana whispered to Joy.

'He fucked with my head,' Alison said, overhearing.

'Marriage is for fools,' Erin declared, refilling their glasses.

'But your son is getting married to Joy's daughter,' Tammy pointed out.

'I know, but don't you think they're too young, Joy?' Erin said, sticking the cork back into the bottle.

Erin's attitude annoyed her. Her presumption that she was an idiot to still be married, her sneering tone of voice. Erin had it all worked out with her freedom, her business, and she still got to have a man in her life. Her condescension was irritating the hell out of Joy, and even though she actually did agree that their children were too young to get married, she found herself responding differently.

'No, I don't think they're too young. If it's love then it's love. Just like me and Eddie. And we're still together.'

'Forever, do you think, Joy?' Erin asked. All the women looked at her.

'Yes,' Joy said, under a spotlight again.

The evening had unsettled her. It felt as if Erin and her girlfriends were in on some big secret she didn't know about. She was the dumb one who'd married at seventeen and had only known one man her whole life. But so what? If she still wanted Eddie, and he still wanted her, then they were good, right?

Joy drove home, trying to silence their words inside her

66

head. What bothered her most was what Tammy had said.

*'You might not have cheated but believe me I bet your husband has. Men like variety.'*

Could it be true? Was she completely naive to believe that her husband was faithful?

That night she went down on Eddie and gave him the best blow job he'd had in years. She listened to his sighs of satisfaction, drank in his pleasure. It made her feel good to have him stroking her hair and saying, 'Oh, baby, don't stop. Oh yes.'

Afterwards he held her in his arms, and it felt so good to be cradled by him.

'Joy, baby,' he said. 'That was amazing. Why don't you do that more often?'

She didn't reply, just kissed him gently on the cheek.

He fell asleep with her arm underneath his back. She tried to settle, but eventually she was too stiff, and her arm was going dead. She pulled it out slowly from underneath him and slipped out of bed. There was no one else in the house. Heather was still out with Darrell. She might even stay over with him. Eddie hated her doing that, but she was an adult now, and soon she would be Darrell's wife. Eddie could no longer lay down the law.

She put on one of Eddie's sweaters, picked up her Walkman and went out onto their tiny porch. It was her favourite spot, sitting on her father's old rocking chair. She put her headphones on and looked up at the stars, remembering the sight of those incredible Northern Lights, and pressed play. It was a new cassette that Ray had sent her, and she'd been playing it non-stop since it had arrived in the mail. At first she hadn't been so sure she liked the music, but now she was hooked. It was a compilation tape of all of her son's favourite bands. Sometimes when she listened to it she felt like all the songs were about her life. How could Ray know? She particularly loved a new band called The Stone Roses, and their track 'Elephant Stone'. She had no idea what an elephant stone actually was, but the song itself seemed to be about broken dreams. She loved the images it created in her head of sunsets, fields of wheat, clouds and a home someplace else where she belonged.

The night air was mild. Already it was warming up for the summer months. She inhaled and smelled orange blossom from a neighbouring garden. The scent made her sad, reminding her of her own orange tree. She pushed the memory away and tried to relax into the music, yet she couldn't. She felt restless, and, as she slowly began to realise, unsatisfied. It occurred to her that even though she and Eddie had sex regularly, she wasn't actually making love with her husband out of desire but out of the fear she would lose him. She was entirely focused on his pleasure, for every time Eddie tried to do something for her, she told him to stop. 'It's okay,' she'd say, shifting over to her side of the bed, wanting space.

Why did she not want her husband to satisfy her? She really was no different from Erin and her friends, for what they were saying was that if you didn't sleep with your husband, whether you wanted sex or not, he would find someone else who would. Just tonight she had been spouting off how Eddie was 'the one'. It had to be true because if not her whole life made no sense. Yet the truth was Eddie didn't turn her on any more.

So what? Sex wasn't the most important thing in a marriage.

Eddie and she were a partnership. But Joy knew that even that wasn't true. Eddie was the leader in their relationship and in their family. She just fell in behind him and always did what he wanted.

Like her, their son Ray possessed wanderlust, and yet unlike her he had actually acted upon it. She guessed it was easier for boys to do that. The last time she'd seen Ray had been at her father's funeral a year ago. It felt like an eternity ago to Joy. Ray had travelled all around Europe, sending her cards from everywhere. She had them all tacked up on a board in the kitchen: Paris, Rome, Berlin, Vienna and London. He had settled in the English capital now. His passion was music, a type she didn't quite understand – alternative rock he called it. The names of the bands were all obscure and rather disturbing like Stiff Little Fingers, The Cult, The Jesus and Mary Chain, The Stone Roses and Joy Division, Ray's favourite. It pleased her that her son liked a band with her name in it.

Ray not only loved music, he made it. He sent her tapes. At first the sounds alarmed her. It was so different from her favoured country music, but gradually she found herself listening to it more and more. She began to understand why her son had needed to leave Scottsdale. Why he had worn only black clothes, had spiky hair and a pierced nose. She wasn't afraid of how he looked any more. In fact she was inordinately proud of Ray's need to stand out from the Scottsdale crowd, although she was careful not to say so in front of Eddie. Her husband had been appalled by Ray's look and seemed almost relieved when their son hit the road.

69

Joy looked up at the night sky again and caught sight of a shooting star. She loved these Arizona night skies, full of so much activity. She wondered if the Northern Lights would be back tonight. The stars to her seemed like breathing entities in an endless celestial dance.

This morning she had been so sure that change was coming into her life. An image of the Englishman she'd met that day came into her head – Lewis. What a quaint name. The same name as the man who wrote those children's books, *Alice in Wonderland* and *Alice Through the Looking Glass*. She had loved those stories when she was a little girl. How you could walk through a mirror and have another life altogether. She used to dream about the idea of living in two worlds, and now it seemed that she did. There was the American side of her, the part she lived with every day, and then there was the Irish side to her, unknown – and undiscovered.

Everyone would talk like Lewis if she ever visited Ray in London. She had to admit she found his accent attractive. And had he flirted with her just a little? He'd said she was too young to have grown-up kids, but then everyone said that. It had been odd the way they had stood next to each other watching the Northern Lights, only to meet again less than twenty-four hours later. She found herself wondering what it would be like to have Lewis touch her rather than Eddie.

She squeezed her hands tight, pinching the flesh between her fingers. She needed to get real. She was a married woman. She couldn't even start with these straying thoughts. She and Eddie were part of each other. How could she even think of being with another man?

Besides, Lewis hadn't been flirting with her for real. He had merely been friendly because of the coincidence of their meeting again.


## SCOTTSDALE, 15 MARCH 1989

No postcard today. Lewis didn't know whether to be relieved or disappointed. Yet even if he never heard from Marnie again, the damage was done.

The two other postcards plagued him, scratching at his subconscious all day long. As soon as Samantha went out after dinner, off he went into the garage to open up his toolbox and retrieve the two cards. They were all he had of Marnie.

He had left London with nothing from their time together. Not one picture or memento of their relationship.

Lewis sat on a stool in the dusty garage, under the buzzing bare bulb, and tried to remember what Marnie looked like. He could not conjure her. Instead, to his consternation, he saw an image of the hummingbird woman from yesterday. Her raven hair, her bluer-than-blue eyes and that northern skin. It was one thing to dream about Marnie, an echo of beauty from the past, but it was another thing altogether to have thoughts about a married woman here in Scottsdale. He felt guilty, as if he had betrayed Samantha already.

Lewis's heart was heavy with regret. After suppressing his memories for so many years, now they were rushing back. Those heady days at Studio M. His self belief, his ambition and his vanity. He had presumed too much.

## London, 14 April 1967, 9.08 a.m.

George Miller was scattering pigeons as he charged through Bloomsbury Gardens, hand in hand with his wife, Eva. Lewis looked down at them from the second-floor window of Studio M. His boss looked like any other middle-aged businessman. Yet despite his uniform of long dark mackintosh, black bowler hat, black umbrella with cane handle and black lace-up shoes, George was far from ordinary. It was Eva who gave him away. Ten years younger than her husband, yet ten years older than Lewis, Eva Miller was an exceptionally beautiful woman. Dressed in a flamboyant Zandra Rhodes full-length coat, with her geometric Mary Quant bob and swinging a Biba bag, his boss's wife was the epitome of all that George Miller stood for. STYLE in capital letters.

George was a small man with a big talent. Eva towered over him, and yet still appeared graceful. Lewis stared down at them both. They had stopped walking and were standing outside the office building. George took out his wallet and handed Eva some money, which she slipped into her handbag. She kissed her husband on the cheek, and he almost swatted her away before charging into the Studio M building. What an odd couple they made. Eva seemed like such a modern woman, yet George's chauvinism was blatant. How did she tolerate him? What did she even see in him? His boss's powers of graphic observation were outstanding. He saw every tiny visual detail in the world around him, yet the subtext of the unseen was lost on him.

72

Lewis watched Eva for a moment longer. He had never really thought about her before. She was just the boss's wife, and he had considered her life enviable. After all, she had a full-time housekeeper, and her boys were now away at school, so she could spend all her time swanning around London, meeting girlfriends for lunch and spending George's money on the newest fashions.

But as he watched her, standing outside the Studio M building, staring at the door as it closed behind her husband, he realised that she was sad. It was as if now that George had walked inside she could stop pretending. Lewis had never seen Eva look like that before. She was always so upbeat and chatty, smoothing out her husband's rough edges, but today she looked lonely as she walked away down the street. No matter how hard he tried, Lewis could never imagine Marnie accepting that sort of life. If he did marry his Irish girlfriend, she would not want to stay at home and look after the children while his career took off. She would want to shine just as bright as him.

# Four

# *Attraction*

## Scottsdale, 20 March 1989

Samantha had called him up at work. It was a rare occurrence; usually she was too busy during the day to even have the time to make a call.

'Let's go to the Botanical Garden after work,' she had suggested. 'I want to get a couple of plants. You like plants, don't you?'

'Sure I do, but what about your no pets, no plants rule?'

'That was when we first arrived in Scottsdale, when I thought we might move on.'

She had hesitated.

'I take your point about my Lady of Guadalupe, okay?' she said, sounding a little defensive. 'I thought we could get something for you. I remember you said you'd like some plants a few years ago ...'

She had broken off, and he could hear someone talking to her.

'I have to go, Lewis. I've a parent–teacher conference. See you later.'

Lewis had pondered over his wife's change of heart. She had always been so resistant to getting any plants – especially cacti, which she claimed made her nervous because of their spines.

'Knowing me I'll end up speared by one,' she had always said.

But since he had thrown that statue away, instead of getting mad he'd noticed Samantha clearing out a few of her kitsch ornaments. She had removed the skulls and beadwork from the bedroom, as well as taking down the Kahlo painting from the living room. She was making small changes. He wondered why.

The desert gardens were a revelation. They were visiting at a time when all the wildflowers were blooming. Before he came to live in Arizona, Lewis had always imagined it as this dust bowl America with hardly any greenery at all. How wrong he had been. He had learned that irrigation had transformed Scottsdale into good farming country. Indeed the first white men to move here had been cattle farmers, drawn by its fertility. Surrounding the city there were still cotton fields, hazy white ground clouds that sometimes took him back to snowy days when he was a child in England.

Lewis and Samantha wandered into a section of the gardens devoted to wildflowers. He instantly recognised the Mexican gold poppies, and the scorpion weed, or desert bluebells; different yet reminiscent of the bluebells in his childhood woods, but there were so many more flowers. All different sizes, shapes and colours. He read the signage beside them: lupin, desert chicory, penstemon and globe mallow. These wildflowers appealed to him so much more than the cultivated garden flowers of his childhood – dahlias or roses. The wildflowers were fragile, yet wild, and seemed to speak their own beauty rather than exist to please. Butterflies fluttered around them, but even more thrilling to see were the hummingbirds. He watched one feeding on a hanging red columbine flower. It reminded him of that vision of Joy Sheldon outside the gallery last week, and her connection with the tiny bird.

'Look at the hummingbird,' he said to Samantha, but his wife was distracted, glancing at her watch.

'Lewis, I'm sorry; I just remembered I forgot to pick up some marking. Do you mind if I run over to the school and come back to collect you?'

'Can't we go together after?'

'Well, it saves time this way,' she said. 'I've a lot of marking to do tonight.'

'You know, it was your idea to come here,' he grumbled.

'I'm sorry.' Samantha bit her lip. 'Just get what you want.'

She looked tired. He was being too hard on her. He knew how devoted a teacher she was, always putting in extra hours. He should be supportive, glad that she had intended sharing the evening with him, even if it hadn't worked out.

After Samantha had gone, he headed towards the garden shop. As he followed the winding path he noticed a woman bending down and removing a candy wrapper that had been speared onto a small shrub. She was wearing a large, wide-brimmed denim hat, but something about her seemed familiar.

She straightened up and he recognised her immediately,

even from the back. It was Joy Sheldon, dressed in jeans and those fabulous blue cowboy boots, her curvaceous figure hugged by a violet T-shirt speckled with white flowers. She hadn't seen Lewis, and he wondered if it was best to sneak away.

Yet he found himself watching her again. There was humility in how she stood, hands clasped behind her back, silently observing nature. This humility was a quality neither his wife nor Marnie possessed. He looked at Joy's long black hair, cascading over her shoulders from beneath the brim of the hat, and he had an urge to run his hands through it.

He wondered whether he should say hello, or maybe that would embarrass her, or it would be awkward because he had clearly been flirting with her the last time he'd seen her and they were, after all, both married. He really should retreat, but just as he was about to do this she turned round. It was clear she saw him, immediately blushing, her pale cheeks blooming.

'Oh,' she said. 'Hello again. It's you.'

'Hi,' he said, feeling like an idiot. 'Nice to see you. How are you?'

'Fine,' she said, her voice a little shaky. Was she shy of him? 'I love coming here. Actually I volunteer occasionally.'

'I didn't know you could do that.'

She took a step towards him, clutching her bag between her hands. 'Yes, my dad and I used to do it together.'

A small cloud passed over the sun and everything fell into shadow. He pushed his sunglasses on top of his head and smiled at her. 'It's my first time.'

'Have you been on the original desert trail yet?'

He shook his head.

'Let me show you,' she offered, not catching his eye. 'Do you have time?'

Joy led Lewis along the Garden's main trail. Despite having lived in Arizona for fifteen years, he had no idea there was such a diverse array of cacti.

'I only ever notice the big saguaros, the prickly pears and the organ pipe cacti. They remind me of the old cowboy movies I saw as a boy.'

'What about the barrel cactus?' Joy asked, indicating a clump of round, bulging cacti. 'I love it when they bloom. The colours are so vibrant.'

'What do they look like?'

'I'll find you one that's flowering,' she said, searching the banks of cacti on either side of the trail. 'Here you go.' She pointed further ahead to the right-hand side of the path.

He looked at the flowering barrel cacti, the cup like orange flowers on the top of its head.

'They look like chicks in a nest, opening up their mouths for a feed,' he commented.

'Oh yes, they do.' She smiled at him.

They paused at the cafe to buy glasses of iced tea. It was hot for March, and the sun was still beating down upon his head although it was well after five. He wished he had put a hat on like Joy.

'So what brought you to the Garden today?' Joy asked him.

'Actually I came with my wife,' he said, feeling self-conscious. 'She had to leave. Work.' He shrugged, trying to look casual. 'I said I would buy some plants for our house and garden.'

'Oh, that's nice,' she said, her cheeks pink again.

'We're trying to put the life back into our life,' he said, immediately feeling stupid by how corny he sounded.

'What do you want to get?' She was clearly trying to steer the subject away from anything personal.

'Something tough I suppose. I'm not great with plants.'

'Well, for your garden maybe you should plant a lemon or orange tree, or even an olive tree?' she suggested. 'It's hard for much else to survive the summer months without constant attention.'

'What kind of plant would you recommend for inside the house?'

Her wide-brimmed denim hat almost concealed her blue eyes. Yet he searched them out. Who *was* Joy Sheldon? This sense of familiarity and yet his inability to remember was driving him mad.

'I think some kind of succulent with bright flowers would be nice,' she said. 'Would you like me to help you pick some things?'

'Do you have time?'

'Sure,' she said. 'I'm just a housewife, you know. Not that busy, stopping over to my mom in a while, but I've time.'

He detected a slight edge to her voice. He got the feeling that she wasn't too happy about being 'just a housewife', but maybe she was trying to be amusing.

For the first time in his life he really looked at plants. He had never had time for them before, but Joy managed to make him enthusiastic. He hadn't liked cacti either because of Samantha, but in the end he found his shopping cart was loaded with the plants. He purchased a sunset aloe for the sitting room, and a selection of succulents for outside, plus a small orange tree for in front of their house.

'Do you want to buy some crimson star columbine?' Joy asked, holding up a fragile-stemmed plant with crimson trumpet petals.

'Well, I'm not sure; I already have quite a lot...'

'It will attract hummingbirds.' She looked at him with hopeful eyes. 'And how about this beaver tail with the pink flowers, and a claret cup cactus?'

He felt compelled to buy everything she suggested.


After he had bought a stack of plants, they stood awkwardly outside the garden centre for several long moments.

'Thanks,' Lewis said. 'Our house and garden are going to be transformed. You know, you should do this for a living.'

Joy looked genuinely pleased. She was clutching a cactus with a white flower bursting out of its top. A birthday present for her mom, she had told him.

'I love coming here so much.' She took off her hat, and he could see all of her face now. He noticed that there was a new cluster of freckles on the apple of each cheek. 'It's my dream to set up my own nursery one day. I've even got a name – Hummingbird Nurseries I'd call it.' She blushed, looking a little embarrassed. 'But that's all a bit of a far-fetched dream. Really I just love helping people create their own gardens.'

'So I bet you have a great garden then?' he asked her.

Her smile faded. 'Actually no. Our pool takes up the whole of the backyard, and we've no room out the front. I used to have some flowers, an orange tree, but that's all gone now. I've some cacti in pots on the porch.'

'That's a shame,' he said.

'Yeah.' She looked uncomfortable all of a sudden, their earlier ease with each other gone.

'Hang on,' he said, reaching into his cart and grabbing one of the hummer-attracting columbine plants. 'This is for you to start up your own garden again. Attract your own hummingbirds.'

She looked mortified. 'Oh, but that's for your garden.'

'I insist,' he said, thrusting it towards her.

She looked a little upset, and he wondered if he shouldn't have been so forward.

'Those invites will be ready on Wednesday,' he said in farewell, pushing his cart away from her.


As he approached Samantha waiting for him in the car, he wondered if Joy was watching him, yet he didn't dare turn around.

'Who was that woman?' Samantha asked as she helped him load the trunk with plants.

'Just a customer,' he said. 'She's getting some wedding invites done.'

His wife gave him a cool look. 'You seemed a little too friendly for her to be a customer.'

'She's just ordered her *wedding* invites off me, Samantha!' he said, stacking the plants in the trunk. 'She knows a lot about plants. She helped me out in the store.'

'I'll say,' Samantha grumbled. 'You went a bit over-board, didn't you? Just how many cacti did you buy?'

Why had he lied to his wife about the wedding invites? He had never cheated. Yet as Samantha drove them home he could not put Joy Sheldon from his mind. He kept seeing her blushing face underneath the shade of her denim hat, the shyness that he found so attractive. It was all this business of the postcards that was stirring him up. It was not Joy Sheldon he wanted but Marnie.

★

Joy watched Lewis as he walked away from her. He had given her a present. She knew it was a departing moment of generosity, but even so she could not remember the last time Eddie had given her anything. Well, actually that wasn't true. She could, of course, but it was not a happy memory.

Lewis pushed his trolley through two rows of parked cars to stop by a mustard-yellow Cadillac. She saw a woman getting out of the car. Even from this distance Joy could see that she was pretty. She looked about the same age as her, maybe older, but well maintained, as her mother would say, with silky blonde hair and long, slim legs clad in white jeans.

Joy's car was parked in the same row. She hesitated for a moment and then turned around. She walked as if with purpose to the far side of the car park, carefully carrying her mother's Easter lily cactus, and the red columbine plant that Lewis had given her. By the time she had done a full circle and made it back to where her car was parked,

Lewis and his wife had driven off. She took a breath; her shirt stuck to her skin with sweat.

Joy tried to work out her odd behaviour on the short drive over to her mom's house. Why had she become so flustered at the thought of being introduced to Lewis's wife? After all there was nothing going on between them. She had only met him a couple of times, and briefly. Why had she interfered and made him buy all those plants? Why had she forced Lewis Bell to buy the sunset aloe and the claret cup cactus for his living room, just because she liked them? She hadn't told him how to care for them. What if he overwatered them, or placed them in the wrong spot, and the spines fell off the cactus, and the aloe leaves withered and died? What if his wife hated those two plants and threw them out? Joy could not bear to see plants neglected. All that potent life wasted through human thoughtlessness.

Their goodbye had been awkward and only had the effect of reminding her how upset she had been about the loss of her own little garden.

She'd had to give up her back garden years ago when they had a swimming pool put in. How would the kids have coped during those punishing hot summers without the pool?

The unspoken agreement between her and Eddie had been that the front of the house was hers. Of course most of the space was taken up by the garage, but she had an area to the side where she'd managed to grow some wild-flowers from seed. Each spring it had got a little wilder, a mix of white daisy-like fleabane, purple arroyo lupin and pink Parry's penstemon. In the midst of them had sat a large agave plant, and shading them all there'd been an orange tree. How glorious those spring mornings had been when the blossom was out and filling her house with the most divine fragrance. At the same time there had been oranges on the tree – the sweetest she had ever tasted.

It had all disappeared a year ago, the week before her father had died, and before he'd told her about the adoption. She had been sleeping over at her parents' house for several days, but that long Sunday Joy had returned home. She had been feeling guilty for deserting Eddie and Heather, and leaving the cooking and cleaning all up to her daughter. Her father had seemed stable, his best friend Larry had arrived to spend the evening by his bedside and she knew that both she and her mom had needed a break from each other. She had been looking forward to collecting some oranges off her tree and sitting out back by the pool, sucking on their sweet juice.

At first she'd thought she was outside the wrong house. She had pulled up on the road and turned off the engine, her mouth suddenly dry with shock. She had listened to the slow ticking of the car as she'd looked up at the burnt sienna sky above her house, the sun sinking behind the roof. Then she had let her eyes drop again. Where was her wild garden? Where was the orange tree?

She had blinked. She couldn't believe it. Whose garden was this? Every single wildflower had disappeared and in their place were orderly rows of red and yellow tulips. Worst of all was the fact that the orange tree was gone. In its place was a miniature artificial pond, a statue of a dancing cupid in its centre, with water trickling out of his mouth.

Joy had stumbled up the drive and stood in shock before the garden. Where was her oasis?

She had felt anger surge up inside her. For the first time in years she was furious with her husband. She would not hold back this time. She had stormed up the steps and into the house, banging the door behind her.

'Surprise!'

Her husband and daughter had been sitting at the table with grins on their faces. They were surrounded by vases, jugs, jam jars and even old tins, stuffed with all the wild-flowers and orange blossom from her garden. Their last fragrant fanfare before they would inevitably wilt and be gone forever. The scent was overwhelming. In the middle of the table was an enormous fruit bowl, filled to the brim with oranges.

She had been thrown by this vision, back-footed. Before she could scream at Eddie and accuse him of murdering all her dear plants, Heather had jumped up from the table, her face bursting with excitement.

'Do you like it?' she had gushed.

She had stared at her daughter dumbfounded.

'Do you like your new garden, silly?' Eddie had said, grinning at her.

She had looked at her husband in shock. He really had no idea what he'd done. He'd actually thought she would be pleased.

'Why didn't you ask me?' she'd managed to whisper, her anger dissipating.

'We wanted to give you a surprise,' Heather had said to her. 'Something to cheer you up because of Grandpa.'

'I thought I'd get rid of all these old weeds for you,'

Eddie had said. 'They look okay once you put them in a few jars, but they were making the front of the house messy.'

'They're not weeds. They're wildflowers.'

Eddie had looked at her, the smile wiped off his face. 'Did I do something wrong, Joy? You don't look very happy.'

'It's just ... why did you have to cut down my orange tree?' she'd said, unable to contain the emotion in her voice.

'It was diseased, Mom,' Heather butted in. 'We had someone out here helping us, and he said that it was going to fall down anyway.'

'I thought you'd like a little pond,' Eddie said, looking forlorn. 'I screwed up, didn't I?'

She had shaken her head, trying not to show her feelings, but it was too hard. She could feel the tears welling in her eyes.

'No, the garden is lovely,' she had managed to say. 'It's just my dad ...'

She had felt her daughter's hand on her back as Eddie got up from the table and walked over to her. He put his arms around both her and Heather.

'I'm sorry, Joy,' he had whispered into her hair.

Shouldn't the care and comfort of her husband and daughter have meant more to her than a garden? Yet she was not only shocked by the destruction of her wild garden but also by the fact that her own husband had known so little about her. All these years and he had never picked up on her passion for wildflowers. If she was so unknown to him, then what did *she* not know about *him*?

That night she had been unable to sleep. She had kept seeing her father's face, his skin like pale yellow parchment, the distance already in his eyes, and she had been afraid he would die while she was away from him. She should never have come home. Waves of dread, of nausea, swept over her, the sensation compounded by the scent of all the dying wildflowers in her house.

She had been unable to bear it any longer and got out of bed, collecting up all the wildflowers and orange blossom in the containers around the house. She had lit a fire and laid out all her dead flowers and blossoms beside it, before feeding them one by one into the flames, watching them curl up and shrivel in front of her eyes. She had tried to let it go.

It's only a garden, she had kept telling herself. What Eddie had done was through love. Yet every time she looked at those rows of tulips it felt like a punch to the stomach. She wanted to rip the cupid out of the fountain and smash it across the bonnet of her husband's fancy silver Corvette.

*

Lewis told Samantha about all the plants that Joy had picked for him. Their names and where they should plant them. It surprised him how much he had remembered.

'But I don't know why you had to go so crazy,' Samantha complained. 'I thought you hated gardening.'

'Maybe I just never gave it a chance,' he said.

'Well, this woman certainly seems to have inspired you,' Samantha said sarcastically.

'Come on, Sam, she was just helping me out. I told you she's getting married.'

Samantha pouted at the steering wheel. Lewis put his hand on her knee to reassure her. He felt her flinch, ever so slightly. He removed his hand, feeling a little wounded.

'Is it true you're going to Ireland?' Samantha suddenly asked him.

He froze in his seat. Had she found the postcards?

'No, course not.'

'But you told Dad you're going for Easter ...'

'Oh that, I don't know why I told him ... I just needed an excuse to not go over to your parents for Easter.'

'So you're not going to Ireland?'

'No,' he said firmly.

'I knew you were making it up,' she said with confidence as she turned into their drive and parked the car.

'Well, maybe, I *will* go to Ireland,' he suddenly said. 'Since you're going away.'

'Driving to Santa Fe is slightly less expensive than going all the way to Ireland, Lewis. I mean, why Ireland of all places?' Samantha gave him what he called her school-teacher look. It used to turn him on.

That night he tried to make love to his wife. He knew she was awake. He could tell. He reached out for her, tried to draw her to him. She was lying rigid and still, her back to him. He kissed her shoulder and put one arm around her waist, tried to caress her breasts, yet Samantha put her cold hand on his and lifted it off her body.

'Not tonight, Lewis, I'm tired.'

She was always tired, or had a headache, or wanted

to be alone. He lay on his back, frozen by her rejection. Eventually he heard Samantha's breathing even out. He slid out of bed and went down to the garage again, opened up the toolbox and pulled out those postcards. Once he had loved a woman who desired him night and day. Once he had been the centre of her world. Marnie. Their desire had consumed them. At the beginning of their marriage, he and Sammy had had good sex, but nothing like those months with Marnie.

He had wanted to kiss Joy Sheldon today. When he had given her that red plant he had wanted to kiss her rosebud lips and see her blush, feel her respond in a way that his wife hadn't for years.

★

'Happy birthday, Mom,' Joy said, presenting her with the Easter lily cactus.

Her mother took it gingerly. 'Oh thank you, Joy,' she said. 'It's a little big though.'

'I'll plant it for you, Mom. I just thought it was so bright and positive.'

'Thank you, dear,' her mother said, putting it down on the hall table. Joy immediately regretted giving her the plant. She had made the mistake of gifting her mom something that her father would have liked. Teresa Porter would much prefer perfume or some jewellery.

Her mother led the way down the corridor into the kitchen. Joy could tell that she was being a little careful with her. The silence between them hung heavy and loaded.

'I baked especially for you,' her mom said.

89

As they entered the kitchen Joy spied a loaf of banana bread steaming on the counter. She didn't have the heart to remind her that it was her dad who'd liked banana bread, not her. It seemed that both she and her mom were unable to let Jack Porter's favourites go.

Joy sat down on a stool at the breakfast counter and looked out the glass patio doors. Her father's garden had been his pride and joy. To her shame she could see that it needed urgent attention. She made a promise that when she planted that Easter lily cactus she would tidy things up a bit.

At the end of the garden were three palm trees in a row, and behind that she could see Camelback Mountain. How many times had she sat with her father and watched the sunset – the screaming purples and clamorous oranges of an Arizona horizon filtering upwards to create the awesome fire in the sky?

To one side of the garden was an orchard of orange and lemon trees, already filling with fruit and blossom.

She turned her attention back to the slice of banana bread before her and picked at it with her fork.

'You're late,' her mom accused as she poured her a glass of iced tea.

'Sorry, Mom, but I'm here now.'

'Can Eddie and Heather not come over? I baked so much.'

'Eddie's working this evening. And Heather is at the Princess Resort with Darrell going over some of the details for the wedding.'

Her mother sighed and shook her head. 'That girl is too young to get married.'

'I know, Mom. But she's made up her mind.' Joy tried to swallow a bite of banana bread. It was a little dry and stuck in her throat. She took a swig of iced tea to help it down.

'Just like you,' her mother said, looking glum. 'I guess this Darrell fellow is sensible enough. Heather told me he's going to be an accountant and that his mother is giving her a job in her beauty salon at the Hyatt Resort.'

Her mom took a dainty bite of banana bread before speaking again. 'It's important for a girl to have a career even if she's a mom.'

Joy tried to ignore the stab at her. Her mom thought she was lazy, or that she didn't want a job. But the truth was Joy fantasised about having her own business and being financially independent. Like she had told Lewis Bell today, she wanted to help people grow plants and do up their gardens. She'd even told him about wanting to name the business after hummingbirds, though she hadn't told him why – that she was fascinated such power could come from something so small.

She wanted to specialise in cacti and succulents. That was one reason she had been volunteering at the Botanical Garden. She had even asked Eddie once if he'd mind if she went to college to study plants. She had told him she wanted to get a job in a nursery, though she'd been too shy to tell him about her big dream.

'Why would you want to go to college to study something like that?' he'd said, looking puzzled. 'All that money to do some course that young people do? It's not a proper job, Joy. It's bad wages. If you want to work you should learn to type, get an office job like your mom.'

So she had signed herself up for a course in basic secretarial skills, but it had been a disaster. She couldn't type because she was unable to memorise the letters on the keyboard, and her fingers had got all tied up in knots. She was terrible at it, and too embarrassed to tell her mom about her failure, though Eddie had tried to be kind.

'You don't need to work, Joy,' he'd said. 'I can make enough money for both of us.'

Then he'd kissed her on the forehead. 'Besides, I like having you here when I get home. I appreciate all that you do for me. Cooking and cleaning is a job as I see it.'

She was pulled from her thoughts by her mother, who was rifling through her handbag. She pulled out a pink envelope and handed it to her.

'Ray sent me a card,' she said. 'Isn't he a sweet boy?'

Joy felt a surge of pride. Her son was so thoughtful. She tugged out the card, which featured a picture of an extravagant bouquet and the words 'Happy Birthday to a Special Grandmother' printed in gold.

'It's lovely, Mom. Shall I put it up?'

Her mother nodded and she popped the card on the windowsill, taking another long look at her father's garden.

'I should come round and tidy up the garden,' she said.

'If you want,' her mother replied, sounding not the slightest bit as if she cared.

Joy sat back down again. She took a deep breath.

'Mom,' she said, ringing her tea glass with her finger, afraid to look up. 'Remember what we talked about last week – about what Daddy said to me before he died?'

She felt her mother tense on the opposite side of the counter. 'I don't want to discuss that now, Joy.'

She looked up, straight into her mother's eyes. She could see the fear in them. 'Mom, please. I just need to know a few facts.'

She reached out and picked up her mother's hand, held it in hers. Her hands were still soft as velvet yet Joy could feel the veins bulging through her skin.

'You're my mom, and always will be. That will never change, but I need some answers.'

Her mom shook her head, her eyes tearful now.

'Please, Mom, I love you, and I loved Daddy. I know I couldn't have had better parents, but Daddy said my birth mother was Irish, and I just want to know who she was ... and her story ...'

Her mom pulled her hands away with a strength that surprised Joy.

'I don't understand you, Joy. It's nothing but selfish of you to keep going on about this when your father is gone.'

'But wouldn't you want to know if it was you, Mom?'

'No, I would not,' her mother said, adamant. 'I would feel lucky to have the life that I have. Why do you want to know about a woman who rejects her own baby? All it will do is hurt you.'

'Please, Mom; I just want to know her story. Life is never so black and white.'

'I thought your father told you the story. Remember – his last words to you.' Her mother became so agitated that she got up from the counter and walked away towards the patio doors. 'I don't understand why he would do such a thing when we always agreed you should never know.'

'Mommy, *why* didn't you tell me?'

Her mother turned round to face her, clutching her

hands in distress. 'We didn't want you to be hurt. We are your parents, and we loved and supported you.'

She walked towards Joy again, a look of panic in her eyes. 'And haven't we? We never made you feel bad about getting pregnant or marrying young ... I mean, I could have persuaded you to have *your* baby adopted. I never wanted you to waste your life with that Eddie ...'

Joy tried not to react. What compelled her mother to say such cruel things?

'This has nothing to do with me and Eddie. It's to do with who *I* am.' She spoke as firmly as she could. 'I need to know.'

'Please, Joy, stop badgering me. I can't take this at the moment.' Her mother's face was pinched into a determined grimace, her tears held back. 'It's my birthday – don't spoil it for me.'

Joy dropped the subject again, although inside she was burning with disappointment. Who decreed that her mother got to control her life even now she was an adult herself? She just wanted to know the story of her own birth. Why did her mom have to block her like this?

And yet maybe she was right. Why should Joy hunt down a woman who never wanted to know her in the first place? She couldn't explain her desire for truth. It was a force that drove her on. A curiosity to find out what she was made of and why she was the woman she was. What had she inherited from her mother, and her father, in Ireland? And what traits had she passed on to Ray and Heather? It was an urge to belong, to be part of something that hounded her. Her mom would say that she was a Scottsdale girl. An American mom, as wholesome as her, but Joy didn't feel like that. Sometimes she sensed the dark edges of her heart curling inward, and a desire to break free from the role created for her. She felt this was the unknown Irish part of her – and it refused to be quiet.

## LONDON, 14 APRIL 1967, 9.23 A.M.

Some of Lewis and Marnie's designs were already spread out on the meeting table when she came into George's office with his cup of tea. She walked around the table, the cup tinkling in the saucer, eventually placing it with care beside her boss. Lewis didn't look at her, but he could feel her hawk stare as George picked up one of her images.

Sensing her more than usual interest, George looked up. 'Yes, dear?' he asked her, peering at her over the top of his spectacles.

Marnie hesitated. Lewis sensed her draw breath. He begged her wordlessly not to say anything – not yet – for the truth needed to come from him.

'I was just wondering if Mr Bell wants another cup of tea.'

'Don't worry about him, my dear. He can go and get himself one from the pot. We can't have you running around after us all the time.'

Yet still she didn't leave the room. Lewis stole a look at her. She was clutching her hands, shifting from one foot to the next.

'Yes?' George snapped. 'Is there something else?'

'I wondered ...' Marnie paused. Lewis couldn't bear to look at her. He stared down at his shiny black shoes.

Please, he silently beseeched her, don't expose me.

'... if you would like a plate of custard creams with your tea?'

Lewis almost slumped with relief in his chair.

'No, no. We're fine. We're busy. Off you go now, there's a good girl. I'm sure you've lots of typing to do.'

George shook his head at Lewis as if to say 'Silly woman'. If only he knew.

Lewis glanced at Marnie as she left the room. She looked right at him, two spots of colour on her cheeks. He wondered if she was very angry or just nervous like him.

The door clicked shut behind her. George lifted one of the designs up and stared at it, then he got up and walked over to the window. Lewis fidgeted at the table.

'Incredible.' George turned back to Lewis, the drawing still in his hand. 'You've hit the nail on the head, my lad.'

'I have?'

'Yes, this is the way forward. All these vibrant colours. You can see it in the culture – fashion, music, art. London is full of colour, Lewis! That's what Eva keeps telling me.'

George walked towards him, flapping one of Marnie's designs up and down as he spoke.

'It's pure genius to merge the letters and create more colours. Simple, yet so effective.'

George shook his hand vigorously. 'I'm impressed, Lewis; I really am.'

Lewis felt as if he was glowing with pride. He couldn't wait to tell Marnie how well their work had been received.

'Good job.' George took another sip of his tea and sighed in satisfaction. 'I have to say that Irish girl makes the most splendid cup of tea.'

Lewis winced. He wished George could know the true extent of Marnie's talents.

'I tell you what, old chap,' George said, going over to his desk. 'Let's give our cuppas a bit of an extra Irish kick, shall we? I have some of that Beagles whisky in here.'

'It's a bit early ...'

George raised his eyebrows. 'Come on, Lewis, you're one of the big boys now.' He poured out two hefty measures of whisky, handing a tumbler to Lewis. 'Besides, there's something I need to talk to you about.'

Lewis gulped back the liquid, harsh at this time of day. Could this be his moment? Would George make him a partner?

But his boss opened a folder on his desk, pulling out a single sheet of typed paper.

'I feel I can trust you with this rather important project.'

He handed Lewis the paper. The letterhead was hideous, like the worst kind of wedding invitation from about ten years ago.

'Phoenix Airlines,' Lewis read.

'Yesterday I heard that they're about to be transformed into Phoenix International Airlines.' George's expression had transformed from jovial to serious. 'In a couple of days they'll be inviting pitches from design agencies around the world for a new corporate identity. They want to rebrand everything from their letterhead to their uniform to the logo on the side of the aeroplanes.'

It was every designer's big dream. The chance to create a whole new visual identity for a big airline. Lewis had fantasised about something like this since he'd started his career.

'I have been lucky enough to procure a dinner engagement with the fellow in charge of selecting the design agency that will create their new identity tonight.' George sat back in his chair, took a slug of his whisky and looked ridiculously pleased with himself. 'Studio M is ahead of the posse, so to speak.'

'That's fantastic,' Lewis enthused.

'Yes, it is. We have a real shot at this. I told Frankie about it last night in the pub.'

Lewis stiffened. He had no idea that George and Frankie were pub chums.

'We're going to work as a team on this one. But after seeing what you've done with your designs this morning, I'd like you to head the team, Lewis.'

George took the whisky bottle and replenished his glass.

'I don't know what to say,' Lewis said, feeling more than a little overwhelmed. George didn't need to spell out how important this pitch was. If Studio M pulled it off, the agency would be top of the big league.

'This job needs to be first class, if you'll forgive the pun. Visually striking without being too unconventional. Pioneering, powerful and reliable. That's the image the airline wants to project.'

George cocked his head to one side. 'If you come up with a top design, you'll have proved to me that you're good enough to be a partner. What do you say?'

'I would be honoured, George,' Lewis said, his heart racing.

'I need to keep hold of my talent,' George told him. 'I could let any of the others go, but not you, Lewis. So do you accept?'

'Of course I accept!'

George got up and clapped him on the back. 'Good man! I know it's short notice but I want you to come up with a few preliminary ideas by tonight. We can meet in the pub to go over them before we have dinner with the Phoenix Airlines man.'

Lewis's elation was short-lived. 'I think I might need a little more time –'

'We don't have that option, Lewis. We have to act now. If you're going to be my partner here at Studio M, this is what's expected of you.'

Lewis could feel the whisky coursing through his veins. He pressed his hot palms together, gripped his hands. *Think. Think.*

'Can we not postpone the pitch until tomorrow morning after we've bonded with the executive over dinner?'

If he and Marnie worked all night long then they had a chance of coming up with something, but to create a design all on his own by the end of business today felt utterly impossible.

'I fear we may lose them to a competitor if we don't win him over tonight. Time is of the essence.'

George polished off his whisky. 'I'm sure you can hook them with your genius. I have every confidence in you.'

Lewis nodded, feeling his face flush again. He had no time at all. And how could Marnie help him when she was busy with her secretarial duties all day long?

Back out in the main office Frankie and Pete were both immersed in work. Marnie was sitting at her desk with her back to him, typing away, but he could see the tension held in her body. He stood gripping the piece of paper with the old Phoenix Airlines letterhead as if it was a telegram of doom.

He sat down at his desk, closed his eyes and searched for ideas. He was a graphic designer, for God's sake. He was that before Marnie came along. He could do this on his own.

It was just that she was so good. She came up with ideas so quickly. He was so tempted to ask her for help, but he couldn't – not in front of the others.

He picked up a pencil and sharpened it then pressed its end against the blank piece of paper on his drawing board, so hard it snapped off. He sharpened it again and dragged it across the page, but his mind was a total blank. His ideas had no definition, and all he ended up with was a twirl of doodles. Could he not even draw any more?

'So?'

Marnie was standing over him. Her dress was a blue placard of calm in front of his face; her thighs perfectly smooth in flesh-coloured nylons.

Lewis looked up at her. He was relieved to see that her eyes were darting with excitement.

'Did he like them?' she whispered.

'He loved them,' Lewis whispered back. 'They were a huge hit.'

She grinned from ear to ear, her face alight with energy, and Lewis was struck by how young she looked.

'Did you tell him about me?'

Lewis looked back down at the Phoenix Airlines letterhead.

'Not quite,' he mumbled.

'What do you mean?' she whispered, leaning over him so close he could smell her Ma Griffe perfume. He noticed the corner of her breast through the unbuttoned top of her dress. It seemed unreal that he had cupped that breast in his hand only this morning. Kissed her pink nipple a few short hours ago.

'I can't talk now,' he said, blushing as he glanced over at Pete and Frankie. 'Look, I'll take you for lunch.'

If they went for an early lunch maybe she could help him with a few ideas for the Phoenix Airlines pitch.

She glanced down at his desk. 'What's that?'

'I'll explain at lunch. It's something big.' He paused. 'For both of us.'

He put his hand on her leg. He checked the others couldn't see him and let his fingers inch up it until his knuckles were hitting the hem of her dress then looked up into her eyes. He could feel her melting beneath his gaze. Without saying a word, she bent down and kissed him on the lips. He gasped at her spontaneity, her daring.

Then the phone began to ring. Marnie pulled away, rushing over to her desk to answer it.

'Good morning, Studio M,' she said in perfect Queen's English. Sometimes it was impossible to tell she was Irish at all.

She thrust the phone out in front of her.

'It's for you. I think it's Lizzie,' she whispered, her hand over the receiver.

What did his sister want now? She never rang him unless she needed something – usually money.

'You've got to come and get me now,' Lizzie said when he greeted her.

No 'hello' or 'how are you'. There never was.

'What's wrong, Lizzie?'

'My name is Elizabeth,' she began, speaking at such a rate of knots it was hard for Lewis to keep up. 'No one calls me Lizzie any more. What kind of a name is Lizzie for an artist? Elizabeth Bell, now that has stature, don't you think? That's what the man at the gallery told me anyway. If I want to be taken seriously as an artist I need a more dignified name. I mean, no one calls the queen "Lizzie", do they? I'm sure even her husband doesn't call her that...'

It was clearly one of his sister's manic days. He didn't want to have to deal with Lizzie's moods today.

'Christ, Liz ... Elizabeth, will you slow down?'

'Don't interrupt me! God, Lewis, do you know how bossy you are? Always telling me what to do? My whole life you've bossed me around. It's worse than having a father, I tell you, much worse!'

'What's wrong?'

'Nothing's wrong,' she said, suddenly softening her tone. 'I just need you to come and get me in that sweet little car of yours and take me somewhere.'

'I can't. I'm at work. I can't bunk off whenever I want.'

'Don't be so condescending. I work too. I sold a painting last night,' she announced.

At last his sister was making money again.

'That's why I need a lift.'

'I'm really busy. Is it urgent? Can I not take you tomorrow?'

'Please, Lewis,' Lizzie begged. 'I don't want to lose the sale. I need you.'

How many times had Lizzie needed him? He told himself his sister was fragile. She'd had a terrible childhood. Her constant demands were understandable. Yet he'd had the same childhood and somehow he managed to be self-reliant. There were the late-night phone calls, the drunken sobbing down the phone, the panicked drives to the emergency room to see his sister lying there, ashen-faced and distant.

'You need to stop feeling sorry for yourself,' is what he'd heard his mother tell Lizzie after her third suicide attempt. And despite his anger at his mother for being so heartless towards her own child, deep down he couldn't help agreeing.

Not long after that incident their mother had decided to have her daughter committed to a psychiatric unit. Lizzie had been diagnosed with clinical depression and prescribed antidepressants.

Six months later, when she had come out of hospital, she had been different. She might still be a handful now and again, but there had been no more suicide attempts and she was so much calmer. Lewis believed those drugs had saved his sister's life. Indeed when she came out of hospital she'd even announced she wanted to do something with her life and be a painter. He was proud of her successes, though frustrated by her ability to blow her money as fast as she made it.

And finally Lizzie had found her own little family of other artists, musicians, writers and various thespian hangers-on of the hip art scene of London. It wasn't hard for his sister to make friends, especially with men. Lizzie looked exactly how you were supposed to look in 1967. She was a lost little waif. Innocent – sexy. It was why she got away with all her attention-seeking behaviour – and Lewis knew that she had no shortage of admirers. Even if they were usually stoned most of the time. The dope must be good for her, Lewis reasoned. It made her happier, more settled.

Yet there had been times recently when he'd been a little disturbed when he visited his sister. Her long legs looked way too skinny in the look she favoured – black tights and short shift dresses like Edie Sedgwick, that druggy muse of Andy Warhol's. Her pretty face was paper pale, her big eyes, layered by thick kohl and long false eyelashes, were darkest evergreen, holes to nowhere.

'Please, Lewis,' Lizzie pleaded.

'I'm right in the middle of something here. Did you take your pills?'

He couldn't just walk out of work. Why couldn't she understand that? Why did she make him feel guilty?

'Yes, of course, I promise I have. Please come, Lewis...'

He could hear her crying, but she had cried too often. So many times he had come running only to discover that her tears were false.

'I'll come tomorrow straight after work.'

'I have to go today,' she whispered.

'It's only twenty-four hours. Why don't you call Mother? She has a car. Why don't you ask her to help you for once?'

Lizzie hung up. Mentioning their mother always got rid of her. Lewis tried to dismiss her persistent whine from his head, but it was hard because he had always felt so responsible for her.

'Everything okay?' Marnie asked, her eyes curious.

'It's just Lizzie being Lizzie,' he explained, trying not to be bothered, but he could feel his tension tightening its grip. He wouldn't be able to relax now until he managed to call over to her tomorrow and check she was okay.

Marnie walked round behind him. She put a hand on each of his shoulders and rubbed them just for a moment. He heard her bangles jangling on her wrists, felt the tension in his body beginning to ease. He remembered his admission of love to her this morning and her lack of response.

As if sensing his thoughts Marnie took her hands off his shoulders and returned to her typewriter. She had never told him she loved him. He didn't understand why he still wanted her, why he let her wound his heart. How had she managed to get under his skin? No other girl had done that to him.

He tried to focus on Phoenix International Airlines. The obvious thing was to create an image of a phoenix, but how to make it stand out? As he took his eyes off Marnie he noticed Frankie sitting at his drawing board, staring right at him through his fancy glasses, his lips pursed tight as if he was in deep thought. When he suddenly smiled, Lewis knew that Frankie had seen Marnie touching him. But so what if Frankie suspected that he and Marnie were having a relationship? Yet the knowledge that Frankie went for drinks in the pub with George disturbed him. Exactly how close were they? Not so close that George was offering Frankie a partnership at least.

Lewis tried to settle at his drawing board. He summoned images of the phoenix to him. A huge bird of prey like an eagle. Rising from the ashes. But he knew that the airline wasn't named after the bird but after the place. So what about an image from Arizona? One of those Western movie cacti? He shook his head. That had to be the worst idea he'd ever had.

Lizzie's call had stressed him. As much as he tried not to, he was now worried about his sister. All they had was each other. They were fatherless, and his mother hardly counted.

It was no good. He got up from his drawing board and went over to Marnie's desk.

'Could you dial Vauxhall 4391 for me, Marnie?' he asked. 'I need to ring Lizzie back.'

She brushed his hand with hers – smiled at him sympathetically.

'Lizzie, it's me again,' he said. 'I'm sorry.'

'It's okay,' Lizzie sniffed.

'It's just I'm really under pressure. I'll come straight after work, I promise.'

'Thanks, Lewis,' she said, subdued. 'Love you. You are the best brother.'

As Lewis sat back down at his drawing board he thought back to all those desperate years of their childhood. They had been like soldiers marching from one battleground to another. Each time more wounded, hurting even more inside, the hope that they would finally be with their mother fading every time. There had been only one oasis in all that time. Just one home.

## BERKSHIRE, 29 OCTOBER 1954

Lewis and Lizzie walked underneath a canopy of chestnut trees, conker shells strewn at their feet. Lewis searched for the shine of the perfect unpicked chestnut with at least the potential of being a winning sixer. He shoved conkers into his pockets until they were bulging. But really it was pointless. He had no one to play conkers with apart from his sister, and she was no good at all.

They trudged up the long drive, each carrying a brown box suitcase tied with thick green twine, as they'd come apart so many times. Their mother had left them at the end of the tunnel of trees, and thus as usual they had to walk up to the house without her. Their shoes were noisy, each footstep swivelling in the wet gravel, as they shuffled as slowly as they could towards the strange house. All around them was hushed, foreboding. A wood pigeon cooed mournfully; a magpie cackled in response. Sunlight showered them through the horse-chestnut leaves, and the smell of wet earth stuck in the back of Lewis's throat. He shivered. The day was early and despite the sun, it wasn't warm yet.

They had reached a shallow stone staircase that led to the front door. Lewis looked up at the tall sash windows lining the front of the house. He wondered if someone was looking out at them from inside, but all he could see was himself and Lizzie reflected in the black glass.

He took a step forward but Lizzie shrank back.

'Come on,' he encouraged her. 'We have to knock on the door.'

'I don't want to,' Lizzie pouted, her eyes still red from spilled tears.

'Nor do I,' said Lewis, 'but we have to.'

Lizzie shook her head, sniffing as tears began to well in her eyes again. She was such a crybaby, but he supposed she was a girl, and younger than him. As his mother has told him so many times, he was the man of the house. He had to take care of his sister.

'What house am I man of, Mother?' he had asked her. His mother had frowned for a moment, thinking. The next instant she had put on a smiling face as if she had to charm her own son, like all the other men in her life. She had squeezed his hand.

'Whatever house you are in, my darling,' she had told him.

Lewis looked at this imposing stone structure, with its two Roman columns either side of the doorway. Which obscure aunt or cousin of his father dwelt in this grand building? What new set of rules were he and Lizzie going to have to learn to please this relative? How long would it take him to charm them into spoiling them, out of pity, rather than love? Such a lovely boy, they always said. Lizzie was the difficult one, whining and demanding attention. But Lewis was so easy. He was a credit to his mother.

Sometimes it mystified Lewis that no matter how good he was his mother still didn't want him. Yet all these old relatives doted on him so that when their mother decided to move them on, some of them even cried on departure day – like Aunt Celia. Lewis had been quite fond of her. She had lavished him with gifts, the best of which had been his own train set. He'd had to leave it behind at Aunt Celia's house in Suffolk, because his mother had said there wasn't room in Mr Bailey's car. That was one time he had actually made a fuss.

He was used to all this moving around, yet sometimes he wished that he and Lizzie could be left alone. Now he was twelve he was sure he could look after them both quite well. He dreamed of having a caravan and a horse, like the gypsies he'd seen in the lanes near Aunt Celia's. He could make things they could sell. Pictures. He was good at art. It was the only thing he was good at. Or Lizzie could sing and dance, and he could collect money with a hat. Exhibitionism was no problem to his sister.

He glanced at Lizzie now. He could see the telltale flush in her cheeks, the lowering of her brow.

'Oh no, Lizzie, don't you dare. You know that first impressions are important.'

Lizzie stamped her foot, spraying gravel about her.

'I want Mother,' she said, her voice quivering with emotion.

'Well, she's gone,' Lewis said brutally. 'And you know you won't see her for a while.'

'Why not?' Lizzie whined. 'Why can't she live with us?'

'Because we have no father, remember?'

'Because Daddy was a war hero?' Lizzie asked.

'Exactly.' Lewis sighed. How many times did he have to explain this to Lizzie? 'So Mummy has to find us a new daddy. She can't do that with us in tow.'

He walked down the steps again and lifted up Lizzie's limp hand.

'Come on, it won't be that bad,' he cajoled her. 'Remember they usually have cake for us the first day.'

'I *am* hungry,' Lizzie said, reluctantly letting him pull her up the steps.

It was the biggest door he'd seen in his whole life. He reached up and grabbed the knocker, which was in the shape of a fox's head, and dropped it against the giant's door. The sound shattered the solemn morning. A gaggle of rooks took off from a nearby tree, cawing loudly and making Lizzie squeal in fright. Despite the smile plastered on his face, Lewis felt a pinch of anxiety in his heart. What if this relative wasn't kind? What if they were made to sleep on the floor in a cold, damp attic and clean chimneys to pay for their keep? What if he never got to eat cake again for the whole of his childhood? It could happen, and his mother wasn't there to stop it.

The door swung open. Standing in front of him was the last kind of person he'd been expecting. It wasn't the maid nor housekeeper of an ancient aunt, nor even the old lady herself, complete with dusty white curls and yellowing lacy sleeves. Nor was it a statue of a butler, unenthusiastically ushering them in. A young man had swept the front door wide open. He had a half-eaten apple in one hand and was holding an excited-looking red setter by the collar with the other hand.

'Oh hello there, you must be Philip's two?'

Lewis was speechless. For once it was Lizzie who spoke up. 'Who is Philip?'

'Why your father, of course.' The man beamed at her. 'And aren't you a pretty little thing, just like your mother?'

He turned to Lewis and looked him up and down, before throwing his apple core away over his head and releasing the dog so that it chased after it.

'Where is Sylvia?' he asked him.

'My mother had to go ...' Lewis mumbled.

'With Mr Drewe, in his car,' Lizzie told the stranger. Lewis coloured with shame. Why did Lizzie always have to spill the beans?

'Ah! I see, no surprises there.' It was said pleasantly enough, but Lewis detected a slight edge to the man's voice. Still he looked very friendly as he stepped forward and picked up both of their cases.

'Well, come in, do; we've been expecting you.'

'Who are you?' Already Lizzie was being rude, but the man didn't seem to mind her question.

'Why I'm Howard,' he said. 'I'm your father's brother, which makes me your uncle.'

He whistled for the dog. That's when Lewis saw it. His uncle had the same smiling eyes as his father. Lewis had been a baby when his father had left to fight, but he had a photo of him. He had looked at it so many times the image of his father's face was tattooed inside his head: wide forehead, greased-back hair, a dicky bow and a broad smile – big teeth and a thick bottom lip with a cigarette stuck to it – with a dapper moustache finishing off the look. A complete charmer. It was not the photograph of a condemned man.

'Come on, slow coach,' Uncle Howard was saying to him as the dog bounded past him into the house. 'Let's have breakfast. I'm famished.'

His time with Uncle Howard had been the best months of his life. For once he had been living in a man's house – a man's world, in fact. Howard had confided in Lewis that although he liked the odd tryst he was a confirmed bachelor. The only female Lewis had had daily contact with apart from Lizzie was Howard's rather dotty housekeeper, Angela, who lived in the local village and cycled over every day. It had been a relief for Lewis not to be fussed over by one of his father's female relatives.

He hadn't even missed his mother. Rather than sending them to the local school, a friend of Uncle Howard's from Oxford had been employed as their tutor, and the house in Berkshire became Lewis's universe. Uncle Howard would often invite his other bachelor friends down from London and they would all go shooting with Alfie, the red setter, Lewis included. Howard had treated him like an equal, not a little boy.

Lewis had never forgiven his mother for moving them on again less than a year later. He'd thought that Uncle Howard would have them for keeps. But that's not how things turned out. He lost Uncle Howard forever, and it was all Lizzie's fault.

# FIVE

## *Escape Velocity*

### SCOTTSDALE, 23 MARCH 1989

#### IT'S TIME

That was all that was written on the back of the postcard in the same block print as before. On the front was a picture of two children and a donkey in a green field. Both children had mops of startling red hair that stood out against the green of the field, especially as the boy was in a bright yellow top and the girl in a red jersey. The donkey had two basket panniers filled with turf on either side of it, and in the distance Lewis could see blue mountains. At the bottom of the card was printed: 'Collecting Turf from the Bog, Connemara, Co. Galway, Ireland'.

Lewis flipped the postcard over again and examined the handwriting. This script in thick black ink gave nothing away: block letters without a twirl of individuality.

It had been over a week since he'd received the second card. He had begun to wonder if that was it, and yet he had a feeling there was more to come. That was why he had got up before Samantha every morning and nipped out to the mailbox before she had a chance to check it herself.

It's time for what? Lewis wondered. Time for him to return to London, or go to Ireland and find Marnie again? Time to face the truth of his life, his failures and his regret?

Lewis slipped the postcard into the inside pocket of his jacket. He had taken to carrying them around with him. Sometimes at work, he might take one of them out and turn it over and over in his hands – raise it to his face, as if he might smell a trace of Marnie upon it. He hankered for the past, and for the man he'd once been.

★

These books soothed her. Ever since her father died Joy had come here nearly every day. At first it was just to sit between the racks of books, on the worn carpet, and hide from her life outside. In the library she could shelve her sorrow, take it out and thumb through it, cry silently within the comfort of the building's sanctuary then put it away again. She could go on home, cook the dinner, wash the dishes, put out the trash and make love to her husband and he would be none the wiser to her grief. Eddie hated death. No. It wasn't specifically death itself he hated but more what went with it: the hospital visits, the hospice – the place of the living dead as he called it – and then there was the funeral, and worse still the wake, if there was one.

It was Joy's mother who had been centre stage the day of her husband's funeral. Teresa Porter had been regal, dignified, yet broken all at the same time. They had walked down the church behind the coffin, hand in hand, her mother's hand cold as ice within her own, and Joy had felt strange and disorientated. The words kept repeating inside her head. *I am not of her flesh and blood. I am not of her flesh and blood.*

Joy had known it shouldn't matter. She should have been thinking of her father, sending prayers skyward for his soul to rest in peace, and yet all she had been able to focus on was her mother's bloodless hand in hers. The big lie had dug into Joy, like the spine of a prickly pear in her flesh. Her whole life had been based upon it. She had felt cheated and, worse, unstable, like a boat adrift, lost from its moorings.

That's how the library helped. Here she could sit for a little while, breathe in the aroma of books – not even look at them, just smell them – and feel the presence of all those minds contained within one building. This building had anchored her after her father's death.

*

At home as he was in galleries, Lewis felt out of place in libraries. And he knew this went back to his childhood. The only thing he'd been good at in school was art. Despite the fact his job dealt with text – typesetting words all day long – he appreciated the visual composition of each individual letter, even the pattern that words made, but had never been that interested in the content. Books intimidated him. It was something Samantha could be cruel about, especially as she taught English literature at the local high school. She constantly acted surprised that he had never read Dickens, or Hardy, or even Shakespeare. Over the years he had tried to impress her, but he had only managed short novels like *The Great Gatsby*, *Of Mice and Men* or *Heart of Darkness*. And those had held little appeal either.

There was a hush in the library that made Lewis want to call out, just to break it. He headed for the reception desk, the stack of freshly printed leaflets in his hands. He put the leaflets down on the counter and rang the bell. He had to get the delivery note signed.

A young guy in a checked shirt with a mess of curly hair appeared. He didn't look in the least like the austere spinster librarians of Lewis's childhood. The guy signed the delivery note and Lewis was released. This was his last job of the day. He was on his Easter holidays now. He should be going home. He had planned to cook for Samantha before she headed off to Santa Fe, but instead of leaving the library, he found himself wandering through the aisles.

Lewis was drawn towards a display of art books. He trailed his fingers along the spines, and just as he was about to walk away again he jolted to a stop. The spine of one book leaped out at him: *British Graphic Art of the Sixties & Seventies*.

He pulled it out, flicking through the pages. It was a directory of all the major British graphic designers of that era. Of course there was no mention of him. Why would there be? He had left before he ever got the chance to spread his wings as a designer, yet Lewis knew several of the other designers listed. Of course he found George Miller. An old black-and-white shot of the pompous bastard, looking sternly at the camera with his black-rimmed glasses on.

*George Miller, born 1917, died 1979.*

So his old boss had been dead for ten years. He wondered what had happened to Eva.

*George Miller made his name designing a series of wartime posters for the Home Office. From the late 1940s he was one of the leading practitioners of International Modernism ...*

Lewis slammed the book shut. It did him no good to read any more. He had chosen a different life. He was part of a family in Arizona. That was more than he had ever had in London.

He reached up to put the book back on the shelf, but it slipped out of his hand and landed on the floor with a loud thud. A couple of other browsers glanced over at him disapprovingly. He bent down to scoop it up, but the book had fallen open. He froze in shock as he stared down. It hadn't even occurred to him to look for Marnie, but there she was in all her glory. A large black-and-white picture dated 1968, just one year after he had gone. She was looking intense and mysterious. The long hair he had known was cut short into a Mary Quant bob, and her eyes were lined with black kohl. She was smoking a cigarette and looking so damn cool it made his heart throb. Had he really known this girl? This super-chic style puss from the sixties had been his girlfriend once.

*Marnie Piper née Regan. Born 8 August 1943. Starting out in 1966 as girl Friday in George Miller's iconic*

117

*graphic art agency Studio M, Marnie Regan quickly advanced into the position of designer. She was the driving force behind the company's award-winning Phoenix International Airlines branding campaign in the summer of 1967. Regan married fellow Studio M designer Pete Piper in August 1967, and Miller made the couple partners in the agency in 1971. Under the joint creative talents of the Pipers and Miller, Studio M grew to be one of the most significant British design agencies of the era, developing not only major branding campaigns but also branching out into album cover design. Major clients include Bosch, Macht, Dalliance Shoes, the National Health Service, the Department of Education, Pepsi Cola, Samsung, BMW, Beagles Whisky and Gordon's Gin. They also designed album covers for The Rolling Stones, Eric Clapton, Fairport Convention and Led Zeppelin, among others.*

*In 1979 George Miller and Pete Piper both died within one month of each other. Marnie Piper and George Miller's widow, Eva, shut down the Studio M agency. In 1982 Piper moved back to her homeland of Ireland. She currently works as an art and design teacher at the College of Art in Sligo. Marnie Piper has been recognised as one of the few female designers who made a significant impact on the development of graphic design in Britain during the late 1960s and 1970s.*

Lewis squatted on the floor, his breath heaving in his chest. He couldn't believe it. He'd found Marnie in this book. He was even more stunned by what she had achieved. So her star had shone. But what about Pete? He was shocked that Marnie had married Pete less than four months after Lewis had left London. He'd never been aware of any attraction between the two of them. He couldn't get his head round it. How could Marnie have gone from him to quiet, geeky Pete?

He turned the page and there was a picture of Pete himself. It had been taken a few years after Lewis had known him, but he still looked as awkward as ever, skinny and tall with his unflattering glasses, and wearing a jacket that was cut all wrong for him. He would have been pleased for Pete, that he had become so successful, but why did he have to go and marry Marnie? Lewis felt furious at his old friend. Ridiculous since the man was dead, and at a young age as well. But how dare Pete swoop in and take over where he had left off? And how could Marnie have let him?

He flicked to the front of the book and checked to see when it had been published – 1984. Five years ago. It wouldn't be hard to find out if Marnie was still living in Ireland. He flicked back to her biography and stared at her face. The photo was in black and white, but he could still see those flaming blue eyes staring back at him. How they had blazed the last time they had spoken. She must have been so hurt. Had her revenge been to marry Pete?

He slapped the book shut and pushed it back on the shelf.

His Marnie had just transformed from a fantasy into a real woman. She had been a successful graphic designer. And now she was a respected art and design teacher. All her achievements were stacked up in front of him. And what had he to offer her? How could he face Marnie now, with all his lost potential? And yet, he told himself, it was she who was looking for him with those mysterious messages on the postcards. That was so Marnie: the intrigue, the game-playing, the secrecy. She was a woman who liked to challenge, to provoke. It was one of the reasons why he had wanted her – why he still wanted her.

## LONDON, 13 APRIL 1967, 11.38 A.M.

In the entrance hall at Studio M, Lewis pushed Marnie up against the damp walls. He could feel her heart beating through her dress, the heat of her penetrating his skin.

'I want you now,' he said, beginning to kiss her lips.

'Are you mad?' she protested. 'Someone will see us.'

Nevertheless she kissed him back.

'You drive me mad, Marnie; I can't stop thinking about you.'

She said nothing, just picked up his hand and led him down the hallway. She pushed the lavatory door open and they fell in. She put her hands behind her, locking the door. It was a tiny space – the toilet and a sink, a mirror over it. She wrapped her arms about him. He could feel the hunger pulsing inside her.

'Say you want me,' he whispered, sitting down on the toilet lid.

She shook her head. He reached out and put his hand up her blue dress. God, he loved minis.

'I know you want me; I can feel you. Say it,' he commanded

'I do.' Her voice cracked. 'Yes, I do.'

She sat on top of him, and he slipped into her. The feeling of being inside her was sublime. He felt so aroused, and safe as well because inside Marnie was exactly where he belonged. She lifted herself all the way up to the tip of his cock and then slammed herself back down again so he was deep within her. He tried to remain quiet, but the intensity of their lovemaking was too much. As he came, a groan erupted from his mouth.

She put her hand over his lips, her eyes a warning. Her palm tasted of erasers and ink. All the girls he had dated before, no matter how free-spirited, wanted to get a ring on their finger, or some kind of commitment after a couple of months. Yet Marnie seemed to want the opposite. She even lived on her own, with no need for flatmates or other girlfriends.

Eventually Marnie climbed off him. She leaned over the tiny sink and splashed her face. He picked up her lacy pants, dangled them off his hand.

'Don't forget these now, Miss Regan.'

She grabbed them off him, smiling despite herself.

'Why do I let you do this to me?' she asked as she wiggled back into her underwear.

'Do what?' he said innocently. 'Make love to you, give you pleasure? Now tell me what on earth could be wrong with that?'

'You know what I mean.' She tried to frown, but it didn't work.

'Go on,' he said. 'Put on your lipstick. You'll be missed.'

She opened her bag and took out her lip sheen, smearing it over her lips so they were fresh and glossy again, then repinned her hair.

He saw her looking at him in the mirror.

'Lewis,' she began, sounding serious. 'It's time.'

'What do you mean?'

'It's time to tell George about me.'

He didn't reply. He looked away from her, out of the little window, which was permanently stuck open. It had started raining again. The wind had picked up and a few stray drops spattered him. An upturned umbrella, abandoned, was being blown across the road in gusts. A taxi drove over it, crushing it on the tarmac into a twist of metal and nylon.

'Do you hear me, Lewis?'

He looked back at her and into her eyes. They were the same colour he imagined those Irish loughs to be. Such a deep blue you would never find the bottom.

'I'll tell him about you, of course,' he promised. 'We're a team.'


## SCOTTSDALE, 23 MARCH 1989

Joy picked out a book on Ireland. Of all the books in Scottsdale library for her to look at, it seemed apt that it was a large reference book stuffed with pictures of Ireland that she should choose.

She carried the book to one of the chairs facing the full-length windows that looked out upon the manicured civic-centre gardens, stretched her legs out onto the sill and began to peruse its pages. It was full of glossy photographs of sumptuous green pastures, white thatched cottages and the sea – oh yes, the tempestuous western ocean. Beneath each photograph was a quote from a famous Irish writer: W.B. Yeats, Edna O'Brien, Eavan Boland and Seamus Heaney.

It wasn't her imagination – she really did feel drawn to this landscape. This land was the essence of her, even though she'd been taken away as a baby.

The pages Joy lingered over were the pictures of the crashing sea. They bewitched her, seduced her, driving her wild with longing.

She had never seen the sea.

As a little girl she used to have daydreams about sitting on a beach and looking at the water – not even having to be in it, just listening and looking at the waves crashing onto the shore. She didn't need to make sandcastles or collect shells. All she wanted was to sit on the sand, sift it through her fingers and count the waves as they lapped further up the beach, inching their way towards her toes.

Yet at the age of thirty-eight Joy had still never seen the sea. Her parents had never been travellers. Her mother was afraid of flying and hated long car journeys. She had claimed that travelling from New York to Arizona was an experience she never wanted to repeat. During the summer months the heat in Scottsdale rarely dipped below 100 degrees, day or night, and with her pale skin, Joy had struggled. She had begged her parents to drive to California, to the coast, or to the Sea of Cortez, but her mother had been afraid of venturing even the few hundred miles to Mexico. Thus every year they went to the same place on their summer holidays, driving up through Prescott (which was only slightly cooler) and beyond to Flagstaff and into southern Utah, where she and her parents would camp by Navajo Lake.

Her father had loved this landscape, with its high pine and aspen forests. Joy had seen snow for the first time at Navajo Lake when one June they had arrived and there was still snow under some of the trees. Her father had told her it was because they were so high up. It had been a moment of utter magic. She had never forgotten the sensation of that icy powder on her hot skin. In years to come she and her father had always managed to hunt out snow. The last time had been in January 1987 when they had visited the Santa Catalina Mountains just after a snowstorm. The image of snow upon cacti had been both incongruous and beautiful. For a man who had loved snow, romanticised about the Northern Lights and the wilderness of Alaska, Joy had found it surprising that Jack Porter had settled in Arizona. She suspected that her parents had stayed in Scottsdale all these years because it was her mother's preference.

When Joy had married Eddie, already six months pregnant with Ray, she had still believed that they would leave Scottsdale one day. After all, it had been Eddie's adventurous pioneer spirit she had fallen in love with in the first place. She'd had hopes. Not only of travelling all around America but of seeing further afield. Yet things hadn't turned out like that. The arrival of a baby had forced them to settle, and then she had become pregnant again. They'd needed the support of their families, and so before she knew it they had been ensconced in their mint-green house on 2nd Street, a stone's throw from her own parents. So young they had had to deal with the responsibilities of raising and providing for two children. But Eddie really had stepped up to the task, setting himself up as a realtor and working night and day to support them.

There had been no time or money for holidays.

And then as the children got older Eddie was so tired whenever he took a break that he just wanted to hang out at home by the pool, have friends over for barbeques or play golf in one of the local resorts with his buddies.

She'd asked Eddie to take her to the sea one day. He had promised her he would, but it had never happened. Now that the kids were both grown up and they had more money, she'd hoped that they would finally get to travel, but every time she mentioned it Eddie told her he was too busy.

'There are plenty of lakes and rivers in Arizona,' he'd said to her. 'It's just the same. Water.'

But Joy knew that Salt River, the Verde River, Apache Lake, Roosevelt Lake, even the mighty Colorado River were not the same as an ocean. She wanted to smell that salty tang in the air and look out at a horizon that she knew she wouldn't reach for an eternity.

She turned her attention back to the book. The image before her was a sweeping seascape in a place called Sligo. Right on the edge of the ocean was the profile of a mountain. It looked as if its peak had been chopped off, like a hammerhead. Below, the sea raged against the coast filtering between dark, seaweed-strewn rocks. She read the text below:

'Come away, O human child!
To the waters and the wild
With a faery, hand in hand,
For the world's more full of weeping
than you can understand.'

The poem had been written years ago by the Irish writer W.B. Yeats, but still it felt as if the words were just for her. She felt for the child inside her. The baby who had been abandoned and yet found. The wild and watery part of her that scratched away inside, refusing to be silenced. It was more than a desire; it was a need to see this country and look into its dark corners so she could understand the other side of herself. It was a place so different from Arizona with its vast, flat desert plains, weighted by the big hot sky. She could sense it. All the twists and turns of Ireland, the hidden rolls and dips, the nooks and crannies. She wanted to search them all. Somewhere there was her mother.

A shadow fell, and Joy heard a voice, that crisp English accent.

'Hello.'

She jolted in surprise and looked up. There he was again. Lewis Bell. He was wearing a red shirt that offset his dark hair and brown eyes. She found herself smiling in greeting while wondering if there was such a thing as coincidence. What kept bringing her and Lewis together in the same place at the same time?

★

Lewis watched Joy's eyelids flicker the moment she felt his shadow fall over her. She looked up, her eyes hazy, as if he had woken her up from a deep sleep.

'Hello,' he said.

He watched a faint blush creep across her cheeks, making the rest of her skin look even more porcelain, as she registered who he was and woke up fully.

'Hi,' Joy said. 'How are you?'

'Good.' He leaned forward and tapped the book on her lap. 'What are you reading?'

'Well, I'm looking at it rather than reading.'

She held the book up to him and he read the title: *Ireland in Pictures and Verse*. How strange that she should be perusing a book on Ireland.

'Can I take a look?' he asked.

'Sure,' she said, handing it to him.

The images were the same Ireland he had seen twenty-odd years ago. He stopped on a photograph of Rosses Point. It was a more picturesque view than he had experienced in the driving wind and rain all those years ago. A rainbow arched above the beach and into the churning waves below; the grass on the top of the cliffs was lush and verdant.

'God, it's so beautiful,' he said. 'And so different from Arizona.'

'Have you been to Ireland?' she asked him.

He felt as if her blue eyes were boring into him. As if she knew his story.

'Yes, years ago,' he said. 'I had a girlfriend who was Irish. I went with her.'

He kept turning the pages, seduced by the expansive sea, the green fields.

'And what about you?' he asked, looking down at her again. 'I have to say you look quite Irish. Do you have family there?'

She bowed her head, uncurling herself from the chair.

'You think I look Irish?' she asked, still looking down at the floor. 'I thought that the typical Irish look was red hair and green eyes?'

'Not at all,' he said. 'It's the black hair, pale skin and the blue eyes that are so typically Irish. Just like you.'

'Really?' She looked up at him, smiling shyly.

'Yes, you're a real colleen. So you do have Irish blood, right?'

She looked away again. She had on her blue cowboy boots. He couldn't believe she was wearing boots when it was so hot outside.

'Sort of,' she mumbled.

'On your father or your mother's side?'

'Both,' she murmured, glancing up again. 'It's a long story.'

She looked more embarrassed than ever, and suddenly he felt rude for asking her such personal questions.

'Well,' he said, changing the subject hastily, 'was your daughter pleased with the wedding invitations?'

'Shush! Can you be quiet please?' a testy voice called out from one of the stacks behind him and they smiled at each other conspiratorially.

'Very,' she whispered as he handed her back the book and she replaced it on the shelf. 'Did you not meet her when she came in to collect them?'

'No, I was out getting supplies.'

They walked together towards the library exit. On the steps outside he found himself stopping, turning to her.

'We seem to keep bumping into each other all the time; maybe that's a sign we should have a coffee together.'

'I'm married,' she said, her voice tense.

'Oh goodness, no, I didn't mean a date.' He held up his hand; showed her his wedding band. 'I'm married too. Twenty-one years actually.'

'Me too,' she said, gentler now.

'I meant just a cup of coffee and a chat. I'm on my holidays, so if you're not too busy …' He trailed off. He felt foolish, but more than anything he didn't want to go home quite yet. The image of Marnie Piper circa 1968 was still burning in his head. He needed distraction.

'Oh,' she said, squinting at him in the sun.

They stood for a long pause and he was just about to apologise and be on his way when all of a sudden she spoke.

'Can you tell me a little more about Ireland?'

'Haven't you been?'

She shook her head. 'Nope, but I really want to.'

'I was only there once, years and years ago, but sure we can talk about Ireland.'

'We could go for an ice cream at the Sugar Bowl. Do you like ice cream?'

'Sure.'

They began to walk through the civic-centre gardens, past the new performance space. It felt strange to be walking in step with a woman other than Samantha. She was so much shorter than his wife, who was nearly the same height as him. Joy made him feel tall, substantial in a way Samantha never had.

'You know,' she said, 'I've not only never been to Ireland but I've never seen the sea.'

He stopped in his tracks, stunned. He had met people before in the mid-western states who had never seen the sea, but not someone like Joy. She looked as if she belonged by the sea.

'You've never seen the sea anywhere – not even California or Mexico?' He couldn't keep the shock out of his voice, although he could see she was looking embarrassed again.

'I've been to Chicago. We've friends who have a place right on Lake Michigan. Eddie says it's like being by the sea.'

'It's a big lake,' Lewis said, 'but still a completely different experience because it's ultimately enclosed by land.'

'It's shameful that I've never seen the sea,' she said with an air of apology. 'I always dreamed of going, right from when I was a girl.'

'Then you must go, you absolutely must,' he declared. 'You must put it at the top of your list of things to do.'

'It's not that easy.' She dropped her head and looked so sad that he had the urge to hold her hand.

'You have to make it happen.'

He heard himself encouraging her – but what right had he to lecture her when he had given up on his dream years ago?

But deep down Lewis had never given up. These postcards had been a small miracle in his life. He knew he was still bound to Samantha. He couldn't actually leave his wife. Yet just to accept that Marnie was still thinking of him, maybe even wanting him, made him feel as if he was worth something again.


ROSSES POINT, SLIGO, IRELAND,
EASTER MONDAY, 27 MARCH 1967

The car was being buffeted by wind and rain, the smell of cow dung in the air as the two of them steamed up her father's Ford Cortina. Yet it was so enticing to sit next to him as he drove the car down the bumpy, twisted lanes, over the crest of little hills snaking up the western coast. Today more than ever Marnie felt inspired by the rare, raw energy of the sea. She took in the leap and shriek of the waves as they slapped against the shoreline, sending a thrill through her then turned to look at Lewis. She wanted to run her hands through his hair, crush his cheeks with kisses, yet she held back. She knew that if she showed him how she really felt she would drive him away.

Marnie pinched herself. She couldn't believe that Lewis Bell was here, with her, in Ireland, becoming part of her life. This man, who was so elusive, so desirable because of his unavailability, had accepted her invitation to spend Easter with her family. Marnie knew full well she was naive to fall in love with Lewis, to expect him to want only her, and yet she just couldn't help herself. He was intoxicating.

They had only been seeing each other since Christmas. Not even three months. Yet right from the beginning the sparks had flown. She had always promised herself that love wouldn't get in the way of her ambition. Yet wasn't Lewis part of her ambition? One day they were going to be partners in their own design agency. Maybe even partners in love and life? The thought made her dizzy with hope.

He was so English in his ways, but still Lewis fitted right in with her family. She was proud of him, chatting away to her mammy in the kitchen as she fed him slices of her home-made brown bread.

'Are you a Catholic, Lewis?' was one of the first questions Mammy had asked him. She had chastised

131

her mother, told her not to be so rude, but much to her surprise Lewis hadn't been cross at all.

'Actually I was raised a Catholic. My mother is Irish.'

'Grand so.' Her mother had nodded in approval.

Marnie had been surprised by Lewis's openness. In London he had refused to talk about his childhood, mentioning only once a mother he never saw and a demanding younger sister.

Lewis was different here. As the days passed she realised it was because he was relaxed, away from London, and Studio M and its constant pressure.

Her father was out most of the time on the farm, and when he was about he didn't say much, but she knew he liked Lewis too when he took him to the pub to meet his pals.

As they sat ensconced in the snug, sipping on glasses of Guinness, Lewis told her he loved listening to her voice in her homeland.

'You sound different here,' he said. 'Your voice is so lyrical, almost singing.'

She laughed with delight at his compliment, not caring if she looked silly or unsophisticated.

He touched her constantly, stroking her hair, her arm, catching a secret kiss off her when her parents weren't looking.

They were in separate bedrooms, and she didn't dare break the rule that separated them, but that made it so much more seductive a weekend. It was Easter and so they went to Mass nearly every day: Maundy Thursday and the Last Supper, Stations of the Cross on Good Friday and then the big Mass on Easter Sunday. Sitting next to

Lewis on the pew, feeling his body pressed against hers and smelling his aroma, she found it impossible to focus on Christ's suffering or the resurrection. Even to ask to be forgiven for her temptation, the sin of unmarried sex. She couldn't be sorry, no matter how sinful it made her. All she wanted was to be in Lewis's arms, and to feel him inside her.

It was their last afternoon and they were driving from Strandhill along the coastline towards Rosses Point. Ireland felt even emptier now than when she had left two years ago. There were more sheep than people, although every now and again they passed a farmer pal of her daddy's chugging along in his tractor, as well as a determined Maureen Farrelly, a friend of her mam's, battling against the wind on her pushbike, her headscarf flapping like a demented seagull upon her head.

At the edge of the cliff on Rosses Point they held on to each other and let the sea wind sweep through them, taking their breath away.

It felt like the happiest moment of her life. To be in Lewis's arms, the two of them clinging on to each other, facing the elements together.

The rain descended and they ran along the deserted beach, taking shelter inside a tiny cave between the rocks. They held each other in their wet clothes, kissing in a frenzy. Lewis filled her so perfectly. He didn't know it, but he was the only man she had ever made love to. Her first time after the Christmas party she had been so drunk she barely remembered it, but she knew she had wanted him. She had not woken up regretful despite the fact that she was now damaged goods. If her mammy knew ... But she didn't. It was all worth it. Her and Lewis's passion inspired her designs. Lewis was part of her, and she was part of him. Their bodies, their minds, their talents, and she wanted this fusion to last forever.

## SCOTTSDALE, 23 MARCH 1989

Why the hell had she suggested the Sugar Bowl? What if someone saw them and told Eddie? His office was only a few blocks away. Moreover she had offered to take Lewis to the very place she and Eddie had first met. How stupid was that?

Joy brought her arm across her chest to grip the strap of her bag on her other shoulder, instinctively protecting herself while trying to look relaxed. She was being paranoid. Where was the harm in having an ice cream with this man? He wasn't a complete stranger. He had printed the invites for her daughter's wedding. They had spent an hour together in the Botanical Garden, accidental though it was. She had been clear right from the start that she was married, and so had he. But she had to admit she was intrigued by Lewis Bell and how he had ended up in Arizona. He didn't seem to belong here at all.

But how she wished she hadn't told him that she'd never seen the sea. He would have deduced that she had never in fact left the States. He must think she was real hillbilly.

The Sugar Bowl had not changed a bit since that day Eddie had sat down with her and Mary Lynn Baxter. The pink furnishings were a little faded, but it was nice to feel she was stepping back in time. It was still the best place in town to eat ice cream.

Joy and Lewis were at a round table by the window overlooking busy Scottsdale Road. To her discomfort a familiar face approached their table to take their order. Looking like a wildcat in a tutu in her pink uniform was Heather's friend, Carla. Joy felt her cheeks grow hot. Would Carla tell Heather that she was eating ice cream with a strange man? She was almost grateful for the fact that Carla and Heather didn't seem to be speaking at the moment.

'Hi, Mrs Sheldon,' Carla said, her big brown eyes curious as she looked from Joy to Lewis. 'What can I get you?'

Carla was not as friendly as usual despite the fact she was almost family. Joy and her mom, Rosa, had been best friends at high school, and Joy had known Carla since she was a baby, yet she was definitely acting a little cool towards her.

Joy looked down at the menu. 'I'll have a Buster Brownie ice cream please and a black coffee.'

'I'll take the Spectacular Banana Bowl and a coffee too,' Lewis said.

Joy felt herself blushing slightly as Carla took in her companion.

'This is Lewis Bell, Carla. He printed Heather's wedding invites,' she blurted out, as if that was a good enough reason for them to be in the Sugar Bowl together.

Carla frowned. 'So she's going ahead with the wedding?' she asked Joy, tapping her notepad against her skirt.

'Of course she is, Carla. Aren't you her bridesmaid?'

Carla shook her head. 'No way,' she mumbled, scribbling down their order and heading back towards the kitchen before Joy could say another thing.

Joy felt floored. She couldn't believe Carla's attitude. She knew Carla hadn't thought the wedding a good idea, but what she was picking up here was more than that. Heather and Carla had been friends their whole lives, even before they'd started school. Carla, like her mom, had been the only mixed-race kid in the class. Moreover, Rosa was a single mother. Most of the other mothers had been wary of her and behaved as if she might snatch their husbands away. Joy wasn't sure whether their prejudices had been based upon the fact that Rosa wasn't married, or that she was Mexican and her child's father was from a Native American family. Some of these women had been Joy and Rosa's former classmates, so it was even more shocking to see how pointed they were in their determination not to let their children mix with Carla. As a consequence, Carla and Heather had stuck together the whole way through school.

The girls were opposites in almost every way. Heather had inherited her fair, pretty looks from Eddie's mother, and she was sporty, but not very academic. Carla, on the other hand, was a dark, sultry beauty, a knockout combination of genes. She was also clever, consistently scoring the highest grades. Yet, despite their differences, the two girls had been inseparable. What Joy had liked about Carla was that she seemed unaware of her own beauty, and the effect she had on others. She had never known her to even date. Her own daughter, she knew, was not so humble, and sometimes Heather's vanity embarrassed Joy, yet her daughter had a big heart and that was what mattered the most. But it disturbed Joy that two such good friends were now at loggerheads over Heather's marriage to Darrell, and she knew Heather would be devastated if her best friend wasn't beside her on her wedding day.

'Everything okay?' Lewis asked her. He was still wearing the glasses he had put on to read the menu. She thought he looked rather distinguished in them, like her idea of an English professor.

'That's my daughter's best friend. They've had some kind of falling-out over Heather's wedding. But I don't know why.'

'Maybe she doesn't like her bridesmaid's dress. They're usually hideous,' Lewis said, slipping his glasses into his shirt pocket.

'I wish it were just that,' Joy said, dropping her voice as Carla reappeared with their sundaes.

★

'This is delicious,' Lewis exclaimed as he dug his spoon into the mound of bananas and vanilla.

Lewis realised that he'd never really eaten a dessert since he was a child and found that he was relishing every sweet spoonful of it.

'So how long have you been living in America?' Joy asked him.

'Too long,' he said, taking another scoop of ice cream. 'Sorry, I don't mean to be insulting, but Arizona couldn't be more different from London.'

'I know, my son Ray says it all the time.' She sighed.

'He lives in London at the moment. I don't think he'll ever come back now if he can help it. He's in love with the city.'

'Oh yes,' Lewis said, feeling a wave of nostalgia. 'To be young and in London can be quite intoxicating! You should go visit him.'

'I will. I've already got my passport sorted.'

Lewis studied Joy, glad to hear that she was going on a trip. Surely her son would take her to the sea in Essex or Kent?

She wasn't his usual type. She was petite, curvaceous, with a heart-shaped face and navy blue eyes. He felt safe to look at her so openly. They'd both made it clear that they were married, although he found it hard not to flirt a little. He still had this feeling that he'd met Joy before. Maybe it was her Irish looks: dark hair, like Marnie, yet a different kind of dark. Marnie's hair had been such a deep chestnut it shone like polished mahogany whereas Joy's was as inky blue-black as the darkest night.

'So why did you come to the States, and of all places here?' Joy asked again.

His normal reticence deserted him. He wanted to tell Joy about his life.

'My wife's family lives in Scottsdale. We came for a visit over twenty years ago. It was only meant to be short-term but we never went back to London in the end.'

'Do you have kids?' she asked, scooping ice cream and brownie into her mouth.

'No. We tried, you know, but I guess it just wasn't meant to be.'

'I'm sorry,' she said.

'And you? I've heard about Ray and Heather of course … any more?'

'No, that's it. Both grown up and nearly flown the nest. It'll be just me and Eddie after Heather gets married.'

★

Lewis was wiping his mouth with his napkin and looking at her in that way he had looked at her earlier in the library. It was an admiring look, and it made her blush. She glanced down at the table and noticed that he had very beautiful hands. Long, elegant fingers with neat, short nails. His shirtsleeves were pushed up his arms, and she could see the golden hairs on his forearms, a splattering of freckles. For some reason she was possessed with a desire to touch his arm. She wanted to feel the warmth of his skin, its texture.

She looked away, down at her ice-cream sundae. She was stuffed, and yet she scooped up another spoonful and shoved it into her mouth.

'I keep thinking we know each other,' Lewis said.

'Maybe I look like someone you once knew. Your girl friend from Ireland perhaps?'

'No,' he said. 'You don't look a bit like Marnie.'

'So who do I look like then?' she asked, her curiosity making her bold.

'I really don't know,' he said, putting down his spoon. 'It's bugging the hell out of me.'

'Maybe I just have one of those faces.' She shrugged. 'I look like a thousand other people.'

'No.' He shook his head. 'I wouldn't say that, Joy.'

There was something so intimate in the way he said her name. She immediately felt guilty to be eating ice cream with this elegant man who wasn't her husband.

'Do you miss London?' she asked, steering the conversation away from the subject of herself.

'I miss it so much,' he said, surprised by the strength of his feelings. 'Everything about London. Even the noise, the pollution, the rain. I really miss the rain. I miss those smoky cafes where you can get an English breakfast and a proper mug of tea. I miss roast beef and Yorkshire pudding and British pubs. I miss the quirky shops down Carnaby Street, and the music in the clubs, and all the art. I know it's different now. I'm sure it's all changed. I mean, it's Thatcherite Britain. Not the same at all. But I'm stuck in my memories of the past, and I wish I could travel back.'

'The world is changing,' Joy said. 'Look at Eastern Europe and what's happening behind the Iron Curtain.'

'Old ways are crumbling,' Lewis said. 'Soon none of us will recognise the world.'

He was overwhelmed by a need to show someone the postcards. His obvious choice should have been Samantha, but of course his wife was the last person he could show them to.

'The thing is,' Lewis said, pulling the cards out of his jacket pocket, 'I've been getting these postcards from Marnie, the girl I used to know in Ireland. I haven't seen or heard from her in over twenty-one years and now these...'

He flung the cards down on the table.

'What does she say?' Joy asked.

'Take a look yourself.'

She picked the three postcards up and he watched her read each card one by one.

'Eventually the truth will come out,' she read aloud. 'Am I your shining star? It's time.'

'I know they must be from Marnie because they're private messages. The things she writes are words that she and I would know have significance for us ...' He took a breath. 'What do you think it all means?'

'I don't know,' said Joy, putting the cards back down. 'I think she wants you to get in contact with her.'

'But if she wanted me to contact her, surely she would put her address or phone number on one of the cards?'

Joy looked thoughtful.

'They're odd messages because they're not exactly ...' She paused and chewed her lip. 'Well, they're not very romantic, I guess. The star one maybe, but the other two are a bit like threats.'

'Do you think I should go to Ireland and look for her?'

She looked at him in astonishment. 'You would do that?' she asked. 'What about your wife?'

He shook his head. 'I know it's wrong to want to go. It's just things between Sam and me aren't great at the moment, and I can't help thinking about Marnie ... I mean, maybe I picked the wrong woman all those years ago.'

He looked down at the table in shame. 'I really don't know why I'm telling you all this. You must be appalled.'

To his surprise, Joy put her hand on his. It felt so soft and light, and he was reminded of the flutter of birds' wings.

'Of course not, but maybe these cards are a sign, not

141

about Marnie, but about Samantha. Whether Marnie wants you to contact her or not, isn't it more important to make sure things are right with your wife?'

'Yes,' he said, astonished by her clarity. 'I'm being a fool.' He put the cards back in his pocket and grinned at her.

Joy couldn't help thinking what a lovely smile he had. She'd never desired another man in all her years of marriage, never dreamed of it. But Lewis was so different from all the cowboy guys she knew round here. Like a breath of cool air refreshing her on a hot summer's afternoon.

'Well,' she said, glancing at her watch, 'I'd better get going. I have to cook dinner.'

'I don't know how you'll eat anything after that giant sundae!' Lewis exclaimed.

'True, but Eddie will be hungry.'

'What does your husband do?' Lewis asked, standing up and offering her his hand.

'He's a realtor. He works really hard.' She found his gesture incredibly charming and blushed to have him help her out of her seat.

'Well, have a nice evening, and thanks for listening to me, Joy.' He shook her hand and the touch of his fingers made her shiver inside.

She let Lewis leave the Sugar Bowl first, making the excuse that she needed to use the restroom. Then Joy went up to the counter to hand Carla her tip.

'Hey, that Buster Brownie was the best.'

'Yeah, it's a killer for the waistline,' Carla said, hands on her own neat hips, her black hair pulled back off her face, her dark skin smooth as if polished. Somehow she managed to look beautiful even in the gaudy Sugar Bowl uniform.

'You should come round and see Heather. She misses you.'

Carla frowned. 'I can't.'

'Did you girls fall out?'

'It's not that,' Carla said, looking uncomfortable. 'It's just easier this way.'

'But why don't you want her to marry Darrell?' Joy persisted. 'I thought you liked him. You were all friends at high school.'

'I do like Darrell. It's just ... well, do you really think Heather is being true to herself, Mrs Sheldon?'

As Joy drove home she couldn't get Carla's words out of her head. What did she mean about Heather being true to herself? She knew Carla thought Heather was too young to get married and that she should go to college like her, but there was more to it than that. She saw it in the other girl's body language. Carla was hurt. Too hurt for it to be about her best friend's wedding, because Carla had never showed herself to be judgemental before. She was like Rosa, her mother. Equanimity was in their blood.

Joy pulled up at the junction on Goldwater and 2nd Street, and suddenly she remembered something. A moment she wasn't sure she'd actually witnessed. It had been about four months ago, when Carla had been staying over and the girls had offered to do the washing-up. She had been in the front room watching golf on the TV with Eddie, but she had been so bored that she'd decided to

143

join the girls in the kitchen. As she had walked into the room she had seen her daughter trailing her soapy finger down the side of Carla's face, and they had been looking at each other in a certain charged way.

They had jumped apart as soon as she'd walked in, yet Joy hadn't imagined it, for the bubbles from the washing-up liquid had left a line of love all down the side of Carla's face.

The realisation hit Joy with full force. *Of course!* She sat at the junction unable to move on, oblivious to the horn blowing from the car behind her. Carla was in love with her daughter. No wonder she had never had any boyfriends – she wasn't interested in men. And Heather, what about her?

In that fleeting moment, it had been her daughter who was touching Carla, not the other way around.

LONDON, 13 APRIL 1967, 12.57 P.M.

Did George know about their secret affair?

Lewis was helping Marnie on with her coat just as their boss appeared in his office doorway, head cocked to one side.

'Are you two going for lunch together?'

'No, I'm just helping Miss Regan on with her coat.'

'The perfect gentleman as always, eh, Lewis?'

George leaned against the doorway and drummed his fingers on the wall. 'Well, my dear, I'm afraid I have to call you back,' George said to Marnie. 'I have a letter I need typed urgently.'

144

Marnie obediently slipped her coat off and draped it on the back of her chair.

'The Plough,' Lewis whispered as she whisked past him, shorthand pad in hand.

George patted Marnie's bottom as she went into his office and winked at him. Lewis felt the urge to punch his boss in the face.

He strolled out onto the street, pulled up his collar against the rain and tried to dismiss the image of George's hand on Marnie's bottom. He told himself that his boss was like that with all young women, but he knew that George might keep Marnie the whole lunch hour. He tried to focus on ideas for the Phoenix Airlines logo, but all he could think of was either the stupid cactus or the cliché of the phoenix rising from the flames. He needed Marnie's help.

Yet Lewis didn't panic. Sometimes he believed that his quota for misfortune had been filled when he was a child. Even then he'd had a knack of turning things round to his advantage. He believed in luck. And, more importantly, he believed *he* was lucky. Just like now, for who should be walking towards him but Eva Miller, laden with shopping bags, one of which was stuffed with a huge bunch of daffodils. He was saved. There was no way that Eva would let her husband spend his lunch hour alone with Marnie.

Eva smiled when she caught sight of him. 'Well, hello there,' she said. 'Are you off to lunch?'

'Yes, I am, Mrs Miller. Where did you get all the daffodils?'

'In Covent Garden. I love daffs – they remind me of home.'

Eva was too old for him, and yet he could appreciate her beauty. George had made quite sure they all knew that David Bailey had once asked to photograph his wife.

Lewis took out his cigarettes, offering her one.

'So how's the big boss?' Eva asked him.

'Working hard as usual,' Lewis replied, lighting her cigarette. Up close he could see the fine dusting of powder on her cheek, the lacing of black mascara on her lashes.

'Well, his lordship is going to have to put down his pencils for an hour at least. He promised me that we would go for lunch today. I need a Campari after all this shopping.'

She threw her unfinished cigarette onto the pavement then twisted her patent scarlet ankle boot over it.

'Don't tell me he has your Marnie working through her lunch hour again?'

The rain had eased off and Eva unbuckled her coat. She looked him right in the eye, and he could feel his cheeks redden. She knew about him and Marnie. How on earth had she worked it out?

'Oh don't worry.' She grinned, patting his arm. 'George hasn't a clue. He doesn't pick up on those sorts of things, but I have a knack for it. I could see it from day one.'

'I don't know what you could mean, Mrs Miller,' he said, embarrassed by her familiarity.

She leaned forward and gave him a little shove with her gloved hand. 'Oh, what a charmer you are! You men really are something.'

He took a final drag of his cigarette. 'We are?'

'I always know when George is having an affair. He thinks he gets away with it, but I just let him away with it.'

146

Her eyes darkened for a moment, the smile wiped off her face. 'There is a difference.'

'But I'm not married,' Lewis protested, not sure quite what he was saying.

'I know,' Eva said. 'But a girl like Marnie is special.'

'I'm sorry, Mrs Miller, but I think you misunderstand – really there's nothing going on –'

'Just be careful, darling,' she said, laughing lightly as her coat flapped open and Lewis saw the outline of a black bra beneath her chiffon blouse. 'Don't abandon her when you've had enough,' she said with a flick of his tie before sauntering off.

He just stood there, astounded. Being the boss's wife didn't entitle her to interfere in his private life.

He had already drunk his first pint by the time Marnie arrived. The ice had melted in her gin and tonic, and the ploughman's lunch he had ordered for them to share was still untouched.

'My God, our boss is an awful lech,' Marnie said as soon as she sat down.

'What the hell did he do?' Lewis demanded in a blaze of concern. 'I don't care if it's George, I'll knock his block off.'

'Calm down, it's all the pathetic sexual innuendoes; he never does anything past the bum pinching. Thank God Eva turned up.'

Lewis was surprised to hear Marnie use her first name. 'Are you friendly with George's wife?'

'A little bit,' Marnie said, sipping her G&T. 'Remember I mind their boys sometimes. We have more in common than you'd think.'

'Well, I hope that doesn't make me like George.'

'No chance.' She smiled at him, her eyes crinkling in amusement. 'So tell me more about this morning. What did George say to you?'

'He was so impressed with the designs, he's going to make me a partner in the agency.' He beamed at her.

'Lewis, that's fantastic.' She sprang up from her seat and hugged him awkwardly across the table. 'So are you going to tell him we worked on them together when we get back to the office?'

'Maybe not this afternoon,' he said. 'But once I'm a partner, I can make you a proper member of the team.'

Marnie looked a little crestfallen. 'Can you promise me that?'

'Of course I can. I'll be a partner at Studio M. I'll have the authority to promote you.'

She pulled a corner off her bread roll and pressed it between her fingers, before dropping it onto her plate, uneaten.

'But I thought you were going to tell George about me today. I don't want to wait until you're made partner. I thought we were a team.'

'We will be a team – soon. Don't you see, Marnie?'

She drew a perfect circle with her finger in the condensation on her glass. 'I don't think it's fair.'

He looked at her in surprise. 'What do you mean?'

'I do all the work. You get made a partner. George thinks my work is yours. It's wrong, Lewis.'

'It's my work as well, Marnie. You've helped me, sure ...'

'Excuse me?' she hissed, her cheeks beginning to bloom.

'Look, George is making me a partner, which is like a promotion for you too. Don't you understand? He would never accept a woman in a senior design position.'

Marnie shook her head. 'Are you so sure?'

Lewis felt a nudge of unease. He hadn't expected her to react like this.

'Why do we have to keep lying?' Her eyes searched his. Her caked black lashes looked like spider's legs.

'Because it's the only way to get what we want,' he told her as gently as he could.

'It's not what *I* want, Lewis.'

He leaned forward to take her hand in his, but she sat back on the pub bench and crossed her arms defensively. 'I don't want to do this,' she said. 'I don't want to lie.'

'We aren't lying to anyone, Marnie. We're just not revealing everything until the time is right. It's different.'

'I told you this morning that it's time now. I can't wait, Lewis.'

He got up and sat next to her on the bench, took her arms away from her chest and gripped them in his hands.

'Remember what I told you this morning, Marnie. I love you. Please trust me. Just wait a little longer, darling. I'll make it up to you, I promise.'

She turned to look at him. He had never seen her so cool, and so serious.

'You were different in Ireland,' she said suddenly.

He didn't understand. What did their Easter trip to Ireland have to do with all of this?

'No, I'm the same. I feel the same about you, Marnie. There's something amazing about the two of us. Please don't ruin it.'

149

'I can't wait until you're made partner, Lewis. I just can't wait any more.'

'If you really feel that way I'll tell George tonight at the dinner with the Phoenix International Airlines guy all right? We'll pitch for that together, okay?'

Her eyes lit up. 'You really mean it?'

'Yes.' He kissed her on the lips, pulling back to stroke her cheek. He wished he could make love to her. 'You're right. It's not fair. I am nothing without you, Marnie,' he whispered into her ear, brimming with his need for her.

When she kissed him back he could feel her love for him. The emotion swelled within him and the years fell away. He was a boy again, looking for someone to love him.


## BERKSHIRE, 7 JULY 1955

A silvery fish leaped out of the river, catching a fly in its mouth before disappearing beneath the ripples. The high summer sun was beating down on the back of his neck. He could feel the tiny hairs there prickling with heat. He was sitting on the riverbank, next to his Uncle Howard, Alfie the red setter snoozing in the sun, as they fished for trout. Lizzie was kneeling in the grass making daisy chains and singing nonsense. Her high-pitched voice was an unwelcome discord in the harmony of his summer's day.

'Shush,' Uncle Howard said to her. 'We have to be quiet, otherwise we'll scare the fish away.'

Lizzie stopped singing, picked up her daisy chain and put it around her neck. Lewis felt a slight tug on the end of his rod and reeled it in. Had he caught his first fish? Would Uncle Howard be proud of him? However, when his line emerged from the river, his only catch was a water-lily leaf, dripping off the end.

'Hard luck,' Uncle Howard said, winking at him.

Lewis disentangled the slimy water lily from his hook. He had to catch a fish. Uncle Howard had already caught two, and he had none. He took another maggot from the box and stuck it onto the hook then swung his rod in a loop behind his head and cast his line. He watched it flying out across the surface of the river, as if it were trying to run away from him.

'Good cast,' Uncle Howard said.

'I need the lavatory,' Lizzie announced.

'You can go in the trees over there.' Uncle Howard nodded towards a copse of trees across the field.

'I don't want to go on my own,' Lizzie whined. 'Lewis has to come with me.'

'Can you not wait, Lizzie?' Lewis said, as he felt a strong pull on his line. His rod bent into an arch. 'I think I've got something this time.'

He could see splashing. Excitement surged through him as he saw the back of a brown trout twisting and flipping in the water.

'Good boy, Lewis,' his uncle instructed. 'Reel him in.'

'I have to go!' Lizzie shouted. 'I can't wait ... I can't wait ...'

'Lizzie!' Lewis cried out. 'I can't let go!'

'I'll take her,' Uncle Howard offered. 'Keep a hold of him.'

He took Lizzie's hand and marched her towards the trees, Alfie trotting along behind them.

It was a big fish. Lewis could hardly believe how strong it was. It pulled him forward, his bare feet skidding on the grassy bank.

'No you don't,' he shouted at it. 'I've got you.'

His rod bent and strained and he pulled back with all his might. Suddenly the trout burst from the water and flew through the air. Lewis fell on his back as it landed on the ground next to him. It stared at him with accusing fish eyes, its gills working desperately to keep it alive. He picked up the big knife, which Uncle Howard used to kill the fish, and stood over his trout. He had to kill it, but he didn't want to. Not now. Catching it was enough. He wanted to put it back in the river, but he couldn't. Uncle Howard would call him a sissy.

He was just about to slice the trout's throat when Lizzie emerged from the trees. She was screaming, running away from the wood as if there were monsters in it. She ran past him, slid down the slippery bank and plunged into the river.

'Lizzie!'

He dropped the knife and ran after her. He waded into the water and tried to drag her out, but it took two of them, him and Uncle Howard, to convince her to come out. Alfie was in the water as well, barking wildly at the three of them. The river had become a churning cloud of brown muck, every fish for miles around scared away. His sister was beyond reason, shaking in her summer dress, her toes laced with riverweed, tears and snot streaming down her face.

Uncle Howard wiped her face with his handkerchief and carried her up to the bank.

'What happened?' Lewis asked.

'She sat on a patch of nettles.'

'Is that all?'

'Well, I believe that *is* quite painful ...' Uncle Howard was unsmiling, not his usual self.

'You got it,' he said to Lewis when he saw the trout, now dead, lying on the ground. 'It's cruel not to kill it immediately though. You have to be a man and do it right away.'

Lewis was about to explain, but in the end he didn't bother. The fishing trip was abandoned. As usual, his sister had ruined everything.

# SIX

# *Resistance*

Joy was late. How long had she sat at the junction just round the corner from their house, cars beeping and swerving around her, thinking about Heather and Carla? Panic rose in her chest as she drove the rest of the way home. She had to get her head straight. Eddie would be mad at her if she was late. He always came home for his dinner at 5 p.m. sharp and headed back out to do more viewings in the evening, often working until late into the night.

It was 5.15 p.m. She had left nothing at home for him to eat, and she had no idea what she was going to cook. Her mind was a blank.

She did a U-turn, driving off to the closest grocery store. Once inside she scanned the aisles, her mind spinning. What should she cook? Burritos? She had made those last night, and enchiladas the night before. She couldn't do any more Mexican food because Eddie would be sick of it. He wasn't as keen on spice as she was.

*My daughter is gay!*

What about steak and fries, nice and simple? But it would take her too long to peel and cut the potatoes, and to be honest she just couldn't face the bubbling fat and the fryer.

*Are Heather and Carla in love?*

If only she and Eddie could go out for a meal, but of course Eddie had to work.

*Should she tell Eddie?*

She could drive to McDonald's and buy a takeaway. She'd never done that before. She could present it as something special – a treat.

*What about the wedding?*

As soon as she burst in through the porch door, clutching her brown paper McDonald's bag in one hand, the holder of shakes in the other, she knew she had made a big mistake. Eddie was sitting in front of the TV, glaring at a golf tournament on the screen. She stood on the threshold, unsure what to say or do.

Dashing past him she went into the kitchen. Nothing had changed since she'd left this morning. The dirty dishes were still in the sink, the empty apple-pie tin on the counter, her coffee on the table, half drunk, her pink-lipstick lips on the rim of the mug.

She bustled about, pulling out two plates and bringing them over to the table. Should she lay out cutlery? Was it okay to eat McDonald's with knives and forks?

'Where were you?'

Joy nearly jumped out of her skin. She hadn't realised he was standing behind her all the time.

'I'm sorry, honey, I lost track of time. I was in the library.'

She turned and smiled weakly. He didn't return her smile. In fact, he looked almost rigid with displeasure. All the features of his face that used to look so handsome, were distorted into a sort of hardness. His brown eyes were black as ink, his blonde hair was no longer so golden and it was receding so his forehead was more prominent.

'Well, isn't that nice for you?' he said. 'So while I'm working my butt off trying to make enough money to pay for our daughter's wedding, you're taking it easy in the library?'

'I was looking at books on Ireland,' she blurted out in defence.

He looked at her with a toxic mix of sarcasm and pity. 'Oh for God's sake, Joy. Ireland?'

'Yeah,' she said nervously, taking out the paper napkins and folding them into triangles. 'I'm thinking about going to find my birth mother.'

'But you know that's a bad idea, honey,' he said, his voice softening.

'I need to know where I'm from and who I am,' she said, feeling defensive.

'That's bullshit and you know it, Joy.' Eddie grabbed her by the shoulders, forcing her to face him. 'Your mother gave you up. She didn't want you. So why would you put yourself through all this hassle, go all the way to Ireland, to find some old woman who doesn't care about you?'

She said nothing. Half of her believed Eddie. What was the point? Surely she would just feel worse if she went to Ireland, but beneath the fear was a driving force, an ambition she couldn't ignore. She needed to go to Ireland and see where she came from. She was going to find a cliff in the west of Ireland, just like the one she and Lewis were looking at in the book today. She was going to stare at that wild Atlantic Ocean and drink it in.

'What the hell is this?' Eddie said, his attention turning to the food on the table. He flicked the end of the McDonald's bag on the counter.

'I thought we'd have a treat. I got you a Big Mac.'

'I don't eat junk food, Joy. Don't you know that by now?'

Her heart sank. She had screwed up again.

'I can't eat this trash,' he said, walking out of the kitchen. 'I'll pick up something after work.'

'I'm sorry, Eddie. I'll cook something.' She heard her plaintive tone, and she hated herself for being so subservient, yet she couldn't help feeling guilty.

'Forget it,' he said, picking up his car keys. 'I told you I'll get something later.'

'Will I cook something for when you get back? A nice piece of steak?'

'Don't bother, it could be late,' he said. 'It's okay, really. I have to go.'

He hardly looked at her as he left the house. The door slammed behind him. She wasn't sure if it was intentional.

She stood trembling in the front room. Half of her was relieved it hadn't escalated into a full-blown fight, and half of her was disgusted at herself. Why couldn't she tell him to get his own dinner? Because that was her job, wasn't it? He looked after her, and she looked after him. That was the deal. And yet it felt to Joy as if she hadn't got to

157

choose. Eddie had always wanted to be a realtor. But had she ever put her hand up and said she wanted to be a housewife?

She walked back into the kitchen and slumped at the table, looked at the fries and burger. She was still full from the Buster Brownie at the Sugar Bowl, and the McDonald's meal didn't look too appealing. Even so she found herself pulling the wrapper off her husband's Big Mac and taking a bite. She took two more bites and ate a couple of fries, which now tasted like sticks of cold, salty cardboard, before giving up and chucking the rest in the trash.

She felt sick. Too much food in her belly plus the tension of letting Eddie down and her worries over Heather. She should make herself a cup of camomile tea to relax, but instead she opened the fridge and pulled out a beer, snapped the lid off and took a slug. She thought of Lewis, and how gentle and softly spoken he was. She couldn't imagine him getting angry about whether his dinner was ready for him or not. But maybe he was just like Eddie. Did all men at some stage lose patience with their wives? What kind of husband was Lewis? Did he expect his wife to serve him? No, she was certain he was a different kind of husband, the kind who cooked dinner for his wife sometimes or took her out. In all their years together she had never known Eddie to cook anything apart from managing the barbeque when they had friends over during the holidays.

Yet, despite her attempt at resentment, Joy couldn't help feeling guilty. Eddie had expected her to be at home with his dinner ready. He had been working hard all afternoon making money for their family, and now he was out again working until late at night. Not many husbands worked as hard as Eddie. It was selfish of her to neglect him.

Joy was seized by a sudden desire to please him. She wanted so much to see the hard edges of Eddie's face dissolve into good humour, for him to smile at her, genuinely – to look pleased with her. She wanted to see that Eddie of old, interested in her, looking into her heart and soul, and loving her spirit, making her feel special. It had been too many years since either of them had felt like that.

She started opening the kitchen cupboards, searching for inspiration. She had to find something to cook. Her eyes lit upon a bowl of fresh figs on the countertop. She pulled out a bag of flour as a memory came to her of Eddie sitting at the kitchen table in her parents' house, licking his fingers as he devoured a slice of her mother's fig cake. Afterwards he had taken her for a drive in his new Plymouth Satellite. He had taken her all the way to the Grand Canyon to watch the sunset. She had still tasted the sweet fig seeds on his tongue when he had taken her in his arms, the rich sienna of the sinking sun burning through the lids of her closed eyes, imprinting an image of their love. Fig cake in the sunshine, kisses in the sunset. Her young lover had been so sweet and comforting beneath his tough exterior of Stetson hat, Levi's, fast horses and even faster cars. She had loved this contradiction within Eddie. She had thought him a rule breaker; the kind of guy who took her all the way to watch the sunset at the Grand Canyon on a whim. A guy who loved her mother's fig cake, and yet could take it or leave it, the spice of life a stronger pull than the safety of a home hearth. She had thought Eddie was an adventurer and that if she stuck with him her life would be exciting.

Joy took her big mixing bowl out of the cupboard along with a wooden spoon. The TV was still on in the front room. To hear that blaring noise and know she was the only one in the house made her feel lonely so she went and switched it off, standing by the window for a moment and staring out at the ridiculous little fountain in the front garden. How could Eddie have known her so little after all these years? How could he not have known that tearing down her orange tree would break her heart?

No one's perfect, she told herself. That was the problem with a lot of wives nowadays. They expected an ideal, and when their husband didn't match up to it they became bitter and ended up alone, even within their marriages. She didn't want that to happen to her. She didn't want to be angry and disappointed in the man she loved. Despite his flaws, Eddie was hers.

★

By the time Lewis got home, Samantha was upstairs packing for her trip to Santa Fe.

'Are you going to stay for dinner?' he asked her, leaning against the frame of the bedroom door and watching her fold up T-shirts. She looked good tonight, in her favourite white jeans and a pink halter-neck top, her long blonde hair shimmering in the evening light. 'You want a beer, or a glass of wine?'

'No, I've got to get going,' she said, piling the T-shirts into a case.

'How long are you going away for?' he asked her, looking at the mound of clothes, the large suitcase. 'Isn't that rather a lot of stuff to be taking with you?'

Samantha paused, lengthening up her spine. He couldn't see her face, but he could sense there was something wrong.

'Is there something going on, Samantha? What's up?'

'I'm not just going for the week,' she said in a quiet voice.

'Okay, how long are you going for?'

She didn't answer. He stepped forward, put his hand on her shoulder. 'Sammy, what's wrong?'

She pushed his hand away and turned to look at him. To his shock he could see that she was crying.

'What's happened?' he asked, confused.

'I'm sorry, Lewis,' she said.

He could feel his heart throbbing in his chest, a constriction of fear in his belly.

'I'm so unhappy.' She wiped tears from her eyes. 'And you're unhappy too. We're miserable together.'

'It's just a slump, Samantha. We'll get over it – we always do.'

'We've never been right, Lewis. You know that deep down.'

'That's not true. We were happy when we first got here, remember?'

She turned from him then continued to pack, pulling random things out of her wardrobe and throwing them into the case.

'Stop, please, Samantha – you can't run out like this. We have to talk.'

'No, it's too late, Lewis.'

'This is crazy. We've been together over twenty years. Nearly half our lives.'

Samantha slammed the lid down on the case and zipped it up. 'Lewis, we've been dead for years. Don't you want to live again?'

She dragged the case off the bed and stood before him. Her hair fell in blonde waves around her face, and she looked him squarely in the eye.

'Tell me you love me,' she challenged. 'Tell me I'm the one, Lewis. More important than any other woman in your life.'

'Of course I love you – you're my wife.'

'Yes, but am I the centre of your universe? Can you let it all go, everything about Lizzie, for me?'

He was shocked at her mention of his sister after all these years.

'This has nothing to do with Lizzie,' he said, hearing his voice tighten, tension filling his body.

'You're wrong, Lewis. Our whole marriage has been about Lizzie,' Samantha said, looking at him sadly. 'I can't live in her shadow any longer.'

She picked up her case and walked past him, out of the bedroom. He stood for a moment, unable to move. He couldn't believe this was really happening.

'Samantha!' he called as he ran down the stairs.

She was still there, standing in the hallway, her case by the front door.

'Please – let's talk. Don't leave like this,' he begged her.

'It's the only way I can do it,' she replied, her voice cracking.

'Haven't I stuck by you all these years?' he said. 'Don't you remember I gave up my career for you?'

He saw her clench her fists, her eyes flashing at him.

'Of course I remember! Have you ever let me forget?' she hissed. 'I won't let you blame me any more.'

She opened up her handbag and took out her dark glasses. 'I'm not coming back. I've thought about this for a long time and I need to get away from you.' She pulled her wedding ring off. 'Find someone else, Lewis,' she said. 'Because we were never meant for each other – you know that.'

'No,' he pleaded. 'Samantha, please, don't do this.'

She dropped the ring on the hall table and opened the front door. Behind her the sky was flaming violet and orange as the sun sank towards the horizon.

'What happened isn't your fault, Lewis, and it's not mine. I'm letting it all go.' She slipped her dark glasses on. 'You have to stop living in the past.'

And she turned on her heel and walked out.

He should have run after her, pulled her back, but he didn't. It was as if his emotions had paralysed him. He could see Jennifer in the driving seat of her station wagon, waiting for Samantha as she threw her bags in the trunk. He waited for his wife to relent. Come back up the path and tell him she had changed her mind – she needed him. He was her saviour and always would be. But she didn't even give him a backward glance.

If Lewis had been a different kind of husband he would have made a scene, run down their drive, begged her to stay, but instead he stood quite still and watched his wife being driven away. And then he stepped back inside, closed the door and pressed his head to the cool wood. He felt hollowed out. A husk. He stared at Samantha's wedding ring on the hall table, glinting in the waning light. His wife had spoken the truth, and deep down he knew it.


## London, 13 April 1967, 5.14 p.m.

Hands in his pockets, Lewis walked up to the front of the house where Lizzie lodged. The path was strewn with rubbish, the front lawn forlorn and abandoned. He could see missing bricks and crumbling plasterwork. The place was even worse than the last time he'd been here. He pressed a loose coin in his palm and tried to suppress his growing anxiety.

His sister opened the paint-peeled door before he had a chance to ring the bell.

'There you are!' she exclaimed, a cigarette hanging from her lips, a drink slopping out of a glass in her free hand. 'Where have you been?'

Lewis's heart sank. Lizzie looked completely wired. She was wearing a paisley minidress so short it barely covered her bottom. Her legs, in regulation black tights, were so thin that her calves were almost the same width as her thighs. What with her red hair, even longer and wilder than usual, and her cat-like kohl eyes, the overall image was disturbing, rather than the bohemian look he guessed his sister was going for.

'I told you I'd be a while. We have an important meeting tonight. I need to prepare for it.'

'Oh yes, the commercial artists all come together to discuss the importance of some brainwashing advertising campaign,' Lizzie said, opening the door wide for him to enter.

'I am *not* a commercial artist. I'm a graphic designer.'

'Same thing,' Lizzie said, stomping up the tattered staircase into her dingy hall. 'None of you believe in anything, do you? Nothing moves you; nothing you say is of any real importance.'

'I'm too tired for this conversation now. I've heard it all before.'

'You see.' She swung around, flashing him a triumphant smile. 'You can't even be bothered to stand up for what you do. It's all just meaningless rubbish about selling that brand-new car, or fizzy drink, or electric shaver ...'

Lewis put his hands in his pockets and jangled his car keys. 'Shut up, will you? Do you want a lift or not?'

Lizzie took a gulp of her drink before slamming the glass down onto a table so thick with dust a puff of it billowed into the air.

'It was inevitable you would end up doing something like this,' she continued. 'You were always a trickster. If not graphic design, you would have been a car salesman.'

'You'd be better suited to that profession, Elizabeth. You're quite the performer yourself!'

'Touché!' She gave him one of her magnanimous grins. Their little tiff was over. That's the way Lizzie was. From one extreme to the next within a moment. She ushered Lewis into the kitchen, which looked like it hadn't seen a mop or scouring pad in weeks.

'Christ, Lizzie!' He gave a long whistle.

'Elizabeth,' she corrected him. 'It's not that bad.' She shuffled some old newspapers off the table and onto the floor. 'I don't have a housewife or a maid at home all day, cleaning up for me.'

'Yeah, but you're at home yourself.'

'I'm working.' She picked her way through the kitchen. 'Come and see my new paintings.'

She led him into the main living area, which was in an even worse state than the kitchen. His sister had set up a sort of makeshift studio in the corner of the room, and a jumble of paint tins, brushes and jars of dirty paint water were heaped around the floor, and on any clear surface. The sofa was covered in pieces of torn paper and tiny sketches, as well as a jumble of sheets and blankets as if someone had been sleeping there. Clothes were scattered on the backs of chairs or hanging off the dado rail; a cacophony of colour and length. A fuchsia miniskirt hung next to a pair of scarlet flared trousers, next to a print blouse in shades of jade and gold.

In the centre of the room were three large canvases in a colour scheme that was an extension of his sister's wardrobe. The first picture was a whorl of green, blue and yellow – a jungle garden. It hurt Lewis's head to look at it. But there was a figure in all that jungle. A small girl with long red hair. Naked, tangled up in the brambles, her bare flesh punctured with thorns.

The second painting was much like the first, but this time the jungle was pulsing with red, as if all the trees were in full bloom, and down the centre of the painting wove a river. A silver fish was leaping out of the river and, next to it, stood the same girl, thigh deep in water, arms outstretched, water flooding from her eyes into the river, as if she had made it with her tears.

The last picture was the worst. It was a clear self-portrait of Lizzie now. Again she had employed garish, psychedelic colours, with more purples and pinks in this one. The background was a confusion of jazzy hues and shapes, and in the foreground there was a giant Lizzie, naked, apart from a long daisy-chain necklace. Her gaze challenged the viewer provocatively.

'What do you think?' she asked Lewis, flopping down onto the jumbled sofa.

'It looks like you've been taking lots of drugs, that's what I think. You know you're not supposed to while you're on the antidepressants.'

'I paint better when I'm stoned,' she responded. 'It's only the odd joint now and again. Don't worry – I'm careful.'

She pulled a shell box out from behind the cushions at the back of the couch.

'Ah, there it is – the missing stash. I was getting worried! Do you want a quick smoke before we go?'

Lewis shook his head. 'I don't have time. I have to prepare for this meeting.'

'Always rushing – you're like a hamster on a wheel.'

Lizzie took her cigarette papers from a pocket in her paisley dress and picked up a Rolling Stones album from the sofa, placing it on her knee.

'Chill out, man, as Jim always says.'

'Who's Jim?'

'One of my lovers.' Lizzie grinned at him, licking the cigarette papers together. 'He's American.'

'*One* of your lovers. How many do you have?'

Lizzie spread a trail of tobacco along the papers. 'You can hardly talk, Lewis.'

'I just have one girlfriend actually. Besides, it's different for me.'

'Because you're a man? I didn't take my own brother for a chauvinist.'

Lizzie lit a match and heated a chunk of black dope. She crumbled the hot dope and sprinkled it along the tobacco before rolling it up into a perfect joint.

'Come on, Elizabeth, you know what I mean. It *is* different for women. You should know that. Look what happened to Mother.'

At the mention of their mother Lizzie frowned. She tore a strip of card from the cigarette-paper wrapper and rolled it into the end of her joint.

'I am not remotely like our mother,' she said, lighting up and taking a deep pull. 'She was always looking for one man. Her dream was to be the good wife. I'm not like that. I'm into polyamorous relationships.'

'Whatever!' Lewis threw his arms up. 'It's all sleeping around at the end of the day.'

His sister offered him the joint. 'Go on,' she cajoled him. 'You look so uptight – as if you might snap.'

He supposed he could do with a quick puff. It might relax him – help him think of some ideas to pitch to the Phoenix fellow. That afternoon at the office he had been completely blocked. By 4 p.m. panic had been about to swallow him. He'd begged Marnie to think about an idea herself. After he dealt with Lizzie he was going straight over to Marnie's flat. They'd have about an hour to get something together.

Lizzie handed Lewis the joint.

'So which painting did you sell?' he asked, taking a drag and passing it back.

'This one,' she said, slapping her hand against the giant nude.

'Why do you have to deliver it today? And do you really have to sell that one, Lizzie?' He was appalled at the idea of any stranger possessing such an exposed portrait of his sister.

'Yes, because the buyer has the money for me now. Jim says he might change his mind by tomorrow.'

Lewis knew how wilful Lizzie could be. There was no point in trying to dissuade her.

'Come on then,' he said taking another toke. 'Where do we have to take it?'

'Jim's place.'

'Which is where?'

'Paddington.' She rasped on the joint. 'And you don't have to bring me back here either.'

Lewis insisted on wrapping Lizzie's painting in one of the blankets off the sofa. He couldn't bear the thought of parading an image of his naked sister out onto the street. He honestly didn't want to be part of this at all. Yet, despite her early successes, his sister hadn't made any real money for over a year, and she'd been sponging off him for months. The pragmatist in him couldn't stand in the way of a sale.

They sped through the streets. The sun was beginning to sink behind St Paul's Cathedral as they drove over Waterloo Bridge. After a day of showers, the evening was clear, the sunset a combustion of sultry fuchsia, mauve and indigo splashed across the sky. For Lewis, nowhere was as splendid as London. In his whole life he would never feel such awe for another city, not even New York. London was as majestic as a wise old king, and as powerful and strong as a modern mogul.

As he drove across its width, from Vauxhall to Paddington, for a few moments he felt a sense of contentment. He began to hum 'Light My Fire', a song by a new band called The Doors that he and Marnie sometimes played on her record player when they made love. Again and again he would drop the needle on vinyl as he and Marnie set each other alight.

For once quiet, Lizzie lit another joint beside him in the car.

'Do you want some more?' she offered.

'Best not.' He was feeling a little heady. Tonight was going to be a big night and he didn't want to crash too soon.

Lizzie took a long toke on her joint and he glanced across at her, worried that she might be overdoing it. 'Are you all right?'

'Of course I am, Lewis.' She patted his knee. 'I was just thinking.'

'What about?'

'I was thinking there's something I've always meant to ask you. Did you ever really believe that Mother was actually going to find us a new father?'

'I suppose I did because she kept promising,' he started, surprised by her question.

'And children always want to believe their parents, don't they?' Lizzie said. 'But you know, the more I think about it, the more I realise that deep down I never believed she would succeed. Lewis, I think the problem wasn't that she couldn't find a husband but that she just didn't want us.'

Lizzie rarely talked about their childhood and now her words were bringing him down. He didn't want to discuss their long-ago misery tonight. He had enough on his plate.

'Maybe we're lucky, Lizzie,' he suggested. 'Mother could have married some bastard who would have made our lives hell. Moving around meant we had a certain amount of freedom.'

'When we were little maybe, but there's not much freedom to be had in a convent boarding school, Lewis.' His sister tossed the finished joint out the window.

'Was it that bad?'

'I missed you so much. It took a while to adjust.'

He said nothing. He couldn't tell his sister he had missed her when he'd been sent to boarding school. The truth was it had been a relief not to worry about her any more when they'd been separated for their education. Plus he'd still been angry with her about why they'd had to leave Uncle Howard's.

They'd circled Paddington Station three times before Lizzie finally picked the right street.

'Stop! Stop – here we are!' she shouted, causing him to slam on the brakes and bring the car to a shuddering halt.

The houses were all pretty grand. The antithesis of Lizzie's shoddy abode. This Jim clearly wasn't short of a bob or two.

Lewis carried the painting up to the entrance. He had an urge to smash it onto the railings either side of the door. Why the hell was he helping his sister to sell this pornographic picture of herself?

'Elizabeth, are you sure you want to sell this painting?'

His sister looked at him in surprise. 'Of course I do.'

'It's just so private ... of you.'

'Oh, don't be such a prude, Lewis,' Lizzie retorted as she slapped the knocker against the glossy black door.

Lewis remembered all the times he and Lizzie had stood side by side on the doorsteps of other people's houses. His chest felt tight. He didn't need those memories to crowd him now.

As if she could read his thoughts, Lizzie turned, her face suddenly gaunt, her eyes steeped in sadness in the fading light. 'Do you remember the day we arrived at Uncle Howard's house?'

'Yes.'

'Remember the two paintings I showed you back at my flat just now? They're set in his garden, did you notice that?'

'No, I didn't ...'

Lewis pictured those blood-red jungle paintings with their poisonous vines, choking plants, and drama of suffocation and pain. They could not be more different from his memory of Uncle Howard's country garden, the gentle roll of the lawn to the river, the shade of the giant cedar tree, the chink of the bails falling off the stumps as his uncle bowled him out at cricket.

'Uncle Howard's garden wasn't like that.'

'No.' His sister sighed. 'I suppose we remember it differently, don't we?'

Lizzie's pupils were black tunnels. He was drawn into the longing in her face, pulled towards some dark secret. Was it just because they were stoned? Or did she want to tell him something?

'What is it, Lizzie?' he whispered. His words echoed on the doorstep, but before she had a chance to reply the door swung open and they were bathed in light.

'Well, hi there.' An American accent floated out above their heads. Lewis turned to see a girl standing in the doorway. She had long blonde hair and a similar slender build to his sister, but she looked a lot healthier. She was tanned, with not a spot of make-up on her honey skin, and wearing flared blue jeans, out from which peeped her bare feet, her toenails painted an innocent baby pink. The overall effect was refreshing and somehow out of place on a doorstep in the chilly London evening.

'Hi, Sammy.' Lizzie hugged the girl. 'I brought the painting.'

'Oh great!' Sammy said. 'Jim will be so happy.'

'This is my brother, Lewis.' Lizzie waved behind her. 'He drove me over.'

Sammy smiled at him. She had perfect white teeth and pale pink lips, no lipstick. He thought how there was nothing fake about her.

'Do you want to come in?' she asked. 'I can make you a cup of tea.'

'I can't, sorry. I have to go.'

'That sure is a shame.' The girl looked genuinely disappointed. 'Lizzie is always talking about you. You're a graphic designer, right?'

'Yes, I am,' he said, looking over at Lizzie. She winked back at him.

'Well, why don't you come back later? We're having a party. We could hang out together.'

Her American drawl snaked down his spine. He could

tell that she liked him, but he wasn't interested. The only woman he wanted to be with was Marnie.

'See you later, bro.' Lizzie dismissed him with a wave.

As the door closed he saw a pair of legs coming down the stairs. Lean and muscular, in tight leather trousers, with strong bare feet. They clearly belonged to the mysterious Jim. Was this man sleeping with both his sister and this Sammy? Lewis felt an intense hostility towards him already, and not only because of the sex thing, but because he was wheeling and dealing with his sister's talent. Now he was the owner of a huge, explicit portrait of a naked Elizabeth Bell. The idea made Lewis squirm.

Again he had the uncomfortable feeling that he'd let his sister down. All his life he'd been her protector, yet he'd never managed to get it right. Their mother had abandoned them both, but that loss had always hit Lizzie the hardest.


## London, 27 July 1955

The London of his childhood was a city still emerging from the trauma of the Blitz – muted, sombre, smoggy. Lewis was thirteen, tall for his age and skinny. With his head hung in embarrassment, his feet heavy, he followed his mother as she stormed up to the front door of a tall red-brick house, dragging Lizzie with her.

He gripped the Swiss army knife Uncle Howard had given him in his pocket.

It had been one of the rare times his mother had lost her temper. It was Lizzie she was angry with though, not him.

'How could you do such a thing, Lizzie?' his mother spat at her. 'The shame of it!'

She opened the door with her own key, dragging Lizzie by the arm into a musty dark hall. Lewis followed, still squeezing his Swiss army knife. He looked around at the pea-green walls, dotted with framed photographs of people he didn't know. He had no idea whose house he was in. Was it Mr Drewe's? Or had he already driven off in his shiny black Rover and been replaced by another lonely widower?

'How can I expect any decent man to want to marry me when I have two monstrous children in tow?'

'This has nothing to with me,' Lewis defended himself. 'I didn't want to leave Uncle Howard.'

His mother's hand flew out and slapped his face. The sound of it hitting his cheek reverberated through the hall.

'You could have stopped her, Lewis.'

'That's not fair,' Lewis complained, his cheek smarting. 'How was I to know that Lizzie would do that to Uncle Howard's house?'

'I didn't burn it all down,' Lizzie piped up. 'Just the west wing.'

Their mother grabbed Lizzie by the hair. 'Just the west wing,' she mimicked. 'In that case I'm sure your father's family will forgive me. Yes, of course they'll take you both back with open arms.'

'Mummy, stop,' Lizzie whined. 'You're hurting me.'

But their mother was in a fury. She pulled Lizzie around by the hair, the hall rug riding up around them like an ocean and his sister's legs kicking out as if she was trying to swim away from their mother.

175

'What am I supposed to do with you?' she asked, her eyes wild. 'I could have put you in an orphanage, but I didn't. I find you a nice home with family, and look how you repay me?'

Lizzie's arms were flailing about as she tried to protect herself.

'Mummy,' Lewis beseeched, afraid his mother might pull Lizzie's hair out altogether. 'Please – let go.'

His mother stopped dragging Lizzie and stared at Lewis. The depth of anger in her eyes frightened him.

His mother had a naturally sunny personality. That was why men liked her. Her smiling lips were always painted cherry red, her blonde hair sculpted into place, her trim figure tucked into a neat suit or a pretty dress. But on this day she was in disarray. Her hair had fallen apart, her lipstick was smudged and her eyes were full of tears.

She let go of Lizzie, and the girl collapsed onto the floor. His mother smoothed down her hair, took a handkerchief from her sleeve and wiped her eyes with it.

'We will have to leave first thing tomorrow,' she said crisply. 'You can't stay here more than one night.'

'But where are we going?' Lewis asked.

'I don't know yet. It seems that Lizzie has literally burned all of your bridges.'

'Why can't we stay with you, Mummy?' Lizzie bleated from the floor.

Lewis looked at his sister in surprise.

'You know why,' his mother said.

'But why is it so hard to find us a new daddy, Mummy? Why is it taking you so long?'

Sylvia Bell looked at her daughter long and hard. A

shadow descended on her face, a conflict of loathing and love.

'They don't want you,' she hissed at her. 'None of these men want you. They just want me.'

Lizzie flinched. She pulled her knees to her chest and said nothing more.

'Can we not go back to Uncle Howard?' Lewis ventured.

'Don't be ridiculous.'

'But he'll forgive Lizzie. I know he will. He loves having us.'

'Do you really think he'll take you back after what Lizzie did?'

'He might be angry right now, but he promised me he'd take care of us. He has to keep his promise.'

His mother sighed. 'Lots of people don't keep their promises, Lewis. But if you really think he might, I could give him a call...'

'No!' Lizzie stumbled to her feet and tugged at his jersey. 'I don't want to go back there.'

He looked at his sister incredulously. 'Why ever not?'

'Stop being such a madam, Lizzie,' his mother said.

But Lizzie was off. She cried, she wailed, she begged. She refused to go back to Uncle Howard's house.

In the end their mother packed them off to bed early with no dinner, long before her widower returned home for the evening.

'Why do you have to spoil everything?' Lewis hissed at his sister in the musty gloom of their attic bedroom. 'I hate you. I wish you were dead.'

His sister said nothing back, just sobbed in the bed beside his. He felt sorry then that he'd shouted at her. He

177

hadn't meant what he'd said. He loved Lizzie, but why, oh why, couldn't she be happy about going back to Uncle Howard's?

When Lewis woke up the next morning, Lizzie wasn't in her bed. He shouldn't have said such horrible things to her. She was his only family, after all. But his remorse was short-lived. His sister was already downstairs, curled up on the sofa beside their mother. When she looked up at him with her doleful eyes, red from crying, he knew she had won, yet again.

His mother glanced up from her newspaper. 'Darling, I've been thinking it over. I really don't think going back to Uncle Howard's is such a good idea.'

He shoved his hands in his pockets, twisting his Swiss army knife around and around. He pressed the edge of one of its blades against his thumb.

'You've never met Great Aunt Dorothy, have you?' his mother went on. 'She lives in a cosy cottage in a darling village in Norfolk, very near the sea. She said she would love to have you both stay until you start school in September.'

He dug the end of the blade into the pad of his thumb, felt it pierce the skin. He didn't care about the pain because he wasn't going back to Uncle Howard. He was never going back.

Lewis and Lizzie spent just one night in that big house in London before they were sent off to Norfolk. It had been a dreadful August; listless days spent in Great Aunt Dorothy's cottage. His only company, apart from Lizzie, was a King Charles spaniel called Pip, a spoilt and petulant creature. It had rained and rained, and he had spent hours with his face pressed against the misted window, staring at the endless downpour, an unread copy of *Treasure Island* on his lap. He hadn't wanted to read about another boy's adventure. He had wanted adventures himself. Lizzie would loll on the sofa singing to Pip and scratching his tummy, while Great Aunt Dorothy plied them with bowls of boiled sweets. But they were so old that some of them were stuck together and they tasted sour, and smelled of mothballs – like her.

That long deadly month the sun had never seemed to shine. On the days it wasn't raining it was foggy. Lewis would drag Pip out for walks on the fens, a flat dull landscape that stretched forever and made him feel even more bored and lonely. How many times had he hoped he would come home from his walk and find his prayers had been answered?

Down Great Aunt Dorothy's front path, through her laden pear trees, past the pansies and the petunias, he dreamed he would find Uncle Howard waiting for him, standing on her doorstep. Alfie the red setter would be sitting obediently at his heels, in marked contrast to the King Charles spaniel tugging on his lead and snapping at the superior beast. Alfie – the epitome of canine elegance, with his glossy russet fur and regal bearing. Uncle Howard would be sucking on his pipe, his eyes bright with mischief as they always were.

'Come along, old chap – let's get going,' he would say to Lewis.

But it never happened. Uncle Howard never came to rescue him.

# SEVEN

# *Reaction*

Joy was taking the cake out of the oven when she heard the front door open and the sound of voices, her daughter's distinctive laughter trailing down the hallway.

'That smells gorgeous, Mom,' Heather said as she walked into the kitchen.

Her daughter's hair was up in a high ponytail. Darrell appeared behind her, immediately circling his arms around her slender waist and drawing her into him. He was even taller than her and able to prop his chin on the top of her head.

'Hi, Mrs Sheldon, that sure smells good.'

'It's my mother's fig-cake recipe.'

'Daddy's favourite,' Heather said. 'You sure are a busy bee today, Mom. You already made us apple pie this morning.'

Joy regarded her laughing daughter. Really she must have imagined the moment with Carla. Looking at Heather now in her yellow dress, enveloped in the arms of her

180

rugged fiancé, she looked not remotely like Joy's idea of what a lesbian might be. Did lesbians wear dresses, grow their hair long, like pink and want to be cheerleaders? And yet, now Joy thought of it, there had always been something about her daughter, a kinship with her girlfriends right from when she was small.

'You know we're real excited about the house, Mr S showed us today.' Darrell beamed at Joy.

'It's in one of those new gated communities, Mom. Only ten minutes away.'

'Remind me again, what's a gated community?' Joy asked, sprinkling brown sugar on top of the cake.

'Do you not know anything, Mom?' Heather rolled her eyes. 'It's like most of what Dad is selling now.'

'They're like prestige communities, Mrs Sheldon,' Darrell told her. 'They have their own security so they're safe, and exclusive. All you need is within them – like stores and leisure facilities – and the gates keep the trash out.'

Joy was shocked by her prospective son-in-law's tone. 'Trash?'

'You know, druggies, illegal immigrants, welfare claimants ...'

She was speechless. The idea sounded horrendous to her. Why would you want to live somewhere that excluded the very colour of life? But she decided to say nothing. After all, she would be undermining Eddie if she expressed her real thoughts on the subject.

'Is Dad at work?' Heather asked.

'Yes, I'm going to take him over the fig cake.' Joy picked up a knife and used it to loosen the cake from the tin.

181

'You sure he wants you to bring him a cake right now?' Her daughter cocked her head to one side.

'Why not? It's a surprise.'

'Hey, I hope you surprise me like that when we're married as long as your mom and dad.'

Darrell kissed the top of Heather's head. It irritated Joy – as if he was doing it just for effect.

'I saw Carla today.' The words popped out of her mouth before she could stop herself, and she tried not to look too closely at her daughter's reaction.

'Oh, really?' Heather was trying to feign indifference, her expression impassive.

She felt guilty for having mentioned it, but now that Joy had brought up the subject of Carla she might as well continue.

'I thought she was your bridesmaid. What happened?' she asked.

Her daughter shrugged, slipping out from within Darrell's arms. 'She's heading off to San Francisco. Besides, she's gone all weird on me.'

'You can say that again,' Darrell exclaimed. 'You'll never guess what she's been saying, Mrs Sheldon.'

'Shut up, Darrell,' Heather said, her cheeks flushing.

Joy watched her daughter as she put the cake tin in the sink to soak. No one spoke for a moment.

'Well, are you going to tell me what she's been saying?' Joy pushed, aware that it wasn't like her to be so persistent.

An uneasy glance passed between the young couple. Darrell looked back at Joy, and she thought how his eyes seemed even bigger and more fish-like than his mother's.

'She's only told Heather that she can't come to our

wedding cos she's in love with her!' He gave a loud guffaw. 'Can you believe it, Mrs Sheldon? Carla's a dyke! What a waste, eh?'

'I told you to shut up, Darrell,' Heather snapped at him.

'Why does it have to be a big secret?' Darrell countered. 'Shouldn't your mom know why Carla isn't coming?'

'God, Darrell, sometimes ... sometimes ... you're so ...' Heather gave an exasperated sigh. 'Don't you think we should respect Carla's privacy?'

Joy avoided looking at the couple, picking up a cloth to clean the table.

'Hey, I'm sorry, okay,' Darrell said, but Heather had already flounced out of the room. They both listened to her thump up the stairs and slam her bedroom door.

'Sit down, Darrell,' Joy said, suddenly feeling sorry for him.

He slumped at the kitchen table, looking forlorn and embarrassed. She finished cleaning up. All the while Darrell said nothing, just tapped his fingers on the tabletop.

'She'll come back down in a minute,' Joy assured him, arranging her cake on a plate.

'I don't know why she's so mad about it. I kinda think it's funny.'

'Funny?' Joy said. 'Imagine if you found out your best friend was gay and in love with you.'

Darrell looked horrified. 'I'd kick his head in,' he said in a low voice.

'Maybe she's angry with Carla,' Joy said, but when she thought about it she knew her daughter wasn't angry with her old friend. It was another emotion that had caused her reaction. It was that defensive flare of anger that comes with a mixture of fear, guilt and shame.

183

Heather had feelings for Carla too, but Joy couldn't quite believe her own daughter was gay. So what if she was? Joy didn't even want to imagine how Eddie would react to the news, let alone the huge financial loss of a cancelled wedding.

She should go upstairs and talk to Heather, but she was afraid of what her daughter might admit. She wished desperately that she had never met Carla today. Why the hell had she brought it up? It could all have been forgotten about.

Before she had a chance to decide what to do, Darrell was making his way to the kitchen door.

'I'm going to go up to her, say I'm sorry,' he said.

*He loves my daughter,* Joy thought. *But she'll never love him back in the same way.*

★

Tonight Lewis wanted to drink himself into oblivion. He'd decided to get properly drunk. He had earned the right to sway on the bar stool ordering Jack Daniel's and chasing each hard-burning shot with a bottle of beer. He was in the Rusty Spur Saloon of all places. He hadn't been here in years. Since they'd sobered up their act in the mid-seventies, he and Samantha rarely went out to bars. They had become restaurant goers, wine drinkers.

The place was packed with Spring Training fans, and there was a band playing. It was the perfect environment to be alone and drinking. No one saw him. The more he drank, the more sober he felt and the greater his sense of loss. He tried to picture his wife returning to him, but he knew Samantha was never coming back. This had been a long time coming. They didn't belong together and both of them knew it, and he felt a particle of relief mixed up in all of his anger, shock and rejection.

This loss he felt was an old pain, a wound he had kept buried for over twenty years. The longer he ignored it, the worse it had become. It was the love he had shared with Marnie and had lost, and it was what had happened to Lizzie. All of their fates entangled: Samantha, Lizzie, Marnie. And now the knowledge that Marnie had married Pete Piper just four months after he'd left London was breaking his heart as much as his wife's desertion. Had Marnie done it on purpose to hurt him? Losing her still hurt after all these years. How could he have blamed her for what had happened with Lizzie? Yet he had.

## LONDON, 13 APRIL 1967, 6.17 P.M.

Lewis was driving again, guilt nagging at him for having left Lizzie behind in that house in Paddington, but he'd had no choice. He had very little time.

He put his foot down and the MG roadster darted through the traffic towards Marnie's flat in South Kensington. He felt the thrill of speed, of the challenge he faced. They had just one hour. They would work together as always. And this would be the last time they kept it secret. Lewis had promised her.

They sat next to each other in Marnie's flat, the table covered by dozens of her sketches. The windows were open and the light was fading fast as night descended. He could still see the fig tree in the square below, its juicy green leaves sensual and forthright. The sunflower-yellow curtains gently rustled, bombarding his vision with shimmering hope. They were looking at all the drawings Marnie had done while Lewis had been out with Lizzie. He began to forget about everything else: Lizzie and her hideous paintings, the American girl Sammy and his ominous glimpse of Jim. He forgot about the office, the partnership, even George Miller.

They were a team. He and Marnie were as one, focusing on creation, passing cigarettes to each other without speaking, focused only on discussing the images before them. They were arguing. He preferred a looser image, more monotone. She was going for a tightly structured design employing fire-engine red and royal blue with a strong symbol: the red phoenix, emerging from the blue flames. She reminded him of the simplicity of Henrion's design for KLM: all one colour, pale blue, with one enigmatic symbol of a crown. Lewis argued that fire was a bad idea. Should connotations of disaster be emblazoned on the side of an aeroplane? Marnie countered that it was a fire of power, of energy, the flames so abstracted that they could be the leaves of a tree beneath the phoenix. It was an image that would last the test of time. Just like her work would last.

He teased her, saying she had a bigger ego than George, but she laughed, and he caught her laughter with his lips. They were kissing, unable to stop themselves. He pushed her back onto the table and lifted her skirt up. They made love there and then. Their drawings showering around

186

them like a multicoloured fanfare, he pushed himself deep inside her. He wanted to feel Marnie was his completely. He wanted to trust her.

## SCOTTSDALE, 23 MARCH 1989

Dusk had given way to darkness as Joy drove into Scottsdale's old town. Eddie's office was close enough to walk to, but she preferred to drive at this time of day. It was cooler now, still a spring night, and she could see the last streaks of sunlight fading away at the horizon.

At night the land lifted. During the day, the heat in the sky could bear down upon the landscape, so that sometimes she almost felt flattened. She looked to the defiance of the cacti sucking what little they could out of the earth, reaching skyward despite the heavier gravity in the desert. How would she have felt in Ireland? To be in such a different landscape, the opposite of all that she had known. Had she ever really belonged in her life? Was she just a visitor to the world of Joy Sheldon, daughter of Jack and Teresa Porter, wife of Eddie? Could she have been a different kind of girl, another woman, if her Irish mother hadn't given her up?

Joy's heart began to race. She called this sensation her hummingbird heart, for she'd read that a hummingbird's heart could beat more than a thousand times a minute. Sometimes it happened when she was excited, or frightened, or a little panicked. Would she and Eddie have found each other if she had grown up in Ireland? Was he her destiny? In truth, she had always thought so.

Joy was filled with a burning desire to touch Eddie, to have sex with her husband right now. What would he say if she stormed into his office, pulled down the blinds and pushed him onto his office table, the fig cake forgotten as they devoured each other?

She pulled into the car park opposite Eddie's office. Her husband's Corvette was parked outside, alongside another car. She'd forgotten that he might be with a client. She bit her lip, unsure now whether she should intrude.

She tried the door of the building and found it was open. What if she waited for him in the reception area? Surely he would be finished soon.

Joy walked into the cool sanctuary of the empty reception. She sat on a chair by the door of Eddie's office, the fig cake resting on her lap. She watched the hands of the clock ticking by. But as well as the ticking clock, she could hear noises. At first she wasn't sure what she was hearing. But she knew it wasn't the sound of her husband talking with a client. Then it dawned on her.

Joy stood up, still balancing the cake in one hand, and gripped the door handle with the other and opened it.

What she saw whipped her heart right out of her mouth. Sitting on her husband's desk, her skirt around her waist and her legs apart, head thrown back, was Erin Winters. Eddie was on his knees in front of his daughter's future mother-in-law, his face buried in her. He was doing something to Erin that he had never done for Joy in all the years of their marriage.

Joy screamed for one sheer second as the couple unlocked. She saw Erin's look of horror and her husband's head turning, his eyes dazed with lust. She didn't run – not yet. She was in that office long enough to see the sparks of ecstasy still flying between Eddie and Erin. Her scream pealed out. She dropped the cake and fled.

★

Lewis knocked back another glass of Jack Daniel's on his pew in the Rusty Spur.

His mind was spinning with sounds and images. Samantha's voice telling him he had to stop living in the past. Lizzie's laugh haunting him, and Marnie's eyes – that last look she'd given him reaching into his heart and torturing him.

He dropped his head. It felt so heavy, as if the weight of all these memories was too much to bear. He was sinking on the bar stool.

'Hey, buddy, maybe you should head home?'

The barman was leaning over him. Lewis mustered himself, pulled himself upright. 'Just one more,' he said, trying to look him in the eye.

'You sure?'

'Yeah, and make it a double.'

'Okay, fella.'

'In fact, do you have any Irish whisky?'

The barman placed the glass of Jameson in front of him. He took a sip. It was lighter than the bourbon, less sweet. He imagined it fortifying him.

'Have you ever been to Ireland?' he asked the barman.

'Nah, but I know plenty of Irish guys. Good drinkers, I can tell you.'

'I'm going to Ireland,' Lewis told him.

'Are you now?' the barman said with disinterest before wandering back down to the other end of the bar.

'I'm going to find the woman of my dreams,' he announced to no one in particular, his voice drowned out by the sound of the band starting up again. He looked around; everyone was caught up in their own private conversations, half watching the band. He must look like a sad case, all on his own, drunk and sliding off his bar stool.

He looked towards the door and, just as he was thinking he should salvage his dignity and leave, in she walked. Her long black hair was loose and wild, her face pale in the gloom. She looked like she'd seen a ghost.

She pushed through the throng, a determined expression on her face. It was clear she hadn't seen him, but as she reached the bar, her eyes finally came to rest on him. Her body seemed to quiver as she started in shock. For some reason Lewis was not surprised at all. It was as if he had been expecting her.

★

'Hello, Joy,' he said. 'Can I buy you a drink?'

His eyes were glittering. He was drunk, but she didn't care. She was glad Lewis Bell was here in the Rusty Spur.

'I'll have a beer and one of those to chase,' she said. At that moment she'd drink anything. She needed to blot out what she had just seen.

The barman placed a tall, frothy beer in front of her. She picked it up and took a sip then followed it with a gulp of whisky. It burned her throat and made her eyes sting, but already she was feeling a little better.

'Are you okay?' Lewis asked. His elbows were propped on the bar, his head lolling slightly.

'Yeah, I'm fine,' she said, although she wanted to scream out and let the whole world hear her pain. 'You want a beer?'

'Don't think I should,' he said, his words slurred. 'I've had enough. Don't you think you should take it easy?'

She felt a sudden burst of annoyance. Why was Lewis here on his own anyway? Was he just like Eddie, looking to pick up some woman?

'What are you doing here, Lewis?' she demanded. 'Where's your wife?'

★

Her directness startled him. Tonight Joy Sheldon was no longer shy. She looked at him with fierce eyes. It was impossible to avoid her question.

'She's gone,' he heard himself telling her.

'Where has she gone?

'Santa Fe,' he slurred. 'Gone for good.'

He waved at the barman to bring him another beer. Joy said nothing; she just stared at him.

'She said it's been over between us for years.'

'Are you sure she's gone for good, Lewis?' Joy said, her tone gentle now. 'She might want to try to sort things out between you. You should go after her.'

'No, she was clear.' He shook his head. 'It's over.'

'I'm sorry,' she said, taking a more genteel sip of her whisky this time.

'Dead. That's what I am. I'm a dead man in my wife's eyes.'

191

'I don't think you're a dead man.'

'You just don't know me well enough yet.' He gave a lame laugh.

'Stop,' she said. 'Don't say such things.' She put her hand on his arm. He looked down at it. He wanted to tuck it inside his, yet he did nothing – just stared at her little fingers pressed into his flesh.

'Hey,' he said, tearing his eyes away, looking up at her. 'We've got to stop meeting like this. It's getting strange.'

'Maybe we've often been in the same place at the same time but didn't know it before because we hadn't actually met ... Scottsdale isn't that big.'

'Maybe.' He considered her. 'And that's why you've always looked familiar to me. We have seen each other before. Many times.'

Joy nodded. He watched her as she drank her whisky. She was wearing a rather fetching green sundress with a pattern of white daisies upon it. Her pale skin gleamed in the dim bar. She looked fresh, and pure – out of place in this throng of rowdy people.

'And what are you doing here, Joy?' he asked her. 'Where's your husband?'

'I can tell you exactly where my husband is.' She paused, taking another sip of the beer. 'Eddie is working late in his office.'

'He's a bit of a workaholic, isn't he?' Lewis asked. For some reason he felt an edge of competition with Joy's husband.

'That's the impression he gives,' she said, wiping the back of her hand across her mouth.

'Hard-working, ambitious ...' Lewis said. 'I used to be

192

like that years ago, but not any more,' he said. 'Nope –'

'I'm glad you're not like that,' she interrupted, fierce again. 'Hey, do you want to get out of here?'

He looked at her in surprise. 'Okay,' he said cautiously. 'Where'd you want to go?'

★

She drove him out to the desert, to the edge of the McDowell Mountains. They got out the car and looked down on the lights of Scottsdale, and further into the distance she could see the glow of Phoenix. They sat on the desert floor in silence, staring up at the star-filled sky. Gradually the horrific image of her husband with Erin Winters began to fade away.

'Look at the comet!' Lewis suddenly exclaimed. 'I'll never get used to the night skies of Arizona. You don't need to imagine other galaxies – you can just see them.'

'Those Northern Lights were something else, weren't they?' she asked.

She couldn't help thinking how soulful he looked in thought. Solemn, distinguished ... so different from her cowboy husband.

'But what were they doing all the way down here?' he asked.

'A massive geomagnetic storm,' she said. 'It cut the electricity in Quebec for nine hours. Just one of those freaks of nature.'

'A miracle,' he said.

'Yes, I guess it is.'

She was acutely aware of his body next to hers. She

hadn't sat this close to another man, besides Eddie, ever. It frightened her, but it excited her too, to be on her own with him. She shivered.

'Are you cold?' Lewis asked. 'Here, take my jacket.'

Despite her protests, he insisted on slipping it on over her shoulders. She breathed in his warmth, his aroma.

'I love the desert,' she told him, calmed by the feel of his jacket around her. 'My dad and I used to go hiking every spring, tracking down wildflowers. Not this spring though; he died last year.'

'I'm sorry,' he said. 'It sounds like you were close.'

'We were.' She bit her lip to stop the tears from coming. She didn't want to dwell on her father's death. It was still too raw. The last thing she wanted was to cry in front of Lewis. She shifted the focus onto him.

'Are your parents still alive?'

He shook his head. 'No, my father died during the Second World War, when I was very little, so I never knew him, and my mother died about seven years ago.'

'Do you miss her?' Joy asked him.

'No, I don't,' he said, and she detected a slight hardness in his voice.

'There wasn't much to miss, Joy. My mother was never really there when I was a child.'

'It's complicated, isn't it?' Joy said. 'The relationships between parents and children. Sometimes I worry that I haven't been a good enough mother. And it's the only thing I've done with my life.'

'It sounds to me like your children have grown up into fine young people,' Lewis said.

She looked at the shadows of his face in the darkness.

His hair was thick and unruly. It needed a cut, but she liked its wildness. 'Are you sad that you never had kids, Lewis?'

'I try not to think about it.' He shrugged. 'I guess so, but I don't think I'd make a good father.'

'I don't agree.'

'You hardly know me, Joy!' He smiled at her, and she wanted to reach out and touch those laughter lines around his eyes. 'I'm struggling just to keep those plants alive, you know.'

They sat in silence, smiling at each other. Where would this evening end? She couldn't go home. Not now. Suddenly she had an urge to confide in Lewis.

'You know, last year I found out I was adopted.'

'Really?' He looked at her with interest. 'How?'

'My father told me just before he died. I was born in Ireland but brought to America when I was a baby.'

'Do you know who your birth parents are?'

'Nope.'

'And does that matter to you?'

She put her hands in her lap and stared up at the sky.

'Yes,' she said. 'It does. It's my dream to go to Ireland to find my birth mother.'

'Then I think you should go.'

She digested his words, surprised at how much they meant to her.

'Thank you,' Joy said, turning to him, 'for being the only person, apart from Ray, to see it from my point of view.'

Before she could stop herself she leaned forward and kissed him.

★

195

He kissed her back, and it felt so good. He knew he shouldn't. She was married, yet it felt so right, so natural to be kissing this woman.

He took her into his arms, feeling the softness of her body pressing into his. She smelled like the lush spring desert air, the intoxicating and tender scent of orange blossom.

They pulled back for an instant, gazing into each other's eyes.

'Lewis,' she whispered. 'Make love to me.'

Her words astounded him, sent a shiver through his whole being.

But before he could think straight she was kissing him again, her hands on the buttons of his shirt. Desire curled within him, more intense than he'd felt in years. Samantha was a beautiful woman but her looks had always left him rather cold. Joy felt different, reminded him more of Marnie, the soft contours of her body melding to his. He felt young again, brimming with need and passion.

They fell back onto the hard desert floor. He slipped the straps of her sundress off, and she unzipped it to reveal her breasts. He kissed each nipple, listening to her sighs. She was alive beneath him, in a way Sammy had never been, lifting her pelvis to his. He could feel her yearning for him, as she unbuckled his belt and pushed her hand beneath his waistband, her fingers curling around his cock.

'Are you sure?' he said, his voice husky with desire.

She nodded, her face serious.

He pushed inside her, and the intensity of it almost made him cry. They moved together as one, a perfect unit of passion, all the restraints of their lives falling away.

There were no others out here in the desert. Just them, making love.

She came first. He heard her cry out – felt her quivering around his cock, the sensation making him climax. He gasped at how deep the vibrations within him felt.

★

Joy woke within his arms, the two of them covered by her old Navajo blanket. Immediately, she knew that she regretted nothing. Already the navy sky had lightened to a rich sapphire shade, as golden and white light began to radiate from behind the McDowell Mountains. She looked at Lewis and found his eyes were open. She wondered how long he had been lying there, watching her sleep.

'Good morning,' she said, smiling at him and stretching her legs, enjoying the sensation of his body wrapped around hers.

'I'm sorry, Joy, if I took advantage of you last night –' Lewis began.

'You didn't take advantage of me, Lewis,' she said, sitting up and putting her dress back on. 'I think it's more likely the other way around.'

'You're married, Joy, and Samantha just walked out on me yesterday. I wasn't myself . . .'

He was leaning back on his elbows, and she could see him struggling to find the right words. He was embarrassed. Her heart sank.

She turned her back to him and zipped up her sundress. To her last night had been more than an act of comfort sex, but to Lewis that was probably all it was.

'Look, it's fine,' she assured him. 'Last night I was on a mission.' She paused and licked her lips, turning to face him again. There was no subtle way of telling him. 'Before I met you in the Rusty Spur, I had walked in on my husband having sex with another woman in his office.'

'God, that's awful.'

'That's why I was in the bar,' she said, trying not to show her emotions. 'I wanted to pick someone up, get back at Eddie.'

'So last night?'

'Rebound sex ...' she said, standing up and trying to look casual. 'Wasn't that what it was for you?'

She saw him blink.

'Yes, I suppose it was.'

'So we're okay?' She tried to look cool, composed, although she felt far from it.

She began to walk back towards the car, and he fell in step beside her. Streaming around them, between the hazy silhouettes of the chollas, were banks of Mexican gold poppies, interspersed with wild hyacinth, lupin and desert bluebells. A golden field beribboned with blue. Her father would have loved it. She could see buckwheat, and purple trailing windmills, mounds of delicate lilac phacelia with white desert chicory. There seemed to be a bonanza of spring flowers. And most of the cacti were blooming as well. The little hats of flowers atop of the tall saguaros, the ring of blooms around the heads of the Arizona fishhook cactus, orange flowers bursting out of prickly pear and the claret cup cactus with its nest of yellow blooms all greeted them as they walked by. The diversity was overwhelming. All this nature lifted her heart. She didn't know what she was going to do about Eddie, but she did know that this resplendent desert landscape made her feel as if she was worth something.

By now the buttery sun had emerged fully from behind the McDowell mountain range blessing her desertscape with an almost divine light. Some people looked at the desert as a frightening place, a land of death. But Joy saw it differently, like her father. It spoke of life against all odds. It was a land for survivors. She would survive her husband's infidelity because she had to, just as Lewis had to survive his wife's abandonment.

Instinctively she took his hand in hers and stopped walking.

'Lewis,' she said, turning to him, 'let's be friends.'

'Sure,' he said. 'Friends.' But there was something to his tone she wasn't quite sure of.

She sensed the changing air, the final drops of chill from the desert night moving over for daytime heat. A red-tailed hawk soared in the sky above, giddy with its liberty. It seemed a fitting symbol for this new day. Despite her heartache over Eddie's betrayal, her anguish at what she had seen in that office, Joy possessed something now that she hadn't had the previous morning. This night had given her a sense of freedom she'd never felt before.

Joy drove them out of the desert. The silence wrapped around them, but it was not uneasy. He sat beside her, watching her drive down Cactus Road to park outside his house. He was still in the fog of his hangover. All of her movements seemed to be in slow motion, the gentle bite of her lip as she concentrated on parking, the flick of her dark hair as she swept it out of her eyes, the slow measure of her hand turning the key in the ignition. The street had never seemed so quiet, and there was a thumping in his head, a rush to his body, as he looked at her. When she turned to him to say goodbye, he saw a little part of himself locked inside her: a kindred kindness. Last night they had looked after each other. This he had shared with Joy. He wanted to kiss her again but stopped himself. For where would it have led? Into his house, up to his bedroom, under the covers? He had to let her go and fix things with her husband.

Alone, his house already felt different. Hollowed out. He went upstairs to the bedroom and took in Samantha's pillaged wardrobe, the trail of clothes on the floor. He knew that she would never come back.

It was only when he was in the kitchen, drinking coffee and thinking of Joy Sheldon again, that he remembered he had forgotten to check the mailbox.

*

Back in her home the stillness was shattering. Although everything looked the same, Joy felt as if the house had been through a hurricane and was now askew, distorted and unbalanced. It was a house of lies.

There was a letter from Eddie on the kitchen table. She ripped open the envelope. One sheet of headed paper – Sheldon Scottsdale Realtors. She skim read it. She didn't want the words to puncture her heart, take a grip of her head and spin her back to who she'd been yesterday. She never wanted to be that woman again. That fool.

*I waited up all night,* she read. *I'm worried. I'm sorry. It just happened the once.*

Now she knew he was lying. What she had seen was not a one-time fuck. She could tell. There had been complicity between Eddie and Erin, and that only grew with time.

*I waited as long as I could. I had to go to work. Come by the office. I love you ...*

*I love you ...*

*I love you ...*

He had to be kidding. Did he really think she would come to him? Stand across from him at the same table where she'd seen him going down on Erin? She tried to hold on to her righteous anger, but it tugged at her like a kite trying to break free. She had done the same as her husband now, had she not? She was a cheater too.

But her cheating didn't cancel his out. It all hurt. Pained her to her core. The betrayals – her husband's, her parents' – ran deep within her life, like the craters of a riverbed parched by drought and cracking right open, sore and needy. She wanted to wash it all away. She needed a storm, a flood, a bolt of lightning to illuminate the desert plains and show her the way forward. She was a mother whose children no longer needed her, a wife whose husband no longer wanted her and a daughter who was lost.

All she had was a friend.

Joy sat at the kitchen table and put her head in her hands. Everything was broken. Years of trust, love, solidarity. She could not stay here.

★

Those were the words he needed to hear. He turned the postcard over in his hand. On the front was a map of Ireland with a shamrock and the words 'Greetings from Ireland' written in green. He looked to the west coast, trailed it north from Galway to Mayo to Sligo: Marnie's land. He was in no doubt now that she had forgiven him.

He heard her.

'It's not your fault,' Marnie had said to him as she'd tried to take his hand in hers, but he'd pulled away from her, tugging the tips of his chilled fingers out of her grasp. He had told her to leave him alone. He'd blamed her, and he'd blamed himself. He would never forget the last look she'd given him. Her emerald-green coat tied tightly around her waist with the collar up, her dark hair like a storm cloud around her pale face, her eyes had brimmed with sorrow, with pity, for him – and he couldn't bear it.

'Just get out of here – get away from me!' he'd yelled at her, and she had stepped back as if he'd hit her. But her last words were etched upon his heart. He would never forget them.

Marnie had turned round and walked away, her heels clicking on the cold lino. Marnie in green, diminishing through the swing doors, disappearing out into the dawn rain. He'd never seen her again.

He had tried so hard to forget those dark hours, the longest ones of his life. He was still shocked at how much his life had changed overnight. He'd lost everything – his work, his girl, his family. He'd spent the past twenty-two years in America trying to reconstruct himself, but the problem was that Samantha had been part of that past too, and he'd never really been free from it during their whole marriage. He had tried to save himself through saving her. It was only natural that Samantha had become fed up. She hadn't asked to be rescued.

Could he go back? Could he find Marnie again? His friendship with Joy had changed him. Her gentle reassurance had given him back some self-belief. Her touch had awoken his passion. Maybe he wasn't the broken man he thought he was. Maybe Marnie really was waiting for him to come back...

## THE IRISH SEA, 28 MARCH 1967

It was on the ferry home that Lewis opened up to Marnie. He told her about his father, Philip Arthur Bell. A man he couldn't remember, who had died in the final months of the Second World War. Bell had been in the Allied bomber squadron that took a hit over Dresden in February 1945. Lewis had been three at the time and his sister Lizzie only two.

'Tell me about your mother?' Marnie asked, tucking her arm into his as they sat on the deck of the boat. Despite the rain, she wanted to be outside for one last look home. The two of them were huddled together, Lewis in one of his black Italian suits, the collar pulled up against the rain, his thick, dark hair misted with raindrops.

'She's Irish, isn't she?' she pushed.

'Yes, but she never spoke about her home. I don't know where she's from in Ireland. We never met our grandparents. In fact, I think they were dead before we were born. The only relatives we knew were my father's, and they lived in England.'

'So where did you grow up in England?'

'Mainly the Home Counties – Berkshire, Buckinghamshire, Surrey. A year in Suffolk; a few weeks in Norfolk. Everywhere and nowhere in particular.' He avoided her gaze, taking out his cigarettes and offering her one.

She could see he was uncomfortable, but she wasn't going to stop her questions. She had just introduced him to her family; now she wanted to know about his.

They turned into each other to shield the cigarettes from the wind and the rain. He cupped his hand around hers. She focused on his long, elegant fingers as he struck a match and lit her cigarette.

'What do you mean nowhere in particular?' she asked, exhaling a plume of smoke.

'My mother found it hard to cope with the two of us on her own so she left us with various relatives of my father's from time to time. She said she was trying to find a new father for us, but really she just didn't want us in tow.'

'That's a little harsh.'

Lewis gave her such a cold look it made her shiver. 'You wouldn't think so if you met my mother.'

'Did you like any of your relatives? Who were they?'

'Most of them were doddery old aunts. Some spoiled us rotten, and some were mean. Best of all was Uncle Howard. He was my father's brother. I loved living with him.'

As the boat began to roll upon the waves, and the soft drizzle spattered their faces, they fell silent. Marnie watched the Irish coastline fading into the hazy distance and felt a pull on her heart, as she always did when she left her home-land. She loved Ireland, yet she couldn't live there. She had dreams, too big for the country where she was born.

She turned to Lewis. He was looking into the distance too, but his eyelids were flickering, and she felt he was further away from her, back in his past. He'd had a sad childhood. No father, a heartless mother and an unstable younger sister who he felt responsible for. She wanted to take away the pain of all that. Eva had warned her about Lewis. Told her he was a heartbreaker, but to be honest Marnie suspected that Eva was a little prejudiced. She didn't seem to think much of any man, not even her husband, the great George Miller.

Marnie squeezed Lewis's cold hand and stamped his cheek with the warmth of a kiss.

'A penny for your thoughts,' she whispered.

'I've never understood why Uncle Howard abandoned me,' he told her quietly. 'I've never worked out what *I* did wrong.'

The look on his face tugged at her heart. She had never seen him so vulnerable. She cupped his rain-spattered cheeks in her hands and kissed him hard on the lips. It was that glimpse of the boy inside the man that made Marnie really fall for Lewis Bell.

# EIGHT

# *Relativity*

## SCOTTSDALE, GOOD FRIDAY, 24 MARCH 1989

Joy knew exactly what time her mom would be out of the house. Every year on Good Friday her mom went to the old mission church in downtown Scottsdale at noon for the Stations of the Cross. She had never missed it, not even when her husband was sick.

Joy parked her car in a street two blocks away from her parents' house. Her mom's old Ford was of course gone from the drive. She walked round the back of the house and lifted up the loose piece of sill on the back washroom window. The key was there. The cold metal stung against her hot palm.

She unlocked the back door and slipped inside. She took off her sandals, dusty from the desert, and padded across the kitchen. Where to begin?

She went to her father's oak desk in the front room. It was unlocked, but as she riffled through the drawers and compartments, she knew in her heart there was nothing there. It was too exposed a place to hide what she was looking for.

She went upstairs and looked in her mother's wardrobe, lingering over the one suit of her father's that her mother had kept. His second-best suit. He had been buried in his best. She stroked its sleeves, smelled it and tried to summon her father's presence. Why had he left her? She hadn't been ready.

She pulled herself away from the wardrobe, leaving it exactly as it had been and looked in the dressing table and the cupboards beside the bed. Nothing. Joy hunted in the bathroom cabinet and the chest of clean laundry, dug through things in the back of the wardrobe in her old bedroom, but again she found nothing apart from mementoes from her childhood, little daggers of memory that speared her heart.

Back downstairs she searched every cupboard and drawer in the kitchen. She looked inside old casserole dishes and in a dusty, cracked teapot on the sideboard. Still she couldn't find a thing. Could it really be that there was not one line in existence about who she really was? No documentation? No original birth certificate? When she had applied for her passport two years ago her mom had given her a certificate. A certificate that showed Joy hadn't been officially registered until they'd moved to Scottsdale. Shocked, Joy had asked her mom about it only to be told that they'd simply forgotten to do it until then. She should have known there was something up, but the possibility that she could have been adopted had been the last thing on her mind.

Joy stood in the middle of her mother's kitchen and

stared out the back window. She felt different. Loosened, undone, but a little better now that she was no longer in her own house. Her night in the desert with Lewis had changed something within her. Her thighs were still trembling; her heart beat as if at hummingbird rate. She felt opened out, exposed, as if all her nerves were on the outside of her body, tingling like antennae. She was not herself. She was another Joy, from another planet. When she pushed her hands through her hair she wouldn't be surprised if she caught tiny stars between her fingers. Lewis had saved her. God knows where she might have ended up last night if she hadn't met him. She had felt so wild she would have picked up any old lunatic.

'Friends,' she whispered, remembering the pledge they had made to each other this morning.

'Just friends,' she reminded herself.

It had only been a few days since Joy had last been in her mother's house and had planted the Easter lily cactus in the garden, and yet looking out into the backyard she could see that the two orange and lemon trees were overloaded with fruit. She knew her father would have collected them by now.

She slipped her sandals back on and opened the patio doors onto her father's pride and joy. It made her sad to see how quickly it was possible to tell a garden was unloved in the Arizonian climate, when living things quickly shrank and shrivelled up under the full glare of the sun. Sometimes Joy dreamed of living in a place that was lush, to saturate herself in its damp essence and not worry about thirsty plants and bleached, bony soil. Yet the desert was her first love. This was where her heart lay, in its blood-red sands, her soul stripped bare by those searing rays from the sun.

Joy looked up at the first orange tree. It was laden with fruit, the scent of the full blossoms intoxicating. She breathed it in.

'Just go get a ladder and pick the oranges, Joy,' she imagined her dad telling her. 'You overthink things, girl.'

The ladder, the rake and net were all in her dad's garage. She also needed to find one of Dad's old sunhats to protect her face. She walked round to the front of the house, pulled up the garage door and as soon as she stepped inside, she was hit by a smell that took her back to her childhood – those Saturday afternoons spent helping her daddy in the garden. Joy felt tears welling. She wished so much that her father was still here so she could talk to him. Would he feel as threatened by her birth mother as her mom did? She felt not. He'd told her in the first place. But why had he waited until he was dying? Had he been afraid that he would lose her love?

She sat down on a plastic sack of soil and took a breath. It was deliciously cool in the garage, and she imagined her dad right there beside her, putting his arm around her shoulder. She looked at all the shelves crammed with jars, pots, and bits and bobs. No one had touched the place since he'd died, and nor were they likely to. None of her family besides her had any interest in the garden.

Right on the top shelf she saw a large shell that her father had bought for her in a yard sale when she was about twelve. Next to it was his special box, as he used to call it, where he kept all the pictures she'd ever made him at school.

She took the stepladder and pulled it open, climbed up to the top step and took down the shell. She remembered its name now – abalone. She held it up under the bare light bulb and saw that the inside of the shell was iridescent, with swirls of green, pink and opal like the Northern Lights. One day, she promised herself, she would baptise this shell in the sea. She would bring the sky underwater.

Next, Joy climbed back up the ladder and retrieved her father's special box. Setting it down on his workbench next to the shell, she unlocked it and started to spread out all the pictures she'd made her father as a little girl. Most of them were of flowers, secret gardens, forests and woods. Joy smiled as she saw how, even as a child, she'd been obsessed with plants. She pulled them all out, something she had never done, and looked at her progress over the years. They were good – bold and imaginative – and carefully composed, but she hadn't painted since school. That part of herself was buried.

She was about to put the pictures back when she saw a brown folder squashed into the bottom of the box. She pulled it out and stared at it for a long moment. She had never seen it before, but still she knew what was inside.

★

His head spinning, Lewis lay back on his bed. He felt as if he had been blown over. Like a tree felled in a storm.

In his hand he clutched the postcard from Marnie.

He gazed up at his ceiling fan, slowly spinning the hot, dry air in his empty bedroom. He felt like a stranger in his own life. How had he ended up here?

210

He closed his eyes and suddenly he was back in 1967 with all the other young Londoners flocking out to play, listening to new music, being daring and adventurous. Lewis had loved being part of it. He had belonged in that bright new world, but the sixties were long over now. In fact the eighties were nearly over. Everything was changing. The Iron Curtain was being torn apart, and the world order was reshuffling. Nothing seemed as abandoned and free as it had been back then.

He tried to summon a memory of one of the many parties he'd been to, the pretty girls with glittering eyes, the throbbing music and the heady clubs taking him to all the corners of his imagination. But he couldn't do it. All he saw was Marnie, in her dark green coat, appealing to him, yet all he felt was Joy's touch, the press of her lips upon his, the feel of her tender body, her softness consuming him. He knew he was in danger of transferring his heartache for Marnie to desire for Joy. Just like he had with Sammy.

Lewis sat up in bed, his eyes open. Suddenly his head was clear. It was obvious what he had to do.

★

A single piece of paper slid out from the brown folder onto her father's workbench.

Joy stood frozen, her hands shaking as she began to read. She started at the top of the page. There was a heading, Department of External Affairs, and an address in Dublin, Ireland. It was printed in green, a small green harp beneath it. The letter was addressed to her parents

211

Mr & Mrs Jack Porter with an address she didn't recognise in Brooklyn, New York. The letter was dated 13 March 1953.

Joy read every word carefully – twice. It was a letter granting permission to adopt an infant from Ireland. In the letter it stated that her parents must produce evidence to show they were Catholics and that they undertook to raise the child as a Catholic.

She put the letter down and took a breath. The brown folder was still in her other hand and she could feel there was something else in there.

She opened the folder up and there was her birth certificate in black and white. She tried to read slowly, but she found herself gobbling up the words.

DATE OF BIRTH:   1951, 26 April

PLACE OF BIRTH:   Ballycastle, County Mayo

NAME:   Joyce Mary

SEX:   Female

NAME AND SURNAME AND DWELLING PLACE OF FATHER:
  Richard Lawrence, Gloucester, Great Britain

NAME AND SURNAME AND MAIDEN NAME OF MOTHER:
  Aoife Catharine Martell, formerly Martell

FATHER'S PROFESSION:   Soldier

There was more. An old black-and-white photograph. She picked it up.

A toddler smiled at the camera, plump cheeks and chubby legs in a little white dress and holding out a tiny bunch of flowers that looked like buttercups. She stared at the child's face and it dawned on her that she'd never seen any photographs of herself as a baby before. Her parents had told her they were lost in a fire at their home in New York before they'd moved. But that had been a lie too.

She flipped over the photo and written on the back in her father's hand it said:

'Little Joyce the day she chose me.'

Joyce. Joy. It was her.

The facts began to filter through. Her real name was Joyce Mary Martell. Her mother was called Aoife. She wasn't even sure how to pronounce her name. Her father was called Richard Lawrence, and he was from Great Britain – a soldier. They were not married. And Joy hadn't been a baby when her parents had adopted her. Her birth certificate stated her date of birth was 26 April 1951, but the permission for her adoption was given on 13 March 1953, which meant she was nearly two when they took her to America. Horror swept through her. Had she been with her birth mother the first two years of her life? What had happened to her, to Aoife?

She opened the folder wide, hunting for more information. A picture of her mother, a letter, an address ... but there was nothing.

Joy sat down on a stool before she keeled over and brought her hand to her pounding heart. The past year, since Joy had discovered she was adopted, she'd assumed she'd been given up as a newborn. But she'd been nineteen months old, nearly two, when her parents had taken her to America. She would have been talking, running around; surely she had some memories of her mother? Yet she couldn't remember a thing.

Joy imagined what she would have done if anyone had

tried to take Ray or Heather from her when they were babies. She would have killed for them – she knew it.

She looked at herself as a little girl in the photograph. That open-hearted baby face, the offering she had for her new father. The sheer innocence of it made her want to cry.

But part of her also wanted to storm into the house now, wait for her mom to return from church and confront her. She wanted to demand that she tell her absolutely everything. *Joy wanted to know*. Where was Aoife Martell? Why had she given her child up?

Yet Joy couldn't bear the idea of a confrontation. She could already see her mom's tears, feel the way she pricked Joy with guilt for wanting to know anything. Wasn't it better to just go?

Joy put the letter and the picture back in the brown folder and slipped it into her bag, along with the abalone shell. She tidied her childhood artwork into the box and placed it back up on the top shelf. As she did so, she was struck by a new feeling – the sense of an ending. Her father's life was over, as was the fiction of her childhood – and her vulnerability to her mom's judgement.

Joy knew she couldn't hate her mom or blame her, yet her love for her was twisted up inside her gut.

She would go for now.

On the way out, Joy picked up the yard brush and pushed it up into the dense foliage of the orange tree, shaking the branches. A single orange tumbled into her outstretched hand. She lifted it to her face and inhaled its sweet juicy promise before popping it into her bag.

★

What if Marnie didn't want to know him when she actually saw him? Lewis thought. He wasn't the successful graphic designer he'd once hoped to be. He was much older now, a worn-out typesetter whose wife had just walked out on him. He dreaded Marnie asking about his life, the list of failures beneath his name.

Yet he had questions for her too. Why had she married Pete Piper? Why had she left London and moved back to Ireland? But, most of all, why had she waited all these years to contact him?

Lewis knew he couldn't tolerate another day without finding out. This was what compelled him to call Doug up and tell his father-in-law he was going to take that Easter vacation to Ireland after all. He probably wouldn't be back for at least a week.

He made no mention of Samantha. It was clear her parents didn't know that she'd left him, and he couldn't face their upset, their questions and well-meaning interference.

The lack of distress he felt today over Samantha's desertion was strange. Yesterday he'd been devastated. Yet this morning, instead of thinking of his wife, or of trying to contact her, his thoughts kept returning to his night in the desert with Joy. He knew that he'd been very drunk, but still something about Joy Sheldon had enticed him. She was too modest and meek to be his usual type. A different breed from Marnie and Samantha, both bold and confident women who turned heads, Lewis's included. Joy had a different effect on him. She made him want to stay still. When he was beside her, inside her, he'd felt a sense of peace.

'Just friends,' he whispered, reminding himself that at this very moment Joy was most likely sorting things out with her husband.

Valued. That's how Joy had made him feel.

And he realised he'd never had a real friend before.

★

The afternoon was warm, but not too hot. Joy walked within the scent of orange blossom, back towards her car. There was a whole beginning to her life that had been hidden from her. All those unknown smells, sounds, feelings that she had shared with her birth mother were part of the fabric of her being.

Her bag swung against her hip, heavy from its load. She had all that she needed in the trunk of her car: her packed case, her passport – never used – and the book on Ireland from the library. She had left a letter for Heather at home. She didn't know what to write to Eddie, and so in the end, she wrote nothing. She had no words for him. Not yet.

As she walked up Scottsdale Road she saw a figure in a pink Sugar Bowl uniform cycling towards her. It was Carla.

As soon as the girl saw her she braked, and Joy smiled at how the bicycle was a little big for her – Carla was balanced on her toes on the sidewalk, wobbling a little from side to side.

'Hi, Carla,' she said. 'How are you?'

'Okay,' the girl said warily. She looked hot, beads of sweat pooling above her lips.

'I heard you're going to California?'

'Yeah, San Francisco. I'm going to waitress there until college starts in the fall,' she said, her eyes dark and glowering. 'I can't wait to get out of here.'

'Me too.'

Carla wiped her lips with the back of her hand. 'Are you going somewhere, Mrs Sheldon?'

'Yeah, actually I am. I'm going to Ireland.'

'Ireland?' The girl looked stunned. 'Why?'

'It's a long story. But will you do me a favour, Carla?'

'Sure,' she said, hesitant.

'Before you leave for California, call Heather and ask her to come with you.'

Now Carla's eyes opened wide in astonishment. 'I don't understand. She's getting married, isn't she?'

'I'd rather she didn't, to be honest. I'd rather she followed her heart.'

Joy said nothing more, but she held Carla's gaze. The girl dropped her eyes to the sidewalk in embarrassed understanding.

'Okay, bye.' She pushed off as if to cycle away.

'Carla!'

The girl twisted round on her seat. Joy could see her eyes begin to fill with tears, her lips trembling. How love could make a fool of you, she thought. There was no worse pain than rejection. Her heart went out to Carla.

'Don't give up on Heather,' Joy called after her, wondering if her daughter even deserved Carla's love.

Still, she had sowed her seed. She would have been furious if her own mom had tried to stop her marrying Eddie all those years ago. But she had been crazy about Eddie, mad to marry him, and she'd been pregnant. It was different for Heather. She was in love all right, but not with her fiancé.

★

Lewis rooted through his wardrobe and threw aside all the jeans, chinos, shorts and checked shirts that had been his uniform for the past few years. He found a couple of pairs of okay Levi's and some plain shirts. But he was looking for something in particular. At last he found it, hanging up behind all of Samantha's old maxi dresses. It was his tailored Italian suit. He took it out and held it up to the light. It was still sharp black, with not a ripped seam in sight. In fact, its straight-leg cut, the height of style in 1967, was now back in fashion in 1989.

To his surprise the trousers still fitted. A little tight on the waist, but comfortable. He took one of his plain white shirts and put it on and found a blue silk tie that his parents-in-law had given him one Christmas. Finally he put on the suit jacket and looked in the mirror. What he saw gave him a shock. His face looked older, and his hair was peppered with grey, but he was still himself, a ghost from the past. To see the old Lewis excited him, as if anything was possible. He blinked, looked again. Memories flickered in the mirror. Was he ready to go back?

He had worn this suit all through that night and into the next morning of his last day in London. He put his hands in the pockets and felt something solid in the right-hand one. It was his Zippo. He flicked the wheel with his finger and amazingly it ignited, a quick flame shooting out. After all this time there was still a spark.

All smartened up in his best suit and ready for the big night, Lewis met with George in the Hereford Arms. Did his boss even know that his secretary lived barely five minutes away, let alone that half an hour ago she'd been naked beneath Lewis? Had he any idea how this same secretary was a hundred times more talented than his whole team of men? Lewis wondered, though, how much Marnie might have told Eva Miller. Either way, George clearly didn't know. There was no mention of Marnie as he asked Lewis to show him his designs for the Phoenix International Airlines brief.

'I'm not going to show Rex anything yet,' he told Lewis. 'But I want a lead on our approach so I can give him a sense of it over dinner.'

Lewis cleared the spindly table of the overflowing ashtray and empty pint glasses. He took a handkerchief from his pocket and wiped the surface clean before spreading out the final design that he and Marnie had plumped for. It was the phoenix, bold red, head turned to one side with its predator's beak, wings curving upwards in abstracted semicircles and its tail feathers in an arrow shape as they emerged from the blue flames to mirror the pattern of its wings.

George perused the design, his face giving nothing away.

'This is the emblem for the aeroplanes – to go on their tail wing,' Lewis said. 'It will be developed into a crest on

219

the crew's uniforms, which will be blue and red, and on all their other material.'

'So no letters on the plane?'

'Just PIA for Phoenix International Airlines – underneath the phoenix.'

George took out his cigars without offering one to Lewis. Instinctively Lewis took his Zippo out of his pocket, flicked the lid open and lit George's cigar for him. His boss took a couple of meditative puffs. Lewis wanted a cigarette but somehow felt unable to light up in front of his boss, as if to do so would be a comment on George's lack of generosity.

'Not sure they'll like the fact that there's an image of fire on the plane,' George said at last.

'But it shows the bird rising from the flames, triumphant, soaring into the sky. It's a powerful image of flight.'

'I guess it's the obvious choice for an airline from Phoenix,' George said as he puffed on his cigar. 'But I like it. Yes, I do. And I think our man from Phoenix will like it too. The colours are so bold and clear.'

Lewis felt relief wash through him.

'This is excellent work, considering how little time you had. Well done, old chap.' He patted Lewis on the back. 'So are you going to buy me a pint to celebrate?'

Now was the moment. As Lewis stood at the bar ordering their pints he prepared to reveal his big secret. Marnie and her talent. He tried to formulate the right words.

*This isn't just my work ... Marnie helped me.*

No, that wasn't enough.

*Marnie and I came up with this design together. You should try her out. She's good.*

Too good.

He returned to the table and placed the pints down, careful not to spill them.

He could have sworn he was just about to tell George when Eva Miller walked in. Elegant, willowy and dressed in a black lace minidress covered in silver cording, beads and sequins, heads turned as she made her way through the crowd.

'Isn't she a sight for sore eyes,' George said, putting out his cigar.

It was true – Eva's beauty was staggering. Her jet-black hair shone as if polished. It was cut into a perfect geometric bob, its wings pushed behind her neat ears to reveal the biggest earrings Lewis had ever seen – two chandeliers of silver sparkling either side of her glowing face. She must have been well over thirty, and yet there was nothing remotely middle-aged about Eva Miller. A man attempted to stop her on the way over, but she smiled at him sweetly, patted him on the shoulder and swung on by.

'Women, eh?' George winked at Lewis.

Could he spit it out now? Tell him quickly about Marnie. But Eva was upon them. He would have to tell him later, after the success of the Phoenix Airlines pitch. It would be easier then. Lewis took a slug of his pint and felt a pit of dread in his stomach. He had no idea how George was going to react when he did find out.

'Hello, darlings,' Eva said, giving George a peck on the cheek. 'Still working?'

She glanced at the folder of sketches that Lewis was putting away in his case.

'Just working out our pitch for tonight,' George told her.

'Always working.' She gave him a mock grimace. 'If I'd known I would have popped round to Marnie's.'

Lewis felt the dread tighten in his stomach. 'You know where Marnie lives?' he asked her.

'Sure I do,' she said, looking at him with mischief in her eyes. 'Don't you?'

George was oblivious, but Lewis had seen the warning in Eva's eyes. What exactly had Marnie told her?

'Gin and tonic, darling?' George asked her.

'That would be lovely,' she said, settling down as George got up to go to the bar.

Lewis felt Eva's gaze upon him. Outlined in black kohl, the lids highlighted in silver, her eyes looked even larger than normal. He shifted uncomfortably on his stool.

'George tells me he's going to make you a partner?'

'Yes, it's looking like that.'

'Congratulations on going up in the world.'

She smiled at him but Lewis wasn't sure whether she was being sarcastic or not. 'Thanks,' he mumbled.

'So now you are establishing yourself, what are your plans, Lewis?' she asked.

'My plans are to create good work for the agency,' he said defensively.

'And what about a wife?' He heard how the word 'wife' was slippery in her mouth. 'Are you thinking of settling down, starting a family? How does a nice semi-detached house in Fulham sound?'

'I'm a bit young –'

'Nonsense,' Eva interrupted. 'I was younger than you when I married.'

*And how happy are you?* He didn't say it, but Lewis

couldn't help thinking it as he watched his boss push his way back to them, Eva's gin in hand. His wife's beauty completely outshone George. More than that, Lewis had witnessed George talking down to Eva in a way that would crush the most confident woman. How did she bear being married to such a chauvinist, and a blatant womaniser? She'd said it herself today when he'd met her at lunchtime that she knew about his affairs. Why did she put up with it?

'Don't let that girl slip away, Lewis,' Eva whispered to him.

'Excuse me?' he asked, feeling his cheeks blush.

'You know who I'm talking about. It's time to make it official. You should get married.'

'I'm not sure it's any of your business, Mrs Miller.'

She said nothing for a second and put her head to one side.

'Us girls have to stick together. I'm telling you to do the decent thing, Lewis.'

Her voice was soft, but he could see a fire in her eyes. Anger. Undiluted. Marnie had promised him she hadn't told one soul about their design work, and he sensed that Eva didn't know the truth about this at least, because she was the kind of woman who would have exposed him to George. Even so it was clear Eva was furious with him. He could feel fury rolling off her.

# NINE

# *Light*

## SKY HARBOR, PHOENIX, 24 MARCH 1989

Joy was leaving the desert behind her, and she was afraid. In among the red stone boulders of Arizona she had always felt soothed, safe. The landscape had taken her out of her loss, helped her begin to let her father go. She could hide here and carry on her life as before. She and her mom could continue their uneasy peace. And she could sort things out with Eddie. In his letter he had begged her forgiveness, written that he loved her. But no matter how much she wanted to, she couldn't return to her former life. Now she was digesting all that was new and unexpected: her husband's affair, her daughter's secret love, her mom's long-standing deceit. And Lewis. Making love with Lewis. She tried to put last night to one side, but the desert heat was searing through her heartache over Eddie. Those feelings filled her with a raw energy and gave her the strength to be brave.

Joy departed under a blazing sunset. She imagined the sinking sun swallowing her up, transforming her into dusty particles of coloured light in the sky. The wind could bring her north, all the way to the Grand Canyon and release her to the spirits of the wild. To return to earth just like her father. She could hide in the desert for the rest of her life.

Yet there was another part of her that yearned for the unknown, the real. Like the cry of a hungry baby, it could be silenced by only one thing.

As the taxi sped her towards the airport, Joy opened her bag and took out the abalone shell, resting it on her lap and looking down at its iridescent innards as they glowed in the encroaching dusk. Each second it changed before her eyes. This must be like looking at the sea, she thought, its constant shift and movement, the opposite of the heat-oppressed stillness of the desert.

Inside Sky Harbor, Joy was adrift. She walked the patterned carpet up and down in front of the check-in desk several times before she summoned the courage to join the queue. Now there was no going back.

She focused on the back of a man in line ahead of her. He was dressed in a smart black suit, overdressed for Arizona, and the unruly dark hair, the height of him reminded her a little of Lewis. Then he turned to bend down and check the lock on his suitcase, and she almost gasped out loud. Joy felt the blood rush to her face. How could it be that Lewis Bell was on the same flight as her to New York?

★

Lewis was hot in his suit, but he was determined to keep the jacket on. People – especially women – were looking at him differently. He was finally taking action. After all these years he was going to find Marnie. He had no idea what he would say to her when he saw her besides sorry. He owed her that at least.

And, afterwards, would he ever return to Arizona? Again, Joy popped into his head, the strangeness of their union in the desert, its sweetness, unwrapping his senses and his passion for the first time in years. He wondered how she was, and what was happening with her philandering husband. He hoped she wouldn't forgive him. His new friend deserved better.

The young woman behind the check-in counter handed him his boarding pass, and he watched his bag as it shuttled away. It was done now. He really was going to Ireland.

His heart swelled at the thought of it – and then at a light touch on his suited arm. He turned, and to his astonishment there was Joy Sheldon in front of him. She was wearing a dress with a pattern of red roses upon it, and her cheeks were deep pink, her jet-black hair falling in loose waves around her face.

'Hello,' she said.

Lewis couldn't believe she was here too. It was only when the line moved forward and Joy was called to the counter that he found his voice.

'Are you on this flight?' he asked.

'Yes ...' she murmured before going up to the desk.

He waited for her, slightly worried now. Was Joy Sheldon following him? Was she going to attach herself to him now that her husband had left her for another woman?

'How did you know I was on this flight?' he asked as she rejoined him, holding her boarding pass.

'I didn't know you were on this flight, Lewis,' she said to him, a little taken aback and defensive.

He immediately regretted thinking the worst of her. 'So why are you flying to New York on your own?' he asked, consciously making his tone much friendlier. 'What about your husband?'

She shook her head. 'I'm not going to New York. I'm changing flights in JFK,' she said, avoiding his second question. 'I'm going to Ireland.'

'To Dublin with Aer Lingus?'

She nodded. He looked at her in disbelief. 'This is incredible,' he said. 'So am I.'

'You're going to find Marnie then?' she asked, her voice so soft he could hardly hear her.

'Yes, I got another postcard this morning.' He took it out of his suit pocket and handed it to her. 'It made my mind up. Now Samantha's left there's nothing stopping me.'

'*It's not your fault,*' she read then looked up at him. 'What does she mean?'

He sighed. 'It's a long story. But what about you? Why have you decided to go to Ireland? You said nothing about it yesterday.'

'A lot has happened since yesterday.' She looked at him, pensive for a moment, before opening her bag and taking out a piece of paper.

'I found my original birth certificate this morning – in my dad's garage.' She flapped the piece of paper in front of him. 'With my birth mother's name on it, and where I was born. I just knew it was a sign. That I had to go, right now.'

Neither of them spoke and Joy wondered again if a name and an address would be enough – after all, forty years had passed. Might her mother still be in Ballycastle? Joy had tried to convince herself that she'd be glad just to see the place, to return at last to her homeland. But she couldn't help hoping.

'Did you talk to your husband first?' Lewis asked.

She shook her head, tears began to fill her eyes. 'I can't face him, Lewis,' she said, her voice dropping to a hoarse whisper. 'I'm so confused. I thought if I focused on this, you know, take time to find some answers about who I am then it might help me sort my marriage out.'

So she was running away. He of all people recognised the impulse for flight.

'I'm a bit nervous,' she said after a moment. 'I've never flown so far before.'

'Why don't we ask them to change our seats and put us next to each other,' he offered without hesitating. 'Then at least I can hold your hand for you – if you need me to,' he added with a laugh.

She looked at him with hopeful eyes. 'You don't mind?'

'Of course not,' he said. 'We're friends, remember?'

He wondered why he was offering to share this peculiar journey to Ireland with her. All he knew was that he wanted to. He was glad she was here.

'You look different,' she told him as they headed towards the departure gates. 'I like your suit. Real classic.'

'It's very old,' he told her. 'And loaded with memories.'

It was time for a seduction night, as George called them.

For their big dinner pitching to a potential client, George, Eva and Lewis met the others in the rooftop restaurant at Bowen's department store in Kensington.

Lewis was tired. The effects of the joint he'd shared with Lizzie had long worn off, and the intensity of the hour he'd spent with Marnie had depleted him. He felt edgy, restless. Eva's cold stares were making him nervous, and he was anxious about how the Phoenix executive would respond to the pitch. On top of all that he had to tell George about Marnie.

The rest of the Studio M team were already seated. Frankie with his wife Gina; Pete and Marnie sitting next to each other. Lewis felt it was a good sign that George had invited Marnie to join them. Maybe he wasn't as chauvinist as all that. Although, as he watched Eva slip into a seat beside Marnie and immediately start talking to her, he had a feeling that she'd had more to do with the invitation than George.

Marnie looked stunning in a black halter-neck dress, her rich chestnut hair piled on top of her head, her blue eyes smoky with slate-grey kohl. She gave him a tiny smile, and he immediately wanted to kiss her. It was all he could do not to go over and take her face in his hands. *You love this woman,* a voice said in his head. The idea of it thrilled him. He made a promise to himself. By the end of the night George would not only know all about Marnie's design work, but they would also tell everyone that they were a couple.

'Big night, boys,' George said after he'd ordered a round of drinks and sat down. 'But I think we'll win the pitch, won't we, Lewis?'

'I hope so.'

'We've a good strong logo – and the Americans like that, nothing too fancy.'

'I didn't know we'd already come up with a pitch, George,' Frankie said.

He was smiling, but Lewis could sense that the Italian was annoyed at his exclusion.

'Well, you know it was all so last minute,' George said. 'I just got Lewis to rattle something off this afternoon … an emblem of a red phoenix – simple but memorable.'

'Let's see it,' Pete said, turning to him with interest.

Lewis could feel the heat of Marnie's gaze. Here they all were discussing her ideas, her drawings, as if she had nothing to do with it.

'I don't think it's a good idea just in case they walk in now,' Lewis said, looking to George.

'Lewis is right. Plenty of time for that later.'

The drinks came and George raised his glass. 'Here's to Studio M and our pioneering design work.'

Lewis was drinking his second whisky when the client Rex Leigh arrived, along with his wife, a statuesque blonde called Meryl.

George snapped into his professional persona, turning on his English-gentleman routine to charm Meryl.

Lewis imagined he was looking down at the spectacle

of the dinner table from above. The half-eaten plates of food, glasses of red and white wine, empty cocktail glasses and flickering candles merging with the women's finery. The men: George in his element, leaning back in his chair, sharing an anecdote with Rex, who was roaring with laughter. Frankie, hanging on every word George was saying. And Pete. As always, the quiet one. Trying to overcome his shyness as he spoke to Gina, Frankie's wife.

Lewis felt something brush against his knee. He looked across the table and found Marnie smiling back at him. Her foot was between his legs. Her toes squeezing either side of his balls. He shifted in the seat. She shouldn't do this, yet the boldness of it excited him. They stared at each other across the flotsam of the dinner table. He imagined standing up and grabbing her with one hand, sweeping all the dinner plates, glasses and candles onto the floor with the other. He would pull her up onto the table, rip her long black dress off and take her from behind.

He slipped his foot out of his shoe and stretched his leg under the table, letting his toes trail up her leg and slip under her dress, until they reach the top of her thighs. They locked eyes as he slipped his foot in further. He watched colour spreading across her cheeks, her eyes widening, her lips parting. She was wanton, and he loved her for it.

Her foot was working his cock now. It was so illicit, so bold – the sexiest thing he had ever done.

He took a big swig to finish his whisky, shaking the ice in the bottom of his glass. He noticed Frankie's eyes upon him, as if he knew what they were doing.

George was about to order more drinks when the waiter

announced there was a telephone call for Lewis. There was only one person he had told where he would be tonight. He silently cursed his sister. Why the hell *had* he told her? He slid his foot out from under Marnie's dress and he felt her leg withdraw, a questioning look in her eyes.

'Excuse me.' He got up and brushed his lap down with his napkin, hoping his arousal wasn't noticeable, and wove through the restaurant towards the receptionist with her outstretched hand and telephone. And, in doing so, he walked unwittingly towards his doom.

# TEN

# *Space*

Joy distracted Lewis from the nerves that rose within him, the doubt that attempted to break his resolve. He could not have sat out that long wait overnight at JFK for the flight to Dublin on his own. He would surely have turned round and boarded the next available flight back to Phoenix, but with Joy by his side he couldn't. He had to go to Ireland now – not only for himself, but also for her.

She was talking a lot. He realised she was the kind of person that chattered when they were nervous, whereas he clammed up. He liked listening to her, though, as she told him about the little garden she had created and her orange tree. How much she had loved it, all the wildflowers she had painstakingly nurtured. She told him about the day she'd come home to find her husband had cut them all down and put in a pond. She told him how hurt, how angry she still was.

'He betrayed me,' she said. 'He must have known how

233

much I loved my orange tree. He went behind my back and he destroyed it.'

Lewis suspected it wasn't just the tree she was talking about. 'You should grow another one,' he said. 'Start again.'

'I don't know if I care to any more.'

Then she told him more about her daughter, Heather, and how she hoped the wedding wouldn't go ahead.

'She's in love with someone else,' she said but didn't elaborate.

When she spoke about her son, Ray, her face glowed. To Lewis's surprise it hurt him a little. He doubted his own mother had ever spoken about him with such pride.

Joy's voice was a patter of words around him, protecting him from his own sense of unease. What would happen when he took off from American soil? Would he go back in time to his younger self, with all his rage, heartache and desolation? It had begun with that phone call in the restaurant. That long night had changed the whole course of his life, and the truth was that he had buried himself in the routine of typesetting every day because anything slightly more challenging panicked him. He had hidden behind Samantha for over twenty years and immersed himself in her family to somehow make amends for his failings. Now Samantha had given him a gift by walking out on him. She had woken him up. Now he had his chance again.

★

Joy's head was in a spin, her heart racing. She knew she was talking too much. She must be driving Lewis mad,

234

but she couldn't shut up. That was until she heard the sea.

She had tried her best to see the ocean through the tiny window but could only make out the glitter of distant lights as they came in to land, the dark shifting shapes of coast and water at night. She had wanted to take Lewis's hand, but she had held back. She had been all mixed up in her head, bubbling with fear, with the shock of the past twenty-four hours – at seeing Eddie like that with Erin and having the truth crash down around her in that single, awful moment. She'd had no idea. And yet she had always known. For the more she thought about it, the more she remembered.

The glances her husband and Erin had shared at all those dinners, the way Erin always seemed to be phoning him up about one thing or another that needed fixing in her house, or to talk about Heather and Darrell's wedding preparations. Joy had remained mute as they'd had long discussions over what photographer to use, whether the event should be videoed, which caterer was the best. They'd even picked Langely Art Gallery as the place to get the invites printed. The only thing Joy had been allowed to do was order them. They must have been laughing at her the whole time. She cringed when she thought of that meal with Erin and her friends. How dare the woman invite her over and humiliate her like that? The poor deluded wife who was so naive as to think her marriage was good.

And how could Eddie do that to her? Joy gripped the armrests tight and gritted her teeth. She'd always thought that if she found out her husband was cheating she would crumble, fall apart. But she hadn't. Instead she had done the same back to Eddie and had sex with Lewis, and though what she'd done with Lewis had been fuelled by the hurt Eddie had caused her, she didn't regret it – not for an instant.

She suddenly felt uncomfortably aware of Lewis sitting next to her, the brush of his arm against hers on the armrest, and the warmth of his body so near to hers. Her thoughts strayed to how it might feel for him to touch her again and she realised she wanted to relive that night under the stars.

She tried to push the thought out of her mind. Lewis was on a mission to find the woman of his dreams. He'd made it clear that this woman Marnie was the love of his life. Whereas she and him were no more than a travelling fellowship. But realising that Lewis wasn't interested in her made her so much more relaxed. She could just prattle on and not care if he got irritated, like Eddie would. She waited for Lewis to snap at her, but his 'shut up' never came. Instead, he seemed genuinely interested in what she had to say and asked her questions about plants. She told him more about her dreams for Hummingbird Nurseries, and how she wanted to create bespoke desert gardens for her clients.

'You should do it when you get back to Arizona,' he said.

'Will you hire me if I do?' she asked boldly.

He looked a little cagey. 'I don't know.'

'Of course,' she said. 'If you find Marnie you won't come back to Scottsdale.'

'It depends.'

He looked at her, and she wasn't sure what to read in his eyes.

Lewis stood in the restaurant lobby, telephone in hand, looking out the French doors. On the other side of the brick walls of the Kensington roof gardens was the real world. Yet he was so high up that he felt like he was in an oasis in the sky. All of life was going on below him; all the filth and the pain; all of what was happening for Lizzie. But for once he didn't want to know. He didn't want to be his sister's keeper, not tonight. But he had no choice. There was less than a year between them, but Lewis had always tried to replace their dead father.

'Lizzie, it's Lewis.'

'Hi.' But the voice was not his sister's. 'This is Sammy, Lizzie's friend.'

'Is my sister there? Can I talk to her?'

'She's here, but she can't talk to you.' Sammy's voice was shaky. 'She's taken some stuff and it's making her crazy.'

'What stuff? Has she smoked too much?' he whispered, aware of the receptionist's beady glare behind him. What state was Lizzie in if she couldn't talk on the phone?

'I guess she has. And she's drunk. She keeps going on and on that she has to tell you something. That it's really important.'

Lewis groaned. He wasn't falling for that line again. This was what Lizzie always did when she'd had too much to drink, and always when he had an important work event. Getting Sammy to talk to him was just another ploy to add to the drama.

'I'm sorry, Sammy, but I'm at a very important business dinner. I can't walk out.'

'I can't handle her on my own,' Sammy begged him.

'What about your friend, Jim? Isn't he there with you both?'

'He's just fanning the flames. He's no use.'

'Well, put her to bed ... tell her I'll come as soon as I can.'

'She won't settle down ... I can't handle this ...' Sammy's voice was sounding a little hysterical. 'You gotta come!'

The American girl was probably in nearly as bad a state as his sister. Lewis chewed his lip. Damn Lizzie. She was always crying wolf. He couldn't walk out on this dinner. George could fire him. He would lose the partnership at the very least. They still hadn't made their pitch to Rex. But how could he turn his back on his sister? What if this time she was in trouble for real?

'Look, I'll come as soon as I can.'

'Thank you,' Sammy whispered, subdued now. 'I'm sorry about ruining your fancy dinner.'

'It's okay. Just try to get some coffee into her. It sounds like you could do with a cup too. Sit tight.'

He handed the phone back to the receptionist, taking his cigarettes out and sticking one between his lips. He didn't know what the hell to do.

He flicked his Zippo open and lit the cigarette, his brain ticking over, looking at the lights of London.

'Are you all right?' It was Marnie. She touched his arm. 'Is something wrong?'

'It's my sister.' He took another pull on his cigarette. 'She's in trouble.'

Marnie put her arm through his and guided him over to the side, by the front door of the restaurant, where they couldn't be seen by their group. She pulled his cigarette from between his lips and took a drag on it. Her scent was intoxicating. He wanted to bury himself inside of her and forget about everything else.

'Lizzie's taken some drugs, nothing heavy just too much marijuana. She's with this American girl, and she can't cope. I don't know what to do.'

'Can you not just take off?'

'George will be furious with me. I could lose my job over it.'

Marnie looked pensive. She finished the cigarette, crushing it out in an ashtray by the desk.

'I was going to tell him about you tonight,' he said, flicking the flint of his Zippo against the wheel, feeling the heat of the tiny flame on his fingertip. 'I thought he'd take it better with a few drinks in him.'

'Tonight?'

'Yes, as soon as that Rex fellow confirmed we had the deal.' Lewis closed the Zippo lid, turning the lighter over and over in the palms of his hands. 'Don't you think it would have been the best moment to tell him? That I want you working on the designs, properly –'

Marnie's blue eyes deepened to indigo; her face became pale, determined.

'You were going to do that tonight?'

'Yes, but I don't know what to do now.' He took out another cigarette, flicked the Zippo open again and lit up.

'I'll go.'

He exhaled slowly, not catching her meaning.

'I'll go and get your sister ... take her back to my flat. I'll look after her until you can get away.'

'You'd do that for me?'

'Of course I would.' She nicked his cigarette again and took a quick pull before giving it back.

He pulled her to him and kissed her quickly on the lips.

'I love you,' he said, balancing the cigarette in an ashtray before taking a notebook out of his pocket and writing down the address of the place in Paddington where he'd taken Lizzie earlier that day.

Marnie took the paper off him. 'Just tell George about me, Lewis. That's all I ask.'

He walked with her to the cloakroom.

'Will you explain to the others that I feel sick? Tell Eva sorry. I know she was counting on me to get through the evening.'

He held her coat for her as she put it on, swivelling round on her heels as he buttoned her up to her chin, all the while looking into her eyes.

'Are you sure about this, Marnie? My sister can be a handful.'

She tapped his nose with her finger and raised her eyebrows.

'I'm used to wild young sisters,' she said. 'I have three. If there's any problem I'll call the restaurant, okay?'

'And when we leave I'll call your flat to let you know I'm on my way. I shouldn't be too long.'

'Fine.'

'Lizzie has a thing about hospitals. They terrify her. So don't call an ambulance or anything, just sit tight, and don't let her take anything else. I'll only be an hour or two.'

He was gripping her collar, pulling her towards him. He didn't want to let go of her. He was battling his instincts. They were telling him not to let her go.

'Lewis?'

He wanted her to tell him she loved him. He needed to hear the words.

'Tell George about me. Don't forget.'

And that was all she said before brushing his lips with hers and running out the door to hail a black cab. He had an urge to run after her. Jump in the cab and tell her to hell with it. They would go and get Lizzie together, and they would never set foot in Studio M again. They would start over and set up their own design company, just like he'd suggested their first night together. Then they would both shine.

## IRELAND, 25 MARCH 1989

*It's not your fault.*

Joy repeated the words on Lewis's last postcard inside her head. Is this what she would say to her birth mother when she found her? It's not your fault your baby was taken from you? Or was her mom right? Had Aoife Martell given her up willingly?

Lewis leaned over and pulled the card out of her hands.

'You see that's where Marnie's wrong,' he said. 'It was all my fault. I should never have let her go on her own.'

'Go where, Lewis?'

He shook his head and sighed but said nothing more, turning away and looking out of the window. The plane was dropping and her ears were popping like mad. She took a bag of candy out of her pocket and offered one to Lewis.

He shook his head. 'I can't stand boiled sweets. One of my father's aunts used to ply me with old sour ones. Put me off for life.'

They waited in the baggage claim area together, and she wanted so much to ask him where he was going now, but she was too shy. Surely he would be setting off immediately to find Marnie?

'So have you booked somewhere to stay?' Lewis asked her as he helped her drag her big case off the carousel.

'No, I didn't think that far ahead when I took off for the airport.'

He lifted her case onto a luggage cart. 'And how are you getting to Mayo? That's where you're going, isn't it?'

'I guess I should rent a car?'

He dumped his own case on top of hers before considering her. She could feel herself blushing. He must think her a big fool.

'Look, Marnie's in Sligo,' he said. 'Which isn't far from County Mayo. Why don't we travel together? We could share the car rental.'

'But won't I be in the way?'

'Not at all. I could do with the company.'

He gave her a big smile and she felt relief wash through her. She wasn't sure she could do this on her own.

'First things first, we should find somewhere to stay tonight. It's too late to drive out west now. Any preference, hotel or B&B?'

'Anywhere.' She paused, took a breath. 'As long as it's near the sea.'

At the information desk in the airport he booked two rooms in a hotel in a nearby town called Skerries.

'The hotel looks out over the beach, and the Irish Sea,' he told Joy. 'You'll see it as soon as you wake in the morning.'

She almost gave a skip of excitement. 'I don't know if I'll manage to sleep.'

Her anticipation was that of a child, eager for Christmas morning.

Joy was unprepared for the cold as they stepped outside the airport terminal. She couldn't stop herself from shivering in her leather jacket. She had assumed it would be plenty warm enough. It was April after all, and she wore this jacket on cold winter nights in Scottsdale, but this was a different kind of cold from home – a damp, penetrating chill that was making her very bones quake.

'Are you all right?' Lewis asked her. 'Your teeth are chattering.'

'It's just so cold,' she said.

A wet wind slapped into her face as a green double-decker bus trundled by.

'Oh, I thought those buses would be red,' she said.

'That's in London. Remember Ireland is an independent country.'

'Of course,' she mumbled, embarrassed.

Why was she so stupid? Of course the buses weren't red. He must think she was a total hick. He was probably dying to get rid of her so he could go to his Marnie. But she was too cowardly to tell him she was okay on her own, because she wasn't.

'Here.' Lewis was taking off his suit jacket and draping it around her shoulders.

'I can't take that,' she said. 'You'll freeze.'

'I'm fine,' he said, rubbing his hands together. 'I'm from this part of the world. I can take it.'

She glanced over at him, but his face was impassive, so she wrapped his jacket around her and inhaled his scent, remembering it from their night in the desert. He smelled very different from Eddie. A comforting, woody aroma. Her husband was always lathering himself in fancy aftershaves, and now she knew why. It occurred to her that maybe Erin wasn't his first betrayal. Her stomach clenched. How many women had Eddie slept with while he was married to her? There were all those late-night viewings, and weekends away at realtor conventions. What an idiot she had been.

'Okay, here we are,' Lewis said, stopping by a red car.

'Lewis,' she said, 'this car is crazy small.'

'It's a Fiat Panda,' he told her. 'It's fine. It needs to be small because the roads are pretty narrow here. You'll see.'

He unlocked the door and they squashed their bags into the trunk.

'Do you know the way?' she asked as they settled into the front seats.

'I think so. They gave me pretty good directions.'

Despite how close they were to the airport, the roads were narrow, like Lewis said, and winding. She found the experience of sitting on the other side of the car, in such a tiny vehicle, disconcerting. Every time another car approached them she flinched. Before long they were off the 'main' road and bumping along an even narrower road with no street lights. She peered out of the car window at the darkness surrounding them. She sensed the sea out there. Like an unspoken whisper.

A short while later Lewis drove into a small town. Everything looked closed and shut up. She spied a lone cat running across the road, and one man with a dog on a leash, walking down the road. It was a Saturday night and yet the place was deserted.

'It's pretty quiet here,' Lewis told her, reading her thoughts. 'Ireland's not like England. There's not much work here. Most young people have left.'

'That's sad,' she said.

'Yeah,' he said. 'I've heard there are more Irish people in the rest of the world than in Ireland itself.'

They found the hotel easily enough. Lewis pulled into the parking lot, and as soon as Joy got out of the car she could hear the sea. It was like music to her. That roll and crash of waves. She couldn't stop herself. She followed the sound, leaving Lewis, the little car and their luggage behind her. She walked round the side of the parking lot, to the back of the hotel, and found that Lewis was absolutely right. The hotel was on the beach.

She stepped from concrete onto sand, and her blue boots sank immediately. She stared down, fascinated. Of course she had stood on sand many times in the desert, but it was a different type of sand. So dry, and rough, interspersed with scrub and bush. This sand was fine as gold dust, though the air was heavy and damp around her, and charged with the essence of the ocean.

She followed the sound of the waves onto the empty beach and her eyes searched for the water. It was a cloudy night, there were no stars and it was hard to make anything out, but after a while her sight adjusted and she could discern movement, a little white crest of a wave, a tiny welcome for her, and the moment of its landing upon the sand.

She ran across the beach, Lewis's jacket open and splayed like wings flanking her, her hair loose and tossed about by the wind blowing off the sea. She inhaled deeply and tasted the salt on her lips. The words came to her instinctively.

'I am home.'


She was gone. All of a sudden Joy was running off down that beach like a wild thing.

'Joy!' he yelled.

But she didn't hear him. His call was carried off into the wind. He was shivering from the cold, and now he was dying to get into the hotel and warm up, yet he followed her. He was worried about her. Maybe she would be so excited about encountering the sea that she would run right into it and drown.

He supposed if he had never seen the sea before he would be this excited too. Imagine never having left America your whole life? He had to give Joy some credit. She was brave to walk out on her life like this. But he was anxious too and felt responsible for her. She seemed so nervous. What if she found no trace of her birth mother? That disappointment on top of her husband's infidelity ... would it tip her over the edge?

'Joy!' he called again.

He saw her running around by the edge of the sea, like a demented dog chasing its tail, and jogged down the beach to join her. She ran over, grabbed his hands and spun him. He couldn't help but catch some of her enthusiasm and laughed along with her.

'It's so incredible ... so damn awesome!'

'You haven't even seen it in daylight yet.'

'But I can hear it, and I can taste it and smell it!' she cried. 'It's like I've found a part of myself, Lewis. It's been missing all my life.'

'I know,' he said.

'I'm Irish. I'm a goddamn Irish woman!' she yelled out to the wind. 'This sea is mine.'

He pulled her up the beach. 'Come on,' he said. 'You'll see it tomorrow. It's cold and dark, Joy.'

She looked at him, her expression contrite. 'I'm so sorry,' she said. 'I've your jacket on – you must be freezing.'

'It's fine.' He smiled at her. 'Let's just get inside.'

It was Easter Saturday, but still the hotel had an off-season air of desertion. The receptionist, a lanky woman with dark red hair, scrutinised them as he booked them into their separate bedrooms.

'Enjoy your stay, Mr Bell and Miss Sheldon,' she said, handing them keys.

'Mrs Sheldon,' Joy corrected her.

'Excuse me,' the woman said, all prim and proper with a glint in her eye.

The smug look on her face made Lewis wish he and Joy really were up to no good.

They said their goodnights in the corridor outside Joy's room. She was flushed from her run on the beach, and not for the first time he thought how young she looked for her age. The more he got to know Joy, the less like Marnie, and Samantha, he realised she was. Those women were more than aware of the power of their femininity, whereas Joy seemed completely unaware of her beauty. Her lack of vanity scattered around her in unexpected and endearing showers. On the whole trip from America to Ireland not once had he seen this woman check her reflection in a compact, or put on lipstick, or style her hair. When Joy had taken off her blue boots on the plane he couldn't help noticing she was wearing odd socks. This was something neither Marnie nor Samantha would ever have done. Yet for some reason her lack of artifice appealed to him.

In his room, Lewis sat down on the bed and stared at the beige walls and a washed-out watercolour of a sea view. He should have been tired. They had been travelling for over twenty-four hours, and yet he wasn't in the least bit sleepy. He felt completely wired. It was like his head was playing catch-up with his body. He had finally done it. He had made it across the Atlantic. Not as far as London, true. But he was here, in Marnie's homeland. He was so close to her now. Just a few hours in the car and he would see her again. He couldn't quite believe it was true.

What would he say when he saw her?

Sorry. That was the first thing he needed to say. Sorry for that long night and what she must have gone through looking after Lizzie. He was sorry for drinking too much whisky with George, Rex, Pete and Frankie and letting the dinner linger on. Sorry for not telling George about all the hard work she had put into those Studio M designs, and the quick talent she'd brought to the Phoenix proposal. He had tried several times to talk about Marnie and her design work with George, but every time her name was mentioned his boss would make some comment under his breath for only the men to hear – about the size of Marnie's breasts or wondering if she was as able in bed as she was in the office.

Most of all Lewis was sorry for not going back to her flat after the dinner, instead agreeing to go on to a club because Rex was crazy about jazz, and George wanted them to see this new jazz musician. Why the hell had he not thought to ring Marnie before they left the restaurant? Yet he'd believed Marnie was so capable. Not for a minute had he doubted that she wouldn't have Lizzie under control.

### London, 14 April 1967, 12.10 a.m.

Lewis was behind Frankie, narrow-hipped in his pinstriped suit, his diminutive wife Gina in polka dots, hooked onto her husband's arm as they descended out of the cool Soho night into the smoky dungeon of one of George's favourite jazz clubs.

Lewis should have been hailing a cab on the street outside. He should have been on his way to Lizzie and Marnie.

But he couldn't go. It was part of the deal. After dinner,

the banter and the pitch, it was sealed in the early hours of the morning in a drinking den, or a club pulsing with the promise of tomorrow. It was the world Lewis had to operate in; the graphic designer had to be a jack of all trades: artist, salesman, psychologist, magician. He was a mirror to his clients, reflecting back to them the image they wanted to see. Lewis had played the game over dinner, convincing Rex Leigh that their image of the phoenix emerging from the flames was not a repetition of a cliché but in its execution a vibrant image of his dynamic airline emerging as powerful and bold into the future. The abbreviation of Phoenix International Airlines to PIA simplified yet strengthened their profile.

He couldn't deny that he got a thrill out of selling their idea to the corporate man. He exulted in that moment when creativity and commerce collided. His sister was wrong. This *was* an art.

The Studio M group wove between the tables to George's favourite spot, a snug tucked to the left of the stage. The waitresses treated him with a certain reverence since he was clearly one of the regulars. There was a band playing already – trumpeter, bassist and guitarist. The music spiralled around them like the staircase leading into the smoky darkness of the club.

Lewis took a slug of his Scotch, scooping an ice cube into his mouth. The whisky burned his throat, while the ice rolled around his tongue. He bit into it. He couldn't get Lizzie out of his head. He hadn't shifted the nagging feeling that had plagued him all evening, but he had to stay until the client left. That was the rule.

'What's wrong with Marnie?'

Eva Miller was leaning across the table at him.

'She felt sick.'

'Yes, but what kind of sick?'

'You know, the normal kind,' Lewis said, trying not to show his irritation. 'When you feel nauseous –'

'Physically sick?' Eva asked, eyebrows raised.

'Yes,' he replied, wishing she would change the subject. She was just making him feel more anxious about Lizzie, and even more guilty that he had left Marnie to deal with her for so long.

'Did she tell you why she's sick?'

'No, she didn't,' Lewis snapped. 'It's just one of those things.'

Eva looked at him with interest. 'Do you love Marnie, Lewis?' she asked.

'That is a very personal question,' he said, affronted. For a moment Eva reminded him of his mother. How could she really love George Miller? She had surely just used her beauty and youth to trap him into marrying her, attracted by his prestige – just like his mother hunting down a new partner.

'Lewis, do the right thing before it's too late,' Eva said, her voice solemn.

He felt panic rising in his chest. She must know about Marnie's design work. He had to tell George about Marnie's designs before Eva did. Otherwise the humiliation, the damage to his credibility as a designer would be disastrous.

He took a big slurp of his fresh whisky and felt the alcohol curling around his brain, fogging his mind. Maybe

251

he was imagining Eva's threat. What she'd said couldn't have anything to do with the designs. She just wanted him to marry Marnie. He supposed married women always wanted to match up their single girlfriends. Marnie had sworn she had told no one about their work, and he trusted her. But should *she* trust *him*? As the drink relaxed him, his resolve began to weaken.

He soaked in the atmosphere of the club. Who would have thought that Lewis Bell, the misfit boy with the scabby knees, every bully's favourite, would be mingling with the in-crowd? He was rubbing shoulders with *the* people of the moment – young actresses with doe eyes and gamine haircuts, unshaven musicians, bespectacled film directors. The faces looked familiar even if he couldn't remember their names.

He should leave right now. He needed to get to Lizzie. Yet this world enticed him to stay, and George expected him to stay, so Lewis didn't budge; he just lit yet another cigarette, crossed his legs and listened to the banter. Life was good, was it not? He was going to be made a partner in one of the top design agencies in London. He had a beautiful girlfriend. What more could he want?

Marnie. Her name flew around his head like a trapped bird. If he loved her, he should do as she asked. He had to speak to George now. There was a break in the conversation and Lewis took his chance.

'All going well?' he asked George.

'An excellent evening,' George said, with shining eyes. 'And I couldn't have done it without you, Lewis. You are stellar.'

'Thank you, sir.'

'What's with this, sir? Call me George!'

'You think the designs are good?'

'Top notch, my boy – you've impressed me. We're on the way up,' he said, patting Lewis on the back.

'I'd like to ask you something – a favour,' Lewis said.

'Indeed, I'm not sure I can grant it, but fire away.' George looked him directly in the eye, and Lewis tried to hold his gaze, but he couldn't do it. In the end he picked up his glass and studied the golden liquid inside.

'Would you consider promoting Marnie?' he managed to say.

'Marnie?' George exclaimed. 'And just what position would I promote her to? Office manager? I mean, she's the only secretary we have, Lewis ... I know you have feelings for her – I mean, we've all noticed it apart from Pete, but that boy is a world to himself –'

'No, I mean promote her to the position of designer,' Lewis interrupted. He had done it all backward. He had meant to tell George first about Marnie's input on the designs and then ask him to promote her. He looked across at his boss's astonished face.

'Why on earth would I promote our girl Friday to a design position, Lewis?' George's eyes narrowed, hardening to flint. In that look Lewis could see there would be no forgiveness. His fall would be fast, and irredeemable.

'Well, she's always told me she was interested in that side of things.'

'It's a ridiculous idea, Lewis. We can't let that girl play around and make pretty little pictures for us. Studio M is cutting-edge, Lewis, with a team of professional graphic designers. Surely you know that? Love has addled your brain, young man.'

'Sorry, George, I just promised her I would talk to you.'

'Well, very nice of you, old chap, but a completely outrageous suggestion. She's a great little secretary. I appreciate her skills, and Eva seems to adore her, as do the boys, so I will certainly give her a raise. How about that?'

'Very kind of you, George –'

'And if she's hitched to your cart, she'll benefit from your successes now, won't she? Your star is rising, young man. Mark my words. What I saw today was the sign of a very great designer in the making. I don't give praise easily, believe me.'

'I do believe you. Thank you, sir.'

'George!' He clapped Lewis on the back. 'Now you're going to have to shut up because the reason I brought you to this rather dingy club has just walked on stage.'

The final act came on, and Lewis was surprised to see that it was a lone guitar player. George was tapping Rex Leigh's arm.

'Amancio D'Silva just arrived in London from Goa. He has an incredible sound,' George enthused. 'A fusion of modern jazz and Indian music.'

D'Silva took his place centre stage, moving with such grace that he didn't look like he belonged in a smoky jazz club in Soho. Lewis imagined him sitting cross-legged on the sand, under a desert sky at night. Each star polished bright by the clear, crystal air.

He began to play. Lewis closed his eyes and the music took him away from his guilt over Marnie – his anxiety over Lizzie. All that was yesterday, and yesterday was over now. But even with his eyes closed, his mind shut down, he hadn't quite stepped over the threshold of tomorrow yet. He was travelling backward, in time to the strum and quiver of the guitar strings, back through this day, this year and all the years of his life. He was himself as a little boy, holding his sister's hand, and they were climbing down the staircase of a house he had long since forgotten. Those big stairs, gripping the rail and his sister's uncertain steps, waddling in her nappy. Yet now as he saw the rosebud-papered walls, smelled the furniture wax on the shiny banister rail and slipped on the Turkish rug in the hall, he knew exactly where he was. This was his home, where his mother and father had lived, and where he and his sister were born. He was three years old, Lizzie two, but he could see with the knowledge of now. His sister's need to be loved, and his too.

They ran down the hall together, these two cherubs, bubbling with excitement because Daddy was home. The hall door was open, rain falling in on the doormat where their father crouched, trench coat swinging open, his officer's cap tilted sideways and his arms open wide for them. The sun came out and a rainbow arched over his head. Daddy was home!

Lewis gasped as if his heart had missed a beat. He opened his eyes. Everyone should have a father, especially Lizzie.

The others around the table were staring at Amancio D'Silva, bewitched by his music, as if they also had been transported into private memories. When he finished playing there were a few seconds of silence, as if the room was collectively drawing breath. Then there was an explosion of applause. The young man made a slight nod of thanks and walked off stage without fuss, his guitar in his hand as if it were an extension of himself. They all looked at each other as if for the first time.

'I guess that was the perfect conclusion to a great evening,' Rex Leigh eventually spoke up.

Lewis, Pete, Frankie and Gina surged up the stairs as one. As they emerged onto the street Lewis could see that the sky was streaked with strands of pale yellow and washy grey light. How could it be dawn already? Had he really been down in that club for all those hours?

Rex and Meryl Leigh, and George and Eva Miller seemed to have vanished in the other direction. The rest of them walked through Soho together. After the crowd in the club, the street felt like a morgue with its shuttered shops, no buses or cars. Gina's heels clicked loudly on the wet pavement, and the noise of Frankie lighting a cigarette seemed amplified.

'That was a long, long night,' Frankie said. 'Did we actually get the deal, do you think?'

'We bloody better have,' Lewis growled. 'That man was a bore.'

He nearly walked into a red telephone box as it loomed up in front of them.

'I'm just going to make a call. You all go on. I'll follow you in minute.'

He went into the phone box, making sure the door was shut behind him. Frankie and Gina meandered on, but Pete waited for him, uneasy at being left with the couple. Lewis waved him away before dialling Marnie's number. To his surprise the phone was picked up almost immediately as he slipped a coin into the box.

'Hello?'

'Is that you, Lewis?'

'I'm just calling to check Lizzie is okay, and to thank you. I don't know what I would do without you.'

'Lewis, where were you?'

Her Irish accent was more pronounced than usual and there was something about her tone of voice. His whisky head was gone in a flash, as if someone had tipped a bucket of ice water over him.

'Everything's all right, isn't it?'

'Lewis...' Marnie's voice came out in a hoarse whisper. 'Your sister...'

The tick, tick, tick of the telephone line echoed in his head.

'What's happened?'

'She won't wake up ... I don't know what to do ... Should I call an ambulance?'

The words seemed to come from the air inside the telephone box, not his own mouth, not his own words about his sister. 'Is she still breathing?'

'Yes, but I can't wake her. Lewis, where are you?'

'I'm coming. Five minutes.'

He slammed the receiver down and hurled himself out of the phone box, running to the end of the street where the others were waiting.

'What's up?' Pete asked.

'There's something wrong with my sister. I have to go.'

He could feel panic swelling inside him. He pressed it down; he had to stay calm and in control.

'I'll drive you,' Pete offered. 'My car's parked just round the corner, and I've only had a couple of pints.'

He felt Pete's hand on his shoulder. 'It's okay, mate.'

Pete's reassurance steadied him. Everything would be fine. It always was in the end. It would just be one more of Lizzie's dramas. Marnie was overreacting.

But as he and Pete rushed off to the car, Lewis knew this wasn't like any of the times before. The whole day he had felt this sense of foreboding, and now he knew why.

# ELEVEN

# *Time*

## SKERRIES, COUNTY DUBLIN, 25 MARCH 1989

'Fancy a nightcap?' Lewis stood in her doorway, proffering a bottle of whisky.

'I don't really drink liquor,' Joy said.

She was embarrassed. She had already put on her pyjamas and was conscious of her face scrubbed clean.

'It's a special occasion.' He smiled at her, although his eyes looked dark and sorrowful. 'For both of us. Let's make a toast to the first night of our Irish quests.'

She opened the door wide. 'Okay,' she said, 'Just one.'

She got two plastic cups from her little en suite, and he sat on her bed, his long legs stretched out in front of him. There was nowhere else to sit but the bed so she climbed up onto it, sitting next to him awkwardly.

'I like your pyjamas,' he said. 'More flowers.'

She blushed as she held out her plastic glass and he poured the whisky in. 'I wasn't expecting company.'

'No, really, I like them. You're always wearing flowers.'

'I am?'

'When you came in to order those wedding invites, you were wearing a shirt with lots of little red flowers on it.'

'That old thing.' She tried to sound casual but was touched that he remembered.

'I thought it looked pretty. And that time in the Botanical Garden you were wearing a shirt with flowers on it.'

'That's my gardening shirt,' she said.

'And you had on a sundress with white daisies on it when you came into the Rusty Spur.'

'Oh yeah.' She could feel herself blushing, thinking now of the moment he had slid the straps of that dress off her shoulders, out in the desert.

'And today you were wearing a dress with red roses on it,' he said. 'You're a floral lady!'

'And you're a man with a really good memory,' she said, astonished that he would remember what she'd worn every time they met.

'A good visual memory,' he corrected her. 'I remember what I observe, what I see, down to the tiniest detail. I guess it's my training, but what actually happens that's much foggier, and words – now words I forget.'

'Not the words that Marnie wrote on the postcards. You remember those.'

'That's because they're in the context of pictures from the past. I remember how Marnie looked when those words were spoken, what she was wearing too, where we were. I don't remember what else was said, or what happened afterwards, or how I felt.'

Joy took a slug of the whisky. It burned her throat but made her feel warmer. The room was so cold, despite the fact the radiator was on. She meant less to him than Marnie. Of course she did.

'Sure you remember,' she said. 'Isn't that why you're here?'

'Maybe this is my midlife crisis. My wife leaves me and I go on a wild goose chase after a figment of my imagination.'

'But she's not a figment because you have the cards,' she reassured him.

'I just don't know why,' he said, looking at her as if she might have the answer, 'Marnie's waited all these years to contact me.'

Joy didn't know how to explain it either.

'You'll find out tomorrow I guess.'

'I haven't even told her I'm coming. It doesn't seem real,' he said. 'That I'll see her again. And yet sometimes it feels like only yesterday when I saw her last.'

'What was Marnie like?' she asked, feeling a twinge of jealousy when his eyes lit up.

'She was something else, Joy. A stunning girl – and clever. She was such a talented designer. I knew she'd make it, with or without my help.'

Joy took another gulp of her whisky. The drink was relaxing her, making her feel generous. She wanted to hear the story of Marnie and Lewis. It would help her remember that Lewis could be nothing more to her than a friend.

'I let her down,' Lewis said. 'We worked together, you see. It was down to Marnie that I got offered a partnership, and I meant to tell my boss about her. I tried ... but I was a coward. She did so much great design work, and I took the credit.'

'I can't believe you'd do that, Lewis,' Joy said.

'Well, I did. I was a selfish, ambitious young man.'

She watched him run his hand through his thick hair, and she wanted to touch him, reassure him. She wanted to tell him that everyone makes mistakes when they're young.

'But I really did want to tell my boss about Marnie. I did try,' Lewis went on. 'He was such a chauvinist, and Marnie was our very capable girl Friday, and he didn't want her involved in the design side of things ...'

'Did you tell him in the end?'

'I tried, but we were all so drunk that last night, and I got it all wrong the way I went about it. Then something happened –'

Lewis stopped speaking. He took the whisky bottle and refilled their glasses. She didn't stop him. She wanted to know what that something was.

'Is that why you and Marnie fell out?' she asked. 'Because you never told your boss about her?'

'No,' he said with a heavy voice.

He got up and walked over to the window, pulling back the curtains. She could see nothing outside, just darkness and a few winking lights. But she could hear the surge of the sea whispering to her from beyond the glass.

'You should leave the curtains open so the first thing you see in the morning is the sea,' he said, his back to her as he stood at the window.

She took another drink and waited for him to speak, but he said nothing for several minutes. He turned round and spied her abalone shell on the top of her case. He bent down and picked it up.

'Is this yours?' he asked, looking up at her.

'Yes,' she said. 'My dad gave it to me. It's the only part of the sea I've ever had ... or seen, I guess.'

Lewis looked amused. 'So you decided to bring it all the way to Ireland?'

'I didn't want to leave it behind ... with Eddie.'

He stood up, placing it on her bedside table. 'It is really quite beautiful,' he said. 'I don't think you'll find any shells like that on Skerries Beach.'

'Can I ask you something, Lewis?' she said, feeling bold after nearly two glasses of whisky.

'Sure.' He came to sit back down on the bed.

'Have you ever cheated on your wife?'

'No,' he said. 'Never.' He paused. 'Well, not if you don't count Thursday night, with you, but then she'd already left.'

He looked into her eyes, and she found his impossible to read.

'I think Eddie has been cheating on me for years,' she said in a small voice. She felt her heart curling up inside, afraid and bruised.

He said nothing, just leaned over and put his hand on her knee.

'He can't love me at all.'

'I wouldn't say that,' Lewis said. 'Every man is different. Just because a husband slips up doesn't mean he doesn't love his wife.'

'How can that be?'

'Nothing is ever black and white, Joy,' Lewis said. 'Maybe Eddie was looking for attention. He didn't really hide his indiscretion, did he?'

'Do you think Samantha might want more attention from you?'

He shook his head. 'No, Samantha was doing the honest thing actually. I can't be mad at her at all. Our marriage had been dead for years. But you and Eddie are different – you told me that, remember? The first time we really talked you told me that you belonged together – that he's the love of your life.'

'I thought he was the one, you know, from the minute he asked me out on a date. I just thought, "He's my guy".'

'So I'm sure he feels the same deep down. You'll sort it out,' Lewis said gently.

She thought about his words. How sure she had been of the love between her and Eddie only a few weeks ago and now nothing was certain. She was confused, too, by Lewis's presence in her life. They'd had sex in the heat of the moment, a mistake, and she knew she should stay away from him. But their fledgling friendship was precious to her.

'I don't know,' she said. 'Maybe there is no one true love but others you can love too. If you marry young, there becomes a point where either you change together or you begin to separate.'

'I guess that's what happened to me and Samantha.'

Joy took the bottle and poured herself another glass. For the first time in her life she was beginning to realise she just might be able to live without Eddie.

'My husband is a cheating bastard,' she said, raising her glass in a toast.

Lewis knocked his glass against hers, and they both downed their whiskies in one.

'Why can't the nice people ever hook up together?' she said.

He shrugged and gave her a lopsided smile. She was possessed by an urge to touch his cheek, bring her hand up to stroke his unruly hair.

'Your wife is stupid,' she said, aware that she was drunk but unable to stop herself. 'And Marnie is stupid to have let you go all those years ago. I'd never let you go. I think you're lovely.'

'Well, I think you're lovely too, Joy.'

She could feel her heart swelling with emotion, and before she could stop herself, she had slid across the bed, put her arms around his neck and kissed him. For a moment she felt him hesitate, and then he kissed her back.

It felt so good to kiss Lewis's lips, to smell him so close to her again and feel his arms around her, pressing into her thin pyjama top. She didn't want to think; she just wanted to feel. She allowed herself to be immersed in sensation, so liberating, because she could be herself. All those years with her husband she had been trying to be the woman he'd wanted her to be. Now her desires were free, and she forgot everything apart from kissing Lewis and feeling his touch upon her. She longed to make love to him again.

Still embracing, she lay down upon him on the bed, kissing him deeply. She brushed her cheeks against his, feeling the surge within her heart as it beat against his. This moment felt so right, so natural, as if it had been waiting to happen her whole life. Joy began to unbutton her top. Yet to her surprise Lewis reached out and placed his hand upon hers, so she could unbutton no further. She stopped kissing him and opened her eyes. He was looking at her, his pupils large and dark, his brown eyes drawing her into their liquid depths.

'We're drunk,' he whispered.

'I know,' she said. 'But I don't care.'

She leaned in to kiss him again, but he put his fingers on her lips.

'Joy, we shouldn't do this.' His voice was gentle but firm.

Her heart fell. She could feel the colour rising in her cheeks, a sense of shame enveloping her.

'Why not?' she whispered.

'Because it's wrong,' he said. 'You have to sort things with Eddie, and I'm here to find Marnie. We're going to screw up our friendship like this.'

She scrambled off him, mortified now.

'I ... I ... I'm so sorry,' she stuttered. 'You're right; I don't know what I was doing. I'm not used to whisky.'

He got up and stood awkwardly in front of her. 'No, it's my fault.' He sidestepped her, heading for the door. 'Please forgive me.'

Then, before she could say another word, he'd run out of the room.

She stood for a moment, just staring at the shut door with the emergency-procedures poster on the back of it, the Do Not Disturb sign swinging on the handle. She was beyond embarrassment.

Devastated, she got into bed and pulled the cold sheets up to her chin. What was she doing here, so far from her life as she knew it? What would she do if she couldn't find her birth mother or, worse still, if the woman rejected her all over again? Could she withstand it?

It was only when she turned out the light, in the dark tomb of the hotel bedroom, she let herself cry, silent tears sliding down her face. She was a fool twice over. Not only had her husband cheated on her, but she had let herself develop feelings for a man who was clearly in love with another woman.

★

Lewis lay on his bed like a fish stranded out of water, a weight pressing down on his chest, his breath short and his body hard with arousal. He closed his eyes and imagined Joy's lips on his again, how good it had felt. He wanted to make love to her so badly. It was all he could do to stop himself from storming back up the corridor to her hotel room.

But he mustn't.

He had to find Marnie.

He had waited twenty-two years for this day. He couldn't change his mind now.

Joy had been drunk. If he made love to her tonight, he would be taking advantage of her.

But why was he overcome with this urge to feel her in his arms, to be inside her again? They had both acknowledged that the other night had been one-off comfort sex. They were friends – that was all – and he was here in Ireland to find the love of his life. Why would he abandon that for one night of passion with a wife on the rebound? It would destroy their friendship. He valued Joy too much to do that to her.

He put his hands on his chest and felt the frantic beat of his heart. He tried to breathe steady and slow, to focus on

Marnie and forget about Joy in her flowery pyjamas. He saw again the image of Marnie in her green trench coat, its collar up, her russet hair uncovered and glistening with raindrops, her eyes swimming with heartache.

## LONDON, 14 APRIL 1967 5.19 A.M.

Lewis recited Marnie's address in South Kensington.

'Thurloe Square,' Pete repeated, sounding surprised. 'Isn't that where Marnie lives?'

'Yes, that's where we're going. That's why she left dinner after the phone call. She's been helping my sister.'

Pete glanced over at him, but Lewis refused to look back. He couldn't deal with explanations right now. What would he find when he got to Marnie's flat? Surely Marnie was exaggerating? Lizzie thrived on drama.

He tried to convince himself that his sister was putting on an act like always.

Pete drove fast, getting more speed out of his old Morris Minor than Lewis would ever have imagined possible. The streets were deserted apart from the odd pedestrian, either returning from a night out, or off to work early. There was the sensation that they were not yet part of the real world. They were driving through the dark truth of their city during that empty first hour of dawn, its black seams visible: concrete, tarmac, bricks and dirt, people and their filth – that's all London really was.

Marnie's kohl was smudged into the dark shadows under her eyes, her fair skin looked almost transparent and her hair was scraped back off her face. He had never seen her like this before. She looked so young – so undone.

'Where were you? Where were you?' she kept saying as he rushed into the flat.

'I'm so sorry.' He grabbed her hands as if praying for forgiveness. 'Where is she?'

Marnie nodded towards her bedroom. Lewis dropped her hands and charged in. Only yesterday morning he had been on this same bed making love to Marnie. Now his sister was lying upon it, her red hair fanning out on the pillow, her skin wet with sweat. She looked like a pale sea creature washed up on a beach, a damaged mermaid. He touched her and found she was warm. When he felt her pulse it was there, if faint.

'I didn't know what to do,' Marnie was saying behind him. 'That American girl told me she'd smoked too much pot, but this is more than that. I was on the verge of calling 999.'

Lewis bent over Lizzie and slapped her face, but she didn't stir. 'Lizzie!' he shouted, 'Lizzie!'

He tried to sit her up and shake her, but she just flopped down again as if she had no spine to support her.

'Christ,' Lewis said. 'Why didn't you call an ambulance?'

'You said not to.' Marnie turned on Lewis. 'Remember? You said whatever happens don't call an ambulance. I just thought she'd smoked too many joints and would sober up. I kept thinking you were going to be here any minute. I was waiting for you.'

'Yes, but I expected you to use your common sense,' he snapped.

'Lewis, stop it,' Pete interrupted. 'This is not Marnie's fault.'

Yet Lewis couldn't help thinking it was. Marnie should have had more sense. She should have ignored his instructions and called a doctor. Even so he held back.

'I'm sorry,' he said. 'Everything's going to be okay.'

'I thought she was all right, you know resting, but now she won't wake up ... she just won't ...'

Pete leaned over the bed. He picked up Lizzie's limp hand and tried to open her eyelids with his fingers.

'You need to get her to the hospital fast,' he said. 'I think she's taken an overdose.'

'But she never takes too many. She's always okay,' Lewis protested. 'She just does this to get attention. Don't you think we can make her throw up, force her to drink coffee?'

He bent over his sister and yelled in her face, his spit landing on her forehead, on her cheeks and lips. 'Elizabeth Bell, wake up now!'

His sister didn't stir. There really was something about her this time. She was so still. Fear crept up his legs. He started to shake involuntarily. Pete was right. They needed to get Lizzie to a hospital.

He carried his sister out of the bedroom, out of Marnie's flat and down the stairs. She was as light as a child. He couldn't bear to look at her face, closed up and lost from him.

'I'll drive you,' Pete offered again.

'No, I'll take her in the MG,' Lewis said. 'It's faster.'

Really what he wanted to say was that he needed to be alone with Lizzie. Away from Pete and Marnie and their desperate faces.

His MG was parked right outside the gate of Marnie's

house, where he'd left it the previous afternoon. That golden glorious evening felt like it was from another era. His head had been full of ambition and passion for Marnie. Now that was all smashed and ruined.

Marnie unlocked the car door for him, and he carefully arranged Lizzie into the passenger seat.

'We'll follow you in Pete's car,' Marnie said, handing him the keys.

'No,' he said, batting her away. 'You've done enough damage.'

His words were harsh, and she stepped back as if he'd slapped her. Pete looked shocked. But Lewis didn't care. He had to save Lizzie. That was all that mattered now.

As he sped away, Lewis caught sight of Marnie's face as it caved in. It was a sight he would never forget. Marnie's hands plastered upon her cheeks, tears spilling over them, as she turned in to Pete, hiding from the horror of Lewis's words. Guilt seared through him. Why was he blaming Marnie? All this was his fault, not hers.

He drove through Kensington like a lunatic, his sister slumped and unmoving beside him in the little car.

'Lizzie,' he pleaded, 'Lizzie, I'm sorry. Please wake up.'

He promised her he would never abandon her again. He promised her that she could call him any time and he would always be there. He wouldn't laugh at her, or mock her paintings, or belittle her. All she had to do was live. He promised her the whole wide world if she would just live.

But it was too late. No one could save his sister. Lewis screamed at the doctors and nurses to do something, but Lizzie never regained consciousness. As minute after

271

minute passed her body shut down, and finally they watched as her heart stopped beating. The official cause of death was a hypertensive attack brought on by a lethal combination of her antidepressants with amphetamines. An accident. After all Lizzie's suicide attempts it was the medication that helped her not to feel suicidal that had killed her. Lizzie died at 9.18 a.m. on Friday 14 April 1967. She was twenty-four years old.

Lewis was there as Lizzie took her last breath. He brushed her hair until it shone like burnished copper. In repose she looked like Sleeping Beauty, waiting to be kissed awake. But there was no prince for Lizzie. There never had been.

Lewis knew that it was all his fault. He shouldn't have brought her over to the house in Paddington where she had got the drugs. He shouldn't have left her there all night and gone to a work dinner. He shouldn't have asked Marnie to go over and get her. He should have gone himself. He should have left the jazz club earlier and gone straight to Marnie's flat. He should have told Marnie to ring the ambulance immediately, as soon as he called her. He should have made Lizzie sick when they had got to the flat. All these regrets tumbled in on him as he held Lizzie's hand and felt the warmth drain out of it. He was turned to stone, unable to let her go.

When the doctor finally announced that she had passed away and tried to persuade him to release his sister's hand, Lewis snapped out of the numb cold of shock. It felt as if he had been stung by a thousand wasps, and the pain of his loss made him bellow like a mad bull. All the anger he'd bottled up during their childhood swelled within him, and he picked up the spindly wooden chair he'd been sitting on and threw it against the wall. It smashed into pieces as two junior doctors restrained him, while Lizzie's doctor gave him a sedative.

'Just to calm you down,' he told him. 'You've had a big shock.'

Lewis entered a world under water. The sounds of the hospital were a background hum, and he could see nothing around him: not the daylight seeping up through the frosted glass windows, nor the cleaners mopping the linoleum floor, nor the pretty nurses trooping by, looking at the distraught young man with his head in his hands. He sat on an orange plastic chair outside Lizzie's room. He was unable to go in. He was unable to walk away. He felt the guilt of a murderer.

Finally Lewis dragged himself out of the chair and stumbled down the corridor towards the public telephones. He called his mother, and with no ceremony told her that her daughter was dead. He could hear her shock, her cries on the other end of the phone, but he couldn't feel anything for her. He was outside of the conversation, as if he were watching himself talking to her.

'What happened? What happened?' his mother screeched. 'Why didn't you call me sooner? Lewis, why couldn't you look after her?'

His fury began to unfurl. 'Don't pretend you care now, Mother,' he snarled.

'How can you say such a thing?' she sobbed.

He slammed down the phone. He hated his mother, but more than that he hated himself. He was just like Sylvia Bell – so obsessed with his own life that he hadn't been able to look after his little sister. He sank onto another chair and stared at the cracked hospital floor.

He heard her footsteps first; saw the high heels of her black boots next, the hem of her green coat. He looked up. Marnie was standing in front of him. At first he couldn't speak. His voice was lost inside him. All he could do was shake his heavy head until the words came.

'She's dead,' he finally whispered. 'It's my fault – she's dead.'

'No, it's not your fault, Lewis.' Marnie kneeled down next to him, bringing her tear-stained face close to his.

'I should have looked after her,' he whispered.

'She needed proper help ... the way things were with your mother and all that stuff to do with Uncle Howard ... Lizzie was very unhappy.'

What was Marnie talking about? What had Uncle Howard to do with any of this? Lewis felt a sudden flare of rage, that she should see him so exposed and vulnerable. 'What are you talking about?'

'On the way back to my flat she was talking a lot ... about what happened. She never got over it.' Marnie reached out to take his hand in hers. 'It's not your fault.'

What was she telling him? That she knew his sister better than he did?

He pulled his hand away from her. 'Go away! Leave me alone!' His voice burst out of him with such violence that Marnie wobbled back on her heels.

'Lewis, please, I want to help you,' she said.

'I don't need your help,' he hissed. 'If it hadn't been for you my sister would still be alive right now.'

'It was an accident,' Marnie told him, her face drained of all colour. She looked so pale she might faint. 'Lewis, please, you know I love you.'

He took the treasure of those words and threw them right back at her. 'I don't care,' he said. 'I can never forgive you. Never. Go away.'

Lewis could see that she was fighting back tears. But he couldn't stop hurting her; it took him away from his own grief.

'You shouldn't be on your own,' she said.

'I'll decide what I need right now. Just get out of here – get away from me.'

His voice was rising, and people were looking over at them. He could see two small points of red on each of her cheeks. He wasn't sure what they signalled: embarrassment, hurt, anger?

'If you need me, Lewis, you know where to find me.'

She looked at him for a long moment, her blue eyes brimming with sorrow. Then she turned and walked away, in that green coat, through the swing door and out into a London downpour, the rain enfolding her, taking her away from him.

He never saw her again.


## SKERRIES TO MAYO, EASTER SUNDAY, 26 MARCH 1989

He could hear that rain again. The pounding of it on the hospital porch, the sheer violence of it, as if Lizzie's rage was being released. He pulled back the sheets and got out of bed, walking over to the window and opening the curtains. He stared through grey swathes of rain down at the windswept beach below. Waves crashed upon the wet sand. It was a picture of desertion apart from one lone figure walking by the sea. He watched as she walked back along the strand towards the hotel, her dark hair swirling around her, hunched over as she pushed against the wet wind. She had to be soaking, but she didn't seem to care. He watched her walk with such determination. Sometimes people were not what they seemed. His memories of Marnie had been of a strong woman with monumental drive who had said that she loved him. Despite this she had not stayed with him in the hospital that day. How could he have expected her not to walk away when he had blamed her for Lizzie's death?

As Lewis watched Joy striding along the beach, against the rain, against the wind, walking into the unknown on the other side of the world he wondered if Joy would have done the same as Marnie. Would she have walked away that day, or would she have stayed in the hospital with him and taken his blame and rage?

★

Joy hadn't slept well. The whisky had made her restless, and what sleep she did get was full of nightmares. She dreamed that her father was still alive but sick with the cancer. She had to find a cure and time was running out. She didn't know what to do and was filled with a sense of her own failure to help him.

She'd woken up devastated with the realisation that it

was a dream and her father was already dead. She was too late.

Afraid to go back to sleep and dream the same dream, she lay awake watching the hours tick by, the light changing in the room from gloaming darkness to a dusky, hopeless dawn.

Joy stared out the window Lewis had left with the curtains open for her, watching a patch of sky change a thousand shades of grey. She could hear the wind whipping the hotel, the rain hammering against the glass. She shivered under the covers, not knowing what to do.

In the sober light of morning she was mortified by her forwardness the night before. How could she face Lewis after she had thrown herself at him? She was a desperate woman, a pathetic creature that husbands cheated on and other men rejected. She considered leaving before he got up. She had no idea how to get to Ballycastle in County Mayo, but she could ask in the hotel lobby where she could take a bus to, or if there was a train out of this little seaside town. Lewis had promised he would drive her, and still she longed to see him one last time, even if it was embarrassing. Before she had kissed him she had been looking forward to their road trip together. Now she had ruined everything. What had she been thinking of, jumping on him like that?

She winced at the memory of him stopping her as she unbuttoned her pyjama top. Their night in the desert had been a one-off. They'd agreed that. He was in love with another woman, and she was supposed to love her husband.

Just because she now knew that Eddie had cheated

on her, did that mean she had stopped loving him? You couldn't just switch it off, could you? You tried to work it out together and repair the marriage. How could she let all those years together count for nothing? She needed to find their love again.

But what if her suspicions were correct and Eddie had cheated on her multiple times? How could their love survive such extensive betrayal? Every time she thought of Eddie, she thought too of her night in the desert with Lewis. It had been intoxicating. As if the two of them were in this cocoon of sensuality, of wanting to give pleasure with no expectation. Eddie had never made her feel like that, and she wanted to experience it again, though her desire was against all reason or logic.

Unable to lie in bed any longer, she got up and made straight for the window. Despite her pounding head and her confused heart, she was uplifted by what she saw. The sea raged against the shore. She pressed her palms upon the cold glass, making handprints in the streaming condensation, and drank in the view. She didn't care if it was freezing outside or a full-blown storm, she had to be by the sea.

The hotel was deathly silent as she made her way downstairs. She wondered if it was empty apart from her and Lewis. In the lobby a young man with tawny red hair was sitting at the desk, reading a newspaper. He looked up and smiled at her. 'I'm afraid breakfast isn't served yet,' he said. 'Not until seven.'

'I was going for a walk first,' she replied.

He looked at her in surprise. 'Out in that dirty weather?'

'That's right,' she said with determination. 'Is there a door out to the beach?'

He got up and walked round the side of the lobby desk. 'Are you from America?' he asked her.

'Yes, Arizona.'

'I like those,' he said, pointing at her blue cowboy boots, 'but they're not the best for this weather.'

'I'll be fine.'

'Sure they'll be ruined,' he said with a grin. 'If you really want to go out let me lend you a pair of wellies and a mac. You're my mum's size I'll bet.'

'Oh, that's very kind.'

'It's no bother. You'll be drowned if you don't put something on. This is my parents' hotel. They always keep some stuff in the press by the kitchen.'

The wind was behind her as she walked up the beach. She felt it pushing her along, like the guiding hand of a parent on the small of her back. Despite the intense chill of the rain, the assault of the wind, she felt an exhilarating sense of relief. She had made it to the sea. Whatever came next in her life, at least she had made it this far.

She hardly cared what would happen to her now. She could not think past this day, and maybe it was just as well. She walked along the beach, looking down at the sand, marvelling at its multi-toned grain and the myriad shells that glistened at her feet. Every few minutes she had to stop and pick one up, slip it into her pocket. Mostly they were blue mussel shells, intense blue ovals fading to indigo, their insides pearlescent like her abalone shell.

The grey sky lightened until it was almost white, yet

filled still with rain. She turned to walk back to the hotel, and the wet wind slapped her cold cheeks. She pulled her scarf up to cover her face as best she could and tied the hood of the mac tight around her chin. She was glad now of the kind young man and his mum's wellies as they dug into the wet sand.

She walked right to the edge of the sea and into its frothy fringe, letting small waves splash against the side of her boots, almost holding herself back from going too far in.

She thought about her husband's betrayal. Could she really forgive him and try to rebuild their love? She had no idea what that would entail; no idea whether she could count on him to commit to her again. She was still reeling from that vision of him with Erin. In that moment, *she* had felt like the intruder, the third party in *their* romance. That's what was so shocking.

What had happened to her and Eddie? She remembered the passion of their early years. How he used to swoop her up in his arms and twirl her all the time. How he used to laugh and say, 'I am full of Joy,' every time they made love. But she couldn't remember the last time Eddie had laughed with her, and now she realised there had always been something missing in their intimacy. He had been angry, detached for years. Was that her fault? She'd thought she and Eddie were special, that their bond was timeless, but perhaps she was merely deluded, blind to the truth.

Could she live on her own? Would her husband move in with Erin – the mother of her daughter's fiancé? Joy's head spun at the horror of it. She felt sick at the memory of

Erin talking about her lover at that awful dinner party with her mean friends. The woman had actually been talking about Eddie – and all her friends would have known that! She couldn't believe anyone could be so cruel. What had she ever done to Erin?

The wind beat her back, and Joy longed to collapse onto the sand and let it carry her away, buffet her into the sea. She wanted the waves to close over her and suck her down so she could give up at last. But her body kept walking. As if it knew best.

She bent into the wind and pushed forward, her arms tight by her sides, each step taken with determination. The rain mixed with her tears and salt spray from the sea so that her cheeks stung.

'Just walk to the hotel, Joy,' she told herself. 'Don't worry about what comes next. Take one step at a time.'

She had come to Ireland on a mission. No matter what, she had to see it through.


Lewis was already seated and eating breakfast when she came into the dining room. They were the only guests there. He had chosen a table right by the window, with a view of the beach.

'Good morning. Happy Easter,' she said, taking the chair opposite him, too embarrassed to look him in the eye.

'Your hair is wet,' he said.

She touched it with her damp hand. 'There's no hair-dryer in the room,' she said. 'I was walking by the sea.'

'I know – I saw you,' he said, sounding relaxed, as if last night had never happened. 'I was wondering who the mad woman out in a hurricane was. And then I realised it was you.'

She sneaked a look at him and saw he was smiling at her. *He feels sorry for me,* she thought, her heart sinking. *I am a woman to be pitied.*

Breakfast arrived on large plates, each one decorated with a fluffy, feathery yellow chick and one small chocolate egg for Easter. Joy dipped her toast in her yolk and drank two cups of weak coffee. She already felt exhausted, and this day, one of the most important of her life, had hardly begun.

'Are you sure you don't mind taking me all the way to Mayo?' she asked Lewis as she poured herself another cup of coffee.

'Of course I don't,' he said. 'It's not that far from Sligo, just a slight detour.'

She reached over to take the jug of milk at exactly the same time as Lewis and their fingers unintentionally interlaced. She quickly pulled back and the milk was knocked over.

'Oh, I'm sorry! I'm so stupid!' She felt tears begin to prick again and tried her best to swallow them down.

'It's just an accident,' Lewis said, picking up his napkin and mopping up the milk. 'My fault just as much as yours.' But his gentle words slid off her. She felt clumsy, useless, unwanted.

By the time they hit the road the rain had abated slightly from a full-on downpour to a light drizzle. Her clothes felt damp and cold on her skin. She was wearing a shirt with a print of tiny purple violets all over, her jeans and cowboy boots, plus her leather jacket. She still didn't feel warm enough. She sat in the passenger seat of the car, shivering. Lewis glanced over at her, his hand on the ignition key.

'You look cold,' he said. 'Your nose is blue.'

'No, really,' she lied, 'I'm good.'

'It doesn't look like it.'

He got out of the car and opened up the trunk. She watched him in the rear-view mirror. He looked like he fitted in to this landscape. He had taken off his sharp black suit and was wearing an old pair of Levi's and a deep crimson sweater. His wild hair had been made even more unruly by the wind. He looked rugged, at one with his surroundings.

'Here you are,' he said, handing her a sky-blue sweater.

She felt herself colouring. 'Really, I'm okay.'

How could she have been so stupid as to not bring any warm clothes with her? She had been in such a rush when she'd packed.

'Put it on,' he ordered.

'Thanks,' she mumbled, pulling the sweater on over her shirt. It was pure wool, incredibly soft, and had a woody scent, like Lewis. She put her leather jacket back on over the jumper and zipped it up.

He was smiling at her.

'What?'

'The rain has made your hair curly,' he said. 'It's pretty.'

'Does Marnie have curly hair?' She felt like slapping herself. Why did she have to mention Marnie when Lewis was actually paying *her* a compliment?

His smile disappeared. 'No, Marnie's hair is straight.'

And, with a frown, he turned on the car and pulled out of the parking lot.

They drove in silence for about thirty minutes. The unspoken words between them filled the air. She wanted to ask him, Why did you kiss me back? Why did you stop kissing me? What will happen when you find Marnie? Will you ever think of me again? Are we really friends?

As each mile passed, as they got closer and closer to her destination, it was harder to speak. There was such tension between them. It was undeniable. Wearing his sweater was making it worse. She was enveloped by his scent, and she wanted so much to touch him, to be touched by him. She opened her purse and rummaged around, trying to find something to distract her. Her hand bumped against the last tape Ray had sent her. It was her favourite of all, a singer called Tracy Chapman.

'Shall I put on some music?' She asked.

'Sure.'

She slipped the tape into the cassette player. 'This song always makes me think of Eddie when we first met,' she said as 'Fast Car' came on. 'I mean, it's not exactly the story of our lives ... but you know he seemed so exciting when I first knew him.'

'Did he drive you around in a fast car?'

'Yeah, a Plymouth Satellite. All the girls in school thought he was so cool. Eddie Sheldon was a catch.'

'I'm sure you were a catch too.'

'No,' she said, shaking her head. 'Not at all. Everyone was real surprised when he asked me out.'

'I can't see why,' he said. 'I can't see that you weren't a catch. You're a very beautiful woman, Joy.'

284

She felt the blush spreading from her chest, creeping up her neck, the heat rising in her cheeks. Why did he have to say such a thing to her?

'No,' she said with vehemence. 'I was real chubby, and I had this terrible haircut. You know these bangs cut blunt in a straight line. Eddie could have had any girl he wanted. I don't know what he saw in me.'

'In my opinion your husband is a lucky man.' He glanced at her, and their eyes locked for an instant before he turned back to the road. 'He's an idiot too.'

She said nothing, for she didn't know quite what to say. She let Tracy Chapman's song reply for her. Despite the fact they were tootling along in a Fiat Panda, Tracy's words seem apt. Joy wanted them to go faster and faster.

She wished that she and Lewis could fly away.

★

Along the twists and turns of the Irish country roads, avoiding potholes, stuck behind chugging tractors, nipping round them between hairpin bends. On either side, banks of green fields had become a viridescent sea, populated by islands of cows and sheep. They passed through small towns that seemed to be stuck in the fifties. Lewis listed their names like beads on an abacus – Maynooth, Enfield, Kinnegad – adding them up. Each town was another step towards the conclusion of their respective searches. He felt like he was driving back in time through his old life in London, all the way to his childhood, lost in the small villages of England, not so different from this rural Ireland of the eighties, he and Lizzie to all intents orphaned. He should have taken better care of her. He should have loved her more. She had no one else but him.

He and Joy hardly spoke during the drive. He could sense how full her mind was, and he wondered what she was thinking about: her unknown mother? Eddie? Him?

Listening to Joy's music, each song presented him with a message just like those postcards. Songs about heartache, mistakes and regrets, but also hope, living for the moment, taking a risk for love. He wondered what these lyrics meant for Joy. He could hear her softly singing along next to him, but it didn't irritate him. This Tracy Chapman demanded that he listened to her words. She told him what to say to Marnie when he first saw her; that he was sorry, that he asked her forgiveness, that he loved her. There was no space for animosity or regret in their lives now. It was as simple as that.

Yet despite how much he wanted to find Marnie again, he was in no rush to say goodbye to Joy. He wanted to make this day last.

As he turned off for Mullingar city centre, the drizzle had turned to heavy rain again. It fell in diagonal lines, crossing out the road in front of him. He drove past a street of narrow brick houses and then parked outside a hotel pub called the Greville Arms on the main street; it looked as good a place as any. They ran through the rain, their jackets over their heads, into the hotel's beamed entrance, and as Lewis shook himself dry again he travelled back in time. The Greville Arms spoke of the past, with its thick red carpet and dark wood furnishings, and the hushed bar reminded him of some of the pubs he had gone to as a young man in England.

They ordered bowls of seafood chowder and two glasses of Guinness off an elderly barman with a resplendent head of white hair and matching overgrown eyebrows, dressed in a crisp white shirt and dark trousers.

'Are you here on your holidays?' the old fellow asked.

'Yes,' Lewis said, with a clip to his voice. He didn't want to get pulled into a long chat.

'Not really the weather for it,' the old man said, ignoring his tone. 'But I've heard we've a good spell coming tomorrow afternoon. You might get a bit of sun yet.'

They settled into seats by the fire. Joy was rubbing her hands. Despite his gift of the sweater she still looked cold.

'I love the way that man speaks,' Joy said. 'It's like a sing-song.'

'I hope you like the Guinness too,' Lewis said. 'You have to try it at least once.'

'I'm sure I will,' she said. 'I mean, I have Irish blood in my veins. To think I probably spoke like that man until I was two years old. My first words were Irish words.'

She stared out of the window, shivering still.

'Are you okay?' he asked.

Her hair had become so curly since they had arrived in Ireland. It spiralled in hypnotic rings around her porcelain skin, a mane of luxurious inky black tresses.

She nodded, but when she turned to look at him her eyes were wide, the blue of them unforgettable.

'I'm scared, Lewis,' she said. 'What if she doesn't live in Ballycastle any more and I can't find her? Worse, what if I do find her and she doesn't want to know me?'

'Well, I'm certain that second situation won't happen,' he said. 'You told me on the plane that she kept you for

287

two years. She must have been forced to give you up. Of course she'll want to see you.'

'But what if she's gone and I never find her?' She opened her bag and unzipped an inside pocket, took out a photograph and handed it to him.

'My real name is Joyce. And that's me the day my parents took me.'

He looked down at the black-and-white photo of a baby girl, smiling with one arm outstretched, grasping a bunch of buttercups in her chubby fingers. To his surprise he found the picture incredibly moving. It fascinated him to see Joy as a child.

'Even then you loved flowers,' he said, handing it back to her.

Their order arrived and Joy took a sip of her Guinness.

'Oh, this is good,' she said, taking another mouthful.

Lewis copied her, the dark beer slipping smoothly down his throat. He had forgotten just how great a pint of Guinness could be. He already felt fortified.

'What are you smiling at?' Joy asked him shyly.

'How much I'm enjoying this pint, and the fact that you've a little white moustache.'

She blushed as she wiped her mouth with her napkin. 'I just can't be sophisticated, can I?'

'Thank goodness,' Lewis said. 'I like you just the way you are.'

There was an awkward pause, as if he'd said something inappropriate, but surely his comment was harmless enough?

'Lewis, you're so kind to drive me, but I shouldn't take up too much of your time. You have to get on to Sligo and find Marnie. I'm holding you up.' She looked at him with a worried face.

'I can't just abandon you in the wilds of Ireland,' he said, and he meant it. He had no intention of deserting Joy to face this on her own. 'We'll see what we find out in Ballycastle and then make a decision. Okay?'

'Okay,' she said as she dipped her spoon into her soup.

'I should take a turn driving,' she suggested. 'Though I haven't driven manual shift since I first passed my test.'

Ten minutes out of town, pulled in on a deserted stretch of road, he retaught her how to use the gears. She sat in the driving seat biting her lip as he put his hand over hers and went through the shift changes. Her hand was cool beneath his, and he liked the sensation of holding it firmly, on top of the gearstick.

'Remember you have to use the clutch at the same time as the gears.'

The car bucked a little as they took off.

'Oh Lord,' she said, biting her lip so hard he could see a bead of blood welling. 'I don't know if I can do this.'

'Of course you can. There's nothing to it. I'll help you.'

He kept his hand on the gearstick, over hers, and reminded her to press down on the clutch each time they changed gear.

'First, second, third, now into fourth. And we are cruising along nicely.'

He kept his hand upon hers as they drove through Longford. He knew he was holding it in place way longer than he needed to. But she said nothing.

She looked for her big sky, but she couldn't find it. It was a country of corners and clouds. The twisting road made her dizzy. She felt like they were being hunted as they spun down the wet tarmac in their tiny car. Her heart felt like it was beating at hummingbird speed.

And all this lush landscape closing in around the narrow road. Green, green – bright, dew-laden, sparkling green. She wished she could tell her father about it. The banks of tousled grasses and wildflowers, some she recognised – buttercups, dandelions, purple irises, yellow gorse and cow parsley – swaying in the rainy squall. Behind them trees – so many different types. She saw a broad oak spread before them and felt awed by its magnificence. It forced her to stop the car. She stepped out onto the verge and just breathed all the green in. She wanted to roll in it, cover herself in its mossy comfort. Lewis stood beside her and took her hand in his. He said nothing, and she had no idea what his gesture could mean.

Strokestown, Frenchpark, the names of towns that sounded like they belonged in old English novels rather than this hidden part of middle Ireland. And then Ballaghaderreen, which she stumbled over, and on towards Swinford, a name that sounded like it was from the Dark Ages, where Lewis took over driving again.

After the empty cheerless towns, after the landscape of green fields, they drove through a different land. Open, treeless – a desert of sorts, with black, moist cakes of earth.

'This is the bog,' Lewis told her. 'Peat.'

She didn't like it. It was as heavy as the desert dust was

light. It bore down on her, and the land looked destroyed, bleak – almost raped.

'The locals cut turf,' Lewis explained. 'To burn on their fires.'

'It looks too wet to burn,' she said.

'They stack it to dry it out,' Lewis told her. 'Actually, I remember, it has a wonderful smell when it burns.'

He had been here with Marnie. None of this was new to Lewis. This landscape was clearly a memory come alive for him of a past he wished to re-enter. Yet for her, too, there was a part of herself buried in Ireland. She just couldn't remember it. Nothing was familiar to her.

In Ballina Lewis drove into the centre of the town, parking the car on the main street. He took the map from the glove compartment and opened it out.

'This is the last pit stop before Ballycastle,' he said, spreading the map in front of them on the dashboard. He tapped Ballina with his finger. 'There are two ways we can go to Ballycastle. The short way across country or the long way by the sea.'

She looked at the map, her heart rushing again when she saw how close they were to the sea. From Ballina to Ballycastle the land billowed out into the blue. She knew exactly which way she wanted to go.

It was already late afternoon as they drank tea and ate scones in a small tea shop.

'When we get to Ballycastle,' Lewis said, spreading a thick layer of butter upon his scone, 'I think the best idea is if we ask in a pub if anyone knows your mother or if

291

she still lives around there.' He spooned raspberry jam on top of the butter. 'It's a small place; someone is bound to know who she is.'

'I can't believe I'll actually find her,' Joy said, tearing the raisins out of her own scone and popping them one by one into her mouth.

'What do you want to do?' Lewis asked. 'Shall we try to find a place to stay overnight?' He bit into his scone, and she found herself mesmerised by the sight of him licking the jam off his lips.

'I hadn't thought ...' She put down her scone and twisted her napkin in her lap. She was too shy to look directly at him. 'Do you think there'll be a hotel there?'

'It's a small place,' he said. 'It's more likely we'll find a B&B. I can ask in the pub when we get there.'

'But, Lewis ...' She forced herself to raise her eyes and tried to look firm. 'You must go to Sligo to find Marnie. I'm delaying you.'

'I told you that I wouldn't abandon you,' he said. 'It's only one more day. What difference could that make?'

She didn't understand why this man was sticking by her. He had made it clear last night that nothing could happen between them again. They were friends. That was all. And yet she saw something in his eyes when he looked at her. She daren't believe it, but could he have deeper feelings for her as well?

★

He took the coast road from Killala to Ballycastle. At first the sea was hidden from them. But he sensed it, a taste

292

between his lips, a stirring in the bushes that permeated the open window, the cry of a gull as he drove by. They made a sharp turn, driving alongside a stone wall, then he rounded another corner and there was the big blue spread out before them.

'Oh, Lewis, look!' Joy cried out next to him.

How must she feel, he thought, to see such a vista for the first time? To him the sight of the western sea shook him deep into the very pit of his soul. The shore swept before them: perfectly smooth, golden sand. In the distance was the headland, its strata of rock slippery and dark with seaweed, the cliff itself topped with a verdant green icing. The sky was pillowed with low banks of pale grey clouds descending into a slither of silver horizon. But most of all there was the sea, a stretch of infinite blue. A sight that filled him with longing.

He parked the car, and they got out. There wasn't a soul on the beach. It was theirs.

A light breeze lifted the hair from her face, revealed her, and again he had this sense that he had always known Joy. She began to walk swiftly across the tufty grassland and down onto the sand. He followed her.

He stood behind her, watching as she presented herself to the sea. She was perfectly still. He could see her drinking it all in, trying to quench that thirst for her roots. He stepped forward to be beside her, and they stood in silence for a while.

'Look – where the sky and the sea meet is the clearest blue,' she said to him. 'I feel as if I am looking to forever. As if time doesn't exist any more.'

She turned to him, and her eyes were as blue as the sea.

He blinked. Joy was lit up. No woman had looked more radiant to him.

'It isn't completely alien to me, Lewis,' she said quietly. 'Something about this place tugs at me. I don't remember anything in particular, but I feel it. I've been here before.'

She began to walk along the beach, and he kept pace with her. Faster she walked until they were jogging up towards the sand dunes. She took a run at them, laughing as her legs sank knee-deep and she became stranded. He chased her up, pulling her out of the sand, and they dragged each other all the way to the top of the dune. Breathless, they collapsed onto their backs at the top, their limbs splayed.

'Whatever happens, nothing can change the joy I feel in this moment,' she said.

Joy.

It was a gift she offered him. One he had never trusted. *She's married*, he told himself. *She's the kind of woman who will forgive her husband. She's too soft and good-hearted.*

And he was here to find Marnie, to lay the ghosts of the past to rest. Whatever had happened between him and Marnie, he had to see it draw to a close. He owed her.

Lewis felt a drop of water on his cheek, followed by another and another.

'It's raining,' Joy said, sitting up.

The sky, which one moment ago had been composed of light, silvery clouds, had turned to heavy slate. There was a roll of thunder, and he saw a sheet of lightning out to sea, ruffled by the approaching storm.

'Come on,' he said, taking her hand.

They slid down the dunes together. He heard her

laughing beside him, and he began to feel giddy too. They ran across the sand as the rain pelted down upon them, but by the time they got to the car they were soaked. They piled into the tiny Fiat and sat staring out the windscreen at the flash of lightning across the beach.

They weren't just witnesses to this storm, but part of it. The wildness of nature was in them, and he was finding it hard not to reach for her, to touch her.

He glanced at Joy. She was shivering, wet through, her teeth chattering but her cheeks blooming.

'You're cold,' he said. 'We'd better change our clothes.'

She turned to him, water streaming down her face, her lips glistening. He felt a physical lurch in the pit of him. He was drawn to her, despite himself. He could see the longing in her eyes and couldn't hold back any more.

★

Wet, naked, they explored each other. It was different from the time in the desert. More measured, less impetuous. They were curled up within each other, rolled up on the tiny back seat of the Fiat, the windows steamed up to conceal their passion from the outside world. Joy was being taken back to the girl she once was. Lewis made her feel young again.

His hands cradled her breasts, his lips caressing her nipples, as he stretched his naked body over hers. She felt him hard, pressed against the soft mound of her pelvis. She wanted to merge with him. Yet Lewis was bringing his lips down the length of her body. He was kissing every inch of her from her breasts to her belly to her hips, and further still. She pushed her hands into his thick hair, her fingers wrapped by his curls, and she rolled her head back upon the seat. Through the mist of the back window she saw the blue sea rolling towards her, the sky clearing after the storm just as Lewis's tongue touched her in a place so sensitive that she could not stop herself from sighing. She had never let Eddie do this to her. She had always felt too embarrassed, convinced that her husband might not enjoy it. But with Lewis she wasn't worried. She could feel that he was deriving pleasure from her enjoyment, and it turned her on. Tiny tremors as he licked her, flicking the tip of his tongue over her clit, then stroked her with his long, elegant fingers. A part of herself that had been dormant for so many years, fallen by the wayside of her roles of mother and wife, was awakening within her again. She began to understand something about why her husband might have cheated. She had turned away from him. She had lost interest and assumed that's what happened between couples with time. When she had made love with Eddie it had been as if she were doing it in her sleep. It was as perfunctory as brushing her teeth last thing at night. Yet now she was awake again, roaring with need and hunger.

Lewis lifted his head and gave her a long look. She had no idea what he was thinking. She didn't want to consider the consequences of their actions. Instead she slid her body, slippery with the glow of their passion, beneath his, so they were almost on the floor of the car. She put her hands on his rear and brought her pelvis to meet his, drawing him to her. She wanted him to rock her, deep down to the core of her being.

# TWELVE

# *Gravity*

What had he done? The guilt sank in as he navigated the car round the bends of the narrow lane running alongside the shore. He focused on the road. He couldn't bear to look at Joy. He didn't know what to say. He was grateful for Tracy Chapman singing about what she would do for her lover. Was that what he and Joy now were? Lovers? What had just occurred was, for him, completely sponta-neous. He couldn't fool himself that it was comfort sex. He'd wanted Joy with that raw, keen, clear-headed need – and more than that, he'd wanted to give her so much, make her thrill with pleasure. What was the source of this passion?

They began to climb a small hill and the car struggled. He shifted gear. They seemed to be rising higher and higher so that if he looked in the rear-view mirror, the land slid away to their beach, a fragile crescent of gold against the blue. He couldn't resist and looked across at

Joy. She was staring straight ahead, her eyes glazed, deep in thought, her curls still wet, her cheeks glowing and he felt that pull towards her again.

Was it all a fabrication, his mind playing tricks on him? Just like he'd felt pulled towards Sammy all those years ago in London. That hadn't been real love. It had been sexual chemistry, and then a sort of companionship – two souls thrown into the same life together by circumstance. He'd married the wrong woman. He should have been with Marnie all these years, in London, running their own design agency. Was he going to let his attraction to Joy stop him from following his heart's desire again?

Before him the landscape appeared as a green shelf poised above the frothing Atlantic. He could see its ragged outline, hear the distant beat of the waves. Fragments of land had broken away, and one in particular stood apart: a tall, multilayered slice of rock valiantly defying all gravity.

This was Marnie's land. Its wildness, its rough, unapologetic edges and lush fields, its deep dark insides buried in the bog like a secret essence. All elements of the girl he had once known. The girl he thought he could never have. To whom he was now returning. And yet Ireland was Joy too, if he thought about it. It was where she had been born.

When he'd first met Joy she'd appeared to embody Arizona. An American girl in her denim and blue cowboy boots. She was as delicate and shy as those rare desert wildflowers that she so loved. And then Joy had taken him to the desert at night. She had made him look up. She had made him wonder, and he would never forget how that sky had looked. He had seen all the activity of space, understood that a star lived as much as a human, and that his dream was not so unreachable.

Lewis drove down the Main Street in Ballycastle, eventually pulling in beside a whitewashed building with fifties-style signage that said 'Polkes' in blue above the door. He took a breath and turned to Joy. 'Shall we ask in here?'

She nodded, still not looking at him.

'Remind me, what's your mother's name?'

'Her second name is Martell,' Joy said, finally turning to him, her face pale and serious. 'And her first name must be Irish. A-O-I-F-E. I have no idea how it's pronounced.'

'Nor do I. We'll write it down and show them.' He glanced at Joy again. She looked crushed in her seat. Small and afraid.

'It's going to be okay,' he said, taking her hand in his.

'Will you ask for me, Lewis?' she whispered.

They walked through a deserted shop and into a small, dark pub at the back. A few stray men sat at a single counter on the right, one of them with a collie dog sprawled by his muddy boots. All eyes were upon them as Joy sat on an upholstered bench to the left. Lewis approached the bar. The dog looked up at him with mournful eyes, and he noticed that its fur was knotted with burs. He leaned down and gave it a pat on the head. It rewarded him with a rough lick on the back of his hand.

'Good afternoon to you,' the barman said as he approached. Close up Lewis could see he was a young man, at least half the age of all the old fellows arranged around the counter. His face looked rubbed clean and was shiny in the gloom.

'What can I get you?' he asked, a welcoming smile on his face.

'Two glasses of Guinness please,' Lewis said.

'Right so.'

He watched the barman follow the lengthy ritual of drawing a Guinness, but he could feel Joy's eyes upon his back, her tension. He had to ask about her mother now. He coughed, and the barman looked up at him.

'Would you happen to know of a family by the name of Martell who live in Ballycastle?'

The barman frowned and shook his head. 'I haven't heard of any Martells, but then I'm not here that long. Married a local girl and moved from County Meath about a year ago. You'd be best to ask one of the lads here.'

Before Lewis had a chance to do it himself the barman put his hands on the counter, leaned over and addressed the group of drinkers. 'Do any of ye know of the Martells of Ballycastle?'

'Course we've heard of the Martells,' a voice from the end of the bar piped up as the owner of the collie turned to them. 'Why do you want to find them?'

He was a red-faced man with a head of wiry grey hair and sharp blue eyes.

'Actually we're looking for someone in particular,' Lewis said, taking out the slip of paper that Joy had given him and handing it to the collie man. 'I don't know how to pronounce her first name,' he explained.

'Eee-fa,' the older man read. 'That's how you say it.' He lifted his pint and took a slow sip. No one said anything.

Lewis sensed Joy behind him, holding her breath.

'Do you know her?' he prodded.

'The Martells weren't like the rest of us,' the man said. 'I knew *of* Aoife Martell, but I didn't know her so to speak.'

Joy rose from her seat and joined Lewis at the bar. 'Is she still here, in Ballycastle?' she asked the man breathlessly.

The man said nothing for a moment. Looked at Joy long and hard. Lewis could tell in that look that the man knew exactly why Joy was here. Yet he didn't let on.

'I'm sorry, darling,' he said, his voice a quiet lilt. 'She's long gone. All the Martells are gone.'

'They had land,' said the voice from the end of the bar. Its owner had slid off his stool and approached them. He was younger than the collie man, with thinning fair hair and a craggy face. 'My ma used to work for them, cooking and whatnot. But like Paddy says, they're gone now.' He cocked his head to one side and gave Joy an appraising look. 'Aoife Martell left for London years ago and no one has heard of her since. She had no brothers or sisters. Her parents, Walter and Kathleen Martell, are dead, and the house went to some cousin in America. It's all fallen apart. Abandoned. Terrible shame – it's a beautiful spot.'

'There's a house?' Joy asked.

'Oh yes, a big old house and land. It's just down the road,' the craggy man said.

'I can show you the way if you want to follow me in the tractor,' Paddy, the collie owner, offered. 'Once you've finished your drinks of course.'

Lewis felt Joy's hand clasping his, squeezing tight. She didn't need to say anything at all. He could hear her thoughts.

301

*Home at last.*

He wanted to take her in his arms and tell her it would be all right. That they would find out where her mother was, one day. But he held back. All eyes in the little pub were upon them, but more than that, he had no right to make Joy such a promise. They were passing through each other's lives. Helping each other, like two shipwreck survivors. They were a jilted husband and a jilted wife. Soon they must part again. For surely his destiny was Marnie and hers was Eddie.

★

Joy stood in front of the old house. It sent a shiver down her spine. The rain had stopped, and the sun had broken through the clouds, lifting the lead out of the sky, but still this did nothing to improve how the building looked to her.

'I'd say its mock Gothic,' Lewis told her. He pointed at the latticed windows with their pointed arches. 'Probably early nineteenth century.'

'It looks haunted,' she whispered.

'It's just been empty for a long time.' He paused. 'Shall we go inside?'

He took the lead, and she followed. They walked up the steps and stood for a moment in front of an arched doorway, with mouldings of vines along its lintel and around its edges. This house must have once been so grand. Her family must have been wealthy. It wasn't what she'd expected. She had imagined that she'd come from a poor home, a peasant's cottage, on a cliff edge, her mother barely a child herself and forced by poverty to give her up. This house told her a different story. Aoife Martell had come from a family of privilege. Maybe she wasn't the victim Joy had thought.

Lewis pushed the door open. There was a flurry of noise, and she screamed as a bird flapped past her. Her heart pounded with dread at the prospect of stepping through the doorway. So far she hadn't recognised anything. Not the roll of green fields surrounding the house that dropped down to the blazing blue sea, nor the spectacle of the old house itself, the granite of its grey walls showing through the whitewash, laden with ivy, the slate roof sagging, its chimneys stuffed with birds' nests.

Inside they walked through a barren hall, the air thick with the penetrating odour of ancient damp, into a large room to the left. It was covered in a crimson flock wallpaper that was peeling off the walls. The house was deathly cold. Joy shivered again.

Before he had driven off in his tractor, his dog at his side, the farmer Paddy had told them that old Walter Martell had died about eight years ago, and the house had been empty ever since. Kathleen's death had preceded his by about twenty years, and his daughter, Aoife, had disappeared well over thirty-five years ago.

'Can you tell me anything about her?' Joy had asked him, hungry for information. Here she was with someone who had seen her mother, maybe even spoken to her.

'Well, like I told you, I didn't really know her,' he'd said to her. 'I saw her at Mass on Sundays, but her family were rich compared to us. She went to school in England. She would never have mixed with the likes of me.'

'What did she look like?'

'A little like you, darling,' he'd replied, giving her a crooked smile. She had felt her blush rising. Was it so obvious who she was? What kind of shame was she bringing on her mother by looking for her? She had been embarrassed, grateful for the distraction of the dog barking at his master from the tractor cab as if to tell him to mind his own business and move on.

Now she stood inside a house she must have lived in for nearly two years of her life, and yet as she walked from one dark abandoned room to the next it raised no memories for her. She climbed the stairs, avoiding broken steps, careful not to put too much weight on the wobbling banister. In each room she entered, through every cracked, mildewed window she could see the sea. From all sides of the house there seemed to be a view, as if her family had lived on its own personal peninsula.

But in the last room she entered something was different. She sensed it immediately. It was the smallest room upstairs, and she could see that the walls were once covered in a vibrant floral wallpaper. Now the blooms were faded, but her mind began to colour them in. She remembered these flowers. The twisting stems of red roses, purple violets, the posies of forever-blue forget-me-nots. In this room she heard a voice. It was her own, and yet it sounded different to her. No longer the cry of the child within her, wanting to find her mother's love, but a voice of assurance. Her adult self.

*This is your room.*

She could feel it, imagine the embrace of her mother's arms around her, the scent of her, the sound of a soft lullaby. It was not a fantasy. She knew she had been loved, held, cared for. So why had Aoife Martell given baby Joyce up and run away to London?

Joy felt Lewis's hand slip into hers. The warmth of his fingers spread into her palm, through her wrists and up her arms to her heart. It made it ache. If only she could pull her hand out of his, but she would take the tiniest drops of affection from him now. His contact kept her from falling apart.

'Why don't we go for a little ramble?' he suggested gently.

They walked back down the stairs and out the front door into the light. She gulped down the fresh sea air.

'I lived here for the first two years of my life and yet I recognise so little,' she told him. 'Apart from that one little room upstairs – there I felt something – but I can't remember my mother.'

'Of course you don't remember, Joy. You were a baby. Who would?'

'There's something missing in me.' Her voice came out hoarse, broken. 'I've always felt that way.'

'Everyone has secrets from their childhoods,' Lewis said. 'Some we know, and some lie buried so deep inside our subconscious that only our instincts reveal them to us.'

'Like the way I feel that my mother loved me,' Joy said.

'You look like her, Joy – that's what the farmer said,' Lewis reminded her. 'You've changed since we got here ...'

'I have?' She couldn't stop herself from looking at him.

She traced the line of his nose, his chin in profile, and tried to commit it to memory. After tomorrow she would never see him again.

'Yes, it's like … I can't imagine you back in Arizona now.'

She smiled at him. 'Not even with my cowboy boots on?'

'Well, maybe those fabulous boots are the only part of you that's American,' he said.

'I can't deny my mom and dad. They raised me.'

'Of course not,' Lewis said. 'But why do you think your dad told you that you were adopted? He wanted you to find your roots.'

'It was his dying wish,' she said.

Lewis squeezed her hand. She wanted him to take her in his arms so much. Her need was burning through her.

They walked through an overgrown garden at the front of the house. The grass was almost as high as her waist. It swished against her, silken and coarse at the same time. Lewis led her round clusters of nettles, past huge rhododendron bushes that blocked their view of the sea. She could feel the ground sloping beneath her feet as they entered a copse of trees. It was then she heard a loud, cooing call, a relentless rhythm that almost sounded like a human voice seeking her attention.

'What's that noise?' she asked.

'It's a wood pigeon,' Lewis told her. 'Have you never heard one before?'

'I don't think we get them in Arizona, do we? But I have heard it … that noise … I know it.'

'It must be from when you were here, Joy,' Lewis told her. 'When you were a baby.'

He was giving her that unsure smile again. His eyes were sweet maple, laughter lines creased at their corners.

'So I do remember something else?' The idea of it thrilled her. She felt already a lightening in her heart.

'Do *you* think my birth mother loved me?'

'I have no doubt, Joy,' Lewis said without hesitation.

She wanted to reach up to him. Stroke that long lean face with her hands, stand on her tiptoes and kiss him. Every part of her wanted to be with him.

The silence hung between them, tantalisingly. She watched his face, tried to read it. Was he looking at her with kindness or was it something more? It had to be after what she'd seen in his eyes in the car down on the shore.

The wood pigeon cooed again and then she heard pattering all around her. For a moment she wasn't sure what it was, until she felt a raindrop on her cheek. It was raining again, the leaves catching the drops. The sun was still shining and the water looked like lines of crystal falling from the sky.

'There must be a rainbow,' he said, leading her by the hand through the trees. They walked back out onto the lawn and looked down across the green valley to the sea beyond. A field of heavenly gold spread before them; she knew them to be daffodils, a sight that thrilled her. A perfect rainbow arched above the field, each colour immaculately delineated.

'Oh, it's beautiful,' she gushed.

'Looks like we found our first rainbow,' he told her, turning and kissing her on the forehead. It was an intimate kiss but fatherly, as if he was blessing her. Despite its tenderness she felt disappointed, confused.

They sat in the tiny Fiat, facing the house of her ancestors. It was hard to imagine that this was where she had started her life. Who would she be if her parents had never adopted her and brought her to America? Would she still be living in Ballycastle, in this very house?

'What do you want to do now?' Lewis asked her, turning on the engine.

She thought of the mess she had left back home in Scottsdale. Was the wedding still going ahead between Heather and Darrell? Was her mom okay? Had Eddie shacked up with Erin? It felt like being stabbed – the thought of Erin Winters sitting in her chair, drinking coffee out of her favourite mug and lying in her bed with her husband. She couldn't face any of it.

'I don't know,' she said.

'Maybe we should stick around here for a couple of days,' Lewis said. 'Find a little B&B. Surely we'll discover someone who knew your mother?'

We? Was Lewis suggesting they stay together? But what about Marnie? And what would happen if they shared a room tonight? Would they make love again? She felt undone as it was.

'Lewis, you can't stay,' she said in a low voice. 'You have to find Marnie.'

'But I can't desert you now. We need to find out more about your mother.'

'You've come all this way to find Marnie,' Joy said, arguing against her true desire. 'What about the postcards?'

They looked at each other. She had never thought it possible that you could search so deeply for answers in someone else's eyes and still find them unfathomable.

'I don't want to leave you,' he finally said in a small voice.

Back in Ballycastle they found a B&B on the outskirts of town. It was run by a Mrs McIntyre, who seemed to be constantly distracted by her flock of five fair-haired children. There was only one double bedroom available. They booked in as Mr & Mrs Bell. After all they were both still wearing their wedding rings. There was no one here who knew them to notice. They could be husband and wife.

Joy Bell.

It sounded like the name of a flower, not a person – a joybell. What colour was a joybell? Yellow? Pink? Purple? No – red, the brightest shade a hummingbird could seek.

Joyce Bell had more substance. Joyce. She whispered the name to herself. Somehow a Joyce seemed like a whole different person from a Joy. More important, the two additional letters at the end grounding the lightness of Joy, the simplicity of her childish name.

After they'd put their luggage in the room, they walked back into town to get some food in Polkes pub. Lewis suggested they talk to the younger craggy man they had seen at the bar earlier. After all, his mother had worked for the Martells. Maybe she knew where Aoife Martell was now.

'I'll go change this five-pound note into coins and call Heather first,' Joy said as they passed the phone box. 'I want to check she's okay.'

309

Lewis brushed her hand with his. 'I'll see you in the back of Polkes.'

She felt a flutter in her stomach as she watched him walk away. What would happen tonight? If she spent the whole night in Lewis's arms in a double bed, she knew there would be no going back to her old life with Eddie.

The bell on the shop door tinkled as she walked inside. The shop was empty apart from an old man sitting behind the counter, smoking a pipe and wearing what looked like a hand-knitted fisherman's sweater.

'Good evening to you,' he said.

'Hello,' she replied, trying to keep her accent as soft as possible.

She wandered around the shop. It reminded her of the old stores in Scottsdale that she used to go into as a child. The sparse choice of groceries on the shelves, mixed up with a random selection of household goods, a sagging chair in the corner with a big black cat asleep on it, and some dusty books on a table in the back. She took a look at them. To her surprise most were books of poetry. She had never read much poetry, although she remembered that her father liked Wordsworth. She picked up a slim volume by the English poet William Blake. The pages fell open and she read:

> He who binds to himself a joy
> Does the winged life destroy;
> But he who kisses the joy as it flies
> Lives in eternity's sun rise.

William Blake's joy of course was a state of being, but she couldn't help thinking of herself as being the joy in the poem. She considered the state of her heart. What she had thought was the right thing, to be bound to the one you love, was not the only way.

She heard the shop doorbell ring again as someone else entered. She was hopeful that it was Lewis who had followed her. She wanted to show him the book.

'Joy!'

She froze in shock. For standing on the shop threshold was not Lewis but Eddie. He looked like he hadn't slept since she'd left him. There were dark shadows under his eyes, and his hair was a mess. He strode the length of the shop and – much to the interest of the old man at the counter – encased her in his arms.

'Oh, Joy! I found you, thank God I found you ...'

He drew her to him, but she couldn't speak. She was motionless in his arms. Her heart, only a moment ago so pulsing with heat, with life, withdrew.

At last he released her, and they stood staring at each other. All she could think about was Lewis. What would Eddie say when he found out she was with Lewis?

Finally she managed to speak. 'How did you find me?'

Eddie grinned. Despite his tiredness, she could see his unrelenting charm beginning to shine. 'Your mom,' he said.

'But I never told my mom where I went,' Joy said, frowning.

'Heather and I worked out from the note you left that you'd gone to find your birth mother in Ireland, so I went over to see your mom and asked for her help to find you.'

Joy held the Blake book limply in her hand. She had found her birth certificate in her father's box in the garage, but she had not fully accepted that her mom had known where she was from and chosen not to reveal that information, even when she'd asked. Yet now she had freely told Eddie. She felt another layer of betrayal between her mother and herself.

'So as soon as she told me Ballycastle in County Mayo,' Eddie went on, 'I booked a flight to Ireland, got into Dublin today, rented a car and here I am ...'

Despite the charm, her husband looked different. Meeker, less sure of himself. She could see that his hand was shaking as he swept his fair hair off his brow.

'Joy, I'm so sorry –' he started.

'Not here,' she said quickly, taking the book up to the counter and paying.

Out on the street she steered Eddie away from Polkes – and Lewis. They walked up a small hill to the other side of the town.

'Let's go in here,' she said, slipping into the dark, cool interior of a stone pub called Heany's. Thankfully it was empty. It was early yet. She sat in the corner, while she let Eddie buy her a glass of whisky.

'Thank God I found you!' he said again as he sat down next to her.

It felt so wrong. She had been joined to this man for most of her life, yet now she was uncomfortable to be brushing legs with him.

Eddie picked up her hands. His fingers were dry and cold, and she felt caught in his grip.

'Joy, I am so sorry.' He looked at her with pleading eyes. 'I don't expect you to forgive me, but I am begging you to try.'

Erin. She saw it again, that moment of passion between her husband and that woman. She pulled her hands away from his. Yet surprisingly she was no longer angry.

'I know it's no excuse, but she came on to me, and ...' Eddie sighed, pushing his hands through his hair again. 'I've been so stressed trying to make as much money as possible for the wedding, and our sex life hasn't been great. I was frustrated ... and ... well, we've been together so long.'

'But that's no excuse to cheat on me,' she said. 'You could have told me how you felt. We could have done something about it.'

'Joy, when we married we were kids. I just sort of panicked imagining that I would never know another woman, you know, intimately ...'

She shook her head. 'Eddie, we're married. Don't you believe in our vows?'

Even as she said the words she realised what a hypocrite she was. She hadn't thought once about her wedding vows since she'd made love with Lewis, but then hadn't Eddie done this to her first?

'I know. I'm sorry, Joy, but losing you these past couple of days has woken me up.'

He paused, and she studied her husband's face. She knew it so well, and yet he looked like a different man. She never would have believed he could betray her like he had with Erin, and she realised she didn't really know him at all.

'Don't all marriages reach a crisis point one day? This is ours,' he said. 'We can choose to give up now or we can fight to save it.'

Eddie picked up her hands again.

'Joy, I can't live without you. It's always been you. It will always *be* you,' he said. 'We belong together.'

She had been so sure. Just a few weeks ago she would have sworn that she and Eddie were the loves of each other's lives. One of those rare couples that were almost a force of nature. She had believed all this before she'd met Lewis. Maybe her attraction to Lewis was a symptom of her marital breakdown, all part of bringing her back to Eddie ultimately?

'I don't know,' she said, her voice wavering.

'Baby, please come home,' Eddie begged. 'I'll do anything if you'll forgive me. I'll take a big vacation and we'll go to Hawaii –'

'I need to find my birth mother, Eddie.'

'Darling,' Eddie said, enfolding her hands within his. 'Don't you think it's better to come back home to Scottsdale? That's where your real mom is. This expedition of yours is breaking her heart.'

Joy brought her hand to his mouth and placed her fingers upon his lips to silence him. 'Stop it,' she whispered.

Why did Eddie suddenly seem to care so much about her mom? The two of them had never got on.

He kissed her fingers and she removed her hand quickly.

'But that's where your real family is, darling, not in this depressing town in the middle of nowhere,' he said, 'where it rains all the time. Hasn't stopped since I got here. You are sunshine, Joy. That's where you belong.'

'But I'm beginning to remember things, Eddie. It's important...'

'What's more important is that I can't live without you, and Heather really needs you.'

She felt a pinch of anxiety at the mention of her daughter. 'What's up with Heather?'

'She's called off the wedding, says she's heading off to San Francisco with that crazy friend of hers, Carla. You have to talk some sense into her.'

'She doesn't love Darrell.'

'Those kids are mad about each other,' Eddie said, frowning. 'Besides I've spent a fortune on the wedding.'

'They're not in love, Eddie. Not like we were. And, really, don't you think it might be a good thing if we aren't connected to –'

She could not say Erin's name. It was toxic in her throat. 'To *her* – you know, Darrell's mom.'

The blood rushed to Eddie's face. She believed it was the only time she had ever seen her cool cowboy husband blush.

'Yes,' he muttered, looking down at the table. 'I guess that would be a good thing. I just don't know what's got into Heather.'

'She's grown up, Eddie. She's being true to herself.'

Her husband nodded, pensive. She saw him really listening to her.

'I guess you're right.' He looked up and gave her a pleading smile. 'I've missed you so much, Joy. I've taken you for granted for too long, but I'm going to make it up to you, baby. I promise. I never want to lose you again.'

His words washed over her. This was what she had wanted to hear her husband say to her for years.

'It's okay,' she said quietly.

'You'll forgive me?' he asked, his face hopeful.

'Just get me another glass of whisky.'

He got up and planted a wet kiss on her cheek before going up to order at the bar. She watched him chat to the barman before striding out the back door to the restroom. His confidence had clearly returned, but she was still in complete shock. She had to get up and go. Lewis must be wondering where she was by now. She'd been sitting with Eddie for over thirty minutes, yet she was stuck to the seat, waves of anger at Eddie sweeping through her.

Just as Joy was about to get up and leave while Eddie was in the restroom, the door of the pub opened and in walked Lewis himself. She bit her lip at the sight of him. She tasted blood, fear, yet a rush of desire too.

How appealing Lewis looked to her in that moment. His hair was dripping with rain, as if speckled with tiny diamonds, and his dark eyes looked as deep as those black bogs they had driven through today.

'Hey, there you are!' he said. 'I've been looking for you all over town. What are you doing in here?'

'Lewis … I …'

Behind him she saw Eddie coming out of the restroom. She began to panic.

'Lewis … something's happened … I …' She didn't know how to start, but before she had a chance Eddie was at the table, her glass of whisky in his hand.

'Can I help you?' he asked Lewis, his voice hostile, his whole body bristling.

'This is my husband, Eddie,' she addressed Lewis in a rush, her eyes trying to reach him with an apology.

She turned to Eddie, unable to look at Lewis's stunned face any longer.

'Eddie, this is a friend of mine – Lewis. He's from Scottsdale.'

Eddie's eyes narrowed.

'He and his wife, Samantha, are visiting relatives in the west of Ireland.' The lie gushed out of her. 'They gave me a lift here in their rental car.'

'Where's your wife now?' Eddie asked Lewis, suspicious.

'Back at the B&B,' Joy interrupted. 'She has bad jet lag, doesn't she, Lewis?'

Lewis turned to her. He was beginning to regain his composure, though his face was drained of all colour.

'Yes,' he said flatly.

'Can I get you a drink?' Eddie asked him, putting his hand possessively on Joy's shoulder.

'No,' Lewis said, shaking his head. 'I have to go ...'

'Are you leaving?' Joy asked, trying to sound normal as dread clawed at her heart. Despite everything she didn't want Lewis to leave her behind. It was insane of her to want this when her husband was sitting right next to her. Eddie had come all the way from Arizona to bring her home.

'I'm off to Sligo,' he said.

'With your wife?' Eddie interjected.

'Yes, with the wife,' Lewis said abruptly. 'To visit relatives. Tonight.'

'Well, good to meet you. Maybe we can all get together when we're back home in Scottsdale?' Eddie suggested, as if blissfully unaware.

317

'Yes,' Lewis said faintly, still looking Joy directly in the eye.

Eddie took out a packet of cigarettes and slipped one between his lips. He hunted around for a lighter.

'Do you have a light?' he asked Lewis.

'No, sorry.'

'Back in a minute.' Eddie got up and went to the bar.

'Are you okay, Joy?' Lewis whispered to her.

She nodded, blinking back the emotion. Was this her farewell to Lewis? 'Fine, yes. Good. Thanks.'

Lewis took a quick glance at Eddie, now chatting to the barman as he flicked out a lighter for him. She could see Lewis was struggling. He didn't want to compromise her, yet it was clear he was concerned.

'You're sure you're okay?' he whispered again.

'Yes,' she whispered back. 'Really, it's for the best. You have to go and find Marnie. You can't just leave that hanging –'

She was interrupted by Eddie's presence at the table again.

'Well, goodbye,' Lewis said, holding out his hand to her.

'Goodbye, and thank you,' she murmured, fighting back the tears.

She took his hand in hers, felt the sensation of his bare skin upon hers. Never again would she touch this man.

Another moment and he was gone. She was back to where she had always been. Mrs Joy Sheldon. Wife and mother. Nobody's lover.

She thought perhaps it was for the best. For even if Eddie hadn't showed up, and maybe, just maybe, she and Lewis could have made a go of it, it would never have

318

worked. Marnie would always have been a haunting presence between them.

## LONDON, 14 APRIL 1967, 10.31 A.M.

Marnie was gone. He had driven her away. Lewis sat on a damp bench outside the hospital waiting for his mother to arrive. A bird was singing to him from one of the plane trees. He looked up, but the branches of the tree were hidden by spring foliage. He twisted round on the bench, trying to see where the bird could be, but it was like a phantom, invisible to his eye. He gave up, looking down at his clasped hands in his lap, the white of his knuckles. He listened to the bird's song. He imagined it was speaking to him in its high-pitched whistling talk.

*I want you with me.*

Such an incessant chirp, the bird calling to him again and again.

*With me, with me, with me.*

He remembered his Aunt Celia telling him when he was a boy that birds always appeared when someone in the family died. A row of jeering magpies on the garden wall the very morning her beloved husband, Ralph, had passed away; a goose that had lost its flock flying above her house when her sister had died two years before; a bright-eyed robin looking in the window when she'd lost her darling nephew Philip – Lewis's father – during the war. He wondered if this was Lizzie's bird. He recognised the call of course. It was a blackbird.

Uncle Howard had taught him all of the native bird calls

319

in Berkshire. Lewis still remembered those dawn-chorus mornings, Uncle Howard shaking him awake while it was still dark, struggling to pull on his trousers quietly so that he wouldn't wake Lizzie. He would tiptoe past her as she slept. She had always lain motionless in her bed, like a dead person, and he'd often wondered if she was actually awake and just holding her breath, fooling him. Had his sister watched him in the half-light, tumbling out of his pyjamas and getting dressed? Sniggering to herself at his clumsy adolescent limbs, his gangly height and moonlit buttocks. Or had she watched in silent jealousy? He'd had an understanding with Uncle Howard that Lizzie never had.

He remembered lying in the long grass by the river, birdwatching. No Alfie the red setter, and no Lizzie, because both of them would have disturbed the birds. Just Howard and him, man and boy, down by the river, a pair of binoculars in his hands, peering at the birds careering through the first burst of daylight. This had been nature in its prime. Not the sleepy image that city folk have of the country, but how intense it really was – the helter-skelter of flying birds shooting through the air, missing collisions with expert precision.

*Quick, quick,* they were singing to each other, *no time to delay. We have to build our nests, lay our eggs, keep the cycle of life and death turning, now, not tomorrow, this morning, right now.*

Uncle Howard had pointed out the different species to Lewis.

'Can you hear that?' he'd asked him. 'Like a squeaky wheel with a puncture.' Lewis had nodded. 'That's a moorhen.'

Thirteen-year-old Lewis had listened to the chaos of sound. The birds were so tiny, like the little wren, yet their songs were loud and urgent, demanding to be heard. He'd wondered if they understood the messages within each other's songs. Had the moorhen noticed the wren? Had the thrush heard the call of the skylark? He had especially liked the sound of the wood pigeons cooing from across the river – comforting, like a mother calling her children in.

But there had been one birdsong that had always dominated – a persistent chirping call.

'That's a blackbird,' Uncle Howard had told him, chuckling. 'Oh Lord, he's desperate for a gal.'

Those distant summer mornings had been so delicious. Sitting in the marshy ground by the side of the river, the mist lifting slowly off the water, curling and burning off in the sunlight. He had smelled the sap of the land rising beneath him, how the river nourished it with her rich cakey bed. He had listened to the birds screaming their hearts out, and then afterwards they had watched the fish begin to wake. The popping of air bubbles on the river's surface. Lewis would strain his eyes and sometimes see a silver flick beneath the water. If the day was going to be hot, he had known it by the arrival of mayflies striding across the surface of the brown river, the bright blue damselflies flickering to and fro – the odd majestic butterfly and the flare of the dragonflies. It had felt to him as if the River Thames was sacred. Like a god, it had emanated liquid light.

Uncle Howard would unscrew the lid of his Thermos and they would share a cup of hot tea between them. He'd pull a slice of thick white bread from each pocket. Dry bread had never tasted so good. Lewis had dipped it in his tea while Uncle Howard took notes.

They would stay like this, locked in companionable silence, until the day had shaken herself awake and the river was flooded with sunlight. Lewis had seen all the way to the bottom of the bed, the clouds of mud as fish swam by, the strands of riverweed, drifting downstream. Then together, Uncle Howard's hand on his shoulder, they would walk back up to the house, and as they pulled off their boots, and hung up the binoculars, Uncle Howard would always say the same thing.

'Remember, Lewis, the darkest hour comes before the dawn.' He would ruffle his nephew's hair, but the smile would be gone from his eyes, and Lewis had always wondered exactly what Uncle Howard had meant.

*With me, with me, with me.*

What would be Uncle Howard's bird? He had no idea if his uncle was dead or alive. He'd not heard from him since the day they had left in disgrace, the night Lizzie had set fire to the house.

Lewis got up and stood upon the wet wooden slats of the bench, peering up into the branches, ignoring the stares of passers-by. He had to find the singing blackbird. Make sure it wasn't a symptom of the daze the sedative had put him in. He had to be sure that Lizzie was not gone for good.

He reached up and pulled aside branches, heavy with their new green leaves, and finally he saw the bird, its black oily feathers resplendent in the morning light; its beady eye seeking him out as its beak opened wide. He watched the warble of its song in its throat. The blackbird was singing a requiem for his sister: the final notes of Lizzie's brief life.

He gripped the branch and shook it, wanting to shoo that bird right out of the tree, but it held on fast, staring him right in the eye, and persisted in calling to him.

Lizzie had died because he'd failed to protect her.

It shouldn't have happened.

She had been his little sister, his only family – for their mother didn't count. No one knew him quite like Lizzie. How could he live without her?

Lewis slumped back down onto the bench, put his hands over his ears and tried to shut out the sound of the blackbird.

Marnie had said it wasn't his fault. He had blamed her, but really whose fault was it that his sister was dead?

He dropped his hands. His head was clear all of a sudden. He knew exactly who he wanted to blame.

The bird had stopped singing. He looked up, catching sight as it took off and flew away, then stood up, dusting down his lap, suddenly calm with purpose. He would not stay here to face his mother. He would abandon her in her hour of need, just like she had abandoned him and Lizzie for their whole childhood. It was exactly what his mother deserved, to lose both her children on the same day.

His body was tight with anger; he felt rigid with it, like a blade. He wanted vengeance.

# THIRTEEN

# *Synthesis*

## MAYO TO SLIGO, EASTER SUNDAY, 26 MARCH 1989

The light was sinking, and the sea was a brooding grey. Storm clouds were gathering on the horizon again. Lewis was driving towards the rain, but he didn't want to go on. He felt pulled backward, back to Joy. But he couldn't go back. She had chosen her husband.

And so she should have. What he and Joy had shared were a few random days in the whole of their lives. They would fade away. What was real was love with deep roots, like her marriage with Eddie – like his feelings for Marnie. These were the relationships that they had invested their lives in. They were what counted. He needed to excavate the past and allow himself to come face to face with it.

A crow swooped down in front of the car as Lewis drove. He felt uneasy, the blurred edges of an old memory beginning to push into his mind. He wanted to obliterate it, but it kept surging in front of him. That black crow, those shiny black feathers and Uncle Howard's black hair;

combed and greased with wax into a smooth helmet. That crow was Uncle Howard's bird.

He saw those sleek crow's feathers in a shaft of moonlight, in his and Lizzie's bedroom all those years ago. He had been excited to see Uncle Howard in their room. Had he come to wake him up? Were they going to watch the dawn chorus? Yet his uncle hadn't come near him, and something had stopped Lewis from letting him know he was awake. Instead he saw his shadowy form leaning over Lizzie's bed, his hand reaching forward. His uncle had become something other than human.

Lewis suddenly felt overwhelmed with nausea. The gloaming road swam before his eyes and he pulled in, his hands gripping the steering wheel, his heart racing. What was happening? Was he having some kind of panic attack?

He closed his eyes, but the picture was still there. Like that painting 'The Nightmare' by Fuseli – Uncle Howard crouching over his sister as the incubus. He had stared at Lewis in his bed without seeing him. It was a piece of horror, fixed forever in his childhood. Why had Lizzie never told him?

He pitched forward over the steering wheel, staring out at the storm clouds about to burst. My God, of course Lizzie *had* told him, he had just never listened to her. She'd tried to tell him the night she'd set fire to Uncle Howard's house. She'd tried to tell him the first time she'd got stoned. She'd tried to tell him when she had showed him those awful paintings. Even through Marnie, that last night of her life, Lizzie had tried to tell him. She'd been trying to tell him for the whole of her short life.

And Lizzie must have confided in their mother. That's

why she hadn't sent them back to Uncle Howard's. She had tried to protect her daughter, but not enough.

Why hadn't he acknowledged the truth all those years ago? Why when Marnie had tried to tell him had he rejected her so dramatically?

He rested his head on the steering wheel, tears he had never cried for his sister only now beginning to fall. He began to suspect that he'd always known but wilfully ignored the truth. It had been too much to accept, to see with any clarity. He'd loved Uncle Howard, and that love had made him betray his sister. Her death had been his fault.

He turned off the car, opened the door and got out. He had pulled in off the road into a layby full of oily puddles and cracked mud. On either side of the road were lush green fields populated by clouds of sheep, behind which was a wood of majestic beech trees. He could see no houses and no other people. He walked over to the metal gate and leaned on it. He felt the weight of the rain yet to arrive pressing down on him. The air was heavy around him.

How could he have been so blind?

He looked up at the sky with its foreboding blanket of mauve-tinged darkness.

'I'm sorry, Lizzie,' he whispered.

He felt a breath of wind upon the back of his neck, a stirring in those beeches as clusters of birds began to take off. The air was filled with their chatter as what seemed like hundreds of birds filled the sky, one moment disparate, the next coming together to create one weaving snake of movement above him. He could see that they were starlings as they wheeled to the left, then to the right, to fly right over him in determined formation. Inside that shouting flock of birds was all the panic, anger, guilt and regret of his relationship with Lizzie. And as he watched the birds fly away from the storm he forced himself to let go. It was far, far too late for any redemption now.

He had the urge to drive back to Ballycastle, believing that just seeing Joy's face would make him feel so much better. Yet he had to keep moving towards Marnie. He had to stop running away.

Twenty-two years. What could he possibly say to Marnie after all this time? She had been a myth for most of his life. An unattainable dream, yet now she was less than an hour's drive away. He swiped away the fear that she might not want to know him. It was she who had sent him the postcards he told himself, again and again.

He got back into the car just as the heavens opened. He watched the rain pelt down, like a shout from heaven. The ditch flooded with water within seconds, and the car was shrouded within a watery cocoon.

He saw a tiny picture of London flicker in front of him, like one of those old slow-time photographic boxes; a square of moving image, as small as a postage stamp. He saw himself and Marnie, in black and white, walking through Kensington Square. He had caught hold of her hand and swung her towards him. They kissed, in broad daylight. He remembered the spectacular abandon of this moment quite clearly, as if it had happened yesterday. He had always wanted his old life back. Could he ask Marnie to come to London with him? They weren't too old to start again. They could set up their design agency together at last. Why not?

Another postage stamp of memory surfaced, this time in colour. It was Joy, that day outside the Botanical Garden in Scottsdale. She was holding the crimson star columbine plant, her eyes the same colour as the violet shirt she was wearing, that delicate blush upon her pale Northern skin. Tiny hummingbirds hovered around her as they drank nectar from the drooping plants.

He shook the image out of his head. He had to forget about Joy.

He turned on the engine again as the rain lightened and pulled out onto the road ahead.

An hour later Lewis was heading along the coast road to Strandhill. Despite the fact he had only been here once, and all those years ago, he had not forgotten this stretch of road. To his right was the distinctive outline of flat-topped Ben Bulben dropping almost at a right angle into the sea, which appeared limitless, daunting, the surf wild and dangerous.

He drove through the town of Strandhill and pulled into the car park overlooking the sea. The rain had stopped, the skies had cleared and the sun was beginning to set, spraying the ocean with fragile pink light so different from the dramatic sunsets of Scottsdale. It was an ungodly light.

He sat in the car watching two brave surfers trying to ride the waves. His mouth was dry, his hands sticky with sweat. He was here at his destination. He took the post-cards out of his inside breast pocket and flicked through them again, reminding himself that he was not imagining this. These cards were of Ireland from Ireland and sent to him by Marnie. No other person could have understood the significance of what this hand had written to him in her neat black block capitals.

He got out of the car. He remembered that the house was very close to the sea, just back along the street a little, past the pub, but on the other side of the road.

As he walked towards it, it dawned on him that Marnie might not even live at the house. It had belonged to her parents, and they could be dead now. But he knew the way of Irish towns. It was likely that someone in Strandhill would know where Marnie Regan now lived.

He stopped suddenly, his heart in his mouth. This was it. He remembered the strange palm tree in the front garden, so much bigger now, the latticed bay window in the front of the house and the side alley with the wooden gate. This was the Regans' home.

He walked up to the front door. He was cold and hot all at the same time. He had never been so nervous in his whole life. What would he say to Marnie when she opened the door?

He rang the doorbell before he had time to change his mind. He heard or saw nothing for a moment. Maybe no one was in. Darkness was gathering in all around him, the sun having sunk below the horizon. He shivered, the wet evening air penetrating his jacket. He remembered that he had never got the blue sweater back off Joy. Why did he wish she was with him now, snug in his warm jumper? The notion was ridiculous.

He was about to back away when through the door's small glass panel he saw a light go on in the hall, the outline of a figure approaching. He stood to attention, as if he was on trial, and the door opened.

## BALLYCASTLE, COUNTY MAYO, EASTER SUNDAY, 26 MARCH 1989

Eddie had slipped into his charming persona again. Joy marvelled at the confidence of her husband, how easily he could chat away to strangers. She let herself disappear behind his chatter as she became the invisible wife once more.

While Eddie sank his fourth pint of Guinness and cracked jokes with his new Irish pals at the bar, Joy slipped out of the pub on the pretext of calling Heather and ran back to Mrs McIntyre's B&B. She had to collect her stuff and find somewhere else for them to stay. She couldn't risk being called Mrs Bell in front of Eddie.

Lewis's things were gone from the room, of course. She took a breath. He really had left her. She knew that if he and Marnie reunited he would never return to Arizona. She would never see him again.

On the back of the chair by the bed was his blue sweater. She picked it up, brought it to her face and inhaled deeply. She could just detect his scent upon it. She folded it and pushed it into her suitcase. As she did so she noticed three ten-pound notes alongside two folded pieces of paper side by side on the table by the bed. She picked one of them up and unfolded it. On it was an abstract drawing of a hummingbird hovering above her name. Below in block capitals was printed:

330

HUMMINGBIRD NURSERIES

JOY SHELDON

CREATE YOUR OASIS IN THE DESERT

She was breathless, could hardly believe her eyes as she stared at the image of the hummingbird. It was perfect. She picked up the second folded piece of paper and opened it. She had never seen Lewis's handwriting before. It struck her as refined, the writing of an artist – a mannered script. She read the letter, her hands shaking.

*Dear Joy,*

*I meant to give this drawing to you earlier. It's just a mock design. Nothing too special, and you might not like it at all. But if you do just let Doug know at the gallery and he will get you some business cards made up. It's all paid for.*

*I have also left the money for the room to give to Mrs McIntyre.*

*Thank you for everything. I will miss you.*

*Lewis*

She couldn't help feeling disappointed that his letter was so formal. No mention of the intimacy they had shared, not even one 'x' after his name. But her reason told her that of course he couldn't leave her a note like that. She was with her husband now.

She picked up Lewis's design again and read the words *Hummingbird Nurseries*, and her name in block print. It

331

occurred to her that this was an instance where actions spoke louder than words.

'I love it,' she whispered as she traced the image of the abstracted hummingbird. Her talisman.

It was exactly what she would have wanted. Lewis's gift showed her that he believed in her – that he knew her.

She sat down on the bed, her heart heavy. For the first time in years Eddie had opened up to her. She had a chance to save her marriage, and yet all she could think of was Lewis driving away in that little red car. He had said he would miss her, and she could barely imagine how much she would miss him.

Unable to face Mrs McIntyre and any awkward explanations Joy left Lewis's money on the sideboard in the hall, along with a brief note telling her they'd had to leave unexpectedly. She knew that it wouldn't be long before their hostess heard of another American woman staying with her American husband in a different B&B in town, but Joy had no other choice right now. The main thing was that Eddie never knew.

By the time Joy returned to the pub Eddie was in the middle of a sing-song with his new friends. They were taking it in turns, Irish rebel song followed by Arizonan cowboy song. She sat by the fire, nursing a whisky, and watched Eddie. It had been many years since she'd last heard him sing. All those old songs come flooding back, all the Rex Allen numbers her husband had loved: 'Riding All Day' and 'Arizona Cowboy'. It occurred to her that Eddie lived in the wrong era. He belonged back when the life of a cowboy could be the best in the world. She could see the shadow of the young cowboy she once knew, the boy she had fallen in love with. Maybe Eddie had never really wanted to live the life they had either. What dreams had he given up for her?

As he sang Eddie kept his eyes on her. He was trying to bind her to him, blowing her kisses when the song ended and the gathering applauded. But for all his bravado she could see he was afraid.

Long past midnight they made their way down the main street of Ballycastle to a B&B that they had arranged through the publican. His sister's place – a Mrs Coffey.

'I'm beginning to like this country,' Eddie slurred. 'Those guys are great company.'

'You're drunk, Eddie,' she said softly.

'So what if I am?' he said. 'I just went through the worst days of my life. Thought I was going to lose you, Joy Teresa Sheldon.'

She stopped walking and faced him in the pewter moonlight. 'Eddie, I don't know if I can forgive you.'

He trailed his finger down her cheek. 'Baby, please give me a chance. I promise I will never let you down again.'

Back in their room, Eddie began to kiss her.

'Darling Joy,' he said. 'I've missed you so much. I want you so bad.'

She searched for those feelings she had held for Eddie through the years. How could they just be gone?

'I want you now,' he groaned.

He backed her against the wall and, with his hands around her waist, he turned her back to him. Her cheek was pressed against the stripy grooves of the wallpaper. Eddie was pushing his body against hers. She could feel his erection on the small of her back. It felt wrong, but this was her husband. If she made love to him maybe her feelings would be resurrected.

Eddie reached round and began to unbuckle her jeans. She started to feel the heat of anger rather than desire. He had betrayed her. Was she going to let him fuck her just like that? What was wrong with her?

'No!' She put her hand on Eddie's to stop him.

'Come on, baby – I want to make things right again.'

'I need more time,' she said, pushing him away and doing up her belt again.

'Okay,' he said, kissing her on the cheek and making for her lips.

'I said no,' she said through clenched teeth, afraid to spill out her rage, her sense of impotence, for if she did where would it end?

She was glad the room was in darkness and that he could not see her tears. He would think she was crying about him. But she wasn't. She was crying for herself. She was weeping for what she had lost.

She sidestepped her husband and hid in the en-suite until she could hear that he had fallen asleep. Creeping back into the bedroom, she curled up in a chair in the corner of the room, lifting the curtain every now and again and waiting for day to break above the silvery Atlantic Ocean. She took out the drawing of the hummingbird design that Lewis had created for her, staring at it while she wondered what was happening now in Lewis's world. Was he with Marnie?

## STRANDHILL, COUNTY SLIGO, EASTER SUNDAY, 26 MARCH 1989

A red-haired young woman stood on the doorstep. She looked to be about twenty. She was dressed like an urchin punk: purple Doc Marten boots, skin-tight ripped jeans and a long stripy jersey with frayed cuffs and collar. Her skin was pale, a tiny smattering of freckles on her cheeks, and her dark green eyes were outlined with black kohl. She was strangely familiar. Not how he remembered Marnie, but like the echo of someone else.

She was staring at him. He might not know who she was, but he had the feeling this girl knew exactly who *he* was.

'Is it really you?' she asked. She sounded a little English, although there was a soft Irish lilt to her accent as well.

He ignored her question, not knowing quite what she meant.

'I'm looking for Marnie Regan ... sorry, Marnie Piper I mean. Does she live here?'

'That's my mum,' the girl said, her face clouding.

'Please excuse me if this is a bad time,' he said, backing away. 'I can come back later if she isn't here.'

The girl shook her head and seemed to gather herself. 'It's fine. I just didn't think you would really come. I'm a bit shocked. I'm Caitlin Piper.'

So Pete and Marnie had had a daughter together, maybe even more than one child. It hurt him to think of it, that Marnie had become a parent without him. It was an experience he would never have now.

335

'My name is Lewis Bell,' he said. 'I'm an old friend of your mother's, and I was passing through –' He paused, swallowed. His throat was so dry. 'I was hoping to see her...' he stumbled on.

'You had better come in,' the girl said.

He followed her down a narrow hall. He could hear loud music pounding from the open doorway of the living room. The exterior of the house was completely misleading. It looked conventional, your average suburban two-up two-down. Inside though he could see Marnie's unique mark everywhere from the open-plan living and dining room to the pure white walls, the modernist leather couch, the iconic sixties Egg chair, the graphic prints on the walls and the shelves packed with art books. In the corner of the room was a pile of boxes; around them stacks of records.

Caitlin pointed to the Egg chair. 'Please sit down. Would you like a cup of tea?'

He could hardly hear her over the music. It was awful, a woman's voice screeching indecipherable lyrics.

'I'm okay thanks,' he said. 'Really I'm here to see your mother. Is she home soon?'

He noticed that the girl's hands were shaking as she clutched them. She looked nervous. Despite the fact he had sat down she remained standing. She walked over and lifted the needle off the record on the player.

'I have to tell you something,' she said.

'But when will your mother be back?' he asked, feeling uncomfortable. He didn't want to be left alone with Caitlin to wait for Marnie. How much did she know about him? On the doorstep she had behaved as if she knew who he was. So had Marnie spoken about him? How had she described him?

Caitlin sat down opposite him on the leather couch. She was really staring at him, her sea-glass eyes glinting in the lamplight.

'I was very angry you see,' she said, 'when I found out the truth.'

Lewis looked at her, confused into silence.

'She never told me,' Caitlin went on.

'Told you what?'

'Do you know when I was born?' she asked.

He shook his head, a sinking feeling in his stomach.

'November the fifth, 1967.'

He stared at her. He was speechless – he could do the maths quite easily. If this girl was born on 5 November it meant she had been conceived sometime in March 1967, during his and Marnie's affair.

Caitlin stood up again. He could feel the anger burning off her. The way she moved ... her nervous energy quite clearly evoked his lost sister, Lizzie. He was so shocked by this vision he still couldn't speak.

'So that means,' Caitlin said in a soft but loaded voice, 'according to my reckoning, I must be your daughter.'

His heart leaped so fiercely he thought he might be having a heart attack. It couldn't be true. This sort of thing never happened in real life.

'No, I ... it can't ...'

'Are you going to deny it?' the girl attacked him. 'Are you going to lie to me like my mother and father did?'

He looked at Caitlin in awe. This magnificent, raging creature was his daughter.

'No, of course not. You look a bit like my sister,' he whispered. 'But I never knew. Why didn't Marnie tell me?'

'Maybe because you ran out on her?' Caitlin snapped, pacing the room. 'And my mum was proud. She was never a victim.'

Something in what Caitlin said jarred with him.

'So when did she tell you? Couldn't she have contacted me then? I mean, she found me eventually.' He took the postcards out of his pocket and put them on the table. 'She sent these to my address in America. That's why I came here.'

Caitlin bent down and picked up the cards. She shuffled through them.

'I sent you the postcards,' she said quietly.

He looked at her speechless, uncomprehending.

'I don't understand,' he said when he finally found his voice. 'What about the messages written on the back of each card. How did you know all those private things between your mother and I?'

'My mum never told me about you. I read her journals and everything was in them. She'd underlined those things you and she said to each other. She wrote about the whole of your affair in great detail.'

The heat rose from his chest, up his neck, to his face.

'Everything, that is, apart from why you walked out on her.'

He felt as if the chair was shifting beneath him, as if he was riding a stormy sea.

'I wrote those things down and sent them to you because I wanted to meet you, but I was too afraid to go all the way to Arizona on my own,' Caitlin said. 'I needed to know

338

that you wanted to come here. I was scared you would reject me ...'

Lewis felt sick. Everything he had thought to be true was turning, tilting upside down. He had a daughter, and she had wanted to find him, but what about Marnie?

'I loved my mum, but she lied to me my whole life because you ran out on her,' Caitlin told him.

The words penetrated his heart. A shiver of dread snaked down his spine. 'Loved?'

Caitlin's eyes filled with tears. He could see her struggling to stay composed, but her emotion was too raw.

'My mum's dead. She passed away just over six months ago.'

His hands gripped the side of the chair.

'She had cancer. There was nothing they could do. She was gone, just like that, in less than a year.'

Caitlin wiped the tears from her eyes. He could see her struggling, trying to stand tall.

'I only found out about you after she died – when I discovered her journal. It was written the year I was born.'

She brought the back of her hand up to her face again to sweep away more tears.

'Nothing is what I thought it was. My dad wasn't my dad. You're my father, and I know nothing about you.'

Caitlin could no longer speak. Her anger seemed to have deserted her. She covered her face with her hands and sobbed. Lewis looked on in horror. He felt her pain like a knife in his own heart. This stranger was his flesh and blood, his own daughter. He acted instinctively, getting up from the Egg chair and taking her in his arms. She didn't push him away but folded into his chest.

## Ballycastle, County Mayo, Easter Monday, 27 March 1989

Just after daybreak Joy crawled into bed, next to the inert form of her husband. She drifted in and out of hopeless sleep, but in the end she gave up trying.

She sat up in the bed and looked down at Eddie. He was still in deep sleep, lost to her. Glad, she slid out from under the covers and went into their tiny en-suite. The shower was a dribbling attachment on the end of the bath taps so she ran a bath instead.

The hot water relaxed her body, soothed her. She tried to convince herself that Eddie was right – that it was time to return to their old life in Arizona. She had seen where she had come from: the lustrous green fields, the eternal blue sea and the ruined old house. If her mother had run away to London all those years ago she had no chance of finding her in that huge city, especially as she had probably married and changed her name. It was best to give up now. Besides, how could she cope on her own, without Eddie? She had no money, no place to go, no job. She had dedicated her whole life to her family. She couldn't throw it all away now, though the idea of Eddie touching her ever again made her feel sick. She was so angry with him. How could she ever forgive him for what he had done?

Joy was the only guest in the dining room, a small glass conservatory with steamy windows and overgrown spider plants on all the windowsills overlooking the sea. Today it was windy. She drank in the view of the white-capped waves, beating against the craggy shoreline. She reminded herself to take some pictures. She never wanted to forget this wild western ocean.

'Would you like a full Irish?' her hostess, Mrs Coffey asked her.

'Yes, sure,' she said, not even knowing what that was.

She was working her way through the huge breakfast of fried eggs, bacon, sausages, beans and toast, big even by American standards, when Mrs Coffey came back into the dining room.

'Sorry to disturb you, Mrs Sheldon,' she said, 'but there's someone here to see you. Shall I show them in?'

She nodded, excitement mounting inside her. It had to be Lewis. He had come back for her. She knew it.

But it wasn't him. Instead an old lady with snow-white hair and a walking stick shuffled over to her table.

'Good morning to you, my name is Josie Whelan,' the old lady said as she took the seat opposite her. 'My son met you and your husband in Polkes yesterday afternoon.'

Josie upturned the empty cup upon her saucer. 'Would you mind if I had a drop of your tea?'

'Sure.' Joy picked up the pot and poured her a cup.

'Thank you – I'm parched. I was hurrying, you see. Wanted to catch you before you left.'

She poured milk into her tea and took a sip. 'Perfect,' she said, smiling at Joy. 'Well now, you really do look like her. There's no denying it.'

Joy could feel her chest constricting. 'You knew my mother?'

'Indeed I did. I worked for her parents for many years up at the house. I was their housekeeper.'

'And did you know about me?' Joy whispered.

'Of course I knew about you, child.' The old lady smiled at her. 'You were a darling baby. Sure I helped care for you for the first year of your life.'

Joy stared at Josie, took in her lined cheeks, her pebble-grey eyes, her wavy white hair, but she couldn't remember her at all.

'I'm sorry,' she said. 'I don't remember you.'

'Of course you wouldn't,' Josie said, clutching the gold cross hanging from her neck. 'It's a miracle you found your way back to Ballycastle. Surely an act of God.'

'Can you tell me what happened to my mother?' Joy asked, the words sticking to her throat as she uttered them. She was afraid to hear the truth, and yet she had to know. Had her mother loved her?

Josie sighed and blew out her cheeks. 'It was never supposed to go the way it did,' she said. 'You must know that your mother was never ashamed of you. She used to walk bold as brass into Ballycastle with you in the pram, head held high. If anyone so much as gave her a bad look she'd flash her engagement ring at them. It helped that her family had money. No one, not even the priest, dared put them down.'

'But then why did she give me up?' Joy asked in a small voice.

'Her father, Walter Martell, wasn't at all happy about the situation, but he put up with it because he believed your father was a gentleman and would marry his daughter when he returned.'

'Do you know anything about my father?' Joy asked the question reluctantly. 'It says he was a soldier on my birth certificate.' While she craved knowledge about her birth mother, she had no such interest in Richard Lawrence, the name on the birth certificate. It felt like a disloyalty to her dead father, Jack Porter.

'Aoife met Richard Lawrence in Gloucestershire in England, while she was staying with an aunt during the school holidays. She went to school in England, you see.'

Josie took another sip of her tea.

'Richard was an army man. He was on leave when he and Aoife fell for each other. They got engaged just two weeks after they met. I always thought it a bit hasty,' Josie sniffed. 'I believe he proposed to Aoife so he could have his way with her before he had to go off and fight in the Korean War.'

She sighed. 'Aoife came home on top of the world. I remember her showing me the ring. She was too young in my opinion, just seventeen, but Kathleen Martell was delighted, and even the old man seemed pleased.'

Joy took up the teapot and refilled their cups.

'So what happened to Richard?' Joy asked. 'Was he killed?'

'Nothing so heroic,' Josie said, looking stern. 'A couple of weeks after his regiment was sent out to Korea Aoife discovered she was pregnant. She wrote to him asking him to return. But he told her he couldn't get leave. He told her to be patient. He promised they would marry before the baby was born.'

'But he never came back?' Joy asked.

'I was told that his regiment got caught up in a nasty battle with the Chinese. Richard was injured and spent weeks in a field hospital. We were told his injuries were quite severe although not life threatening. For months Aoife didn't hear from him. She had to tell her parents about the pregnancy. Oh Lord was Mr Martell furious.'

Josie took out her handkerchief and dabbed her mouth.

'I had a bad feeling all along,' she said. 'But I said nothing. The whole family were praying that Richard would recover and return to marry Aoife. Back then it was a huge, terrible scandal to have a child out of wedlock. Especially here.'

'I can imagine,' Joy said.

'We waited and we waited. Aoife gave birth to you. Her father wanted her to go into a mother and baby home – dreadful places they were – but Mrs Martell, bless her, wouldn't allow it. Every now and again we'd hear how Richard was. He was sent home to England for rehabilitation, but his recovery seemed to be taking so long. Nearly two years. It became impossible to believe that he was still too unwell to marry Aoife. In the end Mr Martell went to his family in England. He demanded that their son make his daughter respectable. That was when he found out.'

Josie clutched the handkerchief in her lap and leaned forward across the table.

'Richard had got married. It seems that he fell in love with his nurse in the sanatorium he was sent to in England. He forgot all about Aoife. He forgot about you.'

Joy pushed her breakfast away, feeling as if she might vomit.

'There was blue murder then!' Josie said, sitting back again, almost relishing her role as storyteller. 'Mr Martell took his anger, his shame, out on Aoife. He demanded that she give you up for adoption because she would never find a husband with a child. He reckoned that if he sent her to relatives in France no one would know her sorry past. She could have a new start.'

'Is that what happened? Did my mother go to live in France?'

'That was the plan,' Josie said. 'Mr Martell contacted cousins in New York about finding a family who might want to adopt you in America. He wanted there to be as much distance between Aoife and you as possible.'

Josie shook her head, mournful now. 'Oh, I will never forget the hysterics. Aoife and Mrs Martell begged him to change his mind, and I was pure torn apart by it. We all doted on you, darling,' she said, patting Joy's hand.

Joy blinked. It seemed impossible to think that this stranger before her used to bathe her as a baby, sing her songs, rock her to sleep.

'I could see the defiance in Aoife's eyes, and I was afraid,' Josie said. 'She wasn't going to give you up so easily, and the night before the American couple were due to collect you, she took off with you on her horse.'

Joy could see it. A moonless stormy night in Mayo, a jittery black stallion, Aoife struggling to mount the horse, her baby girl wriggling in her arms. A desperate young mother with nowhere to turn.

'I don't know what she was thinking,' Josie said. 'She had nowhere to go. No money, no life anywhere else. How could she look after you if her own father refused to help her?' Josie paused. 'Still I refuse to believe what everyone else says.'

Josie leaned her elbows on the table and looked Joy squarely in the face. 'That's why I came to tell you the true story today. I was afraid that you might hear different from someone else.'

'Thank you,' Joy whispered. 'But what does everyone else say?'

Again she saw an image of her mother, a faceless ghost, on her big black horse. It made her shiver, her age-old dread of horses resurfacing.

'They say that she was possessed, that she put you up in front of her on her horse and rode straight towards the cliff edge. They say that she was going to ride her horse into the abyss, throw the both of you off the edge. But I can't believe Aoife would do that.'

Joy could hear the angry sea bashing against the rocks. The call of the ocean, as her mother must have heard it.

'Whatever happened, the horse reared and threw you off before you even got to the cliff. They found Aoife cradling you in her arms, beside herself with fear that she had done you damage. But you were fine. Right as rain. Tough, like all the Martells.'

Josie smiled at her and patted her hand again, took her fingers in her own.

'The next day the American couple arrived. Aoife wouldn't even leave her room to say goodbye to you. She was broken, you see. I think she thought you were better off without her, Joyce.'

Joyce. Her real name. She thrilled at the strangeness of someone calling her by it.

'The night after you left, Aoife disappeared. We never saw her again. It broke her mother's heart.' Josie sighed. 'Kathleen died a year later, and it broke old Mr Martell's heart too, but he refused to speak about Aoife, or you, ever again.'

Joy sat back in her seat. So that was the story of how her life began. It was full of drama, like a fiction, an adventure with people from past times. She couldn't quite believe it.

'Did you meet the American couple who came to get me?' she asked Josie after a moment.

'I did, and they were a lovely couple,' Josie said. 'That's how I knew you would be grand. I remember the gentleman in particular. We had a good chat about all the different flowers in the garden. I remember you gave him a bunch of buttercups. It looked to me like love at first sight.'

Joy nodded, feeling tears prick her eyes. How she wished her father were with her now.

'Tell me, Joyce, did you have a happy childhood?' Josie asked.

'Yes, I did.'

'Tell me, darling, about your life in America. It would make an old woman who once loved you happy to hear all about it.'

So Joy told Josie about growing up in Scottsdale. As she described her childhood, the annual Miracle of the Roses parade that she took part in with their church, how her mom used to fuss over her dress and her hair so she looked just right, the wildflower hikes with her father, meeting and falling in love with Eddie and the birth of her two children, Ray and Heather, she felt a hint of pride. She had always thought she was a failure, a nobody, but in Josie's eyes she could see that her life was something of an achievement.

At the end, when they had drained the pot of its last drop, Josie wiped her eyes with her handkerchief before pulling out a folded piece of paper.

'I have something else to tell you now. A few years ago a lady came by,' Josie said. 'She told me she had known Aoife for many years in London, and that she had been very good to her. Aoife had confided in her and told her about the little baby girl she'd lost. This lady gave me Aoife's address. She told me that if you ever came looking for Aoife to make sure to give this to you. So that's exactly what I'm doing.'

Joy opened the piece of paper with shaking hands. On it in neat black script was an address in London.

'This is where my mother lives?'

'According to that lady it is,' Josie said. 'Although I never got her name. She was Irish, lived in Sligo I believe.'


## STRANDHILL, COUNTY SLIGO, EASTER SUNDAY, 26 MARCH 1989

Moonlight streamed in through the windows as the night closed in on Marnie's house in Strandhill. Lewis and Caitlin, or Cait as she had told him to call her, had been talking for hours. None of this felt real to him, and yet every time he looked at Cait, he saw the striking resemblance she bore to Lizzie and it slapped him in the face again. He had a daughter. He imagined his sister's laughter, the amusement in her voice: 'Now that got you, didn't it, Lewis?'

348

Along with the shock, the trepidation, the joy of this, Lewis also felt grief. He hadn't seen Cait grow up, and now she was a young woman on the cusp of entering the world. Apparently he'd just caught her in time. She'd been sorting through some of her mother's things and preparing to put the house in Strandhill up for sale, and tomorrow she was travelling back to London, where she was based. She was moving in with her boyfriend and working as a waitress for the summer. She already had a place at Goldsmiths art college in the autumn that she had deferred for a year because her mother had been sick.

His daughter wanted to be an artist, just like her mother. It didn't surprise him.

Cait opened a bottle of red wine and offered to make him some dinner, but he wasn't sure he could eat anything. In the end they picked at cheese and crackers while drinking the wine. To eat and drink helped his heart slow down. Every now and again he felt a deep, intense pain in his chest as he reminded himself that Marnie was dead. He couldn't quite believe he had come here to find her gone.

'How did you find out I was in Arizona?' Lewis asked Cait.

'Your address was in one of Mum's old address books. It looked like she'd written it in years ago. I don't know how she had it.'

'She never once contacted me,' Lewis said. 'I promise I had no idea about you, Cait.'

'Do you think you would have come back to see me if you had known?' She looked at him warily.

'Of course,' he said.

'Even though my mum married my dad ... I mean Pete.'

'I would have wanted to know my own child. My daughter.'

Cait gave him a hard stare. 'It's easy to say that now, but you don't know, do you? I mean, you have your own family in Arizona, don't you?'

'I was married, but that's over now,' he said.

'No kids?'

'No.'

He thought of Samantha all those miles away and the years they had travelled together. It made him sad to realise now how they had clung to each other out of loneliness. But she had made him part of her family, and he would always be grateful for that.

'So am I your only child?' Cait asked him, looking at him with her brilliant green eyes.

'Yes. Just you.'

'Damn, I was hoping for some siblings as well.' She gave him a wicked grin before turning serious again.

'Did you know about my mum's diary?'

'No, I had no idea.'

'She kept one the first couple of years she lived in London, until 1967. She just stopped writing them then. I guess she got too busy, what with work and having a baby.'

He thought back to Marnie's little flat in South Kensington. His memory searched the bedroom, the tousled bed, the sunflower-yellow curtains floating in the spring breeze and the rainbow colours of Marnie's clothes hanging in the stuffed wardrobe with the open doors. He saw the bedside table. Was it his imagination or was there sometimes a notebook on it, pen lying across it at the ready.

'After my mum died I had to go through all her things. When I found the diary for 1967 I was curious,' she said. 'You know, because it was the year of my birth. Little did I know what I would find out.' She sighed, tugging on her wild hair. 'I was surprised that she'd only written in it up until 14 April. Then it's just blank pages.'

'That's the last day I saw your mother,' Lewis said.

'So what happened between you and Mum?' Cait asked. 'Why did you run out on her all those years ago?'

Lewis shook his head. 'It's complicated.' He heard his voice trembling.

Cait considered him for a moment, as if waiting for him to expand. But he didn't know where to begin. He had failed Lizzie, and he had failed Marnie. What would his new daughter think of him when she knew everything about him?

'Do you want to hear the last thing my mother wrote?' Cait said, getting up from the couch and walking over to a bag hanging on the back of the door. She took it down and unzipped it.

'I carry the diary with me everywhere,' she explained. 'I like to read bits of it every now and again. Mike thinks I'm obsessed, but I can't help it.'

Lewis watched her pull out a leather-bound notebook, wound with string. Immediately he felt a jolt of recognition. He had seen that diary. It had been lying on Marnie's kitchen table the last time he had been in her flat, but he had always thought it was merely a sketchbook for work.

Cait leafed through it, until she came to one page. She looked up at Lewis uncertainly. 'Do you want me to read it?'

'Go ahead,' he said, his voice barely louder than a whisper.

Cait swept her red hair away from her face as she looked down at her mother's journal and began to read. 'I went to the hospital and found Lewis ...'

Then she slammed the diary shut. 'I'm sorry, I can't do it,' she said, handing it to him. 'You read it. Later.'

She picked up the wine bottle and refilled both their glasses. 'When you read the diary, you'll see why I thought she told you she was pregnant and you walked out on her,' she told him.

Marnie was in the room with them now. Lewis could see her in that green coat. 'The last time I saw your mother was that morning in the hospital – the day my sister died.'

'I guess you were very upset?' Cait asked him.

'Yes. Lizzie was only twenty-four years old when she died. Not much older than you.'

'What happened?'

'She mixed drugs with antidepressants and had a seizure ... She was very sad, troubled; a lost soul, really.'

The phone rang in the hall but Cait didn't move.

'Aren't you going to answer that?' Lewis asked her.

'It's Mike,' she said. 'He said he'd ring at midnight. I'll call him back in a while.'

'I wish I had known Marnie was pregnant,' Lewis told Cait. 'All our lives would be so different.'

'Would you have stayed – married her?'

'Yes, Cait, I did want to marry her. I was just too much of a coward to ask her,' Lewis said.

His daughter didn't reply. He knew it would take more

352

than his words here tonight to make her believe him.

'It's getting late,' she said, 'and I have to get up early tomorrow to catch the train to Dublin.'

'Right.' He nodded, standing up awkwardly. 'Do you have family to see?'

'No, I've cousins in Sligo town, but we've already said our goodbyes. My grandparents aren't around any more.'

'I'm sorry.'

She shrugged. 'I'm used to being alone,' she said. 'For years it was just me and Mum, after my dad – I mean Pete – died. The only other person around is my godmother. I've been living in London with her on and off for the past six months.'

'Cait, you don't have to stop calling Pete your dad. He brought you up. He was your dad.'

'Yes, and I did love him, although he's been gone so long now. I was twelve when he died.'

'I'm sorry. I knew Pete. He was a good guy.'

It pained Lewis to say this, but it was true. Pete had rescued Marnie from the disgrace of being an unmarried mother in 1967. And Lewis couldn't help but be glad that Marnie, and her daughter, had ended up with a gentle soul like Pete rather than someone like George or Frankie.

'Where are you going now?' Cait asked as he picked up his jacket.

'To be honest, I don't know.'

'I think we've drunk too much wine for you to drive. Do you want to stay the night here?'

★

Sometimes when Marnie watched her daughter, she reminded her of Lewis. Cait's fierce concentration when she was drawing with her crayons, the tip of her tongue just visible between her lips; her expression swiftly transforming into a stern frown if she was displeased with what she had created. Her features were similar to Lewis's sister Lizzie though, with her red hair and lively green eyes. At times the similarity disturbed Marnie, but she knew her daughter's destiny would be brighter than her late, unknown aunt's.

Marnie still found it hard to believe that the last time she had seen Lewis was in the hospital corridor just after Lizzie had passed away. If she had known then that he would never show up again on her doorstep would she have walked away so quickly? She had believed she was in love with him. She had wanted him to marry her. Marnie could see now it would have been a huge mistake.

She had been lucky. When it had been clear that Lewis was never coming back, and it had dawned on her that she was unmarried and pregnant, one thing she'd known for sure was that she couldn't go back to Ireland. The shame, the stigma, would have killed her parents. She could have ended up being sent to one of those awful mother and baby homes and forced to have the child adopted. She had no intention of giving up her baby. It was Eva who had saved her. Eva had promised that she and George would take care of her, and Marnie had never forgotten the generosity of her good friend. Many times Eva had lied to her husband, saying that she had needed Marnie to mind her boys, just so she could go round to their house and lie on their couch when the morning sickness overwhelmed her.

Eva had also tried her best to find Lewis but had only come up with dead ends. Apparently his mother had no idea where he was. He'd just disappeared the morning that Lizzie died. Never even went to his sister's funeral. George's rage at the office had been mammoth. He had called Lewis 'the ingrate', swore he would never work as a designer again and became completely paranoid that Lewis would set up his own agency and steal his clients. But none of them had ever heard of Lewis Bell as a graphic designer anywhere else. He had vanished.

In the first few days after he disappeared, Marnie had worried that he might have hurt himself – that Lizzie's death had pushed him over the edge – but a week after he'd disappeared, his car had been found parked at Heathrow Airport. Lewis had run away, and Marnie hated him for it. Granted, he hadn't known she was pregnant, but she'd thought they were in love. How could he have left her high and dry without a word?

Now, seven years later, Marnie had come to understand that what she and Lewis had shared was not real love. It had been passionate, intoxicating, consuming, but it would never have lasted. What she had with Pete was lasting because it was built upon a foundation of understanding, respect and truth.

Pete had been there, all along, right before her eyes, yet Marnie had never actually seen who he was until Lewis had left.

Her husband was strong. He might not look it, being tall and skinny, even vulnerable with his little round glasses, but his backbone was made of steel. He was her rock.

It was Eva who had encouraged her to date Pete just a few weeks after Lewis disappeared and before the pregnancy was showing.

'I can see the way he looks at you, Marnie,' she'd said. 'That man would do anything for you.'

Marnie had seen it too. Pete had adored her. But she hadn't wanted to take advantage of him. She had been heartbroken over Lewis, in bits, a mess, and she hadn't wanted to cling to the first life raft that came along. Yet Pete had surprised her. On their third date Marnie had begun to really talk to him about design, and he'd seemed pleased that she knew so much. They had talked for hours, and Marnie had confided that she had helped Lewis out with his designs.

At Pete's request the next day, Marnie had brought her portfolio into Studio M. It was impossible to hide every-thing she had done on Macht Shavers, Dalliance Shoes and the Phoenix International Airlines pitch. Pete had looked across his drawing board at Marnie, stared right into her true heart with those steady hazel eyes of his and asked her that crucial question.

'Marnie, was it you who really created all these designs, and the corporate image for Phoenix Airlines, not Lewis?'

'We did them together.' She didn't know why she had still protected Lewis. It had been over a month since he'd disappeared, and it was clear he was never coming back.

'Marnie, tell me the truth – that's all I ask,' Pete had said. 'We have to be honest with each other.'

Marnie had thought about the baby inside her, Lewis's

child, and how she hadn't told Pete about that yet. 'Yes,' she'd admitted. 'It's all my work.'

'My God,' he'd replied, shocked. 'Why didn't Lewis tell George? We have to tell him right now.'

Marnie had panicked. 'No, Pete, he'll be angry … he doesn't want to have a woman designer.'

'What are you talking about?' He had stared at her, his eyes huge behind his glasses. 'He's in a fury because we're about to lose the Phoenix Airline job because Lewis left. If you can do it instead, it means you'll save the day. I don't think your sex comes into it.'

Pete Piper had gone right into George's office there and then and told him the whole story. It was as simple as that. All those weeks, months, that Lewis had procrastinated had been so unnecessary. By the end of the day Marnie Regan had a new role as designer.

What Pete had done made Marnie fall for him. He had been her champion; had seen who she really was. He didn't just love Marnie for being a pretty woman; he loved her talent. And Marnie couldn't help being seduced by his admiration. She had known she could no longer deceive him. The next evening, over a celebratory dinner, she had told him she was pregnant. He hadn't batted an eye.

'Lewis might have abandoned you, Marnie,' he'd said. 'But I never will. I've loved you from the first day I met you, and I will never stop loving you.'

He had proposed to her there and then.

Pete had been true to his word. He and Marnie had been married seven years this August, the happiest years of her life. She had fallen in love slowly, unravelling like thread that had been wound tight around her heart, and Pete was the most devoted father to Cait. They had hoped for more children, but Pete had never expressed the need to father his own. 'Cait fills my heart,' he'd told Marnie. He adored her – which was why Marnie didn't understand what he'd done, though she guessed it was all to do with Pete's belief in the value of honesty. To never sweep anything under the carpet.

Last night, as she and Pete had been sitting outside in their tiny garden in Putney, sipping on chilled white wine and relaxing after a tough day at Studio M, her husband had handed her a slip of paper.

'I know where Lewis is,' he had said, for once awkward. 'That's his address.'

'Lewis Bell?'

It had been years since they had mentioned him to each other, although Cait was a living, breathing reminder.

'My friends, Dylan and Rachel, ran into him when they were on holiday in Arizona.'

'Lewis lives in Arizona?' Marnie had asked Pete in shock. The American west was the last kind of place she'd expected Lewis to live. She'd assumed that if he'd gone to America, it would be to a city, like New York or Chicago.

'He works in an art gallery. Dylan just mentioned this English guy called Lewis who helped them pick a picture. They talked about design, and he said that he'd worked as a graphic designer in London in the late sixties. It piqued my curiosity so I did some research and found out that there *is* a Lewis Bell living in Scottsdale, Arizona and working at the Langely Gallery.'

'Why are you telling me this, Pete? I don't ever want to see him again.'

'I would hope not.' Pete had leaned forward and given Marnie a gentle kiss on the cheek. 'He's married, you know. His wife is called Samantha.'

'Bully for him,' Marnie had said, knocking back her wine. 'But I really don't care about Lewis Bell any more.'

She'd stood up, for once annoyed with her husband. Why did he have to rake up the past?

'Marnie,' he'd said softly, reaching out for her. Reluctantly she had let herself be pulled onto his lap. 'Darling, I'm not giving you this address for you but for Cait. One day she might want to know who her real father is, and where he is.'

'No,' Marnie had said, 'you're her dad. I don't ever want her to know the truth.'

'Are you sure?' he'd asked her. 'Remember what you always tell me – the truth eventually comes out.'

'Not this time,' Marnie had said with certainty. 'Only you, Eva and I know the truth, and none of us are going to tell Cait – ever.'

Marnie had started to scrunch up the piece of paper, but Pete had put his hand on hers to stop her.

'Just put it in your address book. You never know.'


## STRANDHILL, COUNTY SLIGO, EASTER MONDAY, 27 MARCH 1989

Lewis woke in the early hours. His T-shirt was drenched with sweat, his mouth so dry he was almost choking. Where the hell was he?

He took a swig of water from the glass by his bed, and

as his eyes adjusted to the darkness, he could make out an unfamiliar wardrobe and row upon row of stuffed bookshelves opposite the bed. The evening came back to him. He put his hand to his heart as he remembered he was in Marnie's house. He was shocked that he was here. That in the room across the hall was a young woman who was his daughter. His life as he knew it was over. The secret dream of Marnie that he had clung to for years was gone.

He lay in bed, trying to still his frantic heart. Apart from the sound of the sea in the distance, all was quiet. Moonlight spilled through the curtains, illuminating the end of the bed and plunging the rest of the room into deeper shadows.

He hadn't found Marnie in time. Lewis closed his eyes, his chest tight with regret. What would Marnie have looked like now? He knew she would have aged well; she would still be beautiful.

Last night he had been unable to sleep, reading Marnie's diary for hours. In it Marnie had written that she had wanted him to marry her. Yet he had run away, and his flight had lasted the rest of Marnie's life.

He turned on the beside lamp, picked up her journal and read her words yet again:

> *I want him to ask me to marry him but not because I'm pregnant, not because he should feel sorry for me, but because he recognises what we have. Eva says I should tell him straight out that I'm having his baby. She says I have to make him marry me. I know she's only concerned for my welfare, but I don't want Lewis to be forced. I will not be pitied. Eva tells me that love is a serious business.*

*She says that unplanned pregnancies are a consequence of the gravity of love. A sobering slap in the face of passion. Yet when she uses that word – gravity – I think of it as a power, a force that you cannot deny. I want to trust in nature, or science. If we are meant to be together then the gravity of our love will bring us together.*

*I wish we were back in Ireland. It was so magical that time together. No wonder we made a child. If only he can see what we are, what we could be. It breaks my heart. That's why I want him to tell George about me. If he can put me before him then I'll know he loves me.*

The diary fell out of his hands as grief tore through Lewis's body. He shuddered, and a tear slipped down his cheek. Marnie was dead. And he had lost Joy. It was the same cruel cycle to his life.

Just as he should have gone to Marnie's flat from the hospital and into the comfort of her love, he should have stayed in Ballycastle and confronted Joy's husband. He should have fought for her.

Yet if he had stayed, Lewis would never have come to Strandhill and found his daughter.

He considered the peculiar symmetry that he and Joy were part of. Him and his lost daughter. Her and her lost mother. It didn't feel like it was over yet.


LONDON, 14 APRIL 1967, 11.21 A.M.

Lewis thrashed his MG down the morning streets like a maniac. He was on fire. His London had turned into hell.

361

It had always been his and Lizzie's city. When they had come to London they had a found a home of their own. No more begging at the table of some relative of their father's in the middle of nowhere. In London they had been free, because they were no longer children. They could do as they pleased. But his sister had gone too far – so far it had killed her.

He screeched to a halt at traffic lights on Bayswater Road. He looked at himself in the rear-view mirror and was shocked by his own reflection. Without his easy smile he looked quite different. Not so handsome, yet more significant. His face was white with fury, and his brown eyes were almost black, the pupils swallowing the irises. He tasted metal in his mouth.

He found the street where Jim lived no problem, his fury guiding him there. He abandoned the car at the end of the road and set off on foot. Everybody was on their way to work for the day, surging forward, like the incoming tide – like he was walking against the whole world. No one was going his way.

The house stood before him: monolithic portico with white pillars, black iron railings and large sash windows. The curtains were still drawn, and the full milk bottles had not been retrieved from outside the door. He picked up a gold top, pierced the foil with his finger and swallowed down a mouthful of milk and cream. He was a warrior drinking blood before battle. Lewis had never been a fighter, had never understood that part of being a man. He was one of the new generation of young men who believed that if there ever was another war, it would be beyond men fighting men; it would be over in a couple of minutes. The whole of London wiped out by an atomic bomb. Lizzie had talked about that often.

Lizzie.

That big white house was where he had left her. It was the place where she had spoken to him last. He clenched his fists, tightened his jaw and banged on the door.

He waited, banging again, but no one answered. Then a curtain flickered. Someone was inside, watching him, hoping he would go away. He walked back down the path onto the pavement and stared up at the house. Again he could see movement behind the curtain of the window on the first floor, but the door didn't open.

The house was on a corner so he walked round it, his hand trailing the rough red-brick wall running the length of the street. He stood on his tiptoes and peered over the wall. He could see an overgrown garden and the back of the house. He looked both ways to check no one was coming and slipped over the wall.

A cat was slinking through the tall grass, its black fur glossy against the emerald green. It followed him as he pushed aside an overgrown blackberry bush, not caring about the pinpricks of blood on his bare hands. Then it jumped onto the lid of a bin and eyeballed him, as if it knew what Lewis was up to. He climbed some broken stone steps up to the back door and tried the handle. It opened.

He walked into a back kitchen. There was a smell of fried onions lingering in the air, and the sink was full of unwashed dishes. The tiny Formica table was littered with half-drunk cups of tea, a random crust of toast, an overflowing ashtray and a heap of broken eggshells. For such a grand house, the kitchen was a dump.

He went into the hall. A slice of daylight from a window on top of the front door lit the way for him, and he paused at the bottom of the staircase, his hand gripping the banister before he crossed the hall and carefully pushed a door open. The curtains were shut, and the room was almost dark. The embers of a fire still glowed in the grate, and the room was hot and stuffy. It smelled strongly of stale cigarette smoke and cannabis.

He peered into the gloom. There could be someone in here, crashed out on the floor, but as his eyes adjusted he could see that the room was empty of people. He flicked the light switch, which shed an unflattering light across the messy room. It looked like a drug den. Cigarette papers were scattered on the coffee table, along with loose tobacco. There was an exotic hookah pipe placed in the middle of the table, its pipe curled around the base. There was no such thing as a couch in this sitting room, for the floor was covered with cushions, of various sizes and colours. There were incense sticks stuck in holders, a large Persian rug and heavy mahogany furniture. A large wooden bowl sat on a side table by the fireplace, next to an antique silver cigarette box.

The owner of this house had more money than taste, for everything about this room was offensive to Lewis's modernist sensibility. Worse than anything was the painting now hanging in front of him. He cried out; he couldn't help it. It was horrific to see his sister in this pose, naked, smiling at him.

He ran across the room, slipping and sliding on the cushions, reached up and took the picture down. Then he punched his hand through the canvas, right through

Lizzie's stomach and ripped it down the length of the picture, through her exposed thighs, right down to her toes.

'Hey, what are you doing?'

Lewis spun round, ready to fight, but behind him was the girl he'd met yesterday – Sammy. He hadn't even heard her coming into the room. She was practically naked, apart from a tiny white T-shirt, which just about covered her backside. Her hair was all over the place, and her eyes were hazy and slightly unfocused.

'Do I know you?' she asked him in her soft American accent, seemingly unperturbed by Lewis's demented destruction of the painting.

'I'm Lizzie's brother, Lewis.' He pushed his fist through the canvas again – tearing through Lizzie's torso this time.

'You mean Elizabeth?' the girl asked.

'We met yesterday. You're probably too stoned to remember.'

'I remember.' The girl stepped forward, and stood right next to him.

'Do you want me to put the pieces you've ripped into the fire?' she asked.

He stopped what he was doing for a moment. Sammy was smiling at him. He could tell she was completely out of it, yet he was glad of her solidarity.

'Sure,' he said.

Sammy knelt down by the fire and started feeding pieces of Lizzie's painting into it. At first it smouldered, but then it suddenly flared up.

He had reached his sister's face, but now he didn't know what to do. He couldn't rip it up. Without the naked body attached to it, her expression looked joyous. He tore around Lizzie's head, carefully, in a circle. Then he folded the piece of canvas up and shoved it in his pocket.

'What the fuck are you doing?'

A voice boomed out behind him. Lewis turned round. Fear and fury conflicted within him as he faced Jim, the man who had bought his sister's painting – and given her those drugs. He was the person Lewis had chosen to blame for her death.

Jim stood before him, dressed in a crimson bathrobe. He wasn't tall, but he was well built, stocky, with a battered face. He looked nearly twice as old as Lewis.

'This is Elizabeth's brother,' Sammy piped up from the fireplace.

'I don't care who the fuck you are, what are you doing in my house, destroying my property?'

'It's my sister.' Lewis's voice erupted out of his mouth. 'And you can't have her.'

He picked up the frame of the now destroyed picture and smashed it on the ground.

'I paid for that,' Jim yelled back. 'That cost me money, man. You can't just come into someone's home and destroy something that belongs to them.'

Lewis walked up to the American so that they were eye to eye. 'Why not?' he challenged. 'You destroyed my sister.'

'Hey, I done nothing, man. Your sister's a junkie slut. I didn't make her that way.'

'Take that back!' Lewis screamed, his spit spraying the man's sneering face.

'No. She was always begging me to give her stuff. She'd

366

fuck me just to get more dope. I even paid for some of that picture with drugs.'

Lewis couldn't hold back any longer. He grabbed Jim's bathrobe with both hands and tried to shake him. But the man was an immovable block in front of him.

'You killed her!' Lewis yelled at him. 'Lizzie died this morning, and you killed my sister.'

'Fuck you, man.' Jim swung forward and punched Lewis in the face. He went flying backward, an arc of blood from his nose spraying the room as he landed on his back. He knew he couldn't win this fight. The American was tougher and stronger than him, yet he scrambled to his feet and launched himself at the other man as if he was entering a rugby scrum. He grabbed Jim by the waist and tried to pull him down, but the American just thumped his shoulders and Lewis crumpled beneath the impact.

He tried to get up again, but Jim kicked him down. 'Fucking pussy.'

He could hear Jim laughing at him and Lewis felt a crack in one of his ribs as Jim kicked him again and again. Pain seared through him, but it was good to feel this pain. He was doing something for Lizzie.

Curled up on the floor now with Jim beating the life out of him, he closed his eyes and waited for Lizzie to come to him – always together the two of them, on every new threshold. Yet she didn't come. Instead he heard a scream followed by a loud crash, and the kicking stopped.

He opened his eyes to see Jim swaying above him, blood trickling down his face, and then he fell with a thump onto the floor next to him. And there was Sammy, a heavy wooden bowl in her raised hands. Tears were streaming down her stoned face. She was saying something, but it was hard to make out the words.

Lewis unwound his broken body, got onto his knees and then stumbled to his feet. He looked down at Jim. He was out cold, but alive. Lewis could see his chest rising up and down.

'You could have killed him.' His voice came out in a hoarse whisper.

She was still standing, arms aloft, holding that heavy bowl and teetering on her feet. Lewis took the bowl out of her hands and put it on the table, and she stared at him, uncomprehending, tears still streaming down her face.

'Elizabeth,' she whispered in a cracked voice.

Then she began to shake. He put his arms around her shoulders and led her out of the room. In the dark hall, she clung to him, clawing at his shirt. Her face was so close to his he could feel her tears wet on his neck.

'It'll be okay,' he said, but he wasn't so sure. The anger that had fed him all morning had dissipated. If Sammy hadn't stopped him, Jim might have kicked him to death.

Sammy tucked her hands into his trouser pockets and leaned into his body.

She pressed her mouth to his chest, but he could still hear her muffled words. 'Jim killed Elizabeth.'

'He didn't actually kill her.'

She pulled her head back. 'He gave her the speed. She said she wasn't allowed to take it because of her medication, but he made her.' Sammy tugged at Lewis's sleeve. 'I told him not to, but he laughed at me.'

Lewis tried to disentangle himself, but the American girl was stuck to him like honey. As he looked down at her straggly blonde hair, her tanned face now pale from fear and her big dark eyes, he imagined she was Lizzie, beseeching him one last time.

'Don't leave me here,' she said. 'Take me with you.'

He took her out of the dark hall into the kitchen. Sunshine was belting through the window, illuminating the squalor of the room as he sat her down on one of the chairs. She was shaking uncontrollably, her teeth chattering. He took a cardigan off the back of one of the chairs and put it round her shoulders.

'You need to get dressed, and we need to get out of here before Jim wakes up.'

Sammy staggered over to the kitchen counter and opened one of the drawers. She began pulling out tons of black-and-white photographs, throwing them onto the table in a pile.

'We gotta take these with us,' she said, her teeth chattering.

Lewis picked one of the photographs out and what he saw made him want to vomit. It was Lizzie and Sammy, the two girls naked, wanton, with dog collars around their necks. He scrunched it up in his hand.

'Jim used to make us,' Sammy said. 'He called us his bitches.'

She was shaking as she spoke.

'I wish you'd killed him now,' Lewis said, his own voice so cold it shocked him.

He drove Sammy to her flat in Camden and they staggered up the stairs together like two drunks. His whole body was aching with the beating Jim had given him. While Sammy collapsed onto the bed, he stumbled into her bathroom and looked at himself in the mirror above the sink. He had a broken nose and a cut lip, but apart from that, his face wasn't too damaged, though when he took off his shirt his chest was covered in large purple bruises. As he touched them tentatively the door slid open. Sammy stood in front of him, looking at his damaged body.

'I thought you were sleeping,' he said to her.

'I can't sleep,' she said. 'I feel okay now, but look at you…' She touched his chest with one of her fingers. He flinched in pain. 'Sorry,' she said. 'Here, it's easier if I help you.'

She made him sit down on the edge of the bath while she took some cotton wool and Dettol out of the bathroom cabinet.

'I think you might have cracked a rib,' she told him.

'I have to get back to the hospital,' he said, squeezing his eyes shut. 'Lizzie.'

'I can't believe she's dead,' whispered Sammy.

He should be on his way back to meet his mother. He needed to organise a funeral for his sister.

'Oh God, Lizzie,' he heard himself sob, the pain of his loss welling up inside him again.

'Just take it easy,' Sammy said, cradling his head against her chest. 'You can stay here as long as you want.'

He hadn't gone back to the hospital. It had felt like the circumstances of his sister's death had marooned Lewis and Sammy in her flat in Camden. Instead, as they drank mug after mug of tea together, Sammy told him about the circumstances surrounding Jim's pornographic pictures of herself and Lizzie. She described orgies in the London house. All the things that she and Lizzie were made to do. Why hadn't Lizzie told him?

370

Sometime during those few hours in Sammy's flat, Lewis decided that the best thing would be if he took the American girl back home to her family. He needed to rescue her. He had failed his sister, but he could still help Sammy. He would call her parents and ask them to wire the money for the tickets. Tell them their daughter needed help. They sounded like good people. Sammy was clearly too fragile to travel on her own, and he needed a break from everything in London.

I'll come back, he had told himself as they boarded the plane at Heathrow. I'll just get Samantha home to her parents and then I'll come back to London, back to Marnie and ask for her forgiveness. I will sort out everything with George. Make it right.

But of course, Lewis never had.


## From Mayo to Dublin, Easter Monday, 27 March 1989

Joy walked all the way through the small town of Ballycastle, still sleepy on this Easter Monday, without seeing a soul. She went down the hill and took a right. She was heading for the sea. She walked past tiny cottages, with scrappy dogs barking at her and tractors parked in the driveway. She walked past fields of tall swaying grass and others ploughed, the earth dark and moist, hedgerows thick with yellow gorse. Then she left the road, clambering over stone walls, prising apart rusty old barbed wire and walking across lumpy fields. She could not stop until she got to the sea.

And here she was, standing on a slab of wet rock, blasted by salty spray, her hair flying around her, her hands tucked into her pockets, clutching that scrap of paper with her mother's address on it. Finally she had a once upon a time.

*Once upon a time there was a raven-haired girl with the bluest eyes, who had a little baby just like her. But the wicked world said she couldn't keep her baby so...*

Had her mother been riding towards the cliff that night intending to destroy the two of them? Could she not bear to be parted from Joy so much that she was willing to kill her own child?

Grief scratched at Joy's heart. No matter how crazy her behaviour had been, she couldn't help feeling sorry for Aoife Martell. She wished she could tell Lewis her story. Everything about their parting yesterday felt incomplete.

She stepped down onto another slab of rock and walked right to the edge of it. She could feel the pulse of the ocean coursing through her. She took the abalone shell out of her bag then crouched down and pushed it under the surface of the icy water. Its luminous splendour was magnified. It looked like last night's liquid moonlight mixed in with the dusky pinks, purples and gold of an Arizona sunrise. She watched the water rippling over the shell, and she let go. The shell was buffeted by waves and then gradually dropped into the clear depths of the ocean. Let the sea carry it whatever way it would.

Joy straightened up. Her fingertips were tingling from their contact with the sea. She wanted to get into the ocean, yet she knew that would be insanity. She resisted the urge just as she heard Eddie calling her.

'Don't you think it's a bit dangerous to stand so close to the edge,' he said as he joined her. 'Step back.'

He put a hand protectively on her arm, and she let him pull her back.

'What are you doing out here?' he said. 'We should get going. I've booked us on flights out of Dublin tonight.'

'Tonight?' She was unable to hide the disappointment in her voice. 'Can we not stay in Ireland longer?'

'I'm sorry, baby; I have to get back. I was in the middle of a big deal when I took off after you. We need the money.' He put his arm around her, kissing her cheek. She felt herself flinching. 'Remember we're going to Hawaii in a couple of weeks. It'll actually be warm enough to get into the sea, rather than just look at it.'

'I was thinking of going to London,' she said, careful to avoid his gaze.

'To see Ray?'

'Yes, but not just that.'

She told Eddie about her breakfast visitor, how Josie Whelan had related the story of her early life in Ballycastle and the tragedy that had befallen her mother.

'So let's get this straight,' Eddie said as they walked back across the field to the road. 'Some anonymous woman gave this Josie lady an address in London where your birth mother is supposed to be living?'

'Yes. I want to go and see if she's still there.'

'But why, Joy?' Eddie asked her. 'Your birth mother has never tried to contact you. It wouldn't be too hard if you were adopted through relatives in New York.'

'But she gave birth to me, Eddie ... she was so young ...'

'Darling, I think you're hoping for something you will

373

never get. This woman sounds unhinged. I mean, she tried to kill you when you were a baby, Joy.'

'Josie doesn't think she was trying to do that,' Joy protested.

'It looks pretty clear to me,' Eddie said.

He looked at her and sighed, and she could hear his exasperation tinged with anger.

'Baby, please give it up. For me. I want to bring you home. Start over. Don't you think our marriage is more important than all of this?'

She wondered what Lewis would advise her to do. She tried not to think of him, but she just couldn't help it. Every second, her body was alive with the sensation of his touch.

★

Lewis dreamed he was in a red stone desert in Sedona on one of his hikes with Samantha. It was a dusty, parched trail, punctuated with fiery rock. They wound their way through prickly pear, crucifixion cacti and star-like desert flowers. Lewis turned to check that Samantha was still following him, but to his surprise he found Marnie walking behind him instead. He waited for her to catch up, but she hung back, forcing him to turn his back on her and keep climbing the trail.

He saw bobcat paw prints in the sandy track, the markings of a predator, the shadow of himself. Up and up he climbed, all the time aware of his true love behind him, pushing him towards the sky. Thunder Mountain was to his left, and now he was on a high, craggy plateau, a finger of rock, jutting into the sky. He sat on the ledge, feet dangling over the edge. He could sense her approaching cautiously, creeping up like a shy animal, so he didn't turn. He didn't want to frighten her away.

The sun was fierce. She slipped in next to him on the edge of the rock, and the sun beat down upon them, yet the intensity of the heat felt good, as if it were cleansing him of the past. They looked at the view spread before them: a valley of red rock, all different heights, widths and shapes.

'People can see all sorts of things in the shapes of the rocks,' she said.

Her voice was different. He turned to see that it was not Marnie who sat beside him, but Joy. She was his dream's companion. He picked up Joy's hand and held it in his. It was cool and soothing to feel the softness of her skin. He looked at the view again.

Yet Lewis didn't see the rocks as anything. He was looking at the spaces between the rocks, the deep Vs of blue sky. It was like the space between characters, holding the letters in, as the rocks were held in a matrix of surrounding space. It was like filling in the silences of his life and all the things unspoken. He understood that what was real might not be seen at first, like his love for Joy.

In his dream he kissed Joy under the hot blue sky in the Arizona desert. He tasted her sweet saltiness, enfolded her in his arms and merged with her. He had never felt so part of a woman before – never been made to feel this complete.

From the sky a storm erupted and rain poured down upon the desert, the ocean's most ancient bed. It filled it in and became the sea. Joy took his hand and together they swam, riding waves of abandon. She took his heart within her hands, as if it was that abalone shell she so adored, and held it up to her ear to listen to it.

When he woke again Lewis was no longer afraid. He was here in Marnie's house, and he had lost her forever, but she had given him something back. It wasn't just a daughter; it was the truth. Over the years he had clung to this fantasy of Marnie, using it to justify his unhappy marriage to Samantha. The feeling that he had married the wrong woman. But his Marnie was an ideal that had never really existed, and Joy … Joy was the here and now.

★

As soon as they left Ballycastle it began to rain. Despite the fact that Eddie had the heating turned up full in the rental car, Joy was cold. She pulled her jacket tight around her and wished she could put on Lewis's sweater, but of course there would be questions about it, so she just shivered, her teeth chattering as she watched the road she and Lewis had taken to the west unwind before her in reverse.

She had never seen so much rain. It felt as if the sky had been pried wide open, the rain falling at an unnaturally accelerated pace. The landscape was pulled taut by the density of it as the car pushed through the tension.

'Christ, this country is miserable,' Eddie said, hunched over the wheel as he peered out the windscreen. 'I can hardly see out the car. What person could bear to live in such a climate?'

'You liked it last night,' Joy said. 'You were singing in the pub with all your new friends.'

'I was drunk, Joy,' he snapped. 'Now I'm sober, I can't wait to get the hell out of here.'

The rain hounded them out of Mayo and through Roscommon. Finally in Longford it lifted and Eddie put the foot down. She wanted to hang on to her past, what she had discovered, but her husband was driving her relentlessly away from it.

Just outside of Kinnegad they pulled into a garage to get more gas. She found a restroom while Eddie went to pay.

Joy looked in the cracked mirror at her own reflection. Lewis was right. Her newly curled hair did make her look a little different. She tried to smooth it down, but it just bounced right up again. She applied some lip salve and pinched her cheeks, but she looked tired, defeated. The spark had gone out of her.

Eddie patted her knee as she settled back into the passenger seat. 'Everything okay?' he asked her.

'Sure,' she said.

To her amazement the grey skies were lifting, and a glorious sun had turned the sky blue, a few stray puffs of white cloud the only reminder of the flood they had just driven through. The sun's rays spilled through the windscreen of the car, blinding them. Eddie pulled out his sunglasses and she opened her bag, searching for her own sunglasses. As she did so she dropped the bag and everything tumbled out onto the floor of the car.

'Still as clumsy as always,' Eddie teased, bending over to help her pick up her stuff.

'Hey, what's this?' He retrieved the sheet of paper with

the hummingbird design that Lewis had made for her, lodged between her seat and the gearstick.

'Hummingbird Nurseries. Joy Sheldon,' he read. 'Create Your Oasis in the Desert.' He chuckled. 'Are you starting up a business, baby?' He was grinning at her. It felt as if he was mocking her.

'No, it's just something a friend designed for me as a gift. In case I ever did want to do something.'

'Hummingbird Nurseries?' She could hear that familiar condescension back in his voice. 'How would you be able to run a business?'

Eddie and his all-knowing smirk. Joy looked past it – really looked into him. She felt jolted awake, for it dawned on her that she was not attracted to her husband any more. In this moment she could see that the young fearless cowboy she had once loved was gone forever.

'You don't need to do anything like that anyway. I keep telling you things are good. I can take care of you. You don't need a job,' Eddie continued.

'It's not just a job, Eddie,' she said, trying not to betray her emotions. 'It's something I've always dreamed of doing.'

'Oh, come on, Joy! Flowers? An oasis in the desert?' He laughed, patting her knee again before turning on the ignition and pulling out of the garage.

In Dublin Airport she followed her husband. He liked to be in charge, although only she could see that he was nervous of travelling, out of place, until he set foot on Arizonan soil again. He asked the check-in staff to allocate them seats beside the wings (the safest spot, he told her) and

378

stocked up on candy to help them pop their ears, and Irish crisps, along with bottles of Guinness in the duty-free, for his friends to try back home. She didn't want to buy a thing. Not one fluffy green shamrock key ring, or box of Kimberley biscuits, or postcard of the Emerald Isle.

Looking at the postcards made her think of Lewis – and Marnie. It hurt her to imagine them together, even though she had never met the woman. She had no right to be jealous, but it twisted her up inside just to think of Lewis with her.

Of course Eddie made sure they arrived at their gate well before boarding. He had bought a copy of *The Irish Times* and was reading it, while she fidgeted beside him. She couldn't even open the magazine he had bought her.

'What a depressing country,' Eddie murmured to her. 'No jobs, everyone leaving.'

She felt defensive of Ireland. It was, after all, her birthplace. And yet she was too tired to argue back – and what could she say? She knew nothing about jobs or emigration.

Their flight was called and Eddie jumped up, anxious to be one of the first to board, but Joy was suddenly gripped by a fierce pain in her belly. Waves of nausea flooded over her. 'I just have to go to the restroom; I'll be back in a minute.' She touched Eddie's hand.

'Now?' Eddie said, annoyed. 'But we're boarding. Can't you wait?'

'No.' She shook her head. 'You go on and board. There's loads of people queuing. I won't be a minute. See.' She pointed at the Ladies. 'It's just over there.'

'Okay,' he said, shrugging. 'See you in a minute.'

She scurried over to the restroom, but once she was

379

inside its tiled walls, the feeling that she was going to be sick lifted. She leaned over the sink and splashed some water on her face then opened her purse and dabbed her cheeks with a tissue. She looked at her sad face in the mirror before pulling out the design Lewis had made her. She traced the image of the tiny hummingbird, imagining Lewis drawing it, creating the words to describe her business. Thinking about her and her dream. She felt her eyes watering. She couldn't cry. Not now – not when she was about to get on a plane and sit next to her husband for seven hours. But it hurt to realise the truth. She loved Lewis. She loved him, and she would never see him again.

She wiped her eyes, folded the drawing up before putting it back into her purse and pulling out her lipstick. She tried to paint some colour onto her wan face. But as she dropped the lipstick back into the purse, she saw the scrap of paper Josie Whelan had given her this morning. She took it out and read again her mother's address in London.

The last call for her flight sounded and yet still Joy didn't move. She gripped that tiny piece of paper within her hands as if it was a treasure map. Something she must never lose again. She could feel her heart rate begin to quicken to hummingbird speed, and her cheeks were flushing with the sheer idea of her rebellion. Could she really do this? Until this very moment she hadn't even considered it, but now she knew: there was no way she was going to get on that plane back to America.

Lewis woke to a loud knock upon his door. He dragged himself out of his dream. Where was he? As he took in his surroundings – the art books, the graphic prints, the tasteful, minimalist furniture – he began to piece together the night before.

The knock came again.

'Come in.' His voice sounded gruff. He didn't mean it to, but he was still half asleep.

Cait's red hair then her green eyes appeared as she popped her head round the door. 'Sorry to wake you,' she said. 'But I have to get going. The train to Dublin leaves in half an hour.'

This was his daughter. This beautiful young woman, this marvel, was actually related to him. It took his breath away, and for a moment he was unable to speak.

'So I can't leave you here. You'll have to go,' she said, sounding a bit abrupt.

'Of course,' Lewis replied, sitting up. 'But why don't I drive you to Dublin? I'm heading back that way today.'

Cait looked surprised. 'Are you sure?'

'I'd like a chance to get to know you more.'

She shrugged. 'Okay.' He could see that behind her nonchalance, she was pleased.

'Cait, you're my only family.'

'And I guess you're mine.'

They looked at each other for a moment, and Lewis could almost see the stretch between them begin to shrink like the tide creeping up the shore. It would take time. But she was his child. Irrevocably they were drawn together.

'There's just one detour I want to take on the way, if that's okay with you,' he said. 'What time is your flight to London?'

'Not until this evening,' she said. 'We've all day.'

'There's someone I need to see,' he told her.

He couldn't leave it. He knew he should. By now Joy and her husband had probably made up. And that was a good thing, he tried to convince himself. How could he want Joy to walk out on her marriage, make a mockery of twenty-one years of her life?

On the other hand, Lewis didn't like the look of her husband. He had met plenty of guys like him in Arizona over the years – macho cowboy types who patronised their wives and cheated behind their backs. He told himself he wanted to spare Joy the misery of this. But really, if he was honest, he just couldn't let her go, not now that he had come to understand his own failed marriage. He had held on to that dream of Marnie because it had explained how unhappy he and Samantha were for too many years, but it had also given him an excuse to do nothing about it. Marnie was unattainable. He had loved her once, of course. But they had been so young. He would never know if things could have worked between them, but it didn't matter in the end, because she was not, never had been, the woman he really wanted. He knew now, with surprising conviction, that the woman he loved was Joy. Deep down he had known it from the first moment she'd stepped inside Langely Art Gallery. There had been this pull towards her, as natural and understandable as if they were two magnets. That was the only way he could explain it.

On the drive from Strandhill to Ballycastle Lewis told Cait a little about Joy's search for her birth mother, being careful to leave out his own feelings about her.

'I want to check she's okay,' he said. 'She might need a lift back to Dublin too.'

'It's a little like me,' Cait commented. 'She's looking for her mum, and I was looking for my dad.'

'And you found him ...'

'Well, you found me.'

'It was you who sent the postcards, Cait.'

Lewis glanced at his daughter. She was slouched in the passenger seat, her legs up and her booted feet pressed against the dashboard. He didn't tell her to put them down. He rather liked her spiky attitude, and her punky look, from the purple Doc Martens, black PVC trousers and leather biker jacket to the cat-like kohl around her eyes and her black nail varnish. If Lizzie were young now, it would be exactly how she'd dress. His daughter was no square, and this pleased him.

The rain hit them just as they approached Ballycastle. He drove down the length of the main street until he reached Mrs McIntyre's B&B, where he pulled in, and they sat in the car, waiting for the shower to pass. Cait offered him a stick of chewing gum, but he refused. He felt tight with nerves. What exactly was he going to say to Joy, especially with her husband there too? He could be about to completely humiliate himself. He clenched his fists. No, he had to listen to his instinct. Joy had feelings for him. He was sure of it.

'What the hell,' he said under his breath, and Cait gave him a curious look.

'I won't be long,' he said, opening the door and plunging into the deluge. He ran up the garden path and knocked on Mrs McIntyre's door.

But he was too late. Mrs McIntyre had told him about the Americans staying at the Coffeys, but by the time he got there, he found they had left not half an hour before.

'The husband told me that they're flying home to America tonight,' she said.

He had missed his chance. He fought the disappointment in his heart. Just as well, he told himself. What exactly was he going to say to make Joy leave her husband anyway? There could have been a fight. And by the look of her husband – shorter than him but well built – Lewis knew who would have come out of that the worst off. He wouldn't have wanted Cait's first impression of her father to be as a brawler and marriage wrecker.

Would he never see Joy Sheldon again? It seemed wrong, unbelievable. Yet he had no intention of ever returning to Arizona. So how could their paths ever cross again?

'Has your friend left already?' Cait asked him as he got back into the car. The rain pounded on the metal roof like a thousand hammers banging in a thousand nails.

'Yes, I missed her,' he said, wiping his rain-spattered face with a tissue.

'Sorry,' Cait said.

He shrugged. 'That's life, I guess. Mine has been remarkable for bad timing.'

'You know, if you're meant to be together, the universe has a way of bringing you together.'

Lewis looked across at his daughter in surprise. How did she know about his feelings for Joy?

'You do know that's a load of baloney,' he said. 'Besides, Joy and I are just friends –'

'I don't think so,' Cait interrupted, her eyebrows arched. 'I believe we're meant to meet the people we're supposed to in this lifetime … at the right time. Maybe if you and Mum had married it would have been a disaster. You would have fought all the time, and my childhood would have been miserable. Pete was supposed to be my dad when I was little. He and Mum were happy – therefore I was happy. I wasn't supposed to meet you until after my mum was gone. Now is *our* time, Lewis.'

He considered his daughter, her words so clear, so direct, so wise. He knew he would never be able to lie to her.

She looked back at him with those searching green eyes.

'How would you feel if I came to London with you?' he asked.

## LONDON, 28 MARCH 1989

I had never stopped thinking of you. In all these years, I couldn't let you go. Every time I was on the Tube, sitting opposite a woman around the same age as you, with black hair, and blue eyes, I wondered if it was you. Would fate one day find a way to bring us back together? If I wanted you badly enough, would my love for you pull you to me?

I had begun to give up. So much time had passed. My whole life nearly lived. A husband and two sons to occupy me, but still I couldn't forget you. I kept you secret, like a tiny garden in my heart. A place I would go and hide and remember small things about you. The tinkle of your laughter. The scent of your skin. The way your little hand felt in mine.

To the world outside, I was Eva Miller, the designer's wife. The mother of George Miller's children, the dazzling socialite, ignoring her genius husband's black moods and his many affairs because I could not face the alternative. In those early years, I would never have left George, for I would have had to step into the howling abyss of my grief.

And yet it never went away. I would dream about the house in Ballycastle night after night. Running up and down its grand staircase, tearing at the flock wallpaper as I looked for something I had lost. I would see my parents walking out the door, their backs turned to me, as they glided across the meadow towards the sea, a trail of yowling cats in their wake. I felt the heat of my black stallion between my thighs as I rode those fields, and still I was searching for what I had lost.

On your birthday every year, I lit a candle for you. It was the only time I ever prayed, because I had long stopped believing in God. But for you I slipped back into my childhood rituals and asked baby Jesus to protect you, even though you had long stopped being a baby. I had no photographs of you, no mementos to help me, but I could still summon your scent. Different from my boys. It was the smell of home, the turf on the fire and Josie's apple pie steaming on the kitchen table. The innocence and joy of our first year of your life together.

Now I lived alone. I had been losing all those I loved, slowly, over the years. My husband first, his heart attack so sudden that, even ten years later, I found it hard to accept the brutality of his end. He never knew about you. And your two brothers, who had long since flown the nest, settling on the other side of the world. I didn't tell them either. I was afraid, you see. Not that they wouldn't accept you. Of course they would have. No, I was ashamed that I had given you up. What would my sons think of me? To know I had rejected their sister?

I missed Marnie. She was the only one who knew about you. Every morning we had spoken on the phone. Around eleven – just a quick hello. *I love you. I care.* But the phone hadn't rung at 11 a.m. in over six months.

I had promised Marnie I would look after Cait. She had trusted me, despite the fact that I had told her about you, and she still wanted me to mind her daughter. Cait was a lot younger than you would be now, but we could have pretended she was your little sister. I think you would like her. Everyone loved Cait.

Today Cait was due back from Ireland, and at 11 a.m. as usual, I came in to make a cup of tea. I looked at the last photograph I had taken of Marnie, Cait and I sitting in my garden, the cats all over us. Marnie was wrapped up in a blanket, despite it being summer. She was already ill.

'Hello, I love you. I care,' I whispered to my lost best friend. I imagined Marnie's soft lilt.

*Eva, darling, how goes it?*

The telephone rang. How did you know that was the best time to call? I answered it without thinking. I thought it was Cait. But it wasn't her voice on the other end. You had an American accent, and you pronounced my name all wrong.

*Can I speak to Aoife Martell?* you said, the final 'e' flat. I couldn't answer you I was so shocked. You asked to speak to me again, and I slammed down the phone. I was shaking

387

like a leaf in the hall. You kept on ringing and ringing. I was so frightened to answer, but then it was as if I felt a hand on my shoulder, a whisper in my ear. It was Marnie. *Answer it,* she said. *You know this is what you've always dreamed of.*

You asked me for Aoife Martell again, and I told you that you were speaking to her. You told me your name, Joy Sheldon, and your voice was shaking. *There is no easy way to say this,* you told me.

But I already knew what you were going to say. Marnie had been right. I had been waiting for your phone call my whole life.

We met at 3 p.m. in a café by South Kensington Station. As soon as I walked in, I knew who you were. The woman sitting in the corner, clinging to the edge of the table. You had my father's dark hair and my mother's blue eyes.

You stood up and shook my hand. Your palm was hot; your cheeks were flaming pink. You looked as terrified as I felt.

You showed me your birth certificate and I read it: the truth of my life, buried all these years. I looked up at you and I could see you as Joyce.

'Are you my mother?' you asked.

I said yes, and we looked at each other, stunned. Neither of us able to speak. I was at a loss. Undone. My sons would say that I was somewhat controlling. I'd had their childhoods organised down to the very last music lesson; every single football practice. I had taken my job as their mother seriously. I had tried to make up for what had happened, you see. Yet here I was with you, not knowing what to do or say, drowning.

I asked you how you found me, and you told me that you had gone to Ballycastle. You had met Josie Whelan, and she had given you my address in London.

'A lady visited Josie last year and gave her your address. Josie didn't know her name – just that she came from Sligo.'

Marnie. Dear Marnie.

'I saw the house. It's derelict.'

I clutched my napkin. Of course my parents were dead. How could they still be alive after all this time? And yet a little part of me had hoped one day, maybe, my mother and I could have seen each other again. And even my father too. It had taken me years to forgive him.

You talked about the views of the sea from the old house. I was haunted by a wisp of memory from my childhood of those western shores. The call of the gulls, the constant beating of the waves, sounds I had never fully been able to silence.

'Josie told me what happened.'

What happened . . . My throat was tight with dread. Had you come to London to accuse me? What had been Josie's version of that dark, desperate night?

'Why did you give me up?'

Your voice was low, and sharp with anger, your meekness gone now as you glared at me. I could feel myself crumbling from the inside. It was for the best, I told you, casting my eyes downward. I couldn't provide for you in the same way that a proper family could, I tried to explain, but it wasn't enough. Of course not. Why had I agreed to meet you? What good had I imagined it might do?

'I have two children and nothing in the world would

have forced me to give them up. Did you not love me?'

My heart was beating tightly in my chest. 'Of course, I loved you.'

'Why then?'

I could see the desperate look on your face. You needed to understand. Yet I had been asking myself the same question ever since I had given you up, and I still didn't know the answer.

I tried the best I could. I told you that the thought of being separated from you had made me want to die. I had wanted to escape from the reality of our lives, torn apart. I had tried to run away with you, on my horse, because I couldn't bear the thought of losing you.

Your anger dissipated. You looked at me with compassion, and that hurt me even more than your rage.

I admitted it. I had wanted to ride my stallion off that cliff edge, just you and I forever lost in the deep blue sea. I had been possessed, but my horse had had more sense. He had thrown us before we even came close to the edge.

You were silent, looking at me, but I could not bear to meet your gaze.

I told you that I had been a danger to you. I had run away to London, for otherwise I would have ended up in the local asylum.

And still you said nothing.

'I am sorry,' I told you, feeling utterly broken.

You reached forward and touched my hand. Your fingers curled around mine. I never wanted to let you go.

We began to peel away the layers. The hours passed as minutes. I told you things I had told no one before. My first few weeks in London back in 1953 and how I had been driven almost insane with loss. The day I had taken the train to Cheltenham and walked all the way to Richard Lawrence's house. I had planned to confront him, hoping that once he saw me he would remember how much he had loved me. I told you how I had wanted him to help me get you back.

It had been a fool's dream. I had hidden behind a tree on the street in front of his house, waiting, until finally I had seen him step outside his front door with his new wife. My hope, and my heart, had shattered as I watched him take her arm. She was clearly pregnant. He had helped her into his car with such solicitude, and I had known he would never give this woman and his unborn child up. I had watched him drive away and the heartache had been so deep and intense that I had thought I might faint right there on his street.

I told you about slipping my engagement ring through his letterbox and taking the train back to Paddington. All I had wanted to do was stop the pain. The gaping hole of the loss of my baby. How my body ached for you. That was when George found me, the moment I was about to step in front of a Bakerloo-line train at Paddington Underground station. He'd grabbed the sleeve of my coat and pulled me back into life. His life. I told you how my husband saved me yet never knew my deepest secret.

I asked you more questions. I wanted to know about your life in America. You spoke about growing up in a town called Scottsdale in the American west. It was odd to listen to your American accent. We sounded so different, yet we shared the same blood.

★

I brought you back to my house. We were nervous together. Careful not to say the wrong thing. Gently we tugged information out of each other as you helped me prepare dinner. I asked you if you always knew you were adopted. You shook your head. Told me you only found out last year. Your father had told you the day he died. You paused in the middle of chopping onions, your eyes loaded with tears, wiping your arm across your eyes.

'I believe my dad wanted me to find you.'

I sent a silent thanks to your father. Watched you as you chopped. Your hands were just like mine. Small, neat and square palmed, with short fingers like a child's and narrow wrists. The visible connection between us shook me. It made me want to cry.

You sat on my couch with a glass of wine in your hand. I was in a daze. Yesterday we had not met, and yet today here you were, in my home, with my cats climbing all over you. You asked me how many cats I had. Five, I told you. I love cats, you confided, but my husband can't stand them.

I spoke about your grandmother, my mother, and how she loved cats as well. There had always been so many of them in the house in Ballycastle. Open a drawer in the hall and you'd discover three tiny kittens mewling inside. You asked me if I would ever go back to Ballycastle. I told you that I didn't know if I could face it, but you suggested that we could go together, speaking so quietly I almost missed your words. I was astonished by your generosity.

I imagined the reality of walking back into the past and I wasn't sure I could stand it. To see the house I grew up in broken. Empty decaying rooms. My mother lost from me forever. There was still a little part of me that imagined it was all still there. My mother and Josie bustling around in the kitchen, cats underfoot, my father out on the farm. If I went back then I would have to accept that was all gone forever. But maybe I could face it with you by my side.

You looked at me without a trace of resentment, and I was overwhelmed with tenderness, and regret. If only I had been braver. I told you that I had thought of you every day. You looked doubtful, but I had to make you understand.

'You're a mother too; you know it's true.'

We were on our second glass of wine when the doorbell rang. My black cat Athene was curled upon your lap, the little ginger, Demeter, tugging at the frayed hems of your jeans, and it looked to me as if you had sat exactly in this spot, with the cats all over you, so many, many times before. As if we had always known each other.

I slipped out into the hall as the doorbell rang again and put a hand to my frantic heart. I was on a high, like the old days, and yet all I had consumed was a glass of white wine with you. *My daughter.*

How would Cait take this? I was sure she would think it was good. The truth eventually came out – that's what she would say.

I walked down the hall, Demeter now at my heels, and switched on all the lights. I wanted Cait to see the joy on my face. I wanted to hug her with all my might and tell her that something very wonderful had happened. You.

When I opened the door, my god-daughter stood before me, looking as edgy as ever in her electric blue miniskirt, black tailcoat and purple boots. Behind her was the shadowy figure of a tall man, his face hidden in darkness.

I felt a hint of annoyance. The last thing I wanted was a stranger at our family gathering.

Cait stepped forward and hugged me. I was a little surprised as my god-daughter was not one to initiate embraces.

'Prepare to be shocked,' she whispered into my ear.

The man stepped into the light on my porch. 'Hello, Eva,' he said.

It was Lewis Bell. Older. A gentler, more humble expression upon his face than I had remembered, his thick dark hair streaked grey, yet unmistakably still that charming young designer from all those years ago.

'Lewis! Is it really you?'

I released Cait from our hug and looked for my answer in her eyes, the green of them as brilliant as two polished gems. I could tell she comprehended who this man was to her. That girl could unearth the truth of life from the deepest grave.

As I opened the door wide and ushered Cait and her father inside to meet you, a star shot across the London night sky as if it were a sign of perfect timing. I had called you to me. And you came.

# Acknowledgements

Thank you to my very special agents Marianne Gunn O'Connor and Vicki Satlow, and to my brilliant editor Emma Hargrave, along with the great team at Black & White Publishing in Edinburgh – especially Campbell Brown, Lina Langlee and Janne Moller. Much gratitude to my first readers Alison Walsh, Ila Moldenhauer, Tracey Skjæråsen, Nina Rolland and my sister Jane Birman. Thank you to my brother Fintan Blake Kelly, my sister-in-law Eimear and the Conyard family for their Mayo hospitality. Thank you to my dear friends Kate Bootle, for her editorial guidance, and Jo Southall, for first bringing me to Arizona. A mention to Kate and Rob at Bespoke Inn in Scottsdale for their hospitality during my time in Arizona.

To all my old friends, especially Donna Ansley, Monica McInerney and Sinead Moriarty for never losing faith. And to my new friends in Scotland, especially soul sister Thalia Vazquez, my fellow cohort at Edinburgh Napier, my inspirational tutors David Bishop and Laura Lam, and my bus pal Becky Sweeney. A shout out to Aurora Writers' Retreats, and especially to Karen Rosenstock, Vanessa Rigby and Melody Nixon. And to all my wonderful friends for their enduring support especially Ann Seach, Emma Cha'ze, Page Allen, Hege Isaksen, Elisa Bjersand and Suzy Wilson. I am thinking also of dear friends lost in the past few years – Jenny, Karen, Jason, Serge and Paula – and those who lost them, especially Cathy, Pat, Cora, Manoushka and Bernie. Their love endures.

A huge thank you to my family. To my Aunty Joyce, for whom Joy is named, and for whom I wrote the small tribute to my late uncle Amancio D'Silva, to my mother-in-law Mary Ansley, my brothers Paul and Jed. Most of all thank you to my son Corey and my stepdaughter Helena. Love you so much! And if this book belongs to anyone it is to my darling Barry, who has fed, watered and provided shelter for this struggling writer, year after year. You are my hero!